WARNING

The contents of this story may ignite feelings of great joy, anger, fear, profound sadness, regret, inner strength, humility, empathy, indescribable compassion, bewilderment, disgust, love, tenderness and amusement—just a handful of the emotions a nurse can manage during a single shift.

To the Nurses!

Other Books by Jen Purcell

Saucy On the Side
The Dirty Mermaid

Prologue

When plans were exacted to add floor space to the Emergency Department at Dixon Valley Hospital, located in Dixonville, North Carolina in late August of 1969, historians and town educators were concerned about the land parcel designated for such purpose.

"It's an old Indian graveyard," reported skeptic and local activist, Tonya Simmons. "*Holy* Land."

So the story goes...

During the War Between the States, a battle broke out on the unnamed Holy Land killing almost everyone involved. Almost. Historiographers like Ms. Simmons believe that somebody must have survived. To move the bodies.

When the first band of travelers happened upon the smoldering lot of dead and mortally wounded soldiers, it appeared that they had been dragged off the actual burial site and their remains piled up around it in heaps, lining the land mass like a giant human fence.

For decades the tainted battlefield remained secluded in the thickest part of the forest, easy for folks to avoid or simply forget. Eventually rumors of the assault transformed into pure superstition, a hoax to keep children from venturing too far into the thicket. But every so often a stranger would appear in local pubs and trading posts, after traveling the wooded region, and re-circulate such claims fantastic as they may be. All the accounts differed to some extent, although each man, woman and child agreed on hearing a similar sound...

...drums beating in the distance.

As years passed, the town of Dixonville grew in population and urban activity. The forest was cookie-cut into dog parks and neighborhoods, schooling districts were founded, malls erected, and yet, somehow, the small patch of Holy Land avoided demarcation. No houses were built upon it, roads seemed to twist around it, and even hospital plans, which were exacted smack dab center, spared the troubling parcel as a garden courtyard. Mere coincidence? Ms. Simmons didn't think so.

When John K. Scott took over the hospital in 1986 and decided that the ED needed even more beds, renovations were designed to floor and cover the courtyard in question. These construction plans did not sit well with the likes of Tonya Simmons. Not that Mr. Scott worried much about the old lady anymore. Rolling into her eightieth year, Tonya was no longer the scholarly and irritating demonstrator that she once was. She had grown hunched and arthritic, and couldn't see past her nose, spending twilight hours lingering on park benches, feeding squirrels, retelling local myths and folklore to anyone willing to listen. Just the same, the ancient historian surprised all by turning up at the annual budget meeting to oppose the action.

This was Mr. Scott's response: "My dear Ms. Simmons, our community has tripled in size. ED wait times border on dangerous! We're working on a very tight budget and yet demand more space. I have reviewed hundreds of proposals, checked every possibility, and the most cost effective way to add hospital beds is to renovate from within. The courtyard needs to go!"

"But it's Holy Ground!"

"Let's be practical, Tonya. Nobody sits in that courtyard, nobody walks in that courtyard; I can't even get our gardener to mow the grass because he's afraid of the goddamned thing. It's nothing but wasted space."

"You can't *build* on a graveyard. It's against the law!" The old woman snarled.

"You know," The director chuckled, shaking his head, clearly out of patience. "I researched this so-called *Holy* Land of yours and couldn't find one single fact to verify its existence. I'm beginning to believe the rumors, ma'am. That it's a fairy tale. One big jumbling hoax."

Of course Ms. Simmons went eighty years of crazy. She contacted the newspapers, six radio stations, the schools, the hospital board of directors; she even touched base with the *Preservation Society of the North American Indian*—a group sworn to investigate and protect old relics, historical sites, and in this case, possible burial grounds of the Native American Indian.

Director Scott was a reasonable man. He wasn't trying to piss anyone off, not even Tonya Whatever-the-hell-her-name-was. He was just trying to run a cost effective hospital. But when forty-some hulking Indians resembling a knock-off version of the Black Panther Party, wearing militia garb, berets and battle boots, offered a silent march in front of the emergency department, the agitated administrator hastily announced that to satisfy all parties involved, he would bring in a crew of forensic anthropologists to search the area and prove once and for all that Ms. Tonya Simmons was out of her tree. (He didn't actually say *out of her tree*, but his tone suggested it.)

Imagine Mr. Scott's surprise when a skeleton was actually exhumed. Surrounding the bones they also discovered a series of scored rocks and oddly shaped instruments believed to be utilized for healing purposes by a remote descendent of the North Carolina Creek Tribes. The newly renovated emergency department, it seemed, was to be built on top of a medicine man's resting place.

When a slightly embarrassed John K. Scott was asked to amend his statement, he retorted with this. "A witch doctor, eh? We'll be haunted by a medicine man? That's spectacular!"

An obviously confused reporter questioned his jubilation, restating for the record how it would delay construction and cost thousands in tax dollars to relocate the remains.

This time Mr. Scott grinned and said, "Anyone misfortunate enough to find themselves at the mercy of emergency medicine will most certainly agree. The department can always use the extra help."

The Nurse Whisperer
By Jen Purcell

Chapter 1

Present Day.

What I recall about the day of my demise is not what you'd think. You'd think a flash of images would blaze across my neurotransmitters, a cumulative barrage of memories I unknowingly and knowingly held dear. Possibly followed by a bright light at the end of a shadowy tunnel, signifying the end or perhaps a new beginning, making you question a broad spectrum of religions, suddenly wondering if you paid tribute to the correct god. *Is there a Promise Land? A gate? Peter Someone-or-other?*

It didn't happen like that for me. Or maybe it did and I was just too busy getting electrocuted to realize the flash came from above and not from the 200 joules of electricity burning holes in my chest. My nostrils flare from the pungent smell of searing flesh. Everyone is screaming. I'm being jabbed and prodded, gagging as another doctor works to cram something down my throat. Still, this isn't what's freaking me out the most.

What I recall mostly from the day of my death was the presence of Ollivander Dick, a man that I am certain was already dead. Now you may think it common practice for a deceased chick to have a run-in with a ghost dude but that's the thing, I wasn't dead yet. Not even close.

Ollivander, or Ollie, as the plaque described, was a guy that had passed long before my arrival to Dixon Valley Hospital. Apparently, he'd been employed in the emergency department some fifteen years back and died suddenly in the break room. He was found blue in the face, slumped over the corner of the dining table. His final act most likely ramming his abdomen into the furniture, a last futile attempt at performing the *Heimlich maneuver* before collapsing onto the table.

I'm privy to this information by relayed accounts from senior colleagues who had been employed at the time and remember the incident as if it happened yesterday. Ollie D. died from asphyxia. They found a hot dog (almost the whole goddamned thing), wedged in a throat full of raisin-speckled coleslaw, containing only two small bite marks, as if Ollie inhaled the pork wiener instead of chewing it.

Time, or lack of it, that's what killed Ollie Dick. In our business, the business of saving lives, "lunch break" is very rarely thirty leisure minutes with our noses in a book, slowly and carefully chewing a healthy home-cooked meal, discussing weekend get-a-ways and family events. Lunch hour is definitely not as prevalent as it is portrayed on the thousand hospital soap operas I've managed to view over the years. (Very rarely are doctors and nurses dressed in suits and heels having coffee while relaxing in cushy lounge chairs at linen-covered tables.). This is a true fallacy. For most emergency medicine staff, meal time is about five solid minutes of shoveling; cramming in a half-sandwich here, a spoon full of pudding there, usually between assessments and IV sticks, and every so often while patients are stewing on bed pans.

Really? On a bedpan? Who could eat half an egg sandwich knowing that Mr. Jones is squeezed onto a plastic shit-pot spewing diarrhea in room six?

That's easy. Any nurse. Truthfully, I can toss Grandpa on a bedpan and quite naturally march into the break room, down half my lunch and return in time to roll him off, wipe his ass and refit him with another diaper. Don't worry. I'm a *Super Hero Hand Washer*. During this process, I have washed my hands six times. Before the bedpan, after it, in the break room before eating, after eating, before removing the bed pan, and after cleaning him up. It's what we do: wash and gel, wash and gel. (Besides, I'm the one eating, remember? Definitely *not* trying to conjure up my own shit party. For this reason alone, nurses are extremely cautious about where their hands have last been.)

As for common lunchroom banter, our normal conversation would sweep any other lounge in the world with sudden nausea and loss of appetite. There's always a chance you could run across a discussion involving vomit and blood, or bloody vomit; or hear stories about mucked up suture lines, seeping infections and strange foreign body insertions. The slew of inquiries and comical discussions that follow are enough to make the average individual watery at the mouth.

Don't worry, we talk about normal stuff too. Who's screwing whom, which kid is selling Girl Scout Cookies, culinary skills, weight loss programs, mall sales—normal stuff. Just count on it being tossed and mixed with a dash of bile and guts.

It's only once in a blue moon that we discuss a specific patient rather than the malady that brought them in. When our brief moment of sanctuary is lost to work related prose, I can assure you that it's not from the really messed up souls with valid life threatening complaints. (If this were the case, lunch would be skipped.) What a health care worker truly can't stand more than anything, enough to ruin their lunch break, is a "support" family full of assholes. (Even as I write this, I'm pondering ways that I can report this observation while maintaining a professional air. But why bother? I'm not worried about annual evaluations or letters to administration. I'm dead.) So if you don't like it, tough luck.

Here's my biggest beef with families.

Many, many folks out there are under the impression that the only person that matters in an emergency department is their relative. They believe that footies and ice chips, extra blankets and pillows, saltines and apple juice, mark the level of care and not the actual medical treatment. These same people frown at the caregivers who arrive to draw blood and give shots, shoot X-rays, scrub wounds and place catheters. They're continually asking the question: *Are such tests necessary?*

My response: *You brought her in, dumbass. You were concerned. Did you really think medical treatment was going to be easy on Grandma? That we could wave a magic wand and conjure blood counts or press a finger on her temple and diagnose her with a bad infection? Sorry. No magic wands in this department; just needles, stethoscopes, pills, and X-ray machines spewing loads of radiation.*

These same people never visit Grandma at home. Never think to buy her a new bra or, God forbid, a six-pack of cheap cotton underwear (available at K-Mart for less than six bucks). They show up on holiday and find their once vital relative, dirty and dehydrated, slumped into an old recliner wearing the shabbiest of dressing gowns, sipping instant coffee out of a grubby cup, and make the unanimous decision that Grandma needs to go to the hospital!

Sadly, this physical condition is nothing new to the old woman, definitely not a medical emergency. She's been tired and weak for many years. Keeping up with the washing and cleaning is impossible and she doesn't have money or strength to go shopping. She eats simply because it's too hard to prepare proper meals and bathes sporadically for several reasons. Most importantly, it takes a lot of energy and she's afraid she's going to fall in the shower. Her nails haven't been cleaned because she can't see well and doing her hair causes terrible pain due to arthritis. Grandma is not sick. Grandma is neglected.

These are the patients who show up around the holidays, followed by the group of assholes who deem it appropriate to call 911 in the first place rather than driving the old lady in a private vehicle. They bombard the ER like it's a Carnival Cruise, yapping and concerned as if this one annual visit puts them in good with the withering soul. They ring the call bell incessantly as if it's the Ritz, more worried about getting cold drinks and graham crackers for themselves and their bratty children than anything else. They glare at the nurse as if it's her fault that Grandma's under garments are soiled, and wonder what's taking so long to order a dinner tray.

Families of ten members or more, who even after being told six or eight times about a two visitor policy, have the audacity to call the nurse out of another room to help Grandma with a bedpan. *Really? Ten of you and nobody can assist the woman to relieve herself?* They all file out of the room laughing and joking like this is fun for them, getting to see what an ER is like on a normal day, commenting as they go. *Out of the way guys, let the nurse do her job. She knows how to maneuver the bedpan after all. Let the expert do her thing.*

I smile and nod, thinking *how does Grandma take a dump at home?* With that I'd like to add, *maybe if you checked in on her more than once a year, cooked her a decent meal or offered to assist with a shower, she wouldn't be in this mess. Guess what happens when old people can't get to the bathroom? They either piss in diapers or hold their urine, two huge triggers for urinary tract infections...*

If you haven't guessed, in life I was an emergency room nurse. I worked at Dixon Valley Hospital in the very same department where Ollivander Dick had perished twelve years before. The reason I bring up the bedpan stuff is because when the Dickman collapsed for good, he did in fact have a grandma on the old pink potster. Five days later, right after returning from Ollie's funeral, the nursing manager received a very official letter of complaint from the old woman's family berating the dead RN for his toileting negligence.

Nobody, not even the director, admitted to the pissed off relatives that Ollie had bit the big one. They blamed it on HIPPA, of course. Against the rules. Can't talk about anyone's medical history without consent. (And the dead Ollivander was in no position to sign any documents releasing his information.) However, I'm pretty certain it was more than that. Hospital administration would be too worried about losing a customer even if the family was a bunch of morons. Tell you the truth; I'm not sure confiding Ollie's death would have been enough to appease these kinds of idiots.

I often wondered why Ollie didn't just walk out of the break room blue in the face. He was ten paces away from two ER doctors and ten nurses, a crash cart, and an entourage of cutting blades. Surely, one of his colleagues could've tried the *Heimlich maneuver*, surgically cut into his throat, attempted intubation, pushed the food into a lung if they had to, anything to dislodge the deathly wiener dog. No doubt, his vocal cords would've been fucked. His nickname could've been changed to Froggy instead of *Dick*, a definite improvement in my opinion.

In memory of the dead RN, they blew up his employee badge photo, mounted it on a wooden plaque, added a generous inscription and hung it over the lunch table to be remembered by all for two reasons: First, as jolly old Ollie Dick, registered nurse extraordinaire, and second, more importantly, as a reminder for staff to chew their goddamned food and not die in the emergency department break room. It was seriously bad for business. (Probably another reason the berated family was kept in the dark. If we couldn't even keep our staff alive then how were we supposed to care for their relatives?)

I obtained most of my information about the Dickman from my preceptor, Bev Martin, eight years ago, when I entered the hospital work force. Dixon Valley is a sister hospital to Dixon Regional, the community's enormous trauma center, where I tortured myself for five solid years before requesting a transfer to the smaller, less chaotic facility, known to many of us as the Country Club. I soon discovered that every ED had its share of drama and trauma, even the Level 2 sister hospitals. Just because The Valley avoided many of the debilitating injuries, like car crash ejections and falls from high buildings, we still got our share of walk-in-the-front-door chaos. Drunk people flying off of three-wheelers or diving into shallow swimming pools. Nail guns chewing up legs because of negligent safety latches. There were also plenty of accidental stab wounds (knifes slipping from counter tops, lopping off toes). Fishhooks snared into the lips and ears of less than skillful fishermen, and, of course, the occasional drive-by gunshot wound. (Side note: Not to confuse anyone, but ED and ER can be used interchangeably. Emergency Department and Emergency Room mean the same thing. Personally, I like to use ER but now a days ED is more common.)

At the beginning of my employment, I can't say I held much love for Bev Martin. She was one of those spiteful nurses that should've been sent to pasture long ago, but due to a delinquent son and frivolous husband (now ex-husband), golden year employment had proved a necessity.

I also think that she secretly despised me because of my hair. It was long and silky, not a split end in sight, and needed relatively no maintenance. Bev had wiry gray with flyaway tresses that, even in her prime, needed loads of treatment, not to mention a barrage of curling and flat irons, hot oil treatments and boxes of color. The reason I say this is because at least once a day she would comment on my beautiful locks and then deteriorate into a bitch rant about her own nest. The monologue would end with Bev cackling about how she finally gave in and the conversation would fold with her repeating the statement, "I've come to appreciate the wiry gray. It brings out my inner witch."

Nobody had the balls to say it aloud, but we all agreed with her.

Over time I have come to appreciate the stand-up and honest qualities of Bev Martin, but in the beginning, I absolutely despised her. She marched around wearing a continuous frown, witch hair flying everywhere, angry with the ex for taking half, angry with her son for being a loser, and angry with herself, I suspect, for choosing nursing as a profession.

After only an hour with the woman, I wished I were back in the trauma bay getting my ass kicked by a gang of gun shot wounds. The idea of having to follow around such misery twelve hours a day for three solid weeks made my last job seem like a walk in the park.

"You can handle it, girl." My nurse manager had consoled. "We've hired so many new people,

Bev's all I got. She may be grumpy but she knows her stuff. Ask a lot of questions. She's tolerable when focused."

I cringed thinking about our second day together, but took to heart my manager's suggestion. The good news was that the morning was so darn busy we barely had time to breathe let alone make small talk. Bev eased up after the fifth hour. I was a good stick and knew how to handle an assignment, which detained my preceptor's comments to the occasional grumble. Seven hours in, Bev tapped me on the shoulder and announced that it was time for a break.

Back in the lunchroom, the uncomfortable silence returned. I concentrated on the click of my silverware as I chopped up my field greens. Bev wolfed down a re-heated plastic container of pot roast and mashed potatoes. Her eyes burrowed into the side of my salad bowl when a colleague breezed through and casually asked where I left the rest of my lunch.

"I'm in a wedding next month." I replied. "Need to shed about four pounds."

"*Four* pounds?" Bev snapped offensively. "Who *cares* about four goddamned pounds?

Me. Bitch.

Chewing very slowly, I forcibly silenced my inside voice. That's another thing about the medical field. Pointed rebuttals offered too early at a new job were greatly frowned upon, especially when they involved attacking the department's signature warhorse. So instead, I shrugged and filled the gap a different way. Pointing at the wall, I asked, "Who is Ollivander Dick, anyway? And what did he do so special to get a plaque on the wall?"

Bev's facial expression contorted in a series of emotions. I suspect she was trying to display respect, but I sensed revulsion. "Ollie worked here. He choked

to death one night on shift and died at this very table."
"That's uh...sad." I said.

"What's *sad*," Bev replied, "is that a nurse can work for this department a good thirty years, go to hours of useless meetings, miss seventy percent of precious holidays with a kid that no longer pays her any attention, and a *moron*, a lazy shit who couldn't properly nurse if he grew a third arm, gets his picture on the wall because he can't chew his fucking food. You done? We've got work to do."

As the weeks progressed, Bev refused to answer any more questions about the *Dining Room Hero* and yet her bitching about the field of nursing in general continued to escalate. Bev was *Old School*, you see. She remembered when caregivers wore solid crisp white uniforms accessorized with sharp caps and bleached hosiery. When mopping floors and bed baths were part of a nurse's fourteen patient workload. "You did what needed to be done! These days' *nurses* only care about PTO and what they *can't* do. They're *lazy*! And the Dickman was laziest of all!"

"For someone who hates the medical field," I commented to Amanda, another RN I better related to, "Nurse Martin is pretty driven."

"Bev is mean as a hornet." Amanda replied. "She's so Old School we call her Neanderthal."

After those first three weeks, I completely appreciated the nickname. For starters, Bev's belief on being brutally honest bordered on blatant cruelness. Embarrassingly evil, in my opinion, to the uneducated folks of the world who showed up on the ED doorstep out of ignorance and fear. Bev had no problem berating young pregnant mothers about considering birth control, because *obviously* they were too stupid for motherhood if they couldn't tell the difference between a true emergency and a visit to the doctor. Type II diabetics she'd scoff at, bluntly discussing their wide girths and the need for preventative running shoes and literally mutter *lost cause* as they walked out the door. Bev was relentless. Just about everyone was ignorant, selfish, or ridiculously wasteful.

And if you think she was mean to patients, wait until I tell you how she treated the doctors. "None of them," she glowered, "have a lick of sense when it comes to proper treatment. Take this kid, for example. Clearly, the little beast is constipated. His stupid idiot of a mother is feeding him soda pop and fried chicken for breakfast. What did she think was going to happen? Kid's going to have coronary artery disease before he hits ten. Mom even admits that he hasn't crapped in four days. And this...this..." Bev flung an irritated arm at the physician. "...*buffoon!* He's going to order the fucking Full Monte—blood, IV, urine. Just watch. By the time we're finished, the kid'll be taking a ten thousand dollar shit."

"Physician's have such liability." I remember saying.

"Don't get me *started* about liability." Bev frowned and shook her head. "Lawyers have made pansies out of these doctors. Their greed, in general, has sucked the life out of medicine. Forget about assessments and medical expertise. Let's just do every goddamned test on every goddamned person and forget about common sense or being *practical*. It's no wonder health care costs are through the roof. The kid doesn't even have a friggin' *fever*. He was downing a bag of chips when I walked in the room. If he has appendicitis then I'm the Queen of friggin' England."

Attempting to make light of the situation, I added, "Well...you do have the Queen's hair."

When I thought all was lost and deduced that Bev Martin was absolutely horrible to everyone, a cancer patient rolled into the room. Bev's demeanor shifted. She smiled and spoke softly. Every action was reassuring and kind. For the better part of an hour Bev used her every resource, working at great speed to make this sickly person comfortable and at ease, which was amazing seeing the woman had end stage bone cancer.

The nurse manager happened to walk by and give me a nudge. "See? Bev Martin does have a heart."

Instead of accepting the compliment, Bev frowned and took no time muttering a response. "The only souls truly thankful are dying ones."

What I learned from Bev Martin more than anything else during those early days at DVH was to never acquire her attitude. Reflectively, I suddenly wondered how colleagues viewed me in the weeks prior to my transfer out of the *Hood*. (Regional is sometimes called the *Hood* because of its location, on the edge of the projects in the sketchy part of town.) Just thinking about the place made my brow furrow. The wait times were ridiculous, the job never ending, and appreciation from administration nonexistent. When a manager, patient, or anyone offered a smidgeon of gratitude, the moment was lost to the next train-wreck screaming in through the back door, most often spewing blood all over the stretcher.

That's how it is in a trauma center. No matter how sickly your patient presents, there is always some sorry bastard worse off. Forget about taking a break, even a tiny one. Nurses are scorned for trying to go the bathroom or chug a glass of water, forget about eating a saltine or a hotdog without choking it down (Yeah, bad joke). Somebody always needs...*you*...right NOW.

What comes next? Burn out. Something inside snaps and all of the compassion and caring that you planned on bringing to the job gets tossed in the trash with the umpteenth shitty diaper. So much work to be done. So many lives to save. So many needy family members to deal with. After awhile even a courteous smile becomes exhausting.

I remember berating a resident because she needed me present for a rectal exam, like standing in a room as a chaperone was way too much to ask. "*Really?*" I bitched. "You're a chick. The patient's a chick. Do you really need a third chick as a baby sitter? Give me a *break.*"

My eyes were rolling at every request, my comments sharp and offensive. Nobody was working harder than me. Nobody knew what the fuck they were doing. Nobody but *me* was burning both ends to get the job done.

Yeah. Right.

And now here I was a transfer at Dixon Valley, working with Neanderthal Bev, seeing in her what I was on my way to becoming in the Hood. All I can say is thank God I got out.

*

Anyway, back to my fateful day. Years after my three-week rodeo with Bev Martin, (who is still stomping around with a constipated glare, by the way), it is my turn to train the newly hired, which in this case happens to be a newbie, fresh out of school. Meghan and I are on lunch break at the very same table when she points to Ollie's plaque and asks about him, which causes a transmission of Bev's initial explanation.

"I wonder why he didn't walk out of the break room and grab a doctor. It makes no sense." Meg questions, after my long-winded narration.

"That's what I've been saying for years. Shoot, even the Indian couldn't save him." I grin and take a sip of water.

That's another thing about Dixon Valley. Not

only did Ollie Dick die in the lounge, but ever since the new wing was erected over the courtyard, rumors swept the region about a ghostly witch doctor and his drumming. The first time I heard the sound was during my second week with Bev. We were in the medication room drawing up antibiotics for a kid when the beating started. Now let me tell you, when it comes to pediatric dosing there is always a two-person check. Two nurses work out the math, one draws up the dose and the other verifies the amount. Nobody skips these steps. Nobody screws with a kid.

Anyway, Bev and I both agreed that the dose needed was seven milliliters. As we poured it, I heard this weird sound. *THUMP, THUMP, TH-THUMP, THUMP...*

Suddenly frozen, I turned to my preceptor. "Do you hear that? It's...is it *drums?*" I gasped. "The Indian! He...he's *here!* The legends are true!" I whispered in a non-whispery tone.

Bev groaned and rolled her eyes. She then pulled me from the medicine room to an adjacent area known as the tube room. Throughout the hospital there is a tube system, like an electronic mail chute, where staff can send medications, supplies, and paperwork to anywhere in the hospital without leaving the department. Bev pointed at the chute and said, "Listen."

I could hear it then, the beating. It was more like a clunking sound. Bev pushed the send button three times and then kicked the wall.

"What are you doing?"

"One of the tubes is stuck. That's what happens when a moronic colleague doesn't latch it properly. It gets holed-up in the walls and pounds systematically until it loosens enough to move. Those're your drums, sister. Now, can we get back to work?"

When I relay this information to Meg, she replies, "So Bev doesn't believe in the Indian?"

"I didn't say that. When we got back to the med room, Bev made me rework my math a third time. She then scoured the chart, double-checked the order and compared the dose to the kid's weight. She reviewed his allergies a second time, even went back to the treatment area and spoke to the kid's mom to re-verify everything. That's when we caught the error.

"*Mrs. Smith* wasn't Mom at all, but Aunty Sue. Bev promptly made the woman get in touch with the child's birth parent, even after she argued that the phone call could get her fired. After finally contacting the correct Mrs. Smith, we discovered that the frazzled single mother had confused her son's medical histories. (Not surprising. She had six boys with similar names...Chad, Charlie, Chuck, Christopher, Christian and Chambry). Charlie, the child in question, did in fact have an allergy to the very drug prescribed."

"So it is true!" I challenged Bev, back in the day. "The Indian does exist!"

"Oh, bullshit!" Bev grumbled. "I always double-check my orders."

"But to that extreme? Admit it! You are superstitious!"

"Superstitious or not, call it what you will." Bev replied. "I never look a gift horse in the mouth."

*

Meghan sighs as she reads the Dickman's inscription. "He must've been something to get his mug plastered on the wall."

"Yeah, uh, no. Not how Bev explains it. He just happened to die here rifling down a hotdog. Choking to death got him the plaque."

"A sad way to go, don'tcha think? Alone in a break room with a dozen healthcare workers on the other side of a door."

"Pre-mature death is always upsetting, which reminds me, time to take my medicine."

Megs begins to ask what, but catches herself. Medication is personal.

"It's for blood pressure." I explain. "My diastolic was creeping up so the doc insisted. I said fine, I'll take one bloody pill but only if it's cheap. I'm not willing to spend my life savings on medication. Not yet. Come on. Break's over."

Chapter 2

"We're back." Meghan chirps cheerfully to the nurse watching our assignment. Her name is Jamie. Bitch Jamie, to me, and in no way one of my favorites. A transfer from the fourth floor, she started out decent, enthusiastic and ready to dig in. Now Jamie saves her smiles for sucking up to senior staff (at least most of them), and is a total condescending bitch to everyone else. By her tone, it is suggested that the mere presence of my trainee causes her severe physical and mental strife.

When Meghan requests an update on her assignment, she gets cut off. "You got a new one in room nine. Waves of dizziness. EKG is done. The doc's got it now. The patient is absolutely fine."

"Did he come by EMS?" Meghan asks.

"Nope." Jamie clips. "Front door."

"Does he have a line?"

"It's on my to-do list." Jamie huffs, clearly annoyed. "He's only been in the room for like *five* minutes. Unlike your *preceptor*, I don't have a *slave* for the day." Jamie turns back to her charting and repeats, "Like I said, he's fine."

As we gather supplies, Meghan murmurs. "What's her problem?"

I shrug. "She's always a bitch to new people. Come on. Let's go check Jamie's version of fine."

"What do you mean?"

"Whenever I hear *he's fine* or *nothing to worry about*, I worry. It's a jinx. Between us, Jamie's jealous because you got hired into the ED right out of school. It pisses her off that you missed out on a fourth floor hazing." I cough. My throat feels suddenly dry.

"You okay?" Meg asks.

I point to my throat. "Allergies."

We walk into room nine and our man is laying flat on his back, a light sweat peppering his forehead, eyes wild like a rabbit. He jumps at the sight of us. "It's *happening* again."

"What's happening?"

"The dizziness and...and I feel like running. I need to get up. To...to *run!*"

I turn to Meg, mumbling. "What does our monitor tell us?"

"What monitor?"

"*Exactly.*" Not only is our guy still in street clothes, Jamie hasn't bothered to put him on the monitor. "I'll wire him down. You start the IV."

As we work, Meghan asks the man a series of inquiries. *When did the dizziness start? Any precipitating factors? Medical history? Daily medications? How about pain?*

In mid sentence he cuts her off. "I just answered all of these questions for the nurse out front. Don't you people *read?*"

"This is the process, sir." I cut in. "Think of it like check points to make sure nothing is overlooked. After us you speak with the doctor. If you're admitted, the storytelling continues."

"I have to *stay* in the hospital?"

"Depends." I cough again and my face feels warm. I reach up and touch my skin. It's scorching.

"Blast it! Here we go *again!*" The man moans, placing a hand over his chest.

The heart monitor alarms.

"What rhythm is that?" Meghan speaks quietly, almost to herself. "It's too fast. SVT?"

"What the heck is SVT?" The patient crows.

"Technical term, sir." I state calmly. "Supraventricular Tachycardia. In English, you're heart is racing, beating faster than 150 beats per minute."

"How fast is fast?"

"Right now you're cruising at around 200."

"*What*!?"

I lay a hand on his arm. "That's why you're dizzy." I speak evenly but my nervous system shifts into overdrive. I turn to my orientee, back in teaching mode. "So what do you want to do about a speeding heart rate?"

"Slow it down."

"Excellent. How do we do that?"

"Adenosine. IV."

"Right. First things first. I'll hunt down a doctor. You pull the meds." As we hurry from the room, I mumble so the patient can't hear. "And get the crash cart."

If the Adenosine doesn't work, our patient will receive a nice volt of searing electricity directly through his chest; a technique referred to as Cardioversion (which, by the way, is NOT very pleasant). Thankfully, the medicine usually works.

I offer Meg a brief yet speedy prelude to the next five minutes of our job. How the medicine needs to be pushed fast, how the heart will momentarily stop and hopefully restart at a slower more functional rate.

We're hustling back to the room when Meghan says, "What's wrong with your voice? It sounds…muffled?"

Almost simultaneously I can feel it. A tickle in my throat. The cough. A flushing sensation. My tongue…it feels thicker. I shrug it off and concentrate on the task at hand. "When you push Adenosine, it has to be done in less than a second. Follow it with a twenty ml flush…" My voice fails as I start to wheeze.

"You're wheezing." Meghan comments. "It's like you're having some type of reaction."

"Allergies. I get horrible…*cough*…let's go give this med."

I begin to freak out when my arms tingle and my face starts to itch, but SVT is a true emergency and I'm precepting. Meghan has never given this drug before and it's very dangerous. I can't just walk away.

Back in the room the doctor is calling for Adenosine as the tech places EKG leads on the patient, attempting to capture any changes in his heart rhythm on paper. My skin is blistering hot. The folds around my eyes have puffed up like pizza dough and my lids feel heavy. My tongue has doubled in size.

The EKG tech nudges me. "You don't look so good."

"I'n okay." I'm acutely aware that I can't make an "m" sound.

The first dose of Adenosine doesn't work so we draw up a second. This time our guy, still sweaty and anxious, heart racing at 190 beats a minute, points at my face. "I don't know if I want her in here, Doctor. She looks…*contagious*."

"Excuse me?" The physician, who has been focused on our cardiac patient, goes rigid when he sees me. Grabbing onto my jaw, he inspects my tongue. At the same time, Meg pushes the second dose of medicine and the patient's heart rate dumps to 110. He's fixed. Without another glance at the sweaty and yet relieved individual, Dr. Bennet speaks calmly to the tech, "Repeat the EKG, Lashon. Nurse…uh, I'm sorry, I don't know you're name. You. *Kiddo*."

"Meghan."

"Nice to meet you, Meghan. If you would be so kind and grab some 0.3mg Epi, Solumedrol and Benadryl and meet me across the way." Bennet squeezes my shoulder. "This gal needs a fixin'."

Dr. Bennet's face scares me. He's a relatively new physician who addresses nurses and techs with endearing terms like *darlin'* and *kiddo* even though I'm personally a decade older than him. Bennet's an approachable man and I sense that he's just trying to fit in, but I cringe visualizing a response from Bev Martin. The Neanderthal isn't any prepubescent medical man's honey pie.

Dr. Bennet pushes me across the bay like a father escorting a toddler, his smile practiced and controlled, but his eyes betray him. They're flickering with panic. I often wonder what doctors think about when challenged with an actual life-saving act. I bet most don't think at all. They just *do. Do the steps. Follow the protocol. Save the life.* Training takes over. It must. But in the beginning, at that very first instant when reality sets in; when they understand a life is in jeopardy and they're Top Dog, *completely* responsible. There's got to be flash of doubt... *Oh hell! What am I supposed to do about this?!* Followed by an internal pep talk... *Don't panic. Smile. Pretend everything's cool.* Then a prayer...*Please God, help me out here. This one...I'm not too sure about.*

Seven is the only vacant room in the joint and it's tiny. It contains the standard equipment—monitor, oxygen and suction—but due to its size is used mostly for tooth aches and simple procedures like finger cuts and sprained wrists. I cringe. It's Jamie's room. The last thing I want is to owe the bitch a favor.

Word travels fast around a twenty-something bed ER, especially when the news involves an employee. The first nurse to arrive is Sandee Jean.

Sandee's a committee girl who loves to teach. Truthfully, in the past three years, I've probably learned more from her than any CEU class or computer teaching site. Sandee stiffens when she catches sight of my tongue. It's beginning to protrude from my mouth. Her demeanor automatically shifts from southern polite to determined militant. She comes straight at me like a trained assassin, cuts off my shirt, tags me full of monitor leads and masks my face with oxygen. I would've laughed if I could. Sandee's tone remains sweet as syrup but it is acutely apparent that her inner Marine has been unleashed.

Seconds into Sandee's scissor attack, Tina Page enters the room with an entourage of IV gear. I'm pretty relieved to see her with the needle stuff. Tina's a career girl, favoring the trenches for almost two decades. On the job she's all business but don't let that fool you. Miss Page lives, breathes, and works to go on vacation. At least four times a year she flies off to her happy place, a magical world in the heart of Florida swampland. (Take a guess where.) A little hint. She wears light-up Goofy Hats at Christmas, Cinderella earrings on Valentine's Day, and owns seven pairs of Snow White underwear each displaying a different dwarf. Staff at Dixon Valley refers to Tina Page as the *Mickey Mouse Junkie.*

While Tina straps a tourniquet around my arm and slaps at a vein, Dr. Bennet resurfaces, immediately drilling me about allergies, simultaneously invading my personal space and inspecting what's left of my airway.

I shake my head.

"Meds, kiddo. Do you take any prescription drugs?"

"Her oxygen is dropping, Charles." Sandee mumbles. (Sandee is one of the few nurses who refer to physicians by their first names.)

"Page respiratory, Sandee, and set up for intubation." He turns back to me. "What medical problems do you have? Anything I should know about? Where *is* Meghan with those *meds*? I need EPI!?" Doctor Bennet is starting to lose it.

Meghan appears white faced and strained. "S...sorry it took so long. There were so many EPI's to pick from!"

DOCTOR BENNET....LINE ONE.

"Hy er en son."

The doctor stops dead in his tracks. "What?"

I tried again. "Hy er en son?"

"*HYPERTENSION*? *Shoot!* Don't say it..." Bennet practically snarls at me. "Are you on an ace inhibitor?"

My eyes shoot open but my voice fails. I nod. *(Remember that tiny little pill I took with lunch. That was a blood pressure pill categorized as an ace inhibitor. Generally speaking, medication reactions occur right away, after ingesting the first or second dose. Ace inhibitors are different. You can be on one of these beauties for years and then...suddenly...your tongue swells. And when your tongue blows up from an ace inhibitor, it can easily occlude your airway, which seems to be my current predicament.)*

"Let me take this call." Bennet's tone is strained. "Hold that thought, darlin', and keep *breathing*. Meghan, get those meds into her."

Easy for him to say. Air is barely passing into my lungs, nothing more than a hissing, squeaky wheeze. My now protruding tongue is cutting into my teeth causing it to bleed. I can taste the salty texture as it pools in my mouth and promptly oozes down the front of my chin. A barrage of muffled conversations and shouts of preparation echo just outside my door. Anesthesia is on the line. They're going to cut open my throat. *Fuck.*

Jamie emerges yapping a flutter of apologies. "Sorry girls, I was stuck in room eight placing a catheter. What's up?" Jamie stops short. "What the *hell*?"

Meghan pipes in. "She's having a reaction to…uh…to I think her blood pressure pill."

"No *shit*, Meghan. A fool can see that, but she's…she's turning blue. Did we give her anything?"

"Doctor wants Benadryl, Solumedrol and Epi. I pulled the meds. Anesthesia's coming down."

Jamie frowns and snatches the vials out of Meghan's hand. "I'll take it from here. Uh…thanks, but now that your preceptor's down it might be prudent to focus on your own patients."

Meghan doesn't need to be told twice. Everyone scatters. Tina goes after the crash cart and Sandee exits to hunt down intubation supplies. Jamie starts flipping caps, preparing to administer the medications just as the tech arrives to get a tracing of my heart. His timing is impeccable. Because right then, several things happen simultaneously. First, Jamie and Lashon argue over positioning.

"You need to move, Jamie. I have to get this EKG."

"And I need to give these meds!"

"So do it on the other side."

"The IV…*DUH*! You'll have to work from the left. It's not rocket science. I'm sure you can manage."

"What are you *doing*? That's not…"

But that's all I hear of their conversation because right then a searing pain rips through my chest. My eyes shoot back to Jamie as I frantically reach out and grip her hand. Together our attention turns to the tiny monitor high on the wall. I watch my speedy, yet normal rhythm transform. The squiggles that translate heart beats take on an odd shape that medical professionals say resemble a tombstone. And there's a reason *why* they call it a tombstone. The loss of oxygen has taken its toll. I'm in the process of having a heart attack.

As Jamie calls for help, Lashon straps me with EKG leads and Tina emerges with a big red code cart. I start to hallucinate, or so I think, because right as a burning madness consumes my torso, you're not going to believe who I notice standing against the back wall...

Ollivander Dick RN, the dead hot dog dude.

The weird part, (besides the fact that he's dead), is that Ollie is...*is he singing?* And...and *dancing?* He has this big cheshire grin on his face and, no shit, the fat bastard is harmonizing whatever music is playing from an I-pod strapped to his arm. It sounds like that overplayed tune...*Moves like Jagger.* When he belts out the chorus, swinging his hips in a gyrating C, I realize that I am exactly right.

My body is drenched in sweat as the searing pain continues. In what seems like hours (but is really about ninety seconds) Anesthesia, Dr. Bennet, Sandee Jean, Tina Page and Bev Martin join the party. While a dead Ollie Dick shimmies across the floor in a frantic sort of locomotion, whistling and chortling, a third and final assault pounds me like a sledge hammer. Jamie points to the monitor as the squiggles change once again, displaying the unthinkable.

"V-TACH."

The room explodes in a flutter of activity; nurses riddling my chest with shock pads, anesthesia surgically preparing to slice open my throat, and Dr. Bennet shouting out orders. To me it is nothing more than back noise, like one giant buzzing sound, as the Dickman shuffles to the forefront. He's really belting out the vocals now... *"I'VE GOT THE MOO-A-OO-A-*

OO-A-OO-A-OOVES LIKE JAGGER..."
"NO PULSE."
"Tina, prepare to shock at 200 joules."
"PREPARING TO SHOCK. CHARGING TO 200 JOULES"
"I'M CLEAR. YOU'RE CLEAR, WE'RE ALL CLEAR." Everyone pulls away from the bed. (Important medical note: When a person is getting shocked, do *NOT* touch the patient or *ANY* part of the bed. Absolutely *NO* contact. That's why they always yell I'M CLEAR, YOU'RE CLEAR, WE'RE ALL CLEAR. It's a final warning that the juice is about to flow. Touch a bed when a patient gets zapped, and become a patient yourself.)

As electricity courses through my chest, the acrid smell of burning flesh and sweat and fear all congeals into one final sensation. I don't have time to try and describe it better because right then anesthesia stabs an eleven blade into my windpipe. Blood sputters everywhere. Sandee Jean pumps on my ribs. Jamie shoots me up with another dose of adrenaline. I'm lucky to be thinking at all.

"V-FIB, DOCTOR." Tina shouts.

"PREPARE FOR A SECOND BIPHASIC SHOCK. 200 JOULES."

"CHARGING AT 200 JOULES."

Right then Ollie's big fat jowls shadow my view. He raises his eyebrows and nods obnoxiously like slapstick Charlie Chapin, palms flat on his cheeks, lips wording silently an exaggerated *OH NO!*

He pauses and repositions next to my left ear. Chuckling softly, he whispers... "Lights out!"

And *POOF...!* I'm gone.

Chapter 3

Meghan drops onto to the couch, emotionally and physically exhausted after completing the most grueling day of her middle-aged life. Peeking into her daughter's room, upset at finding it empty even though it's to be expected, Megs heaves a great sigh. It is Friday night, afterall. Did she really think her beautiful and very popular daughter would be home reading a book? Absolutely not. What Meghan yearns for more than anything else is to push back time, maybe fourteen years or so, to when Kamron was still a cookie of a girl, happy to spend every available second squeezed in next to her momma, be it on the sofa, the car, or city bus.

Sadly, Kamron is no longer a baby. She is a young well put together woman with unbelievable grades, a decent part-time job, and a promising future. Soon enough she'd be off to veterinarian school down in Gainesville and Megs would see her even less.

Time flies.

Meghan allows herself this one prize, a warranted pat on the back for getting motherhood right. She did an awesome job and had a smart and spirited daughter to prove it. The two were exceptionally close and rarely argued. Teenagers had a way of doing the exact opposite when forced. So Meg wisely steered cautiously around certain topics, especially matters of the heart, keeping Kamron's spare time obnoxiously occupied and extremely limited. Sadly for moms, boyfriends were inevitable…

Craig was a senior at a neighboring high school when Kamron, also a senior, met him at her Pet Smart job. (He was bringing in his dog Barney for shots and a bath and they hit it off immediately.)

"Well?" Kamron asked after kissing her first real boyfriend goodbye. The three had just finished a pleasant dinner at the local pizzeria. Craig even offered to pay, which was shocking to Meg. *What seventeen year old kid pulls out a billfold with an adult around?* Meg, of course, picked up the tab, but was surprised and rather distressed to discover that she actually *liked* the boy.

Instead of saying something nice, something truthful, she promptly blurted out the speech she'd been mentally preparing for her daughter since the beginning of time. "Tread easy with boys, honey. Friends are more important right now. Men'll pull you in, infatuate you, suck up every second of your available time. They'll try and take over, make you lose your way."

Shocked and a bit disturbed by her mother's outburst, Kamron remained quiet for the rest of the drive. Arriving at their tiny apartment, she turned to the stove and boiled up a kettle of water. After pouring two mugs of chamomile tea, she spoke gently to her mother. "Is that why you never date?"

Kamron's remark surprised her. "I…uh don't date, dear, because I need to focus on you. On being a mother and making sure you're not having keggers in the back yard. I need to keep you safe, watch your grades, and make sure you're not sleeping around." At the last statement Meg winked but made it clear that she was only half-joking. Soberly, she added, "Boys only care about one thing."

Kamron rolled her eyes. "Not *all* boys are like that. There are a few respectable gentlemen around. There's got to be. You should date."

"I don't need a date, sweetie. I have you." Meghan sipped from her steaming cup, once again baffled at Kamron's ability to redirect a conversation.

"Seriously, Mom. I'll be on my own soon and what will you do all day when I'm not around to pester?"

Kamron, of course, was right. Her baby would be gone soon, off to Florida to save the four-legged creatures of the world and then what? Dating had never quite worked out for Meghan Ford, even way back, when Kamron was still in diapers. The only guy she went out with after John was a complete lunatic, another one of those sporty tough guys, big and brawny, and all too aware of his handsome physique. At the beginning she thought Mr. Sweet Knees (that's what she called him) was quite the catch. Their first date was pretty decent and the second even better. He was smart, witty, and relatively fun to be around. *Maybe this is the guy for me!*

Or maybe not. The problem with Mr. Sweet Knees was his telephone. He called constantly, at all hours of the day and night. Worst part, he never had much to say except, "*I miss you, babe*" or "*Sleep tight my gorgeous angel.*" At first Meg thought it was sweet, but she didn't have time to be dilly-dallying on the phone. Literally. When she wasn't working, she was cooking, cleaning, and chasing after a toddler, who had a knack for squeezing toothpaste into her hair and buttering the kitchen floor. At night it took everything Meg had to bathe and gather her daughter, pack morning snacks for daycare, shower herself, and climb into bed. Any phone conversations would have to wait.

One evening, around nine, minutes after putting Kamron down for the night, there was a hard knock on the front door. Mr. Sweet Knees barged into the room and started cussing up a storm, accusing her of leading a secret double life.

"What? Too good for me are you? Too busy to answer my calls? What are you doing every night, huh, babe? *ENTERTAINING*? Let me guess? You're some kind of escort?!"

Shocked and absolutely enraged, Meg lost her cool. "I'm a *MOTHER*, you dim wit! I don't answer my phone at night because I'M SLEEPING! I'm friggin' TIRED!"

And she was tired. Parenthood had proved absolutely exhausting, especially without a partner. The love of her life had flown the coop only weeks after Kamron's birth. Not surprising. Johnny T. was an adventurer. In the two years that they were together, he talked of European travel, hitch hiking across America and seeing the world. John was five years older than Meg, a graduate from NC State with a degree in communications. He worked at Lonnie's Rent-a-car. Not his dream job he liked to say, but the entry-level position was all he could manage with limited experience during a recession. Still, a paycheck was a paycheck, and in no way did John's job title hinder his enthusiasm.

"The best part, Megs, on weekends I can use any car I want. We can go to the mountains or the coast, or…or anywhere! In style, baby!"

Meg thought Johnny T. was a hoot. He was funny and gorgeous, and treated her like a queen. (Years later, when she got to thinking about it, she realized her fatal mistake. Except for the hair color, Mr. Sweet Knees and self-absorbed Johnny T. could've easily been brothers. It seemed that Meg's type wasn't her type at all.)

Promptly following high school graduation Meg was hired on at the local diner. She had been accepted to NC State but after meeting Johnny T. decided to take time off to save money and travel. Megs' parents warned her about the dangers of young love and more so of delaying an education. Meg didn't listen. She was sick of school and recklessly in love! When John devised a plan to drive cross-country the following summer, Meg was all for it. They both picked up extra hours and worked diligently to pay for the trip. Come spring they were off to California!

Then...well... Meg got sick. Literally. Barfing her guts out every morning, nauseas in the afternoon. For fifteen days she played stupid, blaming her weak stomach on a silly virus, almost certain that it was not. A Dollar Store test and two pink lines verified her fears. Meg couldn't bear to say it out loud, but at the time being pregnant was nothing less than tragic. Of course John understood. Shoot. He seemed *happy*!

So instead of spending summer days camping at Yellow Stone Park and photographing the Hoover Damn, they used their savings to acquire and furnish a small apartment. John picked up a second job and Meg continued to work at the diner. Cross country trips to California were placed on the back burner. School would have to wait.

As Meghan's belly grew in size, John's attitude waned. The seventy hour work weeks were taking their toll. No longer was he the funny, easy going collegiate that she fell in love with, but more like a grumpy old stuffed hat, too tired for anything but slumping on the couch with the clicker, or sporadically perusing a travel magazine that did nothing now but completely disgust him. Once in awhile he'd receive a text from one of his old buddies off on another amazing adventure.

"Ronny's washing sailboats down in the Caribbean," he growled. "Mikie's stationed in Germany with the Army, and Aidan, that bastard... Aidan's in Hawaii selling surfboards. That was *my* idea!" John complained. "I'm stuck here with...with...while my friends are off seeing the world!"

"I'm not sure washing boats is that much fun, Johnny boy."

"You're missing the point, Megs. It's not the work that makes the adventure, it's the change in scenery. You don't understand."

She really didn't. The minute Kamron arrived, Meg couldn't imagine being anywhere else but close to her baby. The fact that John cared more about hiking a friggin' mountain on the other side of the world than raising his beautiful daughter caused additional tension. Could he not see the tiny miracle bundled up before him? Did he not understand that Kamron was far more important than hiking boots and surfboards?

Megs figured he would come around eventually, but she was dead wrong. One month after Kamron's birth, John joined the Marine Corps. He showed up hours late from work, half-in-the-bag, with a sloppy grin on his face, announcing that he was off to save his country.

"Your *country*?" Meg scorned. "What about your *family*?"

But the government papers were already signed and that was the end of Johnny T. The only good thing about the service was that Mr. Wonderful's salary was easily garnished so, if nothing else, Meg received a monthly check. Not once did Johnny T. call or send a card, not even on Kamron's first birthday. In fact, after his four years of service, the love of Meg's life stayed over seas, away from the clutches of government controlled paternity suits, probably climbing a stupid mountain. That was the end of Meg's fiscal assistance.

Out of convenience and desperation, Meg stayed with the diner. Her mother watched the baby at the beginning, and come pre-school the boss was nice enough to let her show up after the morning drop-off time. When Kam turned fifteen Meg transitioned to nights, picking up work at the only high-end restaurant in town. She was well paid but the job did nothing for her self-esteem. There were definite moments, usually while standing at attention waiting on some pompous ass to decide which red wine was dry enough to accompany his eighty dollar steak, that Meg took a second to internally kick herself for not starting NC State back in the day. Oh, how she yearned to be in school! But then, well, would she have her daughter? The idea of turning back time and erasing the most important thing that ever happened to her sounded preposterous. Raising Kam was the only thing that ever made sense.

But waiting on tables, even at a steak house that literally doubled her salary, was beginning to wear thin. Folks it seemed could never quite accept restaurant work as a career. Serving and bartending were just a means to an end, a mere stepping stone to something more important. Something better. Meg was constantly being probed by customers.

"What is it that you do, sweetie, you know, when you're not working here?"

"Uh, oh…I raise my daughter, I guess."

"So you're married?"

"No. Never did manage that."

"What about health insurance? A 401K? Surely you must be concerned about long term security?"

"I manage just fine." Meg smiled easily, maintaining perfect composure. "Your appetizers are ready, sir. Shall I bring them out?"

She could hear their muttering as she walked away, shaking their heads sadly or possibly in disgust, swearing her off as another life long loser. Truth be told, her restaurant offered awesome insurance but Meg was compelled to keep the customers guessing. It didn't matter how she responded. Certain minds were already made up.

Returning to the table, carrying steamed muscles in one hand and garlic spinach in the other, the same asshole remarked, "How does your father handle the fact that his daughter is a waitress?"

"At thirty-four years old, my father doesn't worry much about me anymore." Meg answered lightly, with practiced conviction, but found herself becoming upset. Waitressing was about the show after all, the presentation. To the diner she was nothing more than a stage puppet. No need to discourage the money dumpers.

Characters of all sorts frequented the restaurant. Many were just normal every day steak lovers who expected prompt service, delectable grade-A meat at the requested temperature, replenished water, bountiful bread baskets, clean silverware, and wine glasses always a third of the way full. For these types, Meg would stand in the shadows and only intrude when necessary. Believe it or not, these were the cherished customers, diners who could muster up their own personal conversation and be happy about it.

Not everyone was that easy. Absolutely sick of their companion's company and in constant want of outside stimuli, many patrons were comparable, Meg determined, to that of a nosy next door neighbor. To these customers, the steak house was more like a Dinner Theatre and Meghan the star attraction. They wanted a back story from the very minion serving their food.

Meg was suddenly reminded of Jake, an ancient icon bartender, who offered treasured advice many moons ago. Frustrated by yet another foul round of demonic diners, Meg sat at the bar finishing up her paperwork, complaining as she did so. "I feel like a monkey hobnobbing on stage."

The Bostonian transplant chuckled in a north shore accent as he placed a napkin on the counter in front of her. "You need to sta't thinking of this joint like a *sales* jo-aab. It's not always about the prooaduct. Folks want to eat, shua, but it's more than that. They wanna mem-*ariable* dining *experience*. Keep 'em laughin'. Tell'em a stories. Encourage'm. Make'em *want* to give you money and lo-*ats* of it." Jake winked and poured Meg a glass of cabernet. "You wanna make a buck, sista', stand poised in yar little co'ner. You wanna make *bank*, then put on a show."

Meg could handle a show. But every so often another group of hot shots, the friggin' wrist twisters of the world, would snuggle up to one of her tables and start in with their pompous jabs and almighty attitudes, causing Meg's emotional restraint to wane. Jake referred to the hot shots as clowns, a bunch of *Bozos.*

Like the over-spent piece of shit slurping up steamers commenting about her father, as if berating Meg had great bearing on his very existence. She could see it in his face, hear it in his whispered tones as he murmured snide remarks to the over-milked cow squeezed into the booth next to him. *Lookie there doll, another breeder stuck schlepping drinks to pay for a kid that's probably already pregnant. Another leech sucking the system dry, gobbling up all my hard-earned taxes. Pathetic, if you ask me. A goddamn shame...*

"For some reason being a server isn't good enough for these people. No matter how much money I earn, a waitress is a waitress." Meg complained to Eve during a late night phone conversation. Eve was Meg's best high school buddy, who lived three hours behind in the strange and exotic land of Seattle.

After Meg hung up, Kamron said, "Tell them you're taking classes."

Startled by the sound of her voice, Kamron had

been watching *Die Hard* on AMC so quietly that Meg had forgotten that she was bundled up on the couch next to her. "Tell who, what, dear?"

"Tell the nosy *clowns* that you're taking classes. Better yet, just take a class."

"*Who*? What class? When would I have time for class?"

"You have time, Mom. Come on. I'll be away at college soon and you'll be bored senseless. Since you won't date you might as well work on an education."

"Hey, I...I *would* date...uh, maybe. Besides, I haven't taken a test in years."

"So *what*? You read. A lot. *And* you're smart. I bet you'd breeze right through school. You should be a nurse."

"A nurse? Where did that come from?"

"From you, Mom, *remember*? How many times have you spouted off about trekking the country as an RN? Always blabbing about how they give travel nurses an apartment and set them up with a job. We were going to hit Hawaii that way, remember...*someday*? Well guess what? Someday has arrived."

"Nursing...I kind of forgot about that."

"The next time some dumbass starts busting your chops, tell'em you're in school."

"Why bother? They're nobodies. A bunch of Bozos empowered by expensive wine."

"Why bother?" Kamron grinned. "For starters, I bet your tips get better."

*

Meg's very next shift she was pouring wine for a very well-to-do couple, maybe ten years her senior, and decided to test Kam's theory. They weren't as snide as many of Meg's Friday night regulars, maybe because they had a daughter only a few years younger than Kamron, who sat next to her in band. Still, they had that *way* about them.

"Is Kamron going to *community* college next year?"

Meg pressed a smile. "Oh, no. She's got a full scholarship at State, my little smarty pants. It'll be me at the community college."

Mrs. Waxly jolted up from her martini. "Are *you* planning school, Meg, so late in the game?"

"Late?" Mr. Waxly piped in. "My darling dear, she's still a baby when it comes to the life expectancy of a career girl."

"Oh hush, darling." She slapped at him playfully. "You know what I meant."

Meg grinned nervously. "Kam's off to the dorms so I'll be an empty nester with nothing but time. I signed up for fall. Just the basics, but I'm hoping to enroll in the nursing program."

"*Nursing?* I always wanted to be a nurse. Isn't that right, Stan? What a *noble* profession! I have a cousin who is an LPN. She works in a cardiologist's office. Well good luck to you, sweetheart. If you serve your patients as well as you care for us, you will do most excellent!"

Meg was caught off guard by the Waxly's enthusiasm, and truly shocked when the couple shelled out a bit more green than their usual fifteen percent. After that, Meg made it a habit to squeeze in a bit about school as she worked, and the change in her customers was absolutely baffling. They treated her better, offered kind words, and acted more respectful. Meg actually felt guilty, as if discussing future plans was somehow an assault on her friends in the restaurant business.

"What's so bad about being a waitress, anyway?" She asked Eve during one of their many phone conversations.

"Nothing."

"Then why is it now when I'm thinking about changing careers that people treat me differently? Better?"

"How do you mean?"

"Patrons are definitely nicer, I'm not imagining that."

"School has boosted your confidence, Meg. I think you're finally discovering that a job doesn't make a person. The person makes the person. Now that you have plans to leave the restaurant business, the work seems more bearable. Surprise, surprise, waitressing can be fun! Positive attitudes are contagious. If you're happy and enthusiastic, then guess what? It reflects in your customers."

"That's very insightful, Eve."

Eve laughed into the receiver. "Gandhi's insightful. I can't take credit for that one."

Chapter 4

Meg rifles through the pantry and pulls out a bottle of wine dusting on the back shelf. She isn't much of a drinker but after the day's events feels the urge to chug-a-lug. As she sinks deeper into the couch, both physically and mentally exhausted, she yearns for the old bartender and his consoling ways. She remembers Jake squeezing her hand after her last waitressing shift, remarking... *"You'll be surprised, Megs, how much you'll miss us. Soon enough, sittin' at this ba' and bitching through yar papa wo'k, you'll be considering the good old days."*

Meg's throat tightens and her eyes leak. She lets out a tired, sad sob. *Oh, what a day! What a horrible miserable shift!*

Just recently Megs had been joking about her new duties with Eve. "In a way it's very much like restaurant work. That's why I feel so comfortable. You get pulled every which way. Room One needs an IV, Two wants pain medicine. A doctor's on the phone with orders, Room Three needs to be set up for a pelvic. Two starts vomiting from the pain meds, Four is having chest pain. Truthfully, it's not much different than a busy night at the steak house. I keep calling patient's tables! Can you imagine? My preceptor thinks it's so funny. She says to me... *"You'd be surprised at how irritated some nurses get from a coffee request. They're always complaining...I'm not a waitress!"*

Meg witnessed her first code three weeks prior, when a little old lady was found gasping and blue at a nursing home. Arthritic, demented and contracted into a fetal position, the ED staff was absolutely mortified when EMS wheeled through the back door with a resuscitation in progress.

"It's the son. He won't let go." The paramedic rolled a troubling eye as he attempted CPR on the already departed soul. "I'm sure I've already broken three ribs. Can you call this one, Doc? I need to go vomit."

The demise of an eighty-nine year old woman waiting out her days in a room of shadows was one thing. The unexpected death of a healthy forty-five year old nurse was very much another. Meg didn't realize that certain pills, ace inhibitors in particular, could cause life threatening reactions even after years of consumption. She was under the impression that if you were to have a reaction it would happen right away, or possibly after a couple of doses. But years later? It sounded absolutely absurd. Sadly, it was the state of things. The pill was the culprit.

In Meg's middle-aged life, she had never witnessed such a debacle. The only thing remotely comparable was when the kitchen staff at Charlie's Pub walked off the job during a Friday afternoon lunch rush. At the time, Meg picked up the shift in search of a little extra holiday cash. What a mistake! With a hundred or so hungry business types awaiting salads and chicken, pastas and grilled meats, the kitchen staff, pissed off about no Christmas bonus, waited until at least fifty orders were pending and then marched out the door. The owner, in a frenzy to maintain order, jumped behind the line and attempted to perform what three skilled cooks managed with hours of preparation. (They didn't bother to prep.) He failed miserably.

If only Meg had taken a video of the swarm of berated customers, waiters fighting over salads and half-made sandwiches, stealing orders to appease those seated before them, she could've picked up ten grand on *America's Funniest Home Videos.* Customers were *screaming* like it was a friggin' war zone and Charlie's Lunch Special their last chance at provisions. Card droppers in suits, skin aflame, rushed the hostess stand in droves, demanding to speak with the owner. *Uh...he can't talk right now. He's trying to make a B.L.T.* The situation became so distressing Meg actually dropped her apron, went behind the line, and offered a futile hand at the fryolater.

The half-ass plates and food delays transitioned into one mass exodus. (Meg was relieved to see them go.) The empty dining room was left in shambles. Nobody bothered pushing in chairs. Some were tipped over. Crumpled napkins rolled about like tumbleweed. Unused silverware intermixed with half-filled, over worked water glasses scattered table tops. Checks lay unpaid, scribbled with nasty remarks. *How dare you think about charging me for drinks! I didn't get my lunch!*

Within a month, an *out-of-business* sign was duct taped to the window. You just don't mess up a hundred lunches in a district lined with eateries and expect a come back. Discussing the drama with Jake years later, he had only one thing to say... *"Owner shoulda' paid them bonuses. Cheap basta'd. I know foa ce'tain Cha'lie boy was a sheista'. You wanna pinch a dime, do it on linen. Screw with yar kitchen staff, it'll ruin a joint."*

*

Hypoxia, or lack of oxygen, Dr. Dee explained, was the reason for her preceptor's deterioration. Swelling from the allergic reaction occluded the airway, loss of oxygen premeditated the heart attack, and due to an already taxed cardiovascular system the heart arrested. Game over.

Truth told, before nursing school Meg never realized that a heart attack and cardiac arrest were two different beasts. A heart attack or *Myocardial Infarction* is caused by lack of circulating oxygen, usually due to a blocked blood vessel in the heart. If oxygen isn't restored in a short period, then that part of the organ (heart) dies. CPR and electric shock only come into play when a heart is so weakened, so completely spent, that it fails to pump effectively. The heart begins to quiver causing the victim to lose his or her *pulse*. Only then is it renamed cardiac arrest.

A review of the rhythm strips showed that Meg's colleague went from having a heart attack to ventricular tachycardia, to ventricular fibrillation (the death quiver) in less than ninety seconds. One minute she was good, and the next...

While anesthesia (the airway doctor) cut open the throat attempting an emergent tracheotomy, Doctor Bennet was calling out shock and drugs orders. Nurses were slapping on defibrillator pads, attempting second lines, administering emergent medications. Meg was hailed back into the room to assist with compressions and quickly discovered why the American Heart Association recommended that team members rotate and limit CPR to two minute cycles. Even with adrenaline kicking at a hundred miles an hour, Meg's chest muscles and arms burned from lactic acid build up as she pumped hard and fast, attempting to replace the job of a quivering heart.

Meg's first two codes were not even comparable. Nobody expected the contracted nursing home patient to survive, so her resuscitation lacked enthusiasm. Sure, the team followed protocols and yet deep down they all yearned for a swift departure. It was time for the fragile soul to be released from her prison.

This time it was the exact opposite. Meg couldn't say for certain but she was pretty sure that everyone present, even the not so religious folks, were sending telepathic prayers off to the God of their choice. *Dear God...help us out here. She's YOUNG! Come on, come on, come ON girly...BREATHE! Our Father who art in Heaven... Oh please, oh please, oh please...DON'T TAKE HER!*

The concentration level was past extreme. Team members were in a zone and yet the face of fear continually surfaced. Meg watched Jamie's hands as she screwed together a prefilled syringe of medication. They were shaking so violently, Tina had to assist. Sandee Jean anxiously kept rechecking the monitor, charging the ordered joules; pushing at the skin leads to be certain the rhythm on the monitor was accurate. Tina, the expert IV girl, had to stick twice for a second line. The ER doctor paced as Bev announced rhythm changes and recorded everything on paper. Anesthesia and the respiratory therapist were maximizing the rigged airway, while Lashon, Meg and Mary Catherine took turns pumping on the chest. Everyone had their job. Everyone needed to get it right.

After each shock the whole room would freeze for a smidge of a second before climbing back on the chest, willing the rhythm to change. *Is that a pulse? Yes? Wait...no...* Back and forth, V-Fib, V-Tach...*yes...wait...no!*

On and on the code continued. Defibrillate. CPR. Bag the airway. Administer medicine. Defibrillate. CPR. Bag the airway. Administer medicine. *"Shock her again, then back on the chest!"*

Every option was attempted; the crash cart literally emptied. For ninety minutes the team pushed onward until the victim's bumpy life-rhythm eventually waned and transitioned into a lazy arch that seemed to drop off the screen. Electricity was no longer scattered and quivering through the nurse's heart. It had petered out altogether. The new rhythm: Asystole. Flat Line. The end of the end.

...And yet, Charles Bennet M.D. called for more drugs and functional CPR.

Meg had never seen a physician cry before but could tell both the anesthesiologist and Bennet were having a hard time keeping it together.

"It's been thirty minutes, Doctor. Thirty minutes asystole." Bev reported quietly. Time flies during a code. Time flies when a person needs oxygen. Time flies when nobody wants to discuss the inevitable.

"Prepare another amp of Epinephrine!" Bennet barked.

"Doctor," Bev spoke in a tone unlike her normal critical self. "your efforts have been extraordinary. You did your best. But I think it's time we consider calling this."

Bleary eyed and wild, the physician turned to the staff. "REALLY? But she's our FRIEND! One of *US*! No. No *WAY*! She can't *DIE*! Not today..."

Meg's eyes welled up and a lump developed in her throat. The room stood stock still. Bev shook her head.

"OKAY, OKAY, *FINE*!" The doctor flung an arm over his head. "ARE WE *QUITTERS*? ARE WE JUST GOING TO GIVE UP?"

He glared at the team. Heads dropped. Lips trembled. Sandee Jean started to weep.

"*WELL*? Who wants to QUIT?"

Bev Martin raised a shaky hand.

"ANYONE ELSE AGREE WITH *NEANDERTHALL*?" Bennet spat, enunciating Bev's nickname. "Or better yet, any *PRODUCTIVE* ideas? Anything we might have forgotten?"

"Nothing was missed, Charles." Sandee Jean spoke quietly. "We're just being selfish now."

"Fine. OKAY! *FINE*! Let's take it to a vote. All in favor of stopping?" The physician glared around the room.

Each member slowly and yet firmly raised a hand.

The doctor paused, pinching at his brow. Nobody spoke. Heaving a distressed sigh, he said, "Record the time of death: four fifty-seven." Without another word, he exited the room.

There was a brief moment of silence, and then...pandemonium. The staff of room number seven buckled in a frenzy of emotions. Some shook violently, others blatantly sobbed, collapsing into each other as they grieved the loss of their newly departed friend. By the time Meg removed herself from the distressing area, she was sniveling so badly, she searched for an exit and plunged out of the building, gulping cold fresh air in the heart of the ambulance bay. A paramedic, sensing her mood, emerged from one of the trucks and squeezed her into a bear hug. He was a stranger and yet she clasped hold for dear life. After much consoling and kind words, he directed her back to the nursing lounge already packed with blubbering employees.

As Bev liked to explain, in weeks to come, administration did something right for a change. When it was reported that the resuscitation had failed, nurses were pulled from the floors, new doctors called in, and within forty minutes of the initial shock, it appeared to the untrained bystander that the ER was running business as usual.

A suffocating weariness swept over the staff as volunteers and management passed around juice and coffee. A discussion followed. Dr. Dee attempted to shed light on the medical emergency, requesting that team members express their grief and concerns in hopes of making sense of the insensible tragedy. (Apparently, it wasn't common for a nurse to drop dead in the middle of her shift, and debriefing employees was one way to decrease Post Traumatic Stress Syndrome.) Eventually the phones started to ring. The units needed their nurses back. Devastated or not, The Show must go on. One single hour was spared for the emotionally crippled staff and then it was back to work as usual.

What baffled Meg more than anything, as she retrieved her former assignment from a second floor ICU nurse, was the compilation of complaints bombarding the secretary's desk. Call bells were flashing, people were frowning, standing outside of rooms with arms crossed, mumbling loudly, grabbing anyone that passed to bitch and confront.

"What the hell is my mother waiting on? My sister needs to be turned! She has a bone spurs! Nobody's been in here for hours! We've been trapped in that cramped room forever and there's not even a television set. Do you even have a doctor in this joint?"

Meg peered around at the staff, subdued and blotchy eyed, trying to get through the last hour without spewing obscenities at the mob of dismantled "customers". Nobody was privy to information concerning room seven, even though Meg wasn't convinced that a death confession would help. The patient was a stranger to this crowd. A dead stranger now, that was doing nothing but fucking up the flow.

A fool could see that something terribly wrong had occurred. A life had passed. POOF! The idea of fluffing and stuffing a bunch of selfish *assholes* with consoling and endearing phrases for bullshit PR Scores flat out appalled the new nurse.

Bev muttered to her in the med room as Meg pulled out some Zofran for another nauseous but otherwise healthy individual who had one too many vodkas the night before. He buzzed the call bell three times while she worked to draw up the medication.

"It sickening, don't you think. Human nature?"

Meg didn't know how to respond. Bev rarely spoke to her. Bev, Meg decided, had a knack for muttering. "What are you talking about?"

"Look around. Not one person gives a rat's *ass* about anyone but themselves."

Meg nodded sadly. "You'd think people would have a little more respect for a passing."

"Oh, they do, when it's their *own* relative being electrocuted." Bev growled quietly. "Even now...look at us! We're...*I'm* no better! If that code involved a stranger...I hate to say it, but I would've already moved on. Shoot, I only cry when the family shows up. I'm strong through the ugliness. Even wrapping the body doesn't faze me. Then some long lost aunt shuffles in bumbling for a tissue and I lose it. When it's a friend...someone *close*...I'm not going to lie." Bev's voice was suddenly trembling. "I wish to Christ it had been a stranger..."

*

There is a jumble of sound at the front door. "Ma? Mom?" Kamron barrels into the living room, stricken with fear.

Meg jumps from the couch and rushes to meet her.

"I...I got your call. Oh my God! Are you *okay*?"

Meg can feel the tears before they form. She wraps the only person in the world that really matters into a tight squeeze. "I'm fine, Kam." She whispers. "Now that you're here, everything's going to be alright."

Chapter 5

I wake up in room seven. The lights are off. No call bell is in sight. Shoot, I didn't even get a blanket. *So much for special treatment.* I lay flat on my back staring at the ceiling trying to remember how I got here. I peer around the tiny room and then down at my body. I'm wearing crisp clean nursing scrubs. And they're white. *Who put me in this getup?* They had to be loaners. I always wear dark colors for obvious reasons. Ink marks and coffee stains hide more easily when camouflaged. My thoughts revert to the Neanderthal, back in the day, stories about pristine dress and nursing caps. *This must be some kind of joke.* I check my head. No cap. A very small consolation.

I rub my arms but they're not cold. I feel pretty good, actually. *But how did I get here?* I suddenly remember my blood pressure pill. I reach up and touch my top lip. The swelling has gone down, thank God. *The Benadryl must have snowed me.* I stand up and walk out into the hall. The ER is bustling at top speed with normal everyday bullshit, but somehow the department looks brighter. Cleaner. *Did they paint A-bay?*

The first nurse I run into is Jamie. "Hey Jamie, where are my discharge papers? And when did they paint A-bay?"

Jamie snubs me and turns away, completely focused on her task at hand. That's when I realize she's in the middle of a demonstration; crutch walking practice for the lady in six sporting a newly splinted ankle cast. "Notice that you swing through with the bad foot and use the good one for balance. Like this..."

"I'll be right back," I silently lip the words but, once again, she ignores me. *Typical Jamie.*

I cruise down the hall passing loads of people...Dr. Breezy, Kristi N., Dr. Bennet and Juanetta the tech. I find my orientee, Meg, sitting next to a corridor stretcher placing a line in a sweaty squirming individual, flailing about, begging for pain medicine. My first thought: *kidney stone.* I peer about in search of Meg's replacement trainer. Not a soul in sight. *Figures.* I stand at an arm's breadth and watch her work. Meg sneaks in the needle with utmost precision, easily handling blood tubes, labeling properly as she talks down the anxious individual. *Wow.* A hundred percent better than last time! In previous attempts, her angle had been too deep and she crammed the needle with such brute force it was like she was trying to penetrate a bone rather than a fragile blood vessel.

I softly squeeze Meg's shoulder, and at the same time she squeezes her patient's upper arm. Simultaneously we speak. I say, "Good job, Meg"

She says, "Good job, sir."

I leave Meg explaining the process. "Now that you're medicated, you'll be getting a CT scan. Cat scans are better images than regular X-rays. Let's see if we can locate that little bugger of a stone."

I check back with Jamie who is still detained. Peering at her computer station, I peruse for possible discharge instructions. Not an official form in sight. I know I should sit in my room and wait patiently, but of course I don't. Instead, I hit the lounge. It's where I go between gaps in work load to inspect the fridge for edible snacks, take a pee, or socialize—anything to wear down the clock.

Lindsey, Tina and Morgan are sitting at the table eating lunch, and a fourth nurse is leaning against the fridge downing a container of orange juice. The fourth staff member has her back to me so I don't recognize her at first. This is before she responds to Lindsey in a sweet southern drawl. Only one gal in the department has that voice.

But...but wait.

Sandee Jean? My mind must be playing tricks because just a few hours ago her hair was shorter. And I'm talking ears-a-showin' pixie short. Sandee usually flaunted a thick dark mane that dropped down the small of her back. (Another head of hair that Bev Martin made a fuss over right before crucifying her own mop.) Bev went absolutely *postal*...when was it? Two days ago? Sandee marched into the job, her glorious locks chopped to the bone.

"Why oh why would you do such a thing?" Bev cried.

Sandee Jean smiled sweetly and replied. "I donate ma' haya' every few yea's to the canca' society, to make weeigs."

Bev's eyes went wide. "Sandee Jean, you're a friggin' saint. Where can I get me one of those wigs?" We all laughed but I was pretty certain that Bev wasn't kidding.

These thoughts fire across my synapses as I attempt to link recent events. Over the past seven years Sandee has donated her hair three times. With each chop Bev offered a weekly play-by-play, astounded at the speed in which it grew back. *"Can you believe this shit? My ponytail looks like an aging rat tied to the back of my head and Sandee's designing a third wig!"*

I must be confused from the Benadryl. *No. No you're not. Her hair was in a pixie earlier today. Two days ago she cut it! Two!* I pause, considering the possibilities. Maybe she got extensions? But that didn't make any sense, either.

Before I have the chance to delve any further,

skinny little Morgan stands up to rinse off some grapes in the sink. I gasp. Either she has a basketball under her shirt or...

"Holy Cow! Morgan? You're pregnant? I...I'm so happy for you!" I shout in a mix of excitement and shock. At the same time, Jeanne emerges from the back locker area and rubs at the soon-to-be mama's tummy, Buddha style, and the room erupts in a mix of laughter and spirited comments.

In synchronized harmony Jeanne and I blurt, "When's the big day?"

"October sixteenth."

I bite my lip in attempt to control my facial expression of blatant shock. *October?* That was seven months away. And Morgan is absolutely protruding! *She must have her dates wrong. No way in hell is she only three months...* I refrain from verbalizing any such commentary. No pregnant woman needs to be reminded of increasing girth. I smile enthusiastically, turn to the coffee machine and busy myself preparing a cup of Joe.

Jeanne floors me when she says, "Only a few more weeks, Morgan. Close and yet so far."

Confused, I spin around and gape at my co-workers. "Try again, Jeanne. More like *seven* months."

She doesn't respond because during this brief interlude the break room door swings open and Josh enters. Josh is one of the few male ER nurses employed at Dixon Valley. He moves deliberately, diving into the fridge in search of his lunch bag. "What the JUNK!" He cuts me off, snarling, arms flying up to enhance his rage. "Who's the ASSHOLE that keeps tossing my lunch?"

"Did you have your name on it?" Tina asks.

"Really, T? This isn't second grade."

Tina points to the sign on the fridge door.

"Every Thursday Nancy cleans the fridge. Anything that's not labeled gets tossed."

Josh's eyes narrow as he scans the shelves. "There are at least six bags in here without names. Why the hell was mine tossed? Damn it! I'm *starving*. I was looking forward to those hotdogs."

"HOTDOGS?" The room chirps in unison.

Jeanne groans, disgusted. "Do you have any *idea* what's *in* a hotdog? It's the pig's asshole for chrissakes. Guts and bowels, crap the butcher scrapes off his shoes. How can you stomach such a thing?"

"Nothing like a dog on the grill with a little mustard'n onion. My absolute gosh darn favorite. Dee-*lish*." Josh rubs his tummy in an overzealous pantomime then quickly shifts emotions as he retrieves a "heart friendly" frozen dinner allotted for late-night patients. Sarcastically, he snaps, "If you think this compressed piece of turkey is any better, then you're all a bunch of fools. Just because the slogan has a heart in it doesn't mean *jack*. It tastes like cardboard."

"Better cardboard than pig connective tissue." Lindsey retorts.

"I still can't get over the fact that you even bring wieners for lunch, especially after what happened to the Dickman." Tina adds. "I'm 'bout fearful of a hotdog, now."

"All I can say is the next *dick* who tosses my food is gonna get his or her *ass* kicked. Give me a piece of paper. I need to write anal-retentive Nancy a note." Josh scribbles out a few words as the conversation shifts to Lindsey's Halloween costume.

"Halloween?" I complain. "How 'bout we get through Easter?"

Nobody responds. I'm being completely ignored. Irritated, I turn to leave and knock over my coffee. The brown creamy substance splashes across the floor.

"Be ca'ful."

"I...I'm sorry, Sandee..."

Josh cuts me off. "What?" He's still writing his Nancy Note on the counter next to me. "I did *not* spill that coffee."

Jeanne chuckles. "I guess it just fell over by itself then?"

Tina scoffs. "Maybe it was the Indian."

Lindsey adds, "I bet the Indian ate his hotdog too."

The table snickers hysterically as Josh cleans up the mess. I stand by completely dumbfounded. Peering down at my exactly perfect white scrubs, it suddenly occurs to me.

> ...I don't wear white.
> ...Morgan did *not* eat a watermelon.
> ...Sandee Jean is not a Chia Pet.

I must be asleep. (Have you ever done that? Been confused about a dream but figured it out prior to waking? Then you're like...*okay, now don't forget the details.* And then you wake up completely oblivious?

All I can say is that Morgan is going to be floored when I resurrect the pregnancy specifics. I have this weird gift, you see. If I dream of a big belly, then it grows. So far I had predicted seven babies. Of course I'll never forget Jamie's snide remark after my last announcement. "They were all *trying* to get pregnant you *fool*. You dreamt it because it's all anyone talks about—friggin' burp bibs and pacifiers. You're no seer, sweetheart."

Jamie was a definite Debbie Downer. A non-believer of miracles and visions, not to mention magic or anything remotely supernatural. Even Santa Claus pissed her off. I remember being present when Jamie reenacted her son's troubled reaction after she announced, point blank, that St. Nick was a farce. He was six years old.

"Why would you break a kid's heart like that?" *I scowled.*

"Oh, please! The holidays are much easier now that he knows. I can wrap gifts and lay them under the tree weeks in advance. I don't have to pay ridiculous mall fees for photos with a fool. And now on Christmas Eve, instead of running around like a headless chicken, I can enjoy a nice glass of wine. What's the big deal, anyway? The kid would've figured it out eventually."

Speak of the devil. Jamie flings open the break room door and hollers in for Sandee. "Girlfriend! Juice break's over. You got a newby in seven and he's sick as hell. Chop, chop!"

Sandee sighs and drops an empty carton in the garbage. She turns to go and says, "I don't like the-is assignment. Working in numba' seven ste-ill gives me the che'ills."

Room seven is my room. No, no, no...that's right. This is a dream. Still...never could I recall a dream so real. So vivid! *They must have cranked me up with a bunch of serious drugs during the code.*

I pause. The code?

Yeah, the code. Your code.

But...but wait... My mind shifts to Morgan's belly and Sandee's hair. Josh getting blamed for the coffee spill. An odd sensation cripples my senses as my mouth begins to water. I stumble to the bathroom tucked in the back corner of the lounge, discretely hidden behind a wall divider. My stomach is flip-flopping and I make it just in time to dry heave into the commode. Nothing comes out but the lurching continues for a good five minutes. My head is spinning and I begin to sweat.

Fumbling for the sink nozzles I twist on the cold water. Splashing my face until the top of my scrubs are absolutely drenched, I open my eyes and gaze into the mirror.

Where the hell is the mirror?

Gone.

What the fuck?

I touch my face. Skin and lips over a sharp jaw and thin neck...it's definitely me. But...*who the hell am I?* My mind goes completely blank as I attempt to resurrect a scrap of memory.

It takes a minute but my senses replenish. *I am a registered nurse, yes, going on fourteen years. I work at the Dixon Valley Emergency Department. I am currently studying for my CEN and used to be crazy about trauma. I have taken TNCC four times and teach ACLS every third Saturday. I hate doing EKG's and I'm pretty good with a needle.*

I pause, slightly relieved. But something is off...

When is my birthday? Do I have a house or live in an apartment? Am I a hatch-back or Lexus kind of girl? Do I eat hotdogs?

I freeze. Horrified. Did I have a fucking *STROKE?*

No, no, no...think about this rationally. You're walking, talking and yes, you can feel both arms and legs. You're not slurring. You can speak. Think. Move. You're just dry-heaving.

I stare at a new sticker taped up in front of the sink where the mirror used to be. *Be a Superhero Hand Washer!* But wait... I flip completely around and stare at the wall behind me bearing the same exact sticker. I read the sign again. *Be a Superhero Hand Washer!* I touch the wall behind me and feel the taped sign under my finger tips. It has bubbled in then center and I automatically rub it smooth.

Why would there be two signs?

Because hand washing is important.

For some reason this continues to bother me. I return to the sticker over the sink and trace it with my finger. I feel for a corner but it's smooth...like...like it's *not* a sticker. My body tenses as I re-read the sink sign. The writing is off somehow.

I gasp. The writing is reversed? *Impossible!* As if the sign above the sink is...*is it a reflection?*

How can it be when there's no mirror?

I lean my face into the wall and sure enough, squish my nose on a protruding surface. *Holy crap!* The mirror is invisible. Then I think about it...

Am I invisible?

Watery nausea returns and the spinning consumes me. I drop to the floor of the small employee bathroom and press my glistening sweat soaked face against the cold linoleum. *Shut your eyes. Wake up, damnit. Get the hell out of this nightmare! Chill.* I squeeze my eyes shut and wait.

Every few seconds I peek through lashes in hopes of viewing white linen. Pray for the sensation of snuggling under crisp clean sheets instead of lying sprawled and crooked on a cramped bathroom floor. I take long deep breaths and attempt to shift my thoughts. *Dream about mermaids or babies...or giant robots. Wait...hold up? Did you just say giant robots? What kind of dream would entail mechanical 'bots?*

"You might want to get off that floor." A voice erupts from above. "It may look clean but both you and I know that it's absolutely filthy."

Still disgusted with my alternate robot path, I gaze upward from my germ-infested oasis and discover a man leaning against the open bathroom door eating an enormous mustard-splattered hotdog.

Ollivander Dick wipes his upper lip with a napkin and chuckles. "'Course it really doesn't matter much now, does it?"

Chapter 6

Meg bumps the alarm repeatedly before rousting from slumbering covers. Her dreams are holding her hostage. Having to serve a bread basket and shrimp cocktail to a robot at the end of Main Street puts her behind. All tables must get served! Even robots need to eat.

Meg chuckles at her dream-state rationalization as waking thoughts emerge. "Waitressing nightmares," she mutters. "Will they ever end?"

According to the bed stand alarm she is behind schedule. Meghan hates to rush. Normally she clocks in twenty minutes prior to shift change, early enough to relax and emotionally prepare for another twelve hour beating. Today she will get only ten, which puts her in an undeniable panic. So far, in her very brief nursing career, Meg has never been late. Ever. Not that six months is an exceptionally long time, but the stepping stones to a great beginning were being laid. And according to Elaine Mattern, charge nurse extraordinaire, being prompt was the most important attribute of a prudent and successful nurse. At least that was the impression she gave several moons ago…

*

"Nurses need to stay healthy, get a decent night's sleep and be ready for action. We don't *call out*." Elaine had warned. "Not *true* ER nurses who have any respect for the profession. Sick calls leave *gaps*. Gaps that have to be *absorbed*. Your colleagues will be forced to work twice as hard picking up your slack because, you know what? According to the government, if there's an empty bed and a patient in need, we have to fill the damn thing even if it means overextending the help.

"The paper pushers of the world would like to believe that adding another bed to each assignment isn't a problem. But it's not a bed it's a *PERSON*. And that person can be sick as the day's long, with needs so great they can consume a nurse. Number crunchers have no *IDEA* the time it takes just to get a withering adult *undressed,* let alone *cared* for. And if there's a complaint about delays, which there always is, nobody gives two shits if I have three staff members or ten. The Show must go on no matter WHO calls out. So unless you're dead, I expect you to be prompt and ready to tackle the day."

Management reassigned Meghan to train with Elaine following the tragic loss of her preceptor. The director thought a week of shadowing Charge would be a great learning tool for the middle-aged new grad. *"This will give you a chance to get your confidence back, Meg, and let you see the demanding political aspects of the job. One week with Elaine and you'll be happy to go back to a patient assignment."*

Weeks following the code, Meg's nerves remained tattered. Although in retrospect, compared to the rest of the crew, she was the least affected by the death. More than once had she marched into the break room and found a weeping staff member dabbing tissue at leaking mascara, or stumbled upon nurses whispering tearfully, huddled in tight corners of the med room.

With the funeral looming, an all-consuming emptiness swept over the department. Meg could sense the distressed state whenever there was downtime, before the big rush and during the occasional lapse in patient care. At times she actually witnessed muttering prayers for extra busy work loads. True emergencies, it seemed, did wonders for a person's sanity.

Elaine hadn't been scheduled on the day of the code so Meg had a hard time gauging her reaction. The veteran employee had a knack for skirting emotional issues by focusing on job specifics and training the newest member of Dixon Valley definitely helped. She rambled continuously, spewing speeches and monologues on everything from promptness to acceptable charting. In fact, Elaine babbled so much that first shift Meg wondered if it wasn't part defense mechanism.

It wasn't until months later, when Elaine considered Meg her friend, did she confess how the death personally affected her. It was much easier, she said, to bottle everything up and mourn in solitude when the workday was done. *"On the job, it's crucial that we keep a dry eye." Elaine claimed. "Lock in the sadness. Get too emotional around here and you'll screw something up."*

Meg listened astutely as Elaine's attendance spiel transitioned into one concerning vigilant preparation. "Stocking is another one of my pet peeves. Supplies don't just *show up* in patient care areas. They need to be *put* there. Techs handle the brunt of it, but some days are so brutal they just can't physically get to it all. That's why it's mandatory that you check your gear at the start of each shift. Whenever I get a free moment, I peruse and make sure the nurses are fulfilling this obligation. If shit hits the fan, it'll be me who takes the final beating. Charge gets blamed for *everything*. No kid gowns? I'm flooded with emails. Lead monitors get tossed with the laundry, I'm pulled into the office. No pillows? Call in the Navy. I've been to actual meetings concerning the *texture* of our toilet paper and why a patient didn't have access to wet wipes. I'm not kidding. I couldn't make this shit up."

Meg trailed Elaine and her rattling comments into the patient care area. "Rooms need to be checked for monitor stickers, oxygen tubing, alcohol swabs, tongue blades, suction..." Elaine paused, cursing. "See? Look at this mess! No suction canister. It drives me *crazy*. Just watch. If I don't replace this container, the next patient will show up seizing and Witch Doctor Ribster, wait until you meet her, will have a *cow*! You think *I'm* nit picky. You think *I* bitch. Ribster makes me look like a friggin' *saint*. She'll have the nurse in tears, high-tailing down to the stock room in search of a set up. Then we'll have to hear her RANT about how lazy and ill-prepared we all are. She's called the witch doctor for a reason. On this point, I hate to admit it, but I'm in agreement with the miserable hag. Having proper supplies is a very important piece. Only one thing is certain in an emergency department—if your section is out of sorts, then it's a guaranteed day of chaos.

"So..." Elaine momentarily inhaled. "Now that you've been officially warned, let's get you up close and personal with the stock room."

Charge carried a phone and it rang incessantly. A total of four times, Meg counted, during their rummage of the supply area. Elaine halted her commentary long enough to interject another formal greeting.

"Dixon Valley Emergency Department, this is Elaine." The seasoned nurse's brow crinkled and her lips crumbled into a frown. Expecting a snarled response, Meg was surprised by Elaine's slightly shrill and yet singsong reply. "Get yourself better, sweetie. Hopefully we'll see you tomorrow." As she dumped the phone back into her pocket, Elaine immediately grumbled. "And here we go with the loser call outs. Not even eight in the morning and I'm down a three o'clock nurse."

"Don't you have a scheduled on-call?" Meg asked innocently.

"That's not the point. I'm still stuck wasting valuable time on the horn. Nobody ever answers; even though phones are protected and worn like a third arm these days. God forbid a person can function without a stupid gadget spewing fluffy kitty *Facebook* quotes and constant grammar-less footage. I'm surprised they don't make'em waterproof, although I'm sure it's in the works. Ninety percent of these fools would attempt electrocution in the shower rather than miss a text. But just you wait. It'll take a dozen tries to get even a single staff member on the line."

"So text, then."

"*Text*? I can't text!"

"Why not?"

"Because I'm *old* and texting is *painful*. Why type for-*ever* when I can dial a few digits? You know, every Monday this happens. At least one *reject* has to make my life miserable." Elaine shook her head. "Instead of running the department, keeping the flow, I'm forced to scour staffing in search of a replacement when I'm pretty certain that my "call out" is relaxing by the pool. Don't be that nurse, Meg. We work three days a week with a set schedule two months out. Plan around it."

Meg figured that being charge nurse came with an envelope of responsibilities but to watch it first hand, to witness the hassling debauchery, made her wonder why anyone would ever purposefully step foot into such a position. Governing staff and stocking were bad enough, but managing the cattle crossing of individuals that showed up for treatment on an average day, usually minutes apart—it was amazing to Meg how more people didn't drop dead in the waiting area.

"It's not like the television show." Elaine reported. "Space is limited. We're a twenty-five bed unit which means we have exactly that—twenty-five beds. Most days the department is so full, with EMS trucks rolling in the back and ambulatory folks marching through the front, we're forced to build rooms."

"Build?"

"Patients with simple complaints sit in chairs. We put extra stretchers in the hall. Twenty five transforms into forty five. Forty five active patients. That may not sound like a lot, but it'll put a hurtin' on a facility of this size."

"I wouldn't want a hall bed." Meg commented.

Elaine chuckled. "You're not the only one."

As the day progressed in a frenzy of activities Meg observed and assisted as Elaine, who, true to her word, bed swapped patients out of cozily confined rooms to chairs and stretchers erected in the halls. "Sorry, sir, but now that you've been evaluated we need to move you out for someone sicker."

Meg cringed at Elaine's abrupt language, and yet was truly perplexed at the number of people with less than remarkable complaints. "I expected the emergency department to be full of, I don't know, *emergencies.*"

"Another myth preened by the Idiot Box." Elaine explained. "What really drives the ER these days are overwhelmed primary care doctors and lack of insurance. If it's a late Friday afternoon and "Mr. Smith" calls his doctor with belly pain, he gets sent to us."

"Why is that?" Meg asks.

"Because it's Friday. Primary care doctors don't work late on Fridays. They have golf games and plans in Myrtle Beach." Elaine rolled her eyes. "It's absolutely ridiculous, but if the office can't fit them in then its policy, LAW, that they recommend us. Their response goes something like this: *Mr. Smith, if you feel that your medical needs cannot wait until our next available appointment, then may I suggest the emergency department?* An hour later, Mr. Smith shows up and says: *My doctor referred me here. I shouldn't have to wait.* But he really wasn't referred. It was just a simple mandated reply probably given by a secretary."

"But today's Monday. What's so special about today?"

"It's kind of like Friday except reverse. Many folks wait until the weekend is over to seek medical attention. Nobody wants to waste a play day in the hospital. Offices become inundated with appointment requests so in comes the speech. *If you feel your medical needs can't wait...blah, blah, blah...*"

Meghan pointed at the wait board. "These can't all be bullshit referrals."

"Of course not. Some are real. Many, more than half of our business, comes from the uninsured. By law, the ER cannot refuse a patient. It's a great theory. We wouldn't want anyone to die from acute appendicitis or walk around with a broken bone because they're short on up-front funds. These individuals still accrue a bill but at least they get treatment. However, as you can see it's amazing what folks consider an emergency. We see anything and everything from friggin' bug bites to gunshot wounds. Now, I can always appreciate a decent gun shot wound. Wait until your first one, Meg. The victim is always some punk minding his own business, hanging out at the gas station with wads of money stuffed in his pockets."

"Why would a gun shot come here? We're not a trauma center."

"Exactly my point. If you really were accidentally caught in a gas station face-off, you'd be dialing 911 from the scene and not showing up with a hanky stuffed under your shirt in the back seat of your buddy's Gremlin. It's not rocket science but when you're running from the law that's what you do—run."

What impressed Meg so much about Elaine was her ability to be yanked in twelve different directions while maintaining a level of composure. Everybody wanted a piece of the charge nurse. If it wasn't to assist with an EMS check-in, there was always some brittle diabetic with terrible veins in need of a line. Her presence was requested in the waiting area on several occasions for angry customers grumbling about delays, forever asking the question why certain individuals cut line.

"Why? Because she's sicker than you," Elaine muttered as they moved away from the congested room. Her public reply was a bit more politically correct...

"Please understand that the emergency department is EXTREMELY busy. Everyone will be evaluated but sadly some medical conditions can NOT wait. Due to HIPPA Laws I am not at liberty to discuss these ailments but, rest assured, the risk for DEBILITATION and LIFE-ENDING injury is HIGH." Elaine enunciated like she was speaking to a foreigner or the hearing impaired. *"Please remain empathic to your fellow MAN and thankful that it is not YOU cutting line. Being treated FIRST in an EMERGENCY department is never a good thing."*

No matter what activity Elaine got involved in the charge phone continued it's battering. Another referral, the house supervisor checking on admissions, a mobile unit with transfer questions, random family members seeking updates on loved ones. "Will this phone ever stop ringing?" Elaine crowed. Everything, it seemed, fell into her lap, including periodic rants from the nurses.

"It can't be my turn already!" Jamie huffed. "What about Bill? Bill's had an empty room for over an *hour*! Are you blind?"

"Bill's got two ICU admits. He's hanging blood on one guy almost as fast as the dude's shitting it out. Now if you'd like to switch assignments, I'm pretty sure Bill would be okay with it..."

"FINE! I'll take the new patient."

Elaine winked. "Everyone bitches. Even you, Meg, will complain eventually. I try to be fair but there is no *perfect* in emergency services. Some days you'll feel abused. But hey, at least I *attempt* to keep the peace. Not all charge nurses worry like me. A few, I won't name names, but *a few* run the joint from a *chair*."

"That sounds impossible."

"It makes for a hostile environment is what it does. Amazing what a bit of power will do to a person. One day they're in the trenches with you, the next they're loading your rooms two and three at a time, snubbing off your attitude, announcing that "*it is what it is*" and "*to get over it*", as they walk away without lifting a finger. You find them minutes later in the break room texting on their cell phone, or flirting with a friggin' paramedic, completely unscathed by the fact that you're drowning in A-bay. Don't be that charge nurse, Meg."

"I don't plan on ever taking on that role."

Elaine grinned. "Nobody does."

"Elaine," The secretary tapped her on the shoulder. "Line one. It's Thompson. She's sick."

"*Another* call out?" Elaine snarled. "Monday night and we're down two. This is absurd! Who hired these slackers? If I can't find coverage it's going to be another sixteen hour day."

"What do you mean?"

"What do I *mean?* Do you really need to ask, Meg?" Elaine howled. "Because I refuse to leave a drowning ship is why. Because I'm on a *team.* It's what I *do. Now* do you see? Can you understand why attendance is so important? Don't be that slacker, Meg. This emergency room can't handle another weak link."

*

Memories of Elaine's speech debilitate her thoughts as Meg races the clock. First the breadbasket nightmare and now stuck behind a garbage truck! And still seven minutes away from the hospital. What a disaster! Meg sputters obscenities from the driver's seat, fingers clamped tightly around the wheel as she inches down the final stretch of road, Dixon Valley looming in the distance. Literally sprinting from the parking lot, Meg swipes her badge with only thirty seconds to spare. Relieved, she slows her pace attempting to catch her breath. According to Elaine, "showing up" was twenty-five percent of the job. Meg sighs heavily and mumbles a prayer. *Now to get through the other seventy-five...*

Chapter 7

"Am I dead?"

"As a doornail."

"Then why am I stuck in the emergency department?"

"Stuck? That's one way to put it. You're definitely stuck."

"Forever?"

"No. Not forever."

"Is this heaven?"

"Far from it. Give me a chance and I'll explain everything." Tapping at his head with a meaty finger he adds, "*Loads* of information in this noggin. But first things first. What shall I call you?"

"How do you mean?"

"Your name, sister. *Le signature.* A gal's got to have a *nombre.*"

"Name, right. Well it's...uh... They call me..." I pause. "That's weird. It's on the tip of my tongue. The very tip! Well *you* should know it. You watched me die."

Ollie chortles. "Pick a name. That's what I had to do."

"That's *ridiculous.* You're Ollie Dick."

"Well looky there, another genius. Of course I'm privy to that information *now.* But at the beginning of this...this *Sentence*, things were different. My memory was pure chicken dung. That's how it works. Only now that I've been replaced can I remember."

"Replaced?"

"Yeah. By *you*." Ollie grins. "Yepper. Before you bit the bucket, I referred to myself as Wallie. Wallie Rich. Funny if you think about it. Kinda like a slanted ghost alter ego. Truthfully, I like Wallie Rich *way* better than Ollie Dick. What was my mother *thinking* marrying a varmint with that last name? " Ollie pauses. "Then again, now that I can actually *remember* my old man, I've got to admit he was pretty cool.

"He owned a race track down near Carolina Beach. Not big motors but little-kid jazzed up Model-T roadsters. A step up from bumper cars is how Mom liked to explain. We charged three bucks a pop and the ride lasted a good ten minutes. They were speedy racers for their size and pulled a decent crowd. Dad worked the ticket booth and I handled concessions. We sold cotton candy, tinted popcorn and eventually upgraded to deep-fried taters and grilled delicacies. Onion rings, french fries, big seeded rolls stuffed with peppers and sausages, chicken fried steak, foot long doggers loaded with chili—Carolinians love 'em some greasy vittles now.

"But that's not the point is it? What I'm tryin' to say is that my old man wasn't so bad even with his crummy last name." Ollie sighs. "I really miss that drag strip. Sometimes he let me help with the cars. Flushing the engines, filling the tanks with gas, wiping the windows. We tossed a flag at the beginning and end of every race, and on Saturdays if a kid rode five times they got a ribbon." Ollie's smile reeks of nostalgia. "Those were some serious glory days. Why couldn't I get stuck at the drag strip for purgatory?"

"What about that picture in the break room?"

Ollie frowns. "What pi'ture?"

Ollie follows me out of the bathroom and around to the lunch table. I point to the plaque photograph. "How have you possibly remained oblivious when your face and *name* has been plastered on the wall for over a decade?"

Ollie leans in and carefully inspects the image. "Well I'll be *damned*. That *is* me." Frowning, he adds, "Shoot! Did they really have to use my badge pi'ture? I look like a melon. Check out the double chin! You know, I should've kept my goatee. My wife always said I looked better with facial hair." Ollie's eyes go wide and he practically stumbles.

"What?"

"I have a *wife!*"

"You're just figuring that out?" Crossing my arms in disgust, I snap. "Let's cut the bullshit. I find it pretty hard to believe that this is the first time you've noticed that photograph. And how does one forget a wife?" I shake my head. "Don't say it, moron. *Christ.* I'm in *hell* with a chauvinist."

"Take it easy, lady. I'm only trying to explain. We're *blind* from ourselves. That's how it is in the Up-or-Down or In-Between, or wherever the heck *Here* actually is."

"I don't get it."

Annoyed, Ollie reiterates. "If there's a pi'ture and I'm in it, all I see is a blank sheet. That goes for newspaper clippings, documents, and mirrored images. *Regular* mirrors, anyway. This plaque, before you dropped dead, all I could see was a blank piece of wood, like an award waitin' to happen. But now...well looky there! What a beautiful inscription. I was under the impression that ya'll considered me lazy."

I cringe, thinking how many times we ripped on old Ollie sitting in this very lounge. "Surely, if you've been floating around this long, you would'a been present for a couple Dickman discussions?"

"Hey! *Easy.*" Ollie says. "For your information, I can hear bits and pieces but as soon as my name is mentioned everything jumbles and the conversation trips into freak Charlie Brown teacher mode. A bunch of *wa*, w-*wa*, *wah* crap. But enough about me. We need to move on. Let's pick you a name. What's it going to be?"

"Is this purgatory?"

Ollie pulls open the fridge and reaches in for a mini Coke designated for patients. "One thing at a time girly, girl. Name. What shall I call you?"

"Is it Gloria?"

"Do you want it to be Gloria?"

"Is that my name?"

"It is now. And a last?"

"Errr...House?"

"*House?*" Ollie rolls his eyes. "Trying to infringe on a television series, is that it?"

I shrug, laughing. "It's the first thing that came to mind."

"How about we just stick with Gloria? It's not like you'll need a last name 'round here. Chop, chop!" Ollie double-claps. "Moving on. Let's discuss your new role in the emergency department."

"*Role?*" My eyes go wide. "I have a *job*? Whatever happened to The Kingdom of Good'n Plenty? Heaven? Olympus? Sugar-lovin' Paradise? The Beer Gardens?" "*Really* Gloria?" Ollie frowns. "You can at least *pretend* to be religious. Especially *now*. This is crucial, a *very* crucial period in your journey, so *pay attention*."

"I am paying attention. And who says I'm not religious? I...uh...I'm sure I believe in...in *something*..."

"Don't bother racking your brain." Ollie replies sarcastically. "You wouldn't remember even if you were spiritual. This is my *third* time explaining the rules and *I'm* the moron? *Sheesh*! Like I keep saying, all memories of your personal life have been zapped. *Ka-poo-ee.* Besides, I've got a funny feeling that there's nothing biblical in that noggin' of yours that doesn't involve a coloring book and a couple of plastic barnyard animals."

"Kiss my ass."

"*Easy.* Sky Net is watching." Ollie solemnly points upward and I can't help myself. We both double over in hysterics.

After catching my breath, I say, "How can you reminisce about a childhood racetrack a second ago and claim zapped memories?"

"I *told* you. I've been *released.* You're the *intuition* now. It is *you* that has no history. *Zero* recollection outside of nursing. Think about it? Do you have parents? Children? A spouse? Are you Baptist? Catholic? Were you one of those dark Goth chicks who played up the spiritual by sporting jewel-studded rosaries? *Shoot.* You could've been a porn junkie." Ollie nods deviously with bushy eyebrows dancing across his forehead. "What about pets? Any Fido's licking on those muscular legs?"

"You're disgusting."

"Go ahead. Try and remember. You can't. Your shit's been erased. POOF!" Ollie flicks his fingers like a magician. "Just like you."

"If that's true then what are all these images in my head?"

"Memories of Dixon Valley. Nursing stuff. You're the know-it-all now. The expert witness. Boss Lady. Queen Bee of the ER. Over the years the title will shift. For awhile, I called myself the Nurse Whisperer. Later, when I started getting fed up, when nobody would *DIE*, I renamed myself the King of Shit Mountain."

"Enough with the rants," I snap, already certain

that I like the manic dead Ollie Dick even less than Bev Martin's portrayal of the live one. *Talk about self absorbed.* My death didn't concern him one bit! Not once did he offer condolences or pretend to be upset. The fucker seemed *overjoyed*! I had a mind to mourn myself, but Ollie refused to shut up even for a second. Shoot. Did I even know a prayer? I wanted a moment alone and yet I had so many questions. Sadly, I needed the fat bastard. "So what's the job? What do you mean by *intuition*?"

"You're the official ghost of Dixon Valley Emergency Department. This is your stomping ground. In fact, no matter how hard you try, be it run or sneak, or plunge, you cannot leave. Not yet. You may have acquired the ability to pass through walls and doors *inside* of the department, but like a force field there's only so far you can go. Trust me. I've tried and tried and tried."

"I'm trapped?"

"Technically, yes."

"So I'm supposed to float around here forever? Doing what, exactly?"

"Keeping watch—monitoring."

"Monitoring what?"

Ollie spreads his arms wide and spins in a slow circle. "Everything and anything. Your job is to keep the emergency department running and on task. Kind of like a ghost director. Or better yet, a ghost charge nurse. You're to assist in the administration of medication, become the vigilante for patient safety, contain escalating situations, ward off mistakes, whisper away laziness, and attempt to keep the peace between doctors, nurses, techs, patients, families and ancillary staff members during periods of extreme duress."

"Is that all?"

Ignoring my sarcasm, Ollie continues.

"Technically, your primary goal is to help nurses and doctors avoid slip-ups. You won't be able to prevent them all but you'll catch loads, and I mean *loads,* of careless errors."

"That's a bunch of *bull.* Nurses are *cautious.* I can count on one hand the amount of mistakes I've made."

As if my career life was instantly photographic, a thousand vivid situations backing up fourteen years of service, flash before me. I suddenly recollect my beefy cardiology teacher, Dr. Joan Ramsey, (Doctor meaning PhD) with her bulbous nose and horrible choice in flimsy polyester blouses. The militant bitch preached constantly about the Five Rights of Medication Administration: "It is pertinent; people, to keep in mind the Five Rules before dispensing any patient medication..."

1.   *Is it the correct **T**ime for the medication.*
2.   *What is the **R**oute? Will it be given by mouth, IV, or shot in the muscle?*
3.   *Are you giving the proper **A**mount? Is the dose ordered micrograms or milligrams?*
4.   *Do you have the right **M**edicine?*
5.   *Are you giving it to the correct **P**atient?*

"Tramp!" Ronny Sullivan hollered from the back of the classroom, absolutely proud of himself, during the instructor's dull and very monotone monologue.

Ramsey's blustery smeared red lips flat-lined, one eyebrow lifting as she responded to Rockin' Ronny, a ladies man that didn't last long in the nursing program for oh so many reasons. "Believe it or not, Mr. Sullivan, that is the acronym nurses use to remember the rule. Not surprising that YOU derived such a conclusion on your very own."

"TRAMP." I announce. "I always check the five rights. Trust me. My clinical instructor was a polyester *bear*." As I listed errors in my head, I count on fingers out loud. *"One...Two...Three...Four!* Yes, I'm positive. Four mistakes."

"What about the ones you've completely missed? The *unknown* foul-ups."

"Unknown?"

Ollie shakes his head. "You've made nineteen blunders, Gloria. In the ten years I've been watching. And I saved your ass from another forty."

My face flushes (well as flush as a dead person can get). "BA-*LONE*-EY."

"You've given pills instead of shots. Shots instead of pills. Too much. Not enough. In the grand scheme of things, your mistakes proved harmless. Most of them, anyway."

"What do you mean by *most*?"

"Remember Mr. Knox from room five? August, early millennium? He was an aging biker sportin' a decaled florescent orange t-shirt that read: *Your girlfriend thinks I'm hot.* It was years ago but now with your ninja nursing mind, your memory should be picture perfect. He was diagnosed with a urine infection. You had him sign the paperwork prepping to go home, but then he got all sweaty and his blood pressure tanked."

I pause, frowning. "Holy *Cow*! That *shirt*. What a classic. He was like eighty. His daughter's name, was it Marla? That's right! Marla went to pull the car around while I helped get him into that florescent garb. Said he picked it up at Bike Week in Daytona. What a pisser! And then he started to sweat. BOOM. Down for the count. Crazy. It feels like that just happened, and yet, when was it? Seven years ago?"

"Almost eight. You've been In-Between for awhile."

"What's In-Between?"

"It's neither here no there. Anyway, you were supposed to give Mr. Knox an antibiotic, but somehow pharmacy loaded or another nurse returned a blood pressure pill to the wrong med slot. You read the label on the first pill which was correct, but tearing into the wrapper posed a problem. Frustrated, you dropped it back into the slot and picked up another. The labels were comparable and so were the pill sizes. You didn't notice. Your brain *expected* it to be the antibiotic so you read it that way. Minds can be very convincing. That's why I recommend reading the drug name out loud. Long story short, it wasn't the antibiotic. By the time he got his paperwork, thirty minutes later, Mr. Knox dropped his blood pressure."

My knees buckle. "I…I, oh my God! I didn't realize. It…it was an *accident*! How could I have known? I, oh…*shit*." My natural reaction was to point a finger. Pharmacy must have screwed up. But every nurse, ever doctor, every pharmacist understands human error must be factored into the dispensing equation. No matter how improbable it sounds there is always a risk; the very reason for all of the checks. Check the patient, check the med against the order, check the dose, check the route, check the time, and finally the check rationale. Does administering the drug make sense? Check, check, check. And yet…

"What else have I messed up?"

Ollie shakes his head. "We're moving *forward*, Gloria. No reason to dwell over spilled soup. Shit happens. The good news is that you never killed anybody, which is more than I can say for some of your colleagues. But back to my point. Your new job is to *limit* mistakes. Catch nurses and doctors before they make that fatal nose dive. It'll ruin more than one life. Obviously the patient's and their families, but let us not forget about the person who makes the blunder. Medical people have a hard time forgiving themselves. Some have been known to take their own lives. Crazy as it sounds, it has happened. So much sadness and loss, it's a huge weight to bear. That's where we come in. And yet, when I say we, I mean *you*. You are destined to assist. That is your job, Gloria. You are the intuition now."

"Intuition?"

"That's right. You work through them. Your job is to watch. Listen. Help. Prevent." Ollie eyes twinkle as he raises a Coke can in salute. "So welcome, Gloria. All hail the new Queen! THE QUEEN OF SHIT MOUNTAIN!"

Chapter 8

"Sorry I'm late!" Meg rushes over to her newest preceptor, Tiffany Gouthro, a five-foot-ten bombshell who could've opted for runway work instead of needle jammin' if so inclined. Tiff is one of those mesmerizing types that the male race constantly drools over outside and, yes, inside of work. (Although with the latter, the ogling is done from a more discrete distance.)

Tiffany could care less. She's been dealing with the uncensored male hormone for the better part of her adult life. Most men were harmless, she reported, and yet if any explicit lines were crossed the voluptuous RN had a way of effectively putting them smugly back into place.

Nine hours into their first shift together, Meg was privileged to witness, first-hand, Nurse Gouthro's authoritative wrath. It was four in the morning and one of their patients took a sour turn. Mr. X was being admitted for a possible necrotic bowel. The hospital was at full tilt, with zero beds available, and the surgeon was up to his ass in cases. Instead of promptly taking the man to the operating room, Dr. Harold phoned in some feeble orders for antibiotics and pain meds to bide his time.

"The surgeon's not coming down?" Meg asked, slightly appalled. "This guy is sick."

Tiffany shrugged. "Surgeons are famous for pushing limits, but this time it's not Harold's fault. The OR has been backed up all day. He has to be exhausted. So far, our patient looks good. He's not green. His lab values are decent and his vital signs are near perfect. I'll light a firecracker when it's necessary and if Harold gets obnoxious then I'll pitch my fit."

"Fit?"

Tiff smiled. "Surgeons have horrible schedules. Dr. Harold has probably been awake for over twenty hours. Do you really want someone cutting into your abdomen on negative sleep? Of course not. So if our guy's stable, is it truly necessary to bump another surgical case? Remember, when a patient cuts line another gets delayed. However, you and I are directly responsible for Mr. X, so if his numbers turn we'll do what needs to be done. The trick is to know when to throw the hammer."

Two hours later, Mr. X deteriorated. His fever, heart rate and belly pain had increased in severity three-fold. Tiffany converged on the secretary. "It's time we put a call out to Dr. Happy Ass."

"Happy Ass?" Meg asked.

"On two hours sleep, he'll be so happy that I woke him up early, he'll show his ass."

Sure enough, after three page attempts by the secretary, only ten minutes apart on Tiffany's demand, Dr. Harold phoned back in pure Ass Form. Meg could hear his booming rants exploding from the receiver ten feet away as Tiffany reported the changes in their patient's status. Tiffany rolled her eyes and nodded into the phone. Eventually she cut him off and said, "Surgeon notified of deteriorating status. That's what I'm charting in my notes. Actually, I'll be reporting that after three page attempts, ten minutes apart, surgeon was notified of deteriorating condition. No orders given at this time."

More phone raucousness.

"I appreciate that it's four a.m. but last I heard we were running a twenty-four hour business. I apologize for waking you up." Tiffany frowned. Finally, she snapped. "I'm sorry, DOCTOR, but I didn't twist your arm and demand you follow a surgical career path. With that being said, I expect you down here promptly to perform your duties, and will continue to call your paging service every five minutes until you do so." Tiff winked at Meg. "My name? Yes, of course. It's Tiffany. Tiffany Gouthro." (Pause.) "Yes, that's right. *That* Tiffany." (Another pause.) "No problem, Doc, apology accepted. See you soon."

Tiffany slammed down the phone. "He's on the way..."

Meg has been working with Nurse Gouthro for only a short time, but they hit it off immediately. Stuffing her lunch bag deep into the fridge, she mumbles, "The last thing I need is to start my shift with Charge preaching about lateness."

Tiffany laughs. "Let me guess? Elaine was your day-shift trainer."

"How'd you know?"

"Elaine's a bit of a Nazi when it comes to tardiness and sick calls. Personally, I'd expect a health care worker to drive the speed limit on their way in to stay *safe*. Why risk your life or any others for a couple of minutes on a time clock? It's absolutely ridiculous. And I don't care what responsibility speech Elaine throws at you, puking and shitting peeps need to stay home. The day you show up with a fever, rushing to the commode every ten minutes, it'll be Cancer Day."

"Cancer Day?"

"Illnesses show up in clumps at the emergency department. One day folks'll be writhing around, jumping about holding their sides, screaming in pain. That's Kidney Stone Day."

"Then there's G-Y-N Day," another nurse pipes

in. "when every female in town has contracted some kind of drip."

Josh is sitting nearby drinking a Five-Hour Energy. He can't help but comment. "Makes you wonder what bars they've been hanging out in and if the contaminator is the same scoundrel for the lot of 'em." He pauses in thought. "Come to think of it, Biggie Williams was slutting around last weekend. Bad Habit Biggie, we call him. Betcha he's given us loads of business over the years."

Tiffany's mouth draws thin as she blatantly ignores Josh's cackling sideshow. "There's Chest Pain Day, Abdominal Pain Day, Migraine Day, Back Pain Day, Dental Pain Day and yes, sadly, Cancer Day, when half the patient population has absolutely no immune system. And in comes Meg the Martyr, radiating a toxic temperature of a hundred and two degrees. Instead of helping, you kill off a mother of three whose weakened system can't handle the slightest of viruses. The tragedy of it all, the true kicker, is that you don't even realize the cataclysmic effect of your heroic actions. In fact, you're patting yourself on the back for going the extra mile."

The lounge door swings open and Angela Sollami marches in. Clipboard at the ready, Angela is known for perfectly coiffed hair (due to a hairdressing sister) and as the best cookie chef on staff.

The fluttering in Meg's abdomen returns. This is only her third overnight so the comfort level obtained with day staff quickly dissipates in a room full of strangers. Men and women donned in scrubs and stethoscopes shuffle about in a flutter of conversation, unpacking lunch bags, pocketing pen lights and trauma sheers, searching for calculators and click pens, readying themselves for twelve hours of serious business. It is only then that Meg notices the obvious generation gap between nights and days.

"Generally speaking, fresh meat works the vampire shift." Tiffany says, unfazed by the observation. "A big piece of that is money. New nurses make peanuts compared to the warhorses. We get six bucks extra an hour on nights, which translates into a car payment for me. As the years pass and nurses knuckle up on experience, salary boosts make the shift to days more affordable. And, believe it or not, some of us actually prefer nights. Personally, if I can avoid administration and a bunch of bogus meetings, I'll work in the dark until the cows come home.

"Sleep deprivation," Tiff continues, "is another reason nurses transition before the money hike. New mothers are the first to go. With small children at home, the idea of working the wee hours and returning at the crack of dawn to chase after bright-eyed toddlers in shit-covered diapers makes the stipend lose its flare. Others hit a personal threshold. No matter how much cash is laid on the table, when that five in the morning drag hits, the idea of working two more hours seems physically impossible. Exhaustion wins and another vampire transcends to warhorse."

"Speaking of exhaustion," Angela cuts in. "Did everyone manage the proper sleep today?"

The room buzzes with mumbling comments, and then, to Meg's surprise, one tattered looking female shoots up an arm. "The twins barfed at daycare today. I had to pull them out. I'm running on two hours sleep. Wicked beat."

"Okay then," Angela announces, "I want all eyes on Allison. Now for assignments. Josh, one through four. Katie, five through eight. Jamie, the eleven o'clocker, is already in nine through twelve. Allison, pick up fourteen through eighteen."

"You missed thirteen," Meg reports helpfully.

Angela stops short and chuckles. "My dear, lady. There is no room thirteen in this emergency department."

"You're *kidding* me?"

"Nope." Tiffany adds. "Room thirteen is exempt from most facilities. In fact, I've worked in four hospitals and never seen a one.

"Superstitions run wild in ER wards." Katie cuts in.

"Superstitions my ass! The Indian is real." Josh crows. "Bastard keeps eating my hotdogs."

The room erupts in a buzz of laughter.

"Settle down, folks." Angela says. "We need to focus. Tiffany, you and Meg take nineteen through twenty-two. Bill, twenty-three through twenty-five. Jessica, I have you marked as float. Lindsey, you're in triage."

Several people cry out in harmonious sarcasm, "*Biiiitttccchhh!*"

Angela lifts an arm. "NEWS! Lots of important information so let's take a moment and *pay attention...*"

Dispersing from the break room, Meg asks Tiffany. "Who would ever admit to sleep deprivation? I'd freak if Charge was on my ass all night."

"What Angela does isn't a bad thing." Tiff replies. "Think about it. It takes a lot of trust to admit to your superiors that you're physically exhausted."

"So why do it?"

"For a second, third, and even fourth pair of eyes. We'll all be watching Allison tonight. Now that she's made the announcement, you...me....we'll all feel this subconscious urge to keep her safe. Basic human nature. Angela will be double checking Allison's meds, perusing her charts, rounding more often on her rooms. Without realizing it, so will you.

Nobody wants to screw up and now, if Allison does, it's kind of on all of us because we were informed." Tiffany pauses. "I've piped up over the years. Angela saved me after I had an argument with a floor nurse. I was so angry and absolutely spent that I couldn't think straight. I almost mislabeled a blood specimen. Thankfully, she was paying attention. It could've gotten really ugly since the patient needed a blood transfusion."

"You?"

"It happens, Meg. Don't kid yourself thinking you're never going to be that person. This is a stressful job. Nurses are constantly pulled every which way. Doctors need chaperones, Lab is on the line with a critical value, X-ray wants to take a patient, blood needs hanging, consents need to be signed—your duties are endless. And if you think I'm exaggerating, be advised...I'm *simplifying*. Nurses are forever expected to remain error free, but are rarely allowed a moment alone to concentrate.

"You're new in this business, Meg, so don't bite off more than you can chew. Being a team player is important, but assess every situation before you leap."

"For example?"

"For example: management calls on your day off and offers a bonus for extra time. You're dead dog tired, but let's face it we can all use the extra buck. You want to be that helping hand, but are you physically capable of another twelve hour shift? Step one foot into the department and nobody'll give a crap about how tired you are. As soon as you commit, they expect a hundred and fifty percent."

"You're freaking me out, Tiff."

"Don't be freaked, be prepared. Know your limits. Concentrate. The best ammunition a caregiver can have, especially a night nurse, is a decent amount of sleep. It's the only way to stay focused. Otherwise it'll be you raising a hand. And then, well, it'll be all eyes on Meg."

Chapter 9

Ollie and I are sitting in on the meeting listening to Angela's daily report. According to Charge, we are getting a couple of new doctors, a full time secretary, and two travel nurses. I'm pleasantly reminded of Angela's safety checks when Allison raises a hand to complain about sleep deprivation.

Ollie reaches over and pats me on the back. "I refer to Angela as my personal assistant. She has it exactly right. In fact, I don't think I can explain your duties any better."

"Is there a method to the madness, or do I just zoom around every which way, peeking over shoulders, trying to guess who's about to screw up?"

Ollie rolls his eyes. "When I was new, my guy told me to start in the most frequented areas."

"The bathroom?" I ask mockingly.

"Try again." Ollie says.

I follow Ollie through the department. We march down the hall past bustling personnel and Ollie glides right through a crowd of visitors parked outside of room two. My eyes go wide. Ollie scoffs. "You're a *ghost*, Gloria. It's kind of freaky the first time, but you can seep through doors, walls, and yes, people. Ba-ha-ha-ha-ha! It's easy." Ollie points at a door and instead of opening it, dissipates into the wood.

For a brief second I stand there, contemplating whether I'm psychologically qualified to tackle a phantom skill. As I muster up the courage a hand shoots out from the middle of the wood, grabs my collar and pulls me through. The sensation feels a lot like being immersed under water. Automatically, I hold my breath. All sound is lost and my vision flashes ochre, the color of the door. I smell pine or stripping or something clean. There is a creaking moan similar to the sound of a wet stick breaking, then…*SNAP*. I'm in the medicine room.

"That was weird."

"You'll get used to it."

"Why can't I just open the door?"

"You can. In fact, back in the early nineties one whisperer was prone to doing just that. A lot of people freaked out, some even quit, certain that the hospital was haunted, which of course it is… But we're not here to frighten the staff, Gloria, or the patients for that matter. Our job is to protect. If doors and cupboards continue to open and close for no reason, it'll just scare the be-Jesus out of everyone. Then guess what? We'll have *MORE* mistakes and *MORE* issues. Learn to walk through shit, sister. It's how we roll. Now, back to your duties…"

There is a brief moment of silence as both Ollie and I settle in to the empty medication room. It hasn't changed much. In fact, it hasn't changed at all. "So…*what*? Do I just stand here?"

Ollie hops his rump onto the counter. "Or sit. Sit and watch."

"Kind of boring."

"Boring is good. Learn to appreciate these brief interludes of silence. Very rarely will you have time for chillaxen on the counter, but this is where I tend to linger on a trickling kind of day. Quiet ER's can be dangerous."

"Why?" I ask.

"Save the stupid questions for the end of the tour."

"There are no stupid questions in nursing. That's what they always say."

"Okay then, call it completely asinine. You already know deep in your giblets why *slow* is bad. When it's balls-to-the-walls sickness, nurses focus. They get into a zone. So up to their gills in work, they don't have time for mistakes. Screwing up brings on delays, more paperwork and repetitive tasking, so they try *harder*. Chaos initiates *thinking*. Concentration. On the other hand, when it's quiet, healthcare providers slack. They dilly-dally, chit-chat, skip simple steps. That's when they muck up. That is why on the dullest of days it is essential that I park my fat ass right on top of this counter."

"We don't have too many monotonous days around here."

"Exactly right, but be advised. Be very wary of silence, Gloria. It's usually a precursor to something nasty. The calm before the storm."

"I'm still trying to figure out how you expect me to pinpoint trouble? There are way too many employees, dozens of simultaneous situations. "

"The shades help."

"Shades?"

"Colors. Shades." Ollie says. "Follow the flash."

"You'll have to explain."

"It'll be easier to show you."

Chapter 10

Mrs. Robertson isn't the most pleasant female in the world. She has a history of Crohn's Disease, a debilitating intestinal illness that brings her to emergency more times than she can count. Because of these multiple visits for pain management, CT scans and antibiotics, her blood pipes are not what they used to be. Tiny and sporadic, they lay scattered about like translucent spiders on paper thin skin. When nurses spot Robertson's name on the tracking board, they all pray. Nobody wants to stick the Crohn's Lady. It makes for an ugly hour.

A flustered Meg emerges from the room. She's been on her own for over awhile, but is designated a resource person to help with sticky spots, which included the likes of Mrs. Robertson. Meg cringes. Up until eleven p.m., that resource person is Bitch Jamie. *What a nightmare!* Meg can't help but recall what her first preceptor confessed months before, at the very beginning of her nursing career. *Jamie is pissed because you started directly in the ED and skipped a fourth floor hazing.*

Working with Jamie is painful. Instead of pointing out beneficial tactics, the fourth-floor veteran lets Meg fumble through new procedures, scoffs at her naivety and, like a broken record, croons on and on about the importance of starting on a medical floor where she could have taken the time to perfect such basic and yet necessary skills. God forbid, Meg ask a question or seek out assistance.

With each request, Jamie snarls a rebuttal. "I shouldn't have to watch over you like a friggin baby!

You've been training for what, *ever?*"

Meghan just shrugs.

"You should already have these skills *engrained*. That's why I'm against new nurses in the ED."

"So you've said..." Meg is ten years older than Jamie and not easily intimidated. She suddenly visualizes Jamie on a school bus, a pig-faced bully, punching kindergartners as they pass. "...like a *thousand* times."

"And I'll say it again!"

Meg considers Jamie one of those glass half-empty types. Every establishment has one. No matter how pampered or pathetic the working conditions, there is always that hitch-in-the–side snit who finds fault in everything. Free cookies in the lounge: *"You're killing us with concentrated sweets!"* A two percent raise: *"What happened to five?"* Getting flexed early on a breezy Friday afternoon: *"You're chewing up my paid time off."* That's Jamie in a nutshell. The company whiner. The complainer. The very reason attitude posters are plastered over employee break rooms nationwide.

Meg keeps a poker face as she exits Mrs. Robertson's room. "Sorry, Jamie, but I can't get the IV."

Jamie huffs. "How many times did you try? It better have been more than once. The only way you'll get good at anything is if you..."

"Twice," Meg cuts her off. "That's all I'm allowed. She's a difficult stick."

"They're all hard when you're *inexperienced*. Forget it. I'll do your work, but that doesn't mean you just sit here. There are other tasks..."

"I'll take Two to X-ray and catheterize Three." Meg replies. Jamie huffs a second time, gathers a few supplies and moves purposefully into the room. She doesn't bother shutting the door, which turns out to be a big mistake. Within seconds, the whole ED can hear Mrs. Robertson's wrath. Meg suppresses a smile, quite pleased that Jamie's getting a dose of her own medicine.

"Oh, *LORD,* not *you* again! I'm already a pin cushion and they send you! Where's Marcy or...or *Elaine*? I need someone with *EXPERIENCE*! Not some wanna be HOT SHOT that feels the urge to practice on my arms. *I'M ON STEROIDS!* My skin is like *PAPER!* This is *RIDICULOUS!* Doesn't anyone in this joint know what they're *doing?"*

"I'm just *looking,* Mrs. Robertson." Jamie's voice is slightly shrill. "I need to look!"

"I don't WANT you to LOOK! I want someone *QUALIFIED.* You're like *TWELVE.* Get me a *real* nurse!"

Chapter 11

"The *shades*," Ollie explains, "are hues. Changes in complexion. The color reflects a person's emotional state. Different tints represent different feelings."

"Like the color of flushing skin when a patient's barking mad?"

"Exactly, Gloria. Except 'round here the color green marks hostility. Red, or flushing, signifies humiliation. Like when a grown man is forced to admit that he's got a vibrator stuck up the ol' shit chute. Now that's a flaming fireball moment."

"Eeewwww!"

"Don't play ignorant with me, Gloria. Just last month one dude "fell" (Ollie flinches his fingers to enunciate and then repeats the word.) ...fell in the shower directly on top of his tooth brush holder. Talk about aim. Then another guy, even older, he was like seventy-four; he lost the end of a baton scrubbing his bumby. That rubber stopper was half-way up his colon before he admitted to a problem. You do realize that the colon is like a giant suction cup. Similar to a vacuum, foreign bodies go up and up and up! Sorry bastard ended up in surgery."

"A *majorette* baton?"

"Yep. Said he picked it up at a yard sale for a buck and a quarter."

"STOP Ollie!" I giggle. "You are one sick bastard."

"Hey, this is *relayed* information. I'm not in charge of our client's bathing activities. Although, I have to admit, ever since that day I can't help but refer to batons as shower corkers."

"What if I miss it?"

"Oh you can't *see* a shower corker. The patient's got to fess up."

"No, you fool! The colors. The *hues*! What if I don't notice?"

Ollie laughs. "You will."

Days, possibly weeks later, (I'm still having trouble gauging time around here), I'm sitting on the counter in A-bay parked right next to the physicians' work desk. Ollie is laid out on the floor in front of me, arms pillowed up under his head, peering at the ceiling like it's a starry night and not a bunch of lumpy water-stained tiles.

"Monitoring the doctors is another easy way to pick up action." Ollie announces as he crosses one meaty leg over top the other. "Nurses are obligated to report ugly vital signs and deteriorating situations, so why kill ourselves?"

"Too late for that," I add.

"You ain't kiddin." Ollie agrees. "So we chill. And wait. It's only a matter of time before a job presents itself. Besides, from this ground position, I've got a great view of Nurse Holden's ass. I love it when she wears skirts!"

The Dickman's perverted chatter is beginning to tatter my nerves. I'm about to read him the riot act, but then Dr. Rossi parks his smoking hot physique in the computer station next to me. Just watching him work makes Ollie's sex blab tolerable. In fact, I am seriously considering sitting on the doc's muscular lap when Mrs. Robertson's cursing screams echo down the hallway.

"Chop, chop, Gloria. Let's see who's pissed off the old bugger this time. No doubt this will be a perfect situation for you to practice your hues." Ollie and I converge on the noise as the well remembered Crohn's Lady continues berating another RN. Truthfully, even in death Jamie irritates me, so I'm quite amused at the situation, upset in fact about having to shut it down.

I follow Ollie into the room as he vanishes through the curtain. Once again, I forget my death status and pull back the material. The argument between nurse and patient is so heated that nobody notices the curtain shift except the Dickman, who frowns and shakes his head.

At that exact moment, Mrs. Robertson kicks her feet and Jamie's supplies fly off the bed. "GET THE *HELL* OUT OF MY ROOM!"

When the patient says *HELL* Ollie nudges me, "Check Jamie. Can you see it? The shade?"

"Of course I can see it!" Still, my jaw drops in sudden awe as Jamie's skin flashes a bright green. Like the *Hulk*, the color is so blinding it shimmers about her person in emerald wavy streaks.

"See how easy it is?" Ollie says. "The tints help tremendously, don'tcha think?"

"What's that rippling around her?"

"That's Jamie's aura. Very few people can see these prisms in life, but as a ghost, especially during periods of profound emotion, people literally ripple with color."

"So now what? What am I supposed to do with this newfound information?

"Rectify the situation." Ollie holds up a hand. "Watch and learn, sister."

Ollie walks over to Jamie who is fumbling to retrieve her gear. He gets behind her, grips both shoulders and literally bumps her out of the room. He then pushes her over to the charge nurse and speaks directly in Jamie's ear. *"I NEED HELP WITH A LINE."*

Jamie frowns but repeats the phrase to Melissa. "I need help with a line."

Melissa nods, "No problem."

"*I CAN'T GO BACK IN THERE FOR AWHILE OR I'M GOING TO SAY SOMETHING STUPID. OR MEAN.*" Ollie states firmly, again directly in Jamie's ear.

Jamie mimics the phrase, "I can't go back in there for awhile or I'm going to say something stupid. Or mean."

Charge laughs. "*You*, Jamie? Now that *would* be a surprise."

By her tone, Melissa's sarcasm is obvious. "How about I assist Mrs. Robertson and you have a visit with the nurse manager? She wants to see you in her office."

"About what?" Jamie asks, suddenly cautious.

Melissa shrugs. "No clue. But it'll give you time to cool your jets."

Chapter 12

We trail an avocado tinted Jamie to the office and Ollie blabs the whole time. "Green reflects anger, red, embarrassment...and orange, yes! Check Jamie. See? What a perfect teaching tool! From Jolly Green Giant to Oompa Loompa, and I'm talking the original orange-face Oompa Loompa's from the real *Charlie and The Chocolate Factory*." Ollie crows. "Everyone turns mandarin when they get called to the office."

"Why?"

"Orange represents uncertainty. The unknown'll turn any employee into a Lil' Cutie. Ever eat one of them baby oranges? Dee-lish! And they're seedless to boot. Man, how happy would I be to gobble down a box of Lil' Cuties right now. Even in death, the world would be a perfect place."

Ollie continues his gibberish as Jamie enters the manager's domain. Sadly, we're too slow and the door clicks shut in our faces. Before I have a chance to argue, Ollie pushes me through the wood. Again I shut my eyes. The world goes momentarily silent as my body compresses. This time I taste tree bark.

"Uh, *ooh*, I don't like that feeling!" Grumbling, I open my eyes but my vision is blurry, like viewing a television screen from an inch away. Only then do I realize that I'm standing half in and half out of the manager's back side. I yelp and leap sideways. Ollie hoots hysterically as I dance around like a chicken attempting to free myself of the disturbing sensation.

Two smartly dressed individuals, both women, sit poised in straight back chairs. (Not that it matters, but one is sporting the biggest diamond I've ever seen.)

The female closest to me is wearing a charcoal gray skirt suit, her neck strung with aqua tinted pearls. The second woman dons a dark green pantsuit, accessorized with a printed metallic silk scarf that reflects her perfectly coifed auburn hair. Definite money chicks. No shopping at *Ross Dress-For-Less* for these two.

The women stand as Winnie, the Nurse Manager, offers introductions.

"Jamie, this is Molly Simmons and Betty Lyons."

Jamie nods politely and turns an even brighter shade of mandarin.

"Hello Jamie," Betty, the woman in green, shakes her hand firmly. "Molly and I are lawyers. We work with the hospital."

Jamie immediately flushes an ungodly yellow.

Ollie jabs me. "See that sallow mustard color?"

"Yeah?"

"Do you remember what emotion it stands for?"

"Uh...fear?"

"Exactly. Yellow represents fear."

Betty gets right down to business. "It has come to our attention that on the date listed as such, you were involved in a code that ended in the death of a patient."

"I have been involved in dozens of codes," Jamie snaps, slightly defensive. "You'll have to be more specific."

Betty's smile never waivers. She whips out a file and passes it over to Jamie. The nurse peruses the first few sentences, hesitates, and then blanches. Winnie pushes a chair up under her as Betty continues. "At this early juncture, we're not sure how far the case will transgress, or how seriously the charges will affect you. Nurses are usually released from legal obligation early in the proceedings. But I need to ask. Have you been served any subpoenas as of late?"

"Subpoenas? For *what*?"

Molly cuts in soothingly. "That sounds like a 'no' to me. What do you think, Winnie?"

The three women laugh lightly, trying to ease the tension. It doesn't work. Jamie's skin bursts into a bright shade of saffron.

"The good news," Betty says. "is that the representing attorney isn't an ambulance chaser."

"What's an ambulance chaser?" Jamie questions.

"Those guys you see advertising on late night television. Famous for sending defendants huge formal packages with mocked up accusations and questionnaires, in hopes of a scribbled confession or a typed-up lengthy rebuttal claiming their side of the story." Betty lifts a wavering finger. "Never reply to these inquiries, Jamie. Do you understand? Contact the hospital. Call me. If you write anything down, anything at all, they'll use it against us. We don't need an Exhibit A."

"I haven't been contacted."

"Which means," Betty pauses, trying to slow the escalating conversation. "Not much. The courier might have missed you. The file should show up any day now."

"How can you be so sure?" Once again, Jamie's response sounds defensive.

"The hospital as an institution is also being sued. We have received our own special white package. You are Jamie Lynn Baxter, are you not?"

"I am."

"See here?" Molly flips to a certain page and shows it to Jamie. "You've been named in the grievance."

"What the heck does THAT mean?"

"It means that we're going to get very near intimate in the next few months preparing for your deposition."

Jamie's eyes go wide. "My *what*?"

"That's how it works. The opposing attorney gets a chance to probe everyone they want who has been sighted in this chart. Deposition is a nice word for interrogation."

"I can't wait." Jamie says flatly.

"Don't worry," Betty grins. "Nurses rarely stay on the charge. Unless, of course, you have private insurance. Tell me, Jamie, that you've never been conned into purchasing a private plan."

"I...I was meaning to."

"But did you?"

"First explain to me why it's bad."

"Attorneys cannot confiscate personal possessions. Unlike physicians, no law mandates that nurses require private insurance, which keeps them safely out of the courtroom."

"I'm confused."

Winnie cuts in. "If you have a policy, then you're worth a buck. People sue for money."

"But I don't *have* private insurance. You'd think they would've figured that out before all this crap." Jamie whines.

"Ahh, but here in lies the tricky part." Molly cuts in. "An individual's insurance history is confidential until they're named in a lawsuit. It is the very reason attorneys initially charge everyone involved with the patient's chart. Those caregivers *without* private policies get dropped."

"So," Jamie frowns, "what you're saying is that only the responsible parties get screwed?"

Betty nods. "Pretty much."

"You gotta love this friggin' country." Jamie growls. "That's *ridiculous!*"

Winnie winks and places a soothing hand on the young nurse's shoulder. "Thankfully, you're not that, as you say, responsible."

"So what happens now?" Jamie asks.

"Like I said, you will be deposed." Betty adds. "Pray we can settle out of court. Very rarely do these cases go to trial."

"TRIAL?" Jamie scowls.

"Possibly, but hospitals don't like long drawn out lawsuits and definitely not trials. It's bad for business. Think about it? What CEO wants investigators and television crews snooping around? Not this place. Already with its Indian graveyard, and remember the nurse that choked to death on his lunch break?"

"Ollie Dick?"

"Yeah, that guy. Dixon Valley can't handle any more bad publicity. I'm surprised we even *have* customers."

"So why not just pay?" Jamie complains, "Get it *over* with!"

"I'm sure Mr. Scott would love to skip the dramatics." Molly agrees. "Problem is the world has changed. People have gotten far too greedy. Nobody sues for a pidily ten grand anymore. It's more like ten million and your left foot. Claims have become so exorbitant; hospitals would rather fight than pay, especially when the charges are questionable."

"I don't understand." Jamie says. "How can there be a trial if a case is bogus?"

"Lawyers are experts at word manipulation." Winnie remarks. "They can cause reasonable doubt in just about any document, let alone a frantically scribbled code sheet. Their finger pointing will be endless."

Jamie flashes avocado. "This isn't right! Why am I being attacked for doing my *job*?"

"People die all the time, Jamie." Molly says. "In their homes, cars, on park benches; they keel over in movie theatres. For some reason, if an individual expires in a health care facility, families automatically assume negligence. They need a scapegoat. Call it human nature or the after mass of sudden death, but people feel better when they investigate."

"So I'm being charged with *negligence*? Is that the bottom line?" Jamie's aura shimmers mustard and relish.

Betty sighs. "The family is upset. However, let's not get into that now. I was hired to review the chart and gauge your side of the story."

"I don't have a story!" Jamie cries. "I came to work. Shit happened. Shoot, we emptied the friggin' crash cart during that code. We tried everything. *EVERYTHING!*" Jamie halts suddenly, her bottom lip quivering. "Sometimes people just die."

Betty slides a paper packet across the table. "Are these your initials?"

"Yes."

"And what is this **JB/ BM** ? There appears to be two sets of initials."

"That's because during codes we have scribes."

"A scribe, as in a recorder?"

"Exactly."

"How does it work?"

The scribe charts while others do the work. Some nurses write *SCRIBE* on the bottom. Others double initial."

"Meaning?"

"The first initial represents the person who did the actual task; the second denotes the person charting."

"Are you J.B.?"

"I am. My job was to administer medications."

Betty peruses the chart. "It states here the time the patient deteriorated. And here, when the code was called."

"Your point?"

"It's charted by the same recorder."

"That's right."

Betty frowns. "I'm confused. How did the scribe know the patient would deteriorate? How could he/she have recorded events *prior* to the code?"

"The patient was barely *breathing*. A nurse can't chart and work at the same time!" Jamie huffs. "You'd think that would be a no brainer."

Betty tilts her head. "Perhaps it is obvious to a nurse. The jury will need an explanation."

"In cases like this, abrupt emergencies, we scribble notes on scrap paper until there is time to chart properly. Since the patient coded, the recorder did me a favor and transcribed my cheat sheet." Jamie pauses. "That's what kills me about you people. Lawyers, administrators, the bigwigs, you pick apart our charts like it's the words that matter and not the patient."

"Even so," Molly exclaims, "it'll be you and your chart under fire in the courtroom. You need to review this document thoroughly and make sure the recorder didn't miss anything."

"What if she did?" Jamie frowns. "I can't fix it now. Or so I've been told over and over and *over* again."

"Told what?" Betty questions.

"That if I didn't chart it, then I didn't do it. They've been spewing that phrase since the first day of nursing school."

"And that, my friend, is a very old and ridiculous nursing myth."

"You're kidding?"

"No, ma'am." Betty smiles. "I am absolutely not kidding. Just because you forgot to write something down doesn't mean it never happened. As long as you're willing to amend your statement in a court of law, it's as good as a written document."

"Really?"

"Yep. For example: In this specific chart nobody recorded an IV site even though, clearly, several medications were administered intravenously."

"I didn't chart an IV?"

"Nope. But that doesn't mean that it didn't happen."

"So what am I supposed to say?"

"State the obvious. That you were so busy caring for the patient, which in this case was true, that you forgot to write it down. A lot of uncharted actions can be blamed on your primary role as a nurse."

"Primary role?"

"To keep your patient alive."

"Oh, right." Jamie picks up the paper stack and thumbs the edges. "I can't believe I didn't chart the IV."

"That is why I need you to review this document with a fine-tooth comb. If you discover a missing piece, or an error, we want to know about it."

"This is *ridiculous*." Jamie shakes her head. "I can't remember specifics from that long ago?"

Again Betty offers a practiced smile. "You'll be surprised at what you can remember."

I sneak a peek over Jamie's shoulder trying to get a glimpse at the script, but a cover page is hiding the material. She rolls it up like a newspaper and stands. "I need to get back to work."

KNOCK, KNOCK, KNOCK.

"Come in."

Serena Grady peers in the door. "Uh, excuse me. I'll come back later."

Jamie pushes past. "No worries. I was just leaving."

*

I find myself suddenly gawking at Serena Grady. She is shimmering an exotic coppery gold.

Chapter 14 (Like hospitals rooms, this nursing book doesn't have a chapter thirteen either.)

"What does gold represent?" I ask Ollie who is already two steps through the door.

"Ah, Serena...The Golden Child. Yes, well, I wouldn't worry too much about that hue. Gold members are usually old or very, very young. And extremely rare. Serena is an extraordinary case." Ollie says. "Gold puts a soul in saint category."

"How do you mean?"

"Let's just say if Serena drops dead tomorrow, she won't be replacing either of us sinners. She'll skip right on through to the Promise Land."

"Why?"

"Because Serena lives by code. She does everything *right*. Please tell me you're not surprised. Nurse Grady's been on the righteous path since the beginning of time."

The Dickman isn't kidding about that. Serena Grady was designed from a special mould, like our Great Creator reached out of the sky and sprinkled her with special Angel Dust (not the bad kind), relinquishing her of any sinister faults. Before Ms. Grady, I had never met a twenty seven year old virgin, especially not a five foot ten, blue-eyed beauty, in perfect physical shape, chock full of brains. A woman with such exquisite qualities rarely surfaced in the singles market. The first guy propositioned, when high standards revolved around decent teeth and a driver's license, usually scooped them up.

Serena was relentlessly selfless, spending her afternoons volunteering in soup kitchens and delivering Meals-On-Wheels. She worked excessively, overtime up the wazoo, and her version of a vacation was three weeks of missionary work in some random third world country where she tended to the poverty-stricken souls of the region. During these trips, the missionaries labored endless hours with limited breaks, all on their own dime, and yet Serena confided that no paying job has ever offered greater satisfaction.

She coached a junior high basketball team, drove the youth group activity bus on Sundays and never wasted time streaming computers or watching television. Serena loved wearing dresses, confessing frankly that the only pants she owned were nursing scrubs. She was always respectful, every stranger was either ma'am or sir, and remained faithful to her God.

Living in the Bible belt, being religious isn't at all that uncommon. What I found truly inspiring about this young adult was the way she managed to be spiritual and true without getting all up in your face about it. Serena didn't preach or push those funny little pamphlets. Serena did not use her Lord's name in vain. A true servant of God, Serena's faith was apparent in her every day actions which, by the way, is absolutely rare.

I remember staff was always hounding Serena, constantly trying to play matchmaker, or at the very least encouraging her to practice her God-given womanly skills on a select few residents. Serena hushed our perverted minds by repeatedly confiding that she favored very specific traits and, *no*, none of the men we mentioned made the cut.

Victoria, a float nurse with a devilish tongue, kept nagging Serena about the importance of mastering the perfect blowjob, while Mary Catherine and I questioned Serena's unyielding requirements. *I mean, really? What could a funny and smart medical resident with a hot body possibly be lacking?*

When the gold-plated nurse listed what she required in a man, Mary Catherine was the first to comment. "*Seriously*, Serena? Is that even *possible?*"

I continually questioned where or *when* did she expect to find such an impeccable counter part? For that matter, was there even a single man left in the world that didn't drink alcohol (*ever*) or smoke *anything (ever)*, who placed God and family first, and would rather feed lousy homeless dudes on a Friday night than lay on the couch mugging a bag of Doritos. Oh, and he had to be a virgin.

I racked my brain, wondering if any such person existed in my personal circle. The answer was simple. No. I didn't know a single soul in the universe that fit *all* of Serena's requirements, especially not a mid-twenty-something male that had any game. *"What's one beer, Grady?"* I remember asking. *"A man's got to live! Surely, having a causal drink now and again can be overlooked?"*

Serena rolled her eyes as if *I* was the one being ridiculous, laughed aloud and replied, "Sorry. No can do."

Serena Grady did not intend to drop her standards for any man. Truthfully, if you ever met the girl, or watched her in action, saint category made perfect sense.

*

Trailing Ollie back into the ED, it's as if my eyes have been opened for the very first time. Colors flash everywhere. I spot another gold dude stumbling around in room six, drawers down at his kneecaps, trying to aim into a urinal, missing by at least two inches and pissing on the floor. Repulsed, I say, "I thought you said gold was saint material?"

"It is."

I point at the disheveled character twinkling a

coppery metallic. Are you really trying to suggest that that beat down grubster has never had a cocktail? *Shoot.* He must be seeping vodka."

Ollie chuckles. "Actually, Denver's a bourbon man. In fact, glugging spirits was the reason why his first wife left him so early on in their marriage. She claimed that he was more in love with whiskey than her and asked their pastor for an annulment. Denver had been honeymooning at the saloon with his life long pal, Jim Beam, when Sweet Jane took action. Six months passed before Denver even realized that his young wife had flown the coop."

"Now I'm really confused."

Ollie grins. "Truth is that Denver Coggins was born with a thirst for the excessive. He smokes cigars, bets horses, plays the Tuesday night money pools over at McKenzie's Pub. Back in the day, he used to sneak down to the Dusty Bucket on his lunch break and drool over his favorite stripper, Rosie Bottoms. The long-legged creature sniped his heart the very minute he stuffed that first crisp five-dollar bill into her garter belt, initiating a decade long courtship. Years later, at least twenty after the loss of Sweet Jane, Rosie finally agreed to marriage. So..." Ollie inhales. "not only does he love bourbon, but Denver's married to a pole dancer."

"And *that* guy's a saint? I thought you said..."

"You don't have to do *everything* right to maintain gold status. You just have to do the right thing *when the time comes.*" Ollie shrugs. "The logistics get confusing and, truthfully, I'm not privy to a complete list of rules." Ollie points a thumb up at the ceiling as if to explain. "It is what it is."

I inspect the old dodger. On closer exam, he appears better maintained than I first perceived. Street folks wear layers of clothing and carry backpacks crammed full of their meager possessions. Nail beds are usually dirt encrusted and men keep beards because razors and skin cream are extremely low on the essentials list.

Denver's skin is clean shaven and his clothes are crisply pressed. Truthfully, all he needs is a break from the bourbon, a cheeseburger, and good night's rest—the very cure for most alcoholic binges.

"I'm surprised as old as he is, the man is still carrying on."

"Oh, Denver's not carrying on," Ollie replies. "He's as sober as a Priest on Sunday *before* Mass."

I point into room six. "That guy is *sober?*"

"The day Rosie married him he went into rehab, cut back his drinking and carousing to only the summer months. Nevertheless, a lifetime of whisky and tripping over his own two feet, smacking his noggin no less than a dozen times, has played havoc on Denver's sodium levels. Now, about once a year, he shows up deranged and disheveled, slurring his words and staggering about like a stroke victim. Today his sodium is down to 118. That'll make the soberest of individuals appear drunker than hippo in heels."

"How do you know so much about him?"

Ollie grins. "Me? *Shoot.* I've taken care of Denver on several occasions, in life and death. I'm surprised that you haven't. He's been admitted at least seventeen times in the past twenty years. We almost killed him once back in 1998. The doctor thought he was just intoxicated. Ordered me to give him a turkey sandwich and call it a day. He seized five minutes before Rosie showed up, and that's when we realized his alcohol was absolutely zero. As you know low sodium causes seizures. But then again, so does sober alcoholics. As we're loading him up with seizure medication, I remember Dr. Dee commenting on

Denver's cleanliness, convinced that the aging alcoholic must have recently visited the homeless shelter for a shower and a new set of duds. Rosie Bottoms over heard him as she entered. She got all red in the face and coughed to make her presence known.

"Dee and I were shocked at the absolutely pristine specimen standing before us claiming to be Denver's wife. The tall muscular creature donned a light pink business suit, hair flipped up just so, looking and sounding more like a business woman than a lunch-time dairy-air swinger. (Denver had later explained that Rosie paid for college working the pole, but in the end found secretarial work and transcription a complete bore so continued dancing two days a week to keep from going completely insane.) This is what she had to say..."

"Excuse me, doctor. What did you say is wrong with my man?"

Now Dr. Dee could be sharp with the tongue, but in the female's presence attempted a civil stature. *"My dear woman, it is of the nature that a life time of bourbon, suddenly removed, leaves a needless hunger in the veins of a man causing seizure-like activity."*

Rosie placed both hands on her hips and scowled. *"English, Doctor, and not Old English. I'm a Bronx girl at heart with zero medical training. So get off your high horse and speak like a normal human being. I don't appreciate your humor. This is my husband we're talking about."*

Dr. Dee flushed. *"Denver is sober."*

"No shit," Rosie snapped. *It's January twenty-fifth."*

"That's his problem. A life-long bourbon man can't just give up the juice over night. He'll seize."

"My dear doctor," Rose retracted, *"I'll have you know that my husband is no longer a bourbon*

man."

"*He's not?*"

"*No, sir. He's switched over to Slims years ago.*" She added smugly, "*That's light beer, for your information.*"

Dr. Dee said, "*Sweet maiden, a man can get just as buttered on a case of Slims as a bottle of Beam.*"

"*But it's winter!*" Rosie repeated. "*Mr. Coggin's hasn't had a thimble of nothing but sweet tea since Labor Day. I can assure you. It's in our contract.*"

"*Contract?*" Dr. Dee questioned.

"*That's right.*" Rosie marched past, snubbing the physician, situating daintily in a metal chair reserved for visitors, and proceeded to tug off a pair of white gloves one finger at a time. After a dramatic pause, she spoke with chin up and eyes lowered, as if addressing a large crowd. "*I married Mr. Coggins under contract. This shouldn't surprise you. I am a stripper after all. Being of the female origin from this particular trade makes me an expert on the philosophy of empty promises. I can't count the amount of cars I should be driving, the vacations I've been pledged, or the apartments I was to luxury-ize. Men have big mouths shouting guarantees for their frenzied penises. That's the way it is in the pole business. So a gal like me learns not to trust. A gal like me starts considering contracts.*

"*Mr. Coggins had been fussin' for my hand going on ten years. I explained to him as best I could about my philosophy on men's bullshit, how it was impossible to believe anyone, even sweet old Denver. I loved him I did, but would never confess. The world's too cruel a place for lovin' on the pole. It rarely works out.*

"*And then, well, the old coot surprised me. The*

very next day Mr. Coggins shows up with a ring, a lawyer and a big stack of legal papers. That's right, my contract. So now, if this decent man screws up, I get all of his hard-earned money. You do realize that he's a contractor by trade, worth a bucket load. With that being said, I can all but assure you, Doctor Sir, that Denver Coggins does not have a lick of the good Lord's piss running through his veins on no January twenty-fifth of any year. So...if you would kindly run some tests and figure out what the dickens is going on. Believe it or not, I'm in love with the nutty bugger and would like to keep him around."

Ollie chuckles at the memory. "That was the last time Dr. Dee stereotyped a person as homeless or blamed booze for confusion without running a couple of lab tests. Shoot, it makes you wonder. How many times do you think we've missed head bleeds on alcoholics? Quoting Rosie Bottoms: *'a bucket load'*."

"Probably not that many," I resist.

Ollie scoffs. "Oh be *honest*, Gloria. Homeless folks can be a serious pain in the rear. How often do inebriated street people check in because of the weather? It's too natty and humid, and their tents don't have air conditioning. They want a fucking cheeseburger and two cans of Coke, shouting for extra ice when you head off to retrieve it. They get angry when they're designated a room without a television set and would rather piss on the floor than ring the call bell for a urinal. I can't count the amount of times I've wiped the shitty ass of a more than capable middle-aged adult on account of White Lightening or a bottle of friggin' Listerine. Caring the screw-ups of the world gets ridiculously old and we both know it."

"You're right," I confess.

"So what happens? We hustle 'em out with a

turkey sandwich and a new pair of footies, off to stumble in front a car or collapse roadside pillaging pennies, and nobody's the wiser. Homeless folks don't get autopsies. They just die. I believe that Rosie Bottoms would've skinned Dee alive if he killed off her husband."

"I'm confused. How does marrying a stripper and drinking light beer make Denver Coggins angelic material?"

"I want you to understand that living up to a specific standard means something different to everyone. We all follow codes of varying degrees; what we truly believe deep in our hearts to be the right thing. That's the ticket for a golden pony ride. Denver made a promise to Rosie and so far he's lived up to it. He's generous and kind. He helps people, desperate folks in need of assistance. Denver never flaunts his generosity or holds it over people's heads, and he was always good to Desi. That's what really got him in."

"Who's Desi?"

"His mother,"

"What he do?"

"He let her die."

"You'll have to explain..."

Chapter 15

"Mother Coggins was ninety-six years old the day she keeled over, and would proudly announce to anyone listening that she hadn't been to a doctor or a hospital ever. And by that I mean *never* ever. She had four daughters and one son. She birthed each and everyone on her own kitchen table with the assistance of Lottie Springer, the unofficial mid-wife in the neighborhood. (*Lottie was a pig farmer by trade. One day, Suzy Thomas, the pig stalls cleaner, a portly girl that had no idea she was with child, birthed a set of twins on the job. Thankfully, her water broke in the kitchen of the farmhouse where she was having lunch— sausage and biscuits with a double cheeseburger on the side. It was no wonder the pregnancy went unnoticed. Nevertheless, it was Lottie who realized what was happening, Lottie who facilitated the birth, Lottie who smacked those tiny juicy butts and cleared those flaring nostrils. Word got around. That's how shit happened in 1926. One day you were a pig farmer and the next, a mid-wife.*) I know this because as Denver stood vigil, hunkered close at Momma's bedside waiting on the ambulance, he told these stories over and over again."

"Were you the nurse?" I ask.

"Nope. All bones and whispering. But the medical staff that night, they all got an earful. Second to beauticians, people love confessing epics to nurses. Truth is, Denver's story simmered with nostalgia, which made you want to listen. This is what he had to say..."

...Momma started slowin' down 'bout six months ago, but only with the heavy stuff. Until then

*she did the mowing and weeding, even dumped her own
garbage. Now we help. She is ninety-six, after all. But
she gardens and keeps her house spic and span. She's
a seamstress by trade. Long retired, she's still fixin'
hems and patchin' knees. Every spring Desi's a basket
case. With all the proms and weddings, every girl in
Benjamin County comes a knocking, knowing that my
Momma does the best work in the area. I think she's
busier now than when she punched a time clock. I told
her she should slow down a bit, but you know old folks.*

*Momma's favorite expression, "I'll quite movin'
when I'm dead."*

*Every day I stop by at lunchtime, and she
always has company. A neighbor sipping tea on the
couch, chatting her up while she pins another dress or
works her magic over the sewing machine. I check the
fridge; make sure she's getting on okay. Never has to
shop, my momma. Every new seam or replaced zipper
promises a dozen biscuits or a green bean casserole.
Customers bring sweet tea and coffee, sugar cakes and
briskets, lasagna and shredded pork. On Sundays she
invites me over to finish leftovers. I eat like a king on
the Sabbath. You sure, Momma? I say. Her response
never changes. "There'll be more tomorrow and I don't
like to waste."*

*Momma is paid more often with food and
services, like painting the fence and tasty cobblers, than
precious green backs. It took me awhile, her own son,
to realize that money really isn't that precious to people
like my momma. They need help with the every day
stuff. Momma's friends have more physical and
cooking capabilities to offer than cash, anyway, so the
system works.*

*Everyone in town watches out for Mother
Desi. Everyone except her good-for-nothing daughters.
Careless creatures who bedded down with sweet-talkin'*

men and birthed way too many young'ins. And they bust my crackerjacks for marrying a stripper? Snakes in suits, the lot of 'em! Big peckers with tiny pockets, that's what my Rosie says. Not a one stuck around. Child support? Forget about it. But their faces flash every where, running about Momma's house at month's end, reminding us all that sex is more than just a romp in a cornfield. It's a life time. Who do you think supports all of those little'uns? Not those sweet-talkin' snakes! It's me and Rosie who buys their clothes and shoes, socks and mitts in the winter. We provide their school supplies. Rosie leaves everything with Momma so they think it's all her. Those good-for-nothin' witches have no idea. Painted nails and 'spensive hair is all they care about. But the babes, well...Rosie feels for the children. Says they can't be blamed...

"According to Denver," Ollie continues. "The only time the sisters ever stopped by was to borrow money and that was usually a week before their state checks rolled in. They'd pilfer frozen casseroles, drink all of her tea and borrow gas money for the ride home. The kids would ram-rod through the house, tearing it up as the daughters sat idle on the front porch, calling long-distance friends, racking up Desi's phone bill. Never once did they offer to mow the grass, throw in some laundry, or help the old lady with a shower. Mrs. Coggins served them!

"They'd show up with dollar-store labels, randomly tagging furniture and dishware around Desi's house, announcing that when Momma *finally* did kick the bucket they were, in fact, first in line for the dining room table. It seemed the only thing the sisters wanted from Mrs. Coggins was her heart to stop. Then they could sell her house, have one big yard sale, and go on a proper vacation. To Disney or the beach, and stay in a hotel with a nice indoor pool!

"In the end, what truly amazed Denver was how the circling vultures made such a racket on that final fateful day. Desi, you see, made the children promise to let her die peacefully, in the comforts of her own home."

"Then how did she end up in the hospital?" It was my first question since the Dickman's monologue.

...Mimi-Jo was getting her pants hemmed. Mimi was young, fifty something, and a member at Mrs. Coggins church. She had dropped by with a cucumber and blueberry pie, services rendered for obtaining the right fit. While Mimi stood on the little step stool describing the actual parts needed to cook such a delicacy, Desi started calling her Momma. With pins positioned between her teeth, she then hurried off to the bathroom and returned with toilet paper wrapped around her head. When Mimi-Jo questioned the toilet paper, Desi replied, "The rain, dear, I don't want it to mess up my curls."

Let me remind you that at ninety-six Desi barely had any hair let alone a head full of curls that needed a toilet paper covering from a rainstorm that didn't exist. It was a bright, sunny day with not a cloud in the sky. Anxiety got the best of Mimi-Jo, a non-relative who had no idea that Desi's dying wish was to avoid an ambulance, promptly dialed 911. After the EMS squad swaddled up Mrs. Coggins and drove away with sirens blaring, Mimi rushed back to the kitchen and found a telephone list of friends and family. She called all the children, four daughters and one son, listed in alphabetical order, which was also in accordance with their age. Addie was first, then Amy, Beverly, Christina and finally, Denver.

By the time Mimi had dialed Denver, Desi's Power of Attorney and custodian of the old woman's Living Will, poor Mrs. Coggins was bundled up in a hospital bed, strapped to machines, a head scan already performed exacting a life-ending prognosis. Desi had popped an artery and was bleeding in the brain. The doctors claimed that without an operation she had only hours to live, and even with surgical intervention could not guarantee any quality of life thereafter...

"Of course that's not how physicians convey information. They circle vaguely, let families believe that surgery's a snap and patients like Mother Coggins will march out of the hospital in a couple days and get back to sewing and churchin' and shittin' on the commode like regular folks. Even if they spelled it out exactly, which surgeons never do, both you and I know that a complete recovery from a ninety-six year old with an enormous head bleed is slim to none."

The Dickman is dead on about rehabilitation. Surviving such a catastrophic event was one thing, returning to the living was entirely something else. A person loses up to thirty percent of bone density after only ten days of being holed up in a bed. After that the risk of falling from pure weakness is so high many patients break a hip or pelvis just trying to take a leak. If that happens a tube needs to be placed in their bladder because a bedpan causes too much pain. They develop bedsores from decreased mobility, a hospital-born infection like pneumonia or MRSA, and *boom...*

The little seamstress with the nimble hands becomes contracted and feeble. Left alone in a nursing home to fend for herself, with a staff so overwhelmed due to mandated budget cuts, she's lucky to get bathed. Forget about feeding assistance or implemented physical therapy. Friends visit at first. As days transition into weeks, and weeks fold into years, the friends get busy, the friends die—friends forget they were friends. And the little old lady that everyone pilfered for casseroles and cheap hems slips into the shadows.

I wish I was exaggerating.

By the time Denver, covered in concrete and grime from the job site, parked his clay-splattered Ford F-150 and raced into the hospital, the neurosurgeon had come and gone, consents for surgery had been signed, and all of the sisters were circled in prayer, dribbling hysterically, begging God for a complete recovery.

"STOP! HOLD UP!" Denver roared as he entered the room. "POWER OF ATTORNEY!"

"Oh Lord, Denver. You're a mess!" Addie, the oldest sibling, decked out in a red two-piece number with nails to match, dropped hands to her hips and glared. "Who let this man in here in such a state? You're mother is sick and you can't even take a shower?"

"Sorry, Sis." Denver snapped. "In the world of honest livin' sometimes a man gets dirty. I would've showered but I had to make sure that none of you lazy, good-for- nothing vultures hadn't started prematurely strippin' Momma of all her jewelry!"

Voices escalated, an argument broke out, and soon enough security arrived. The girls demanding that their slovenly stripper-lovin' brother be removed from the premises. The whole time Denver was crowing in an almost delirious tone "POWER OF ATTORNEY!"

Desi pointed to Denver and chortled, "CHICKEN SOUP IS IN THE OVEN, DEAR! HURRY WITH YOUR SHOWER OR WE'LL BE LATE FOR THE WEDDING!"

The siblings paused, suddenly embarrassed, and Denver reached for his mother's hand. "Did you hear that, ladies? There's no time for surgery. Momma needs to get ready for the wedding. We need to get to the beauty parlor!"

Beverly was next to speak, her voice anxious and shrill. "But she'll diieee, Denver!" The sisters nodded in agreement and then blubbered into another round of histrionic wailing.

Denver's eyes went wide at the sheer irony of it all, his mouth drawing thin. "Whatever ya'll think you're planning—I'd like to remind you what Momma wants. And this...all of this..." Denver flung his arms about in wide abrupt circles. "...is not ANY of it."

The bickering continued. Denver demanded to speak with the surgeon, the ER doctor and a hospital administrator. Within minutes, Denver hand delivered the paperwork. (Desi had very specific documentation about end of life rituals and a number for a lawyer in bold print at the bottom just in case anyone got any stupid ideas. Under that, another paragraph defining who would NOT get their favorite furniture and jewelry if they opposed her wishes.)

When Christina read the clause, the greediest of the sisters, she dramatically retreated from the group, obviously more worried about a certain china set than pursuing brain surgery. She cried out breathlessly as she left. "Heaven help you, Denver. God is going to get you for this one."

The nurses wrapped Desi in warm blankets, repositioned her for comfort and kept her lips moist with a wet towel. As the last of the sisters withdrew from their beside vigil, off to pray with Desi's Pastor in the family room, the surgeon patted the youngest Coggins on the shoulder. Only then did Denver realize that the medical staff was on his side.

Denver quietly requested an ambulance for home, attempting to honor Desi's dying wish. He signed waiver after waiver, as the techs helped clothe Momma in a chiffon blue dress with ivory flowers, personally delivered by the good Reverend himself. The sisters eventually returned and this time Denver joined hands, circling their mother in prayer.

For a brief instance, Desi opened her eyes and scanned her adult-sized children with lucid comprehension, whispering each of their names. "Amy... Addie... Bevi... Christy... and Denver..." She reached out and squeezed his hand. "That's my boy."

*

"Right about then, I could see it." Ollie finishes. "Denver Coggins was shimmering gold."

Chapter 16

"It's gonna screw up your sleep!" Katie from California exclaims from the end of a phone line three thousand miles away. "Aren't you a little old for vampiring?"

Meg laughs easily. "If you think about it, I'm an adolescent in nursing years. Now let me go. My blood thirst beckons and Vegas won't be any fun without a paycheck."

*

From the very beginning of her graveyard rotation, Meg favors the night crew but can't pinpoint why. It was only after an especially grueling shift, dealing with seriously critical patients, that she finally figured it out. It boiled down to four basic emotions: fear, anxiety, excitement and doubt. The difference between days and nights, she determined, was the nurse's level of enthusiasm.

By moonlight, the department pulsed with undeniable tension. Crew members were constantly attempting to conceal their terror, and yet remained steadily fearful of the unknown. *What kind of disaster is showing up next?* It was GO time, afterall. The Real Deal. That rushing sensation a new nurse feels every *single* time a sick patient rolls into the department, when skills and personal nerve are put to the test.

Just the other night, when a fifty-seven year old man abruptly flipped into a lethal rhythm and needed a jolt of electric juice; staff members crowded the room to assist. Everyone *wanted* a piece of the action. When it was over, with the guy snuggled up in the ICU relatively safe and sound, the night crew couldn't shut up about it, reliving each moment like it was Super bowl XXX.

"Oh my God, did you see that twin-cath I plunged into his forearm. I almost missed it, dude. He was all thrashing around and sweating like a pig."

"How about I almost killed the guy!" The triage nurse exclaimed. *"Did you read his original complaint? Nausea, vomiting and diarrhea. I was getting ready to send him back to the waiting room! But then, right when I was feeling his pulse, it jumped up to like two hundred! If I checked it just a minute before that son-of-a-gun would've keeled over on the front sofa..."*

Meg rarely felt that kind of enthusiasm on first shift. (Strike that. It probably existed, but was definitely not as prevalent. Either that, or Meg was just too deer-in-the-headlights fresh to feel it.)

It makes sense if you think about it. It takes years for a daytime position to open up. By then, *most* candidates have been in the trenches a good while. Saving lives becomes old hat. Nobody flips out. Nobody beats the scene to death with play-by-plays and what-ifs. When a patient shows up circling the drain, warhorses gather their gear, march steadily into the room, seek out the complaint and fix it. End of story. There is no fervor. No freaking out. It's just another day at the Meat Plant. One hour closer to clock-out. Enthusiasm has gone the way of the Do-Do bird year's back, along with fear, anxiety, excitement, and doubt.

That was definitely the difference. Night staff displayed passion like a badge of honor. They wanted the world to sense their determination and applaud their efforts. *Truthfully, how many people could leave work on average day and say, "I saved a life."* Meg was now one of those few, and for the first time in her middle aged life, her confidence surged. She *loved* being a nurse! Especially with this crew. They had mojo.

Drive. The desire to do well.

The second reason Meg favored evenings was purely social. Ninety percent of the night crew was single afterall and not yet strapped down by family obligations. They were always posting invitations for pub nights and zip-line gatherings, house warming's and cookouts; requesting the presence of anyone interested, absolutely certain that bigger crowds demanded better laughs.

When it came time to fill out holiday schedules, Meg was slightly perplexed at the battle for time off on Halloween and New Years Eve, some actually scribbling in *will work* on Christmas and Turkey Day to seal the deal. Meg commented to Kristin, a twenty-something diva, who was offering extra Christmas hours in an attempt to secure a three night Vegas retreat for December 31ˢᵗ."

"I'm surprised that you'd be willing to give up Christmas for Amateur Night." Meg questioned.

"Amateur?"

"That's what we call New Years Even in the Restaurant Biz." Meg explained. "A holiday that does nothing but promise over crowded lounges, cheap champagne and expensive venues. A bunch of pretenders spending so much money they keep screaming that it's the *BEST TIME EVA'* when deep down they know it really sucks. By midnight, when they're barfing in the back alley, they get to thinking, wondering if maybe next year they'd be better off lounging on the living room couch."

"I'll take a mobbed casino at *Caesar's Palace* garbed in sequins over Christmas morning anytime." Kristen replied.

Meg suddenly envisioned her daughter at age three, the first year Kam actually caught on to the whole Santa thing. Dressed in a snowman printed flannel zip-up, pitter-pattering with great speed down the hallway in search of Santa's offerings. The way she fist-pumped her tiny hand and shouted, *YYEEESSSS!* It was, by far, Meg's most cherished holiday moment. "But Christmas is such a magical day."

Kristin frowned. "For you, maybe. My family lives four hours away. It's almost impossible for me to get both Christmas Eve and Christmas Day off, especially with all of the young mothers employed here. I'd be an asshole if I made a stink so my choices are limited. I can work until seven in the morning and suffer through the day with no sleep, or rush home early afternoon on Christmas Day and play beat the clock. It's completely exhausting. I'll get to hear my family bicker, watch my bratty nephews whine because they didn't get enough X-Box games, and if I drink I'll be trapped even longer. Last year I opted out, which ended up being worse. Alone, lying around my dismal living room, eating Cheerios and watching *A Christmas Story* over and over again. Talk about depressing. I'm sure my tune will change post motherhood, but right now my top priority is a hot date and possibly getting laid." Kristin winked. "Just kidding, but not really…"

Meg cringed at Kristin's Cheerios visual. Kamron's glory days with Santa were passed. *Poof!* Her daughter lived in Jacksonville now. They already had the discussion. Kam would not be home for the holidays. And Megs would be…*where*? Working. That's right. She had already signed up.

Meg's face visible dimmed. "This'll be my first year alone."

Kristin slapped her on the back. "So? Come to Vegas with the girls! I have an idea. Invite your daughter. That would be so fun! If she's anything like you, I bet we'll have a blast."

"She can't get away. I offered to fly her home,

but she's got school and a new job. But...*wait a minute*. I have a girlfriend in California. *Katie*. We've been talking about a reunion for the better part of five years."

"Round her up! The more the merrier"

Suddenly all of the sadness of losing Kam at Christmas slipped away. Speaking of Katie, she went ballistic when Meg breeched the Vegas subject. They had already spent all afternoon on the telephone discussing outfit options and how much money they were willing to lose at the craps table. So long in fact, that she had to rush off to work, applying her make up at stop signs and traffic lights along the way...

*

These thoughts jumble and dissipate as Meg locks up the car and heads into the job, once again shifting into stress mode. Another major difference between nights and days is the pattern of chaos. Dayshift begins slowly. Cloaked in early morning darkness, nurses trudge in quietly, carrying backpacks and shoulder bags, sipping from percolated thermoses. Huddle is subdued, employees stagnant, periodically rubbing sleep from their eyes. They slink like cats into the bays, receive a few scattered reports on lingering patients and then begin the short yet tedious task of checking equipment.

Some sneak off to the cafeteria for bacon and eggs, while others (fearful of cooties) sanitize work-stations with alcohol wipes the size of washcloths. Not-so-stringent co-workers catch up on gossip, review daily e-mails, and text family members from private phones even though it's against policy.

A line of injured and ill-appearing individuals trickle in through the front door, one in particular starts howling bloody murder, holding tight to his thigh, shouting something about a *fucking nail gun*...

EMS calls abruptly commence. (Warhorses swear that the radio battering is directly proportional to when surrounding Rest Homes take morning vital signs.)

"...Unit 52 coming in with an eighty-eight year old female, short of breath with blue lips. Initial oxygen in the mid-eighties. IV established, 125 mg of Solumedrol administered, breathing treatment in progress

...EMS 1 calling in with a seventy-four, that's SEVEN FOUR. Resident of the Mayberry House found sleeping in the fetal position on the bathroom floor with a 6 cm laceration to the head. Bleeding is controlled. Pt is demented and unable to recall the incident.

... EMS 16 coming at you with a twenty-seven year old female involved in a motor vehicle crash. She was a restrained driver hit from behind at a stop sign. There was limited damage to vehicle but the patient is sixteen weeks pregnant, complaining of back and neck pain. C-collar and backboard are in place. There was no airbag deployment.

The morning lull dissipates and then...BAM. Day shift is rolling.

Evenings start out the exact opposite. Night shift clocks in during the height of chaos. The ER is loud. Bustling. Day nurses race around tidying up assignments, scribbling last-minute notes while the new crew waits, many with arms crossed, some frowning, anticipating the worst. If the day nurse is spinning, anxiety kicks in and many will reach for the charts and begin to read, attempting to get a handle on what lies ahead. They understand that the longer it takes for hand-off, the further behind they will become. Nobody wants to start twelve hours knee deep in shit, but that's the way it usually is. Seven p.m. madness is as common as narcotic induced constipation.

For night shift, there will be no relaxing chats, no e-mail perusing, and definitely no bacon and eggs. *Ready. Set. Hurry your ass up.* Staff will be in an all out frenzy to get the admitted patients upstairs and everyone else treated and out the door. They work under the motto: *If one nurse is standing, then all nurses are standing.*

"Let's go people!" Charge bellows. "The faster we move the sooner we can sit down! Gettum up or gettum out!"

Lines eventually shorten, phones stop ringing and the surge of clients all but disappear. *Most* of the time. Only then does the initially stressed out and anxious crew begin to wind down. Some check e-mails, others eat, many text or play *Candy Crush* on private phones even though it's against policy. Stocking commences and, by twilight, the trickle effect begins and the cycle repeats itself.

Come morning, Meg exits the building like a battered warrior. Although she's emotionally and physically exhausted, this never seems to hinder her overwhelming sense of accomplishment. Only then does she relive the ugly moments of her shift. Like when she couldn't get a line in room seventeen and the patient rotated between screaming out in pain and ridiculing her efforts. She visualized Doctor Raj ranting in the background, hyped up on Red Bull, crazy for results. At the time, she yearned to retaliate with a *shut the fuck up,* not actually sure who was more deserving of the comment, the manic doctor or the histrionic patient.

In the morning twilight the moment loses its fervor. She chuckles at the scene as she replays it in her head. *Who would've thunk it?* Meghan Ford—Steak Pusher to ER nurse. She couldn't deny it. The new shoes felt good.

Chapter 17

To Meg's surprise, the biggest transition from food to medicine wasn't her daily duties. Serving food, she quickly recognized, was very similar to nursing. The white boards posted in each room, advertizing personal wait times and plans of care, reminded Meg of over-sized menus. Call bells had her at patient's beck and call. Shots were administered in both professions (ha-ha), and proved evenly painful. And truthfully, cleaning adult diapers wasn't any more disgusting than clearing off a late night cocktail table cluttered with muddled ash trays and sticky beer bottles. The biggest shock, getting back to the point, was Meg's paycheck.

"They take half! *Half!*" she whines to a random group of colleagues a few weeks later as they gnaw through another two a.m. lunch break.

Mary Catherine rolls her eyes. "They always take half."

"Not when you're a waitress. We claimed tips, at least eight percent of our sales, but I was in a steak house. I always made more than that. I guess I didn't realize how *much* more that actually meant until…well…this!" Meg slaps at the flimsy check stub. "I think overall I'm bringing home less money."

"Let's not forget about our benefits." Ingrid pipes in.

"I had benefits."

"What about a 401k? Paid time off? Sick leave? Did you get dental? It's all about long term security." Mary Catherine nods encouragingly.

"True," Meg admits. "But more than anything else, I'm happier. With myself. I needed a change. I'm just, I don't know…surprised."

"I bet you had to put up with a bunch of shit as a waitress." Ingrid adds. "I waited tables for a summer back in school. I couldn't stand playing servant."

Meg grins. "What do you think we're doing *now*?"

"This is different. People respect nurses." Ingrid pauses her yogurt spoon in mid flight. "Waitresses…not so much."

"I'm beginning to discover that people respect nursing as a profession, but only in theory. In reality, when I'm trying to save their ass, it's a whole different ball game. Truthfully, I got more respect uncorking cheap bottles of wine from morons trying to impress their high-maintenance girlfriends. As for my take on nursing, just yesterday I called room twelve *table twelve. Table twelve wants to know if he can have drink,* I said. Doctor Breezy was howling."

"You're funny, Meg."

"I can't count how many times I've answered the EMS phone, *Giorgio's Steak House.* That, Ms. Ingrid, is how much this place reminds me of waitressing."

"You know what?" Ingrid cries. "We should dress up and have a girl's night! I wouldn't mind a dirty martini and a huge steak."

"Sorry. I'm on for the next four."

"*Four*? Already caught up in overtime?"

Meg frowns. "I've got to make up for these government deductions!"

The conversation wanes as Meg chews her last bit of salad, but Ingrid's invitation gets her to thinking about her pathetic social life. She didn't have any pastimes or hobbies. Meg had always been too poverty stricken to spend frivolously. She was never a big partier. She had witnessed, first hand, the debilitating effects the bar industry had on her restaurant friends. One cocktail after work always turned into ten. Every night drinking and smoking, some even snorting their cash away. They'd wake up with empty pockets and horrible headaches only to repeat the cycle over and over again. No, Meg definitely steered clear of the party train. But she needed to do something! Committing to the Vegas trip had been a big step, but maybe she needed to knit or paint or join a gym.

"Are you married, Meg?" Mary Catherine asks thoughtfully.

"Nope."

"Dating?"

Meg stands up. "Time to get back to work."

"So *that's* the problem." Young Ingrid points a finger in the air and shouts with enthusiasm, "We need to get Meg a date! Next week we'll plan a dinner party. And tomorrow I'm going to bring in cupcakes!"

Meg and Mary Catherine turn to her, confused. "Cupcakes? What the heck do cupcakes and dating have to do with each other?"

Ingrid giggles. "We're nurses. Cupcakes go with everything."

*

A muffled overhead page echoes through the break room. *DR. KASSEL TO THE PARKING LOT. DR KASSEL TO THE PARKING LOT...STAT.*

"That's my cue, girls. Kassel's in my bay." Meg drops her trash in the nearby receptacle and heads for the door.

"Next week, Meg. I've got some cute friends!"

"You're almost twenty years younger than me, Ingrid." Meg adds, "I could date your father."

"Yeah, but that'll piss off Mom."

Meg laughs quietly as she exits the lounge. She has already decided to bow out of any external dinner engagements. Meg isn't ready for a man in her life. Not today. Not next week. Not ever.

Chapter 18

"Why are you always *eating*? You're a *ghost!*"
I snap.

We lap the ER three times and briefly linger near the Pixis before the Dickman announces that it's time for a snack. Sitting on the couch in the lounge, within earshot but just around the corner, we listen as the nurses consider future dinner plans. During this time Ollie manages to scarf down three hospital prepared turkey sandwiches, fourteen graham crackers and three pints of milk. He pauses briefly, walks over to Ingrid, and shouts the word *CUPCAKES* directly in her ear.

"Any special orders, Gloria? Now's the time. Ingrid's a beast in the kitchen."

"I'm not hungry."

"Of course not. You're a ghost."

"Then why are *you* always eating?"

"Because I can," Ollie replies. "It's my only form of enjoyment in this mad house. Cupcakes and hotdogs keep me sane."

"When do you leave, anyway?"

"I've been wondering the same thing." Ollie shrugs. "It was different when I dropped. My predecessor, Dr. Clarence was his name; the minute I showed up he spouted a few rules—I dare say the most limited of instructions, shimmered gold and disappeared."

"But *you're* not gold. What does that mean?"

Ollie frowns, clearly irritated. "I don't *know*, Gloria."

"Mr. Dick knows perfectly well why he's still

here."

Both Ollie and I turn to the voice and find a petite, smartly dressed woman standing behind us. My first thought: a hospital administrator spying on the night staff. But then I notice that she's flickering a silvery blue, her voice slightly echoes, and...well, she can *see* us.

"Where did you come from?" Ollie demands.

"It's me, remember? Deloris? I work for..." The short woman nudges her head in an upward direction. "...the man upstairs."

Ollie springs to his feet. "Speak of the devil...or angel, I guess. Hot *damn*! Are you here to fetch me? THANKYOU *JESUS*! I'm out of here, Gloria." His voice deepens in full Sinatra mode. *"Fly me to the moon! Let me sing your blah bl-blah blah..."* Jovially, he adds, *"In other words..."* He stops abruptly and points at me. "Remember what I taught you, kid. And someday we'll reunite, once again, in the..."

"You've been reassigned, Ollie." Deloris cuts him off.

Ollie's brow furrows and then he winks, playfully. "You're kidding, right?"

"Not kidding," Deloris replies flatly. "You are now a Retrieval Specialist and the job starts pronto. Stay close to A-bay. Room five is a DNR and he's beginning to shimmer. After he transitions, take him to Peter and then report back to me." Deloris hands Ollie a silver bracelet.

"What's this?"

"Your beeper. It glows purple when I need you."

"But...but what about the Promise Land? The House of Good-n-Plenty? I've been WORKING! For ten years I've been trapped in this HELL HOLE! Saving LIVES!"

Deloris pinches her lips together and shakes her head.

Ollie's eyes go wide. "Is this about the *CUPCAKES?* So WHAT if I whisper orders to nurses every once in awhile. A dude needs a perk now and again."

I stand off to one side not sure what to make of the situation. The new ghost frightens me. Her aura exhibits power. Authority. A boss so high up the totem pole, her mere presence feels God-like. I consider kicking Ollie's leg to halt his whining, but no matter if she's watching or not, I'm absolutely certain the boss lady will see.

"It's not the cupcakes, you dumbass." Deloris glares. "Or the hotdogs. Or the turkey and cheese dip..."

"BUT I'VE DONE *NOTHING WRONG!* Moreover, if I missed something...I had a SHITTY preceptor. THERE. I said it. The good doctor SUCKED with explaining the rules."

Deloris guffaws, turns to me and points a thumb at the Dickman. "This guy! Don't let him fool you, Gloria. I showed up seconds after Dr. C. shifted. He got his training."

"I DID WHAT YOU SAID!"

"It's not always about doing *nothing wrong.*" Deloris snaps at a seething Ollie and then re-shifts her attention to me. "Sometimes, Gloria, you have to make sure you're doing *everything right.*"

"Is this about Case 674?"

"It is."

"Oh, this is *BULLSHIT!*" Ollie swoons. "Pure fucking *NONSENSE!* The patient was DEAD! Nothing would've changed that."

"And, as we have already discussed, this isn't about the patient. It's about the primary nurse."

"Oh…this…this is RIDICULOUS!"

An overhead page goes off. *DR. KASSEL TO THE PARKING LOT! DR. KASSEL TO THE PARKING LOT….STAT!*

Silver waves a flickering hand. "Enough. This topic has been beat to death already. You have work to do, Mr. Dick. Help Gloria one last time. There's a shit show coming in from the parking lot. After that, stay where you are. Mr. Drake in room five is about to transition." Deloris huffs. "Seriously, if you screw up the transporter job I'll have you reassigned to the tippity top of the tallest Carolina Pine whispering to squirrels for the next fifty years. Don't think I can't make that happen." Deloris pauses pointedly. "Let this be a lesson to you, Gloria. The chosen path is a righteous one. Weigh the odds. Do what's right. Unless it's wrong."

"What is *that* supposed to mean?" I say.

"It means exactly that, Gloria." Ollie mumbles as he drags me through the door. "Don't mind Deloris. She's here to confuse the crap out of us."

"Who is she, anyway?" I ask, when the coast is clear.

"Think of her as a very important administrator."

"Funny. I thought she was a bigwig. Some kind of hospital spy."

"You got that right, sister, but she's more than that. She helps run the show from a private fucking cloud in the sky and picks apart situations *after* the fact, when options seem obvious. I couldn't stand management when I was *alive*. It's worse in death! They flutter down off their puff cotton thrones and speak in tongues like I have ANY clue to what they're gibbering about." Ollie turns and shouts at the ceiling. "IF I WAS DOING SUCH A BANG UP JOB…WHY

NOT BOOT ME *SOONER*? I WOULD'VE BEEN HAPPY WITH REASSIGNMENT! But NOOO! They wait until I have a replacement and then pull this crap. YOU KNOW WHAT? I *LOVE* SQUIRRELS! Aww…forget it. Come on, Gloria. We've got work to do."

Chapter 19

Meg makes a quick pit stop at her locker to grab a sweatshirt. Eating always chills her to the bone so she figures now would be a good time to layer up before heading back to A-bay.

There are two pods in the Dixon Valley Emergency Department. A and B bay. B-bay is used for the less acute; certain abdominal complaints, persistent fevers and chronic respiratory disorders, just to name a few. A-bay is where most of the serious action takes place. (Side note: this is purely hypothetical of course and rarely, if ever, works out. When beds are tight—like they always are—B-bay is sometimes the only place to go.)

Regardless, Meg views an A-bay assignment with much disdain. She loves the challenge, but with the arrival of every rescue and each debilitating injury, her body trembles with unease, her heart flutters like a rabid butterfly, and she silently repeats the only prayer that matters. *Please, God, don't let me kill anyone.*

She passes Jeanne in B-bay, a woman of equal physical age but twenty years her senior in the nursing role. Jeanne is standing outside of room nine respectfully coaxing a hyped-up drug addict that safety at Dixon Valley is an attainable goal. Meg notices that the druggie has a visitor of the female variety, slumped over and snoring in a nearby chair.

"Now Douglas," Jeanne says, "I empathize with the fact that you're bursting with heat. It's the PCP. Gives you a fever and makes you want to rip off those clothes. I'm pretty sure that the Safety Council here at Dixon Valley will frown upon you jumping up and down on the bed in your birthday suit. Let me bring you a fan. It'll blow the air through your testicles better than swinging about like a monkey. I promise. So take a seat while I go and hunt one down. Tell you what? How about I bring you a nice, extremely cold glass of water and a turkey sandwich? ...What? Oh, we certainly do have mustard. ...*and* pepper. Maybe you're girlfriend wants a sandwich? Oh wait, she's drooling. Tired, I suspect, from all that hard work she does. ...She's not employed? Well *that's* a surprise. Now put back on your gown, Douglas, and lay down. That's right. I'll be right back." Jeanne turns to Meg and winks.

The water fountain is on the way to A-bay so the nurses walk together. Meg can't help but comment. "You're so amazing, Jeanne. How do you remain so composed *ALL* of the time." Meg tosses a thumb over her shoulder. "For fools like that?"

Jeanne smiles. "I've made peace with the horrors of this job decades ago. I used to get mad. *Angry*. I'd go home after a disastrous night, toss and turn, grind my teeth so badly that I ended up with TMJ and had to wear a mouthpiece. Then one day I realized that certain things in life were inevitable. Like drug addicts, for instance. There are a lot of Douglas's in the world. I can't change Douglas. Douglas needs to change Douglas. It's sad really. When he's straight, the man is kind of a charmer."

"You've seen him straight?" Meg asks.

"Loads of times. Every other month he finds God and reunites with his wife."

"That chick snoring in the chair?"

"Nope. That's his girlfriend. When Beastie rounds the corner I know I'm dealing with the tanked up Douglas. But he's got a wife. I call her Peaches." Jeanne shakes her head. "There's been many a cat fight in this joint between those two. Peaches must love that fool to make such an ass of herself. Ugly times, my friend. Ugly times."

It's closing in on three a.m. when Meg arrives back from lunch. Personally trekking her last patient up to the ICU prior to eating, she left an empty assignment. Angela had ordered her to hit the lounge while she had the chance. "Go Megs. Have a proper break. Sit down. Eat. Laugh."

The first time Charge said this to her Meg didn't quite understand, but as her career progressed it became noticeably apparent that lunch breaks rarely ran the allotted thirty minutes. For Megs, leaving her assignment for any length of time brought with it great anxiety. She kept visualizing her rooms filling up with train wrecks and "everything" work-ups. The last thing she needed was to return from eating to a huge mess, and spend the rest of her shift behind the eight ball. It had happened before, too many times to count.

So when the overhead page ordered Kassel to the parking lot, Meg packed up lunch early. She had three empty rooms, afterall. Surely whatever was brewing in the parking lot was heading her way.

Meg's thoughts linger on Jeanne and Douglas as she enters the pod. It takes a second, but wait... A slight shiver tickles the small of her back. Something is wrong. The bay is absolutely silent. Too fucking quiet. Meg peers in a couple of rooms. The same few lingering patrons are chilling on stretchers waiting on results. One is drinking for CT scan. Another is watching television. No one appears too strained.

That's when she realizes... Nobody, not one single medical person is in the bay. Meg's eyes automatically shift to the secretary's desk. Empty. She visualizes Ronnie snoozing on the beat-up lounge recliner. The secretary was still at lunch. Reluctantly, the young nurse turns toward the lobby. Before she makes it to the door, it crashes open. Crowding around a single stretcher, the doctor, three nurses and two techs blast through, moving in unison, buzzing like a swarm of angry hornets.

"Room two! Get her to room two!"

Meg's heart pounds furiously. Her mouth dries up like a crusty cactus as adrenaline shifts into overdrive. She follows the stretcher into the treatment room, *her* room, and automatically reaches for leads, the blood pressure cuff and hi-flow oxygen. The whole while (a matter of seconds) she examines her next customer.

On the stretcher lays a young woman. At a glimpse, Meg guesstimates her age between fifteen and eighteen—twenty tops. Sucking sounds emanate from her airway. Her body spasms violently. She's in the midst of a full blown seizure. This, a mere child convulsing on a stretcher is bad enough. But that's not what horrifies Meghan Ford, RN. What really catches her attention is the sobering cord snaking out from between her legs, connected to a very bloody and slippery limp baby.

Intense is one way to describe it. Even Dr. Kassel's voice, attempting authority and coolness in a moment of toppling hysteria, carries an urgent tone. Very swiftly Brooksie double clamps the umbilical cord while the physician snips in between, releasing the tiny patient from its internal oxygen source. Brooksie whispers more to herself than anyone else. *"It's a girl."*

The tiny fetus is then whisked over to Althea, a Caribbean born nurse pushing sixty-five. It was reported by many of her peers that Althea had only one pace. Slow. But what the semi-retired RN lacked in speed, she quadrupled in skill, especially when handling obstetric patients.

In the late sixties, Althea had been an island midwife, delivering babies for the remotest of village folks dwelling in the heart of Jamaica. "The local Bush Nurse," Josh had joked. "And by that I mean literally!"

All clowning and complaining aside, on this particular late Tuesday evening, every staff member in A-bay, especially the emergency physician, were thanking their lucky stars that the seasoned veteran was on shift.

In previous months Althea had shared a few of her old stories with Meghan Ford. How she was paid with fruits and knit blankets, yard work and baked goods, for delivering the tiniest of souls under the most barren of circumstances. "Nut'in is more gratifying, Miss Meg, dan to bring such happiness to a poor and simple people. Never in me life have I been treated widt such respect or felt so appreciated."

Meg responded by saying, "They were lucky to have you."

The aging nurse shook her head. "Dat's what you'd t'ink. But looking back, I believe it was me lucky to have dem."

A burst of halting silence mutes the room as Althea sweeps up the neonate and rubs it down in a gentle yet vigorous motion. Swaddling and suctioning until the fragile spirit burps out a weak but glorious cry.

Surround sound returns as the room exhales.

Crying is a good thing.

With the mid-wife handling the baby, attention quickly shifts back to the mom. Brooksie and Josh insert lines as Meg and Juanetta strip her down. Ativan is administered to halt the seizure and a suction cord is set up to handle mouth secretions.

"She's been convulsing for four minutes, Doctor." Josh's tone is serious. (The way the male nurse can shut off his funny button during moments of duress impresses Meg.) "The Ativan isn't helping."

"I need 6 grams of magnesium sulfate, IV." Dr. Kassel orders. "STAT."

Confused, Meg pauses. "Six grams, sir?"

"That's right. Six. Six grams of magnesium sulfate. Now."

Anxiously Meg skitters off to the medicine room. She doesn't like the order. *Six grams is too much!* A normal dose is one or two. And this guy wanted six? She pulls the drugs from the machine and, sure enough, even the pre-mixed bags contain two grams. Meg scrambles for the medication book, but on second thought decides to call the pharmacy. *But the patient is seizing!* She reminds herself. *There's no time!*

BRING THE BAGS TO THE DOCTOR AND QUESTION THE ORDER. DO IT NOW.

Meg grabs the medicine and runs back to A-bay. She marches right up to the physician and shows him the three separate bags. "Doctor, did you say *six* grams or two?"

"Six. Six grams."

"I'll need to call the pharmacy." Meg says.

Kassel shakes his head. "There's no time."

SHOW ME.

"Show me where it says this is a normal dose." Meg replies.

Kassel frowns. Grabbing one of the three bags, he tosses it to Brooksie. "Get this started, will you? Josh, set up for intubation please. If she doesn't stop seizing in the next few minutes, I'm gonna tube her." He turns to Meg. "You, come with me."

Meg's stomach flutters with unease. For some reason Doctor Kassel scares the shit out of her. It's partly because he's the director of the physicians' group. *Big Daddy*. But it's more than that. Much more. Dr. Kassel rarely smiles. He never jokes or converses with staff. She's heard the rumors. Much like Jamie Baxter, the director shares the belief that newby nurses should steer clear of the emergency department.

After a year on the job, Meg is beginning to agree. The more she learns, the more she realizes she needs to know. And her skills, although improving, continued to border on amateur. Memorizing steps and procedures could only get her so far. Repetition was the key to success. Repetition and experience. As Bev Martin liked to crow, *"There's a reason they call it medial practice."*

Now here she was questioning Dr. Kassel, the director himself, on a life saving order. The very same man who would love to disrupt her career in emergency services for good. *I must be an idiot.* Meg cringes, already visualizing her next visit to the manager's office.

Dr. Kassel moves briskly. Meg jogs to keep up. Even under certain duress, Meg finds herself admiring the man's lumberjack frame. *I'm ridiculous!*

The anticipated verbal lashing never comes. Instead, the physician marches to his desk, pulls out a medication book and flips to magnesium sulfate. He points with an authoritative finger, reading the insert out loud. *"Magnesium Sulfate. 4-6 gram loading dose over twenty minutes for eclamptic patients.* Are you happy now?" Kassel doesn't wait for a response, snaps the book shut, and retreats back to his patient.

Meg rushes up to him. "Doctor...I...uh...I'm sorry."

The director pauses. His brow furrows and his mouth draws thin. What he says surprises Meg. "That's your *job*, Nurse Ford. Do not apologize for doing it properly. Now, if you would be so prudent as to hang the remaining bags. We have a life to save."

Chapter 20

"Watch how she teeters between orange and yellow. It's sometimes hard to distinguish, but there…yes, can you see it?" Ollie announces as we trail Meghan and the doctor.

"That bright burst of retina burning sunshine? How could I miss it?"

Ollie ignores my sarcasm. "The nurse is uncertain about the order, and fearful of making a mistake. Fear and uncertainty. Yellow and orange go hand in hand."

I have an afterthought. "Ollie, you knew the order was right. Why not just whisper in her ear to give the medication? Why make her go through the rigmarole of confronting a physician?"

Ollie's tches a finger. "Now *now,* Gloria. Be careful or you'll end up a friggin' retrieval specialist like me."

"How is that bad?"

"Because *your* job is not to do *their* job for them. Watch your step, lady. Remember that it's not enough to do everything *right.* You must also avoid doing certain things *wrong.*"

"I don't get it."

"Tell me about it."

Right then I notice that Mr. Drake, the old timer circling the drain from room five, is standing next to us. He taps Ollie on the shoulder to get our attention and I recognize that he's shimmering coppery gold. Minutes before he lay contracted in the fetal position, curled up like a withered infant, white hair matted on the pillow. Now he's parked on scrawny but firm legs, arms folded across his chest, hair sticking up every which way, engulfing a concerned and highly educated expression. The physical changes in his resurrection astound me, but not as much as when he speaks. (Mr. Drake has done nothing but suck his thumb for the better part of three years.)

He frowns, pointing back into room five. "There's something's wrong with my wife."

I had forgotten about Mrs. Lorraine Drake and how she accompanied her husband on every hospital adventure. Sitting quietly at his bedside like a permanent fixture, she was always knitting or reading, and periodically discussing the news as if expecting the demented ex-banker's participation.

Lorraine is spunky and agile at eighty-four years of age. She lives in a quaint little apartment in the same complex as her son's family, who are currently on holiday in Florida. It is their first vacation in four years…

Ever since the already slightly confused Bobby Drake tripped on his slippers and cracked a hip, he lost the ability to walk. Immobility and isolation got the best of him bringing with it great depression and a severe drop in body mass. To further complicate the situation, Mr. Drake acquired a urinary tract infection which left him weak, frail, and on the verge of death. "He could pass any day," is what the doctor had said. Phone calls were made and vacations postponed, so every family and friend could visit with the dispirited soul and do their part in making Bobby's final days memorable.

"Any day" turned into four years.

Bobby was eventually moved from the hospital and placed in a long term care facility. From then on Bobby's visits to The Valley were periodic, for the occasional skin tear or questionable cough. Lorraine never failed to make the trip. DNR status was breeched the day Bobby's overwhelming urine infection dumped his blood pressures in the toilet and almost ended his life, but the subject distressed the old woman so greatly that serious discussions were put on hold. When Bobby's thumb sucking started, Lorraine, to her own dismay and grief, requested the life-ending forms herself.

The same elderly creature is now stretched over Bobby's limp body, weepy and spent. She hasn't hit the call bell or cried out for help. Lorraine wants this moment alone to grieve and say goodbye to her loving husband of umpteen years. I feel a lump growing in my throat, once again reminded why death in the presences of loved ones is so hard for me to stomach.

Ollie reaches out with both hands and softly grips Mr. Drake's shoulders. "You've crossed over, Bobby."

"I *know* that!" The old man wrings at his hands anxiously. "But *Loraine*! She's so...so *upset*!"

Ollie sighs. "There's not much time, Bob. Go to her. Give her a squeeze. Tell her how you feel. Say goodbye."

Bobby scratches at his wiry scalp. "Can she hear me?"

"Today she will."

Bobby nods and returns to his room. We watch as he wraps his arms around his wife's back and latches on. As he begins whispering, Lorraine's eyes clench tight and tears trickle down her creviced face. Bobby's murmuring is so tender and soft that I don't have to hear the words, his body language says it all. Automatically, I reach out to close the door thinking if anyone needs a moment alone it's these two.

That's when I notice Lorraine's forehead.

Ollie spots the image as well and blanches.

"What *is* that on the woman's forehead? Is that a *tattoo*?"

"No." Ollie's reply sounds grim. "It's a number."

"Was it there earlier?"

"No."

"What does it mean?"

"It means exactly that." Ollie's whispers. "Lorraine's been numbered."

"Is it something I should understand? Explain please! You're leaving any second and I...I don't want to be kept in the dar..."

"Like individual fingerprints, souls are unique." Ollie cuts me off. "When a physical number emerges on a person's forehead, it means that their soul has been marked. Death is imminent. In this case, the reason is pretty obvious. Lorraine Drake will die of a broken heart. That's a medical condition, you know, an actual diagnosis. Bobby's death will take it's toll. If an autopsy were to be performed, the chambers of Lorraine's heart would show a very specific demarcation pattern triggered by severe emotional stress."

"That's an old wives tale."

"It's not. The technical term is *Takotsubo Cardiomyopathy*. *Takotsuba* translates into the words *Octopus Pot* because of how the heart muscle actually bulges, resembling a slippery eight legged sea creature. A very remarkable and yet sad phenomenon."

"Are you saying that Lorraine's going to *die*? When?"

Ollie shrugs. "Soon. Today. Tomorrow. A week tops."

"How can you be so certain?"

"Because of the brand on her forehead. It's a ticket to ride. Lorraine's number has officially been punched."

"Why haven't I ever seen this before? The numbers?"

"It's a pretty rare occurrence in an emergency department. Numbered folks aren't necessarily sick so they have no reason to be here. I've seen it a few times—once on a police officer and a second time on a priest. The cop showed up escorting a wounded prisoner and not two hours later got mowed down in a gang fight. The priest happened to be in the ER performing *Last Rites*. The next morning he stumbled stepping off a curb and a taxi driver took him out. I only know the details because the staff couldn't shut up about it."

"Is there a way to warn these people?"

Ollie shakes his head. "We're not privy to the specifics. Consider Lorraine. I suspect *Disease of the Broken Hearted*, but do you think me whispering *Hey, Lorraine. Go easy. Don't stress out about poor Bobby. He's better off,* will help? Doubtful."

"So I'm supposed to do what? *Nothing?*"

"Nothing is all we can do." Ollie frowns grimly. "We're dead."

"And if we were alive?"

"With every marked individual a soul must pass." Ollie pauses, thoughtfully. "Hypothetically speaking, a living person could take the place of a numbered victim."

"Except living people can't see dead people."

"Exactly."

"So...what? We just wait? Wait on death?"

"Death and taxes, Gloria. Death and taxes."

Chapter 21

Time is a blur in the side slots between life and death. I best appreciate the seasons by way of hallway decorations and select nursing attire. Autumn brings purple and orange scrub tops scattered with black cats and witches. Gobbling turkeys and cornucopia horns follow, intermingled with flashy wreaths and gaudy, decorated trees. Tina Page's wardrobe is always helpful. Donning character prints for every season change, Snow White and Cinderella totter about with painted packages at Christmas, Minnie and Mickey sport bunny ears in early April. And, come mid-August, Goofy's Gang rides the surf. Hearts prevail in February, followed by March which is always inundated with shamrocks and golden rimmed leprechauns.

Not only am I physically trapped inside the emergency department, I can't see *out* either. Not grass or sky or dirty, mucked up weedy gravel. Nothing. Nada. This really sucks. I have managed to whisper in a bunch of flowers and potted plants via the nursing staff, but it's not the same. Truthfully, I'd chop off my left tit to be standing on the edge of a grassy cliff, surrounded by wild flowers, a cool breeze lapping against my skin with a panoramic view of a coppery ocean shimmering in the distance.

Oh, how I long for the great outdoors! Sky. Sun. Wind. Rain. I often wonder if the day is snowy and gray or scorching under the blazing sun. Would a bar of chocolate positioned on the dashboard of a car be frozen solid or a syrupy mess? Are the grounds keepers salting the icy side walks of winter or mowing the fresh-green grass of late spring? Is it pouring rain or

Claritin clear? On slow days I fantasize educated guesses by way of bundled scarves and saturated umbrellas, but it's not the same. Not even close. I vaguely recall a few scattered windows at DVH even in the emergency department. In life I was always too busy to bother with the passing clouds of another disintegrating afternoon, and here now I yearn for them.

So what happened to the windows? They still exist. For normal folks. (By normal, I mean the ones with beating hearts and smelly coffee breath.) For the walking dead, these port holes of sanity have transitioned into mirrors. What once displayed gardens and fireflies and bright open skies, is now nothing more than a place for ghosts to check their teeth.

That's why I was completely caught off guard by Geraldyne Dixon.

Geraldyne Dixon, or Geri Mae, is somewhat famous around these parts, especially in the ER. Whether or not it was true, it has been reported that her great-granddaddy, Braden Lee Dixon, was one of the founders of Dixonville, our quaint Carolinian town, referred to by many as the '*Trailer Park Capital of the World*'. Even with bragging rights on the outstanding selection of Doublewide's in the area, I assure you, Dixonville has its share of money folks.

Geraldyne is a rich kid. Or...*was* a rich kid, many decades ago.

Nobody knows for certain what led poor Geri Mae down a less than noble path. Rumors circulated that she got busy with some dumbass, had a secret abortion and then promptly lost her shit. Others whispered the exact opposite. That she fell madly in love with a trailer park boy and, at the ripe age of sixteen, bellied a youngin' that didn't quite meet the expectations of her father, one Braden Lee Dixon III. Family and close acquaintances deny both sets of accusations and no evidence has ever surfaced to verify either story. Nevertheless, something fucked her up. I say this with great certainty because during my thirteen years of service at Dixon Valley I've taken care of the rich poly-substance abuser on numerous occasions.

One thing everyone in town could agree upon was that the young Geri Mae was a *Teen Beat* disaster. According to her father, Geraldyne was a movie junkie. He would brag that his beautiful daughter had seen every movie at the local cinema at least three times. Geri, you see, had big plans of becoming a Hollywood icon like her very favorite, Marilyn Monroe. She studied technique, he said, by way of viewing flicks over and over again.

The young Ms. Dixon was naturally beautiful, adorably sweet, and extremely manipulative. Her father bought every word. In reality, the young Geri Mae hadn't been to the theatre in years. Money designated for tickets and popcorn was spent on malt liquor and cheap beer purchased by Shep, a homeless dude that lived in the woods behind *Manny's Gas & Go*. Instead of memorizing lines in the safe confines of the Dixonville Movie Theatre, Geraldyne was carousing in fast cars, skinny-dipping with young men and smoking marijuana that locals, back then, referred to as *The Pot that Killed Elvis*.

Braden Lee Dixon the *third* was not a complete idiot. Eventually he caught wind of Geraldyne's shifty antics. Embarrassed more than anything, he sent his only daughter away, off to study at a ritzy but strict private school, well beyond the reaches of Boone, in the midst of the Appalachian Mountains.

Sadly, Geri's situation deteriorated. On the brink of her seventeenth birthday there was incident, far more bizarre and debauched than any prior episode. This one was photographed and displayed on the front cover of the local paper. (Thankfully for Brady Lee, the school was a hundred miles away and the Internet still a pipe dream, so very few Dixonville townies were privy to the visual.)

Absolutely certain that money could fix anything, Mr. Dixon spent the better part of his inheritance trying to get his daughter straight. Geraldyne was hospitalized in numerous mental facilities, pumped full of drugs, her mind psychologically dissected and explored by the most adept of head quacks. Some say she improved. Others, not so much.

On Geraldyne's eighteenth birthday, after a very lucid and expressive therapy session, she fired her psychiatrist, dumped her pile of prescriptions in the trash, and went on her merry way. Some days, months even, her mindset bordered on exceptional. During those periods of wellness, Geri was said to be incredibly smart, sarcastically sweet, a great story teller and a complete adventure junkie. She traveled endlessly. Destinations like South America, Mexico, the Dominican Republic and the Caribbean, spending money and partying mostly, wasting another stack of daddy's big pile of money. Some whispered that she was running. Others said she was searching. To ask Geri Mae Dixon, she'd simply reply, "I call it living."

During these traveling frenzies, Geri Mae was high as a kite manic. Living each day carelessly and free, as if it were her last. She would tailgate at weddings and crash political dinner parties. She liked riding horses and would occasionally wrestle with sheep. Geraldyne favored hiking at midnight and having wild sex with dark handsome strangers. Every Sunday she'd have brunch at The Ritz, ordering Fruit Loops and strawberries drowning in champagne, then spend a blurry afternoon shopping for fashion wigs and custom-made Barbie jewelry. Geri was fond of bungee jumping and golf, paying exorbitant greens fees so she could ride around in golf carts eating Triscuits and sipping canned beer.

Truth is, Geri Dixon would try anything. She would go anywhere. On and on. Until eventually...she hit that overwhelming, too fucking enormous to get over, hypothetical brick wall.

And then...

...*CRASH*.

She was usually in this state, on the verge of collapse, when the illness took Geraldyne to her bad place. The place controlled by family secrets nobody was ever entirely certain about, when Ms. Dixon popped one too many pills and chug-a-lugged lethal mixes of Mad Dog and Veuve Clicquot. That's when she came to see us but, truthfully, she was rarely happy about it.

It was early in my Dixon Valley career when I first cared for Geraldyne. The 911 call that activated the EMS team was phoned in as a *ten-fifty-nine* (which translates as a shit show of crazy). A chick lunatic was off the hook. Anxiously pacing the streets of The Jolly Roger Trailer Park in the wee hours of morning, she was knocking on doors, frantically searching and screaming for a man named Joey, who'd supposedly stolen her diaper bag.

The final door she plagued was owned by a young Hispanic woman, who spoke little English and lived alone with two small children. Fearful of the bizarre creature she immediately dialed 911. They caught up with Geraldyne two streets over banging on the cellophane wrapped windows of a camouflaged Doublewide, shrieking like a banshee... "JOOOO-*EEEY*! JOOOO-*EEEEY*!"

Ms. Dixon was in such a state, so exceptionally

irate and out of control, the EMS squad was forced to bind her up in four point restraints and medicate with a series of strong sedatives. She arrived late night via ambulance, hissing and snarling at paramedics through bared teeth, clothed in Marilyn Monroe attire, platinum blonde hair pinned just so, a light pink chiffon dress billowing off the stretcher.

She ignored me when I first introduced myself, shifting into a religious rant, spewing hymns and methodical hyperboles. Chanting about God and redemption, she insisted we were all going to PAY for what we were doing before abruptly reverting back to her aggressive shrieking search of JOOO-*EEEY* and the missing diaper bag.

That was years ago, before Braden Lee Dixon III went. and got himself dead for whatever the reason, leaving any normal person enough money to invest and live an easy life for the better part of many moons. Of course Geri Mae wasn't quite normal and continued down a debauched path, wandering and squandering, until hundreds of thousands of dollars disintegrated into nickels and dimes. Thankfully, she smartened up at the last minute and purchased a small apartment off Main Street, but inevitably had to take up work at the local 7-11 to pay the electric bill and afford her daily staple of kidney beans and Colt 45. Extravagance to Miss Dixon these days involved ticketed bus fare into C-town, to the Crystal Mall, where she was still known to purchase the occasional high-end dress.

Sometimes EMS was activated by a Good Samaritan worried because it was pouring outside and Geri lay shivering, curled up on a street curb, drunk as a skunk. Other days she checked herself in, concerned about spider veins or lip cancer or in need of a muscle relaxer because the city commissioner refused her written request to pad the park benches. Ninety percent of the time, Ms. Dixon proved harmless, but once in awhile, when she arrived tied up in another wrecked cocktail dress screaming for Joey and the pampies, her actions transcended into committable.

The first few hours of those visits were always horrific. Obtaining blood and urine, cutting off clothes, trying to avoid being bitten or spit at as the beat down mental patient fought us off tooth and nail was pitiful and grueling. Snoring would come soon, but never soon enough, and Geri Mae would slip into a drug-induced haze. Hours later, upon awaking, Miss Dixon would sit up and stretch like a cat, completely refreshed, unfazed by her less than desirable situation. She'd ring the bell and, using terms like *Sugar* and *Hon* in her most sincere southern drawl, request the lipstick and compact buried at the bottom of her purse. The crooked pins sticking out of smashed platinum curls didn't seem to bother her, nor did the soiled cut-up satin dress or bits of grass clinging from her ripped stockings. She would peer at her lips like they were separate from her body and sit there applying lipstick, inspecting her mouth for the better part of a morning while awaiting her fate.

Geraldyne knew the drill. Behavioral health would be in shortly; if she didn't say the right things or act appropriately sane, she'd be trapped in a psychiatric ward for the better part of ten days. Most often this was her destined path, but there were times when she actually convinced the behavioral guy that she was in no way trying to harm herself, or anyone else for that matter. It was just another night of one too many cocktails. In her most reserved and suitable manner, she would promise to schedule an appointment with her fictitious psychiatrist A.S.A.P.

During one of those interactions, I happened to be working with Peggy Lee, a Yankee transplant who spent the better part of her nursing career treating the mentally unsound. This is what she had to say about Ms. Dixon's condition:

"Geraldyne is a true schizophrenic." Peggy preached. "Not like most of the bullshit manipulators who consume anti-depressants like tic-tacs rather than face basic everyday challenges. She has an actual mind altering illness. The real deal. She sees shit. She suffers hallucinations. I've personally watched her carry on more than one conversation in an empty room, and I'm talking long, drawn out, lucid chats. To witness it first hand is quite disturbing."

"Have you ever inquired about her imaginary friend?" I had questioned.

"Absolutely not. Playing into delusions is bad business. Our job is to reel in the patient, keep'em focused on what's tangible while simultaneously analyzing their emotional state. For example: When I find Geri Mae in a heated conversation with the wall I wouldn't say...*what are you fools gibbering about?* I would say...*there's nobody in the room, Geri, that's a wall. But I sense that you're upset, what's bothering you?* focusing on the underlying emotion." Peggy paused and grinned, "Although, one time, I remember Geri just glaring at me, completely baffled, directing my attention to the corner of the room as if doing so was stating the obvious. *"You can't see that dude stuffing his face with a hotdog? Are you serious? He's why I'm upset!"* I remember shaking my head and repeating, *"It's a wall, Geri."* Her response was to sigh dramatically and holler over to the wall. *"Get out of here you fat bastard, before you get me in trouble!"*

*

Anyway, back to the ghost mirrors and why I reeled in the part about Geraldyne Dixon. I'd already been trapped in purgatory for God knows how long, when one night, in the wee hours of what appeared to be a Halloween weekend (everyone was wearing witchy and pumpkin scrub tops), she arrives donned in another platinum wig, a white sequined dress, boobs protruding, practically touching her chin, and lips smeared crimson red. Some comment on it being Halloween and all, but others know better. Geraldyne always dresses like Marilyn during her ugliest of episodes and, to top it off, she's completely smashed.

Geri's condition is anything but emergent, so I let her be. Hours later I have all but forgotten she's in the department until I'm in need of a physician. I'm not surprised to find Rodriguez sitting in a chair next to her bed discussing face cream and Jenny Craig. As I recall, Geri favored Dr. Rodriguez, having a knack for showing up "sick" on the nights she worked.

Rodriguez is a relatively young female doctor who respects urgency, and yet has a hard time limiting her assessments to the physical. She spends far more than the time allotted with patients and so much more with the mentally unsound. Rodriguez has a soft spot for the lunatics. Geri Mae is also one of her favorites.

When colleagues complain that Rodriguez is slowing up the process, wasting time on another lost cause, she smiles sadly and says, *"The biggest problem for our psychiatric population is isolation. Loneliness. Geraldyne is a very unique and interesting woman. She just wants to talk."*

I try not to bother Dr. R when she's with a patient, especially one like Geri Mae, but an asthmatic in room five needs her immediate attention.

I march into the room where I've found her and bark sternly into her ear nurse whisperer style: *I NEED TO GO NOW, GERI. I'LL CHECK BACK LATER. THERE'S AN ASTHMA PATIENT IN ROOM FIVE WHO'S NOT BREATHING VERY WELL.*

Dr. R pauses. "I...I need to go, Geri."

"Asthma, smasthma." Geri slurs. "Don't pay her any attention."

Stunned, I turn to the crazy lady, but she isn't looking at me directly, she's gazing at both mine and her reflection in the window. (Remember what I said about windows? They're like mirrors to ghosts.) I'm not completely sure, but it's as if Geri can actually *see* me. She's staring at my reflection in the darkened glass. I don't give it much thought because I'm focused on the kid with asthma. I'm about to restate my cause when Geri winks. I gasp and stumble back. "You...you can see me?"

She giggles.

"What is so funny Ms. Dixon?" The doctor asks.

"Nothing. You'd better go." Then speaking directly to me, *"You really need to rethink that color selection. White's no good for you, sweetheart."* Back to the doctor, she finishes, "There's an asthma patient in room five."

"Geri," Dr. Rodriguez remarks sternly. "You know how we feel about confidentiality. There's no roaming. This isn't a coffee shop."

"I'm not the one traipsing through rooms, making announcements about other patients. Besides, I don't *do* coffee shops."

The doctor rises, advising "Get some sleep, Ms. Dixon," as she exits the room.

I find myself gaping at the drunken woman, who, on the doctor's departure, rolls to her side and faces the wall. I peer at our reflections feeling confused as to whether the mirror is a regular one or a ghost one. Either way, both images should not be seen.

Before I utter another sound, Geri Mae speaks. "Can you hit the lights? I'm trying to get some shut-eye."

"So you can *see* me?"

"*And* hear you," Geri mumbles. "What happened to the fat guy?"

"The fat...oh, *Ollie*? He...he moved on."

"Good. He stunk like sauerkraut. Now if you don't mind, I need to follow doctors' orders."

"Wait...I...do you recognize me?" I shake her and she turns irritably towards me. "Do you know my name?"

"Listen," Geri snaps, "I can't talk to you. The behavioral counselor will be here soon and if they catch me blabbing with the wall again, then I'll be stuck in the nut house for a month. So please LEAVE!"

"But I need your help. To get out of this place."

"Float away, ghost girl."

"I can't. I'm trapped here."

"You and me both."

"I need to figure out who I am."

"Who are you?"

"Gloria, I think."

"There you have it. You're Gloria. Now go...*please.*"

"But I'm not *really* Gloria. I'm somebody else."

Geri Mae shakes her head. "And they call me crazy."

"It's not much to go on, I realize, but if you could fish around, I used to work here. I'm sure of it. I need a name. My real one. Do I have children or a...a husband? That's another question that's been chewing me up. Was I alone in the world? Or did I have a family?"

Geri drops a pillow over her head and shouts, "TMI!"

"What the heck is TMI?"

"TOO MUCH INFORMATION!"

"Promise me you'll check around! Or...or I'll *HAUNT* you to your last breath."

At this, Geraldyne cackles. "Join the club, bitch."

I pause, dumbstruck, and suddenly wonder how many ghosts have been tormenting this woman. All this time, I thought she was seriously off her rocker. But now... My brow furrows. It dawns on me that blackmailing a schizophrenic isn't going to gain me any points with the man upstairs. I didn't want to end up transferred like Ollie, at least I didn't think so.

"I...I'm sorry Geri, for bothering you. Just forget it." I turn to leave. I'm halfway through the wood when she calls to me.

"Hey, you; blabbermouth."

"Yeah?"

Geraldyne remains facing the wall. "Gloria, is it?"

"Yeah."

"I'll think about it."

*

Geri snores for twelve solid hours. She wakes up groggy and somewhat irritable, but plays her usual game. Nurses are *Sugar* and *Hon*, lipstick is applied while staring in her personal compact. She downs three turkey sandwiches and a vat of orange juice, brooding when alone, show girl with any semblance of an audience. She refuses to look at me or respond in any way. When the behavioral counselor shows up, I try and catch to capture her attention in the ghost mirror, and that's when I realize her reflection has disappeared. It seems that stone cold sober Geri has lost her ability to speak with ghosts.

My hopes fade.

On discharge, Geri surprises me. While signing

her papers, she turns to a young nurse I'd never worked with and says, "Gloria says *hello*."

"Who's Gloria?"

Geri shrugs, "I think she used to work here."

"I don't know anyone by that name."

"Uh, okay. Well, good bye then."

My dead heart lifts. I skip along side this ragged Marilyn as she happily departs the building, unexpectedly yearning for her next visit, never thinking such a notion possible!

Maybe Geri Mae isn't such a lost cause after all.

Chapter 22

"How many years have you been an emergency room nurse?

"Prior to this case, less than two, but I worked upstairs before that on a medical floor. I couldn't get in the ED as a new grad. They made me wait."

"What about the doctor? Do you have any idea how long he's been practicing emergency medicine?"

"Uh. He's younger than me so probably not that long. He had just started working at Dixon Valley when this all went down."

"So was he less experienced than you?"

"Probably."

"Two years from you and one year from him... Let's see. That adds up to less than a high school diploma. Does that right, Miss Baxter?"

"Uh...I...I guess."

"Okay, stop. Stop right there." Betty Lyons, Nursing Attorney extraordinaire pauses the mock session abruptly. "Now Jamie, let's discuss. How can this line of questioning be better handled?

*

For months, I've been following Jamie around in hopes of bearing witness to her deposition drama. I had been through one myself, years back, and figured it would be hilarious to see her squirm. But watching my evil counterpart tortured by the grueling process, even for a few minutes, brings out the worst in me, flooding my thoughts with horrible memories of the darkest and lowest point of my thirteen year career.

For me it had been a trauma patient, a ten-year-old kid flipped and thrown from an ATV. The boy concealed the belly pain from his parents for hours before his older brother, a twelve year old, admitted that they had taken out the dangerous four-wheeler without adult supervision. By the time the kid rolled into the department by private vehicle, he was sweaty and pale with absolutely no blood pressure, his abdomen taut, filled with blood from an oozing liver laceration. Nobody cared about the gallons of blood we dumped into him, the profound resuscitation efforts or the inevitable emergent surgery. Our efforts had proved fruitless.

Four years later, I received a big white envelope in the mail, my first and last legal package. The family, it seemed, was charging the hospital and everyone involved with negligence.

"But that's ridiculous!" I remember saying. "He was practically gone when he got here."

The attorney explained it this way: "It's the way of the world. Tragic accidents bring out the worst in people. But just because the family pursues a settlement doesn't mean the staff is automatically guilty."

"They have to prove negligence."

"Exactly." The lawyer words sound weighted. "But it's a grueling process. Your efforts will be perceived through words, pieces of paper, and the defending attorney has a knack for making medical professionals, especially nurses, feel guilty. By the time it's over you may very well believe that the kid died by your hand, even though we both know that that was not the case."

I lost eighteen pounds preparing for that day and seriously considered dumping my nursing cap in the trash at the end of it. A shit show is what it was. The young boy's death transformed into a word game—a *debate*; a fucking hypothetical pissing contest. Every single charted word they picked apart and analyzed. They questioned me like an undercover spy, accusingly. Lawyers twisted my words, corralled me into lose-lose corners and directed my answers. By the end of my deposition they had me feeling one hundred percent guilty about, I don't know, *everything*. I went home and cried and cried, wondering how the job of saving lives could condemn a person working in good faith to such a sinister evaluation.

The case eventually settled out of court, thank God, even though the family barely had a leg to stand on. The hospital couldn't risk bad publicity and a private settlement was far cheaper than paying for trial. In the end, nobody left a winner and the lawyers took all the money. A decade later and it still pissed me off.

*

I lay sprawled out on the floor next to the manager's desk. Molly is sitting across from Jamie and Betty as they practice by mock deposition. It's hard to believe but I'm beginning to feel sorry for the nurse. She's fucking up.

Jamie crosses her arms, disgusted. "What do you mean, *better handled*? I'm answering truthfully!"

"Ah, truth." Betty sighs. "A very interesting concept, Jamie. How about we run through it again but this time pretend you're running for Presidential Election."

"How do you mean?"

"By choosing words that *maximize* your status."

"For example?"

"For example, when I asked about your years of emergency experience you said *less than two*. Then negated your status even further by adding that you couldn't get hired in the ED straight away. It makes you sound third string."

"That's not what I meant and you know it."

"Do I? No, I do *not* know." Betty turns to her colleague. "Question me, Molly. I'll pretend to be you, Jamie. Pay attention and *listen*. Elaborate your strong qualities and play down your weaknesses. If you think a certain line of questioning is meant to make you look bad, then keep your answers vague. Make the lawyer pry it out."

Molly repeats the same inquiries, but this time to Betty. "How long have you been an ER nurse?"

"A long time."

"How long is a long time?"

"Many years."

"How many years are many?"

"On the date in question, I was going into my third year."

"Is that all?"

"No, ma'am, it is not. Before that I worked on a very busy medical unit where I had gained undeniable skills and great confidence. I am also certified in ACLS, BLS, PALS, and Trauma."

"How long did you work the medical unit?"

"A long time."

"How long is a long time?"

"Many years."

"How many is many?"

"I was going into my third when I accepted transfer to the emergency department. I am a very accomplished and seasoned nurse."

Both lawyers pause and turn to their contemptuous client. Betty smiles. "Was I lying?"

"No."

"Which nurse would you rather have sticking a needle in your arm? My version of you or yours."

Jamie coughs. "Uh…yours."

"Exactly." Betty continues. "Now let's discuss this young doctor you threw under the bus. Is he your husband?"

"What?"

"Boyfriend?"

"*No.*"

"Were you college roommates?"

"No."

"Do you know anything about the man outside of work?"

Jamie sighs, miserably. "No."

"Then *why* are you answering questions about his job history?"

"Because you asked?"

"WRONG. Instead of saying *he's younger than me and probably less experienced,* say something like *Dr. So-and-so is an excellent physician. As for his background, you'll have to ask him.*" Betty pauses. "Keep your comments about co-workers limited and always positive."

Jamie rolls her eyes. "This is *exhausting.*"

"You're telling us," Molly replies.

"Which brings us to your overall likeability?" Betty trumps her colleague's sarcasm.

Jamie responds in a growl. "You'd think intelligent and competent would be enough."

"Those are basic ingredients, Miss Baxter, no good without a little sweetener."

"A pound of sugar and a gallon of cherries might do the trick." Molly adds.

Betty holds up a playful finger. "I'm thinking more like *two* pounds." The lawyers maintain poker faces but share a moment of internal hysteria,

Jamie hunches back in the chair, crossing her arms defiantly. "I don't get it."

"You need to be likeable *and* compassionate." Molly says. "Or, how shall I put it... *less* abrupt."

"I am compassionate!" Jamie whines.

Betty's practiced smile returns. "Now, if you could just display those emotions on the *outside* that would be most beneficial."

*

I laugh out loud at this statement. Man, I'm loving Molly and Betty! But I was sick of being kept in the dark. I wanted a peek at the chart. Ever since that first day, I bet myself that I could find the error, the primary reason for the grievance. I'd been patiently waiting for weeks to gain access, but frustrating for me, all of the meetings so far had been outside of the department. This might be my only chance.

I speak directly in Betty's ear. LET'S REVIEW THE CHART.

Betty coughs and suddenly shifts gears. "Moving on. Let's review the chart. Have you been doing what I've asked, Jamie? Checking for discrepancies? We can't afford any second-guessing at this stage."

"I'm *dreaming* this friggin' chart. Is that good enough?"

"Practice that tone, Miss Baxter," Molly warns, more sternly this time. "Your deposition is in a few weeks."

"Sorry."

I'm parked right between Betty and Jamie now, practically sitting on Jamie's lap, waiting for someone to flip the page. They're both staring at the cover sheet like morons as Molly reviews a particular insert from across the table. Frustrated, I yell.

TURN THE PAGE, JAMIE!

Jamie flips the paper.

"What are you doing?" Molly scowls. "We're still on page one. Get your head out of the clouds."

"Uh, sorry." Jamie turns back to the cover page.

Betty points a finger half-way down the blank

sheet. "We're here, Jamie." Her voice, soothing. "I know it's hard, but try and stay focused."

I stand there dumbfound. *What the fuck is happening?* I get up and move around the table to Molly, attempting to check her sheets. They're all empty. Blank.

It takes a second and then my knees buckle. I recall a conversation I had with Ollie on my first day to the in-between, as he attempted to explain the rules concerning our lost identities... *"This plaque, before you dropped dead, all I could see was a blank piece of wood like an award waitin' to happen. But now...well, looky there! What a beautiful inscription. And I was under the impression that ya'll considered me lazy..."*

The paper isn't empty. It's invisible...*to me.*

This case is about my death. Jamie is being deposed because of me.

I promptly barf nothing into a nearby trash canister, although it feels like something. It feels like a whole lot of raw bile and disgust and angst and sorrow all in one pile of invisible beanie brown vomit. I stumble back and slide to the floor. My thoughts are jumbled, a scattered mix of wonder and fear. Then, deep from within, way underneath the anxiety and doubt, I feel another emotion attempting to break through.

Hope.

Someone must have cared enough to seek legal council.

So I did have a family! Was it a...a husband?

My thoughts darken. What if he's like Bev Martin's sorry sap of a spouse? A credit card spending couch potato?

No. You're being ridiculous. He's kind and smart and...wonderful!

So wonderful that he's attacking the very

medical staff that attempted to save your life?

He's either dead broke or broken hearted...

I can't help but speculate.

Oh, stop it! You're not even sure it is a husband. It could be your mom. Or dad. Or son...

Snapping out of my trance, I realize that the meeting has ended. Jamie is shaking Molly's hand, and Betty is exacting a final practice session a week from today in her office.

"The trick is to stay calm, Jamie." Betty restates. "And *listen*. Listen to the whole question. Repeat it. Make sure you understand what is being asked. Then answer with very simple statements and only elaborate when asked. Now go home and practice."

*

I wait with the lawyers this time, as the nurse promises to do her homework and turns on a heel. Betty waits until the door clicks shut before dropping the facade. Frowning she says, "There's one that skipped charm school as a child."

"What a nasty little know-it-all." Molly agrees.

"She's confident, I'll give her that. Let's hope she can maintain that buoyancy under fire."

"Do you think it's the right thing, keeping her in the dark?"

Betty nods assuring. "Absolutely. The deposition is in ten days. Let her report exactly what she believes."

"But what if she realizes, what if Lashon tells her?"

"I've given Lashon strict instructions to not speak with her about the case. Besides, I already have the tech second-guessing himself. Before I'm done, the only thing he'll be reporting with any great certainty is that he ran the EKG."

"I hope you're right."

"I'm always right. Now let's get a drink. Jamie, the bitch, has gotten me really effin' thirsty."

*

Had something gone wrong? What was it that Lashon questioned? Could it have saved my life? Heaving a weighted sigh, I march straight through the door unfazed this time by the sensation. I needed to stay close to Lashon and wait for my moment. He would confront Jamie soon enough. If not...I would make him.

Chapter 23

"And here she is, folks!" Bill announces as Meg enters the triage booth. "The newest Bitch-in-the-Box!"

Meg smiles easily, not at all upset by the slang. There is nothing derogatory about the nick-name hand selected for the triage nurse and yet until Meg trains for the position she has no idea what the fuss is about. If anything, she's happy. It is Meg's premature perception that the job of triage is easy-peazy.

"Patient's are seen by acuity. We listen to their side of the story, gather a medical history and evaluate how they physically present. With this information we triage or 'sort' them into categories of stable and unstable." Bill blabs his spiel quickly. Meg has already taken the special triage class so the information is more of a review. "A Level One is a patient that has no pulse or limited airway. These folks rarely come through the front door because they're just about dead. They usually roll in on a stretcher. But every once in awhile, just last week in fact, Douglas pulled up in a Honda with his barely breathing girlfriend strapped into the passenger seat completely blue after shooting heroine. She was a One."

"Isn't that the guy that jumps up and down naked on the bed?"

"Yep. Our PCP boy." Bill shakes his head. "Douglas doesn't have much time left on this earth. Moving on. Level Two's are potentials, high risk peeps. Cardiac patients with ugly stories. Feverish abdominal pains with shaky vital signs. Questionable strokes or head bleeds. Threes and Fours are your more stable customers. Flu-like symptoms, simple coughs, lacerations, STD issues."

"What about Fives?

"Fives?" Bill scoffs. "Bullshit work notes and script refills. Truthfully, they just need to go home."

"What if I'm not sure, you know, about the level?"

"It's called medical practice for a reason, but I like to see that your on edge. You should be. This is the most dangerous job in the department." Bill's tone borders on serious. "Listen to your gut. There are times when I'm about to return a patient to the waiting area and this weird little voice pops in my head. It's screaming, *BRING THIS GUY BACK.* Pay attention to that voice, Meg. It can save a life."

"So you believe in nursing intuition?"

"I believe it that voice," Bill says. "And what's really weird, when I hear it I always smell onions. That's when I know it's something serious."

"You're kind of weird, Bill."

"Thank you." The male nurse regards the statement as a compliment. "When in doubt, triage up. That'll keep your patient and your Nursing License safe."

"It sounds simple enough"

"Yes, it does."

What seemed like forever, Meg had jealously watched her colleague's breeze into the triage booth and whiz through patients like it was the take-out window at *Grille Burger*, never once lifting a finger to draw blood, wipe ass, or sweat out a possible deterioration. They just sat there in cushy chairs, surfing their phones between check-ins, chillin' and relaxing. Meg could be that boxy bitch. And she could do it with a smile.

"So you've taken the triage class and passed the

test?" Bill clarifies.

"Yep."

"You ready."

"I think so."

"Let's see what'cha got."

Megs finds her first customer sitting in a wheelchair, robust and thick, scarfing down a bag of Doritos, talking loudly into her cell phone. She immediately starts sobbing inconsolably as Meg wheels her into the private area and promptly requests a box of tissues. The patient reports that she has been plagued with torturous belly pain for over a month. Today it was so bad that she couldn't go to work. She starts shivering dramatically and requests a warm blanket. Meg retrieves it, takes vital signs and a history, and eventually sends her back to the waiting room.

"What level did you make her?" Bill asks from the corner where he's observing quietly while simultaneously playing *Candy Crush* on his phone.

"Three."

Bill shrugs.

"Is that wrong?"

"Nothing's wrong. You're the boss."

"I made her a Three because with abdominal pain she'll need some tests."

"Belly pain for a month eating Doritos." Bill rolls his eyes. "But you're right. As Bev likes to say, these moron doctors will definitely run tests."

"Anything else?"

Bill taps his watch. "You took too long. Fifteen minutes. Each patient gets five." Bill points out the triage window. A woman is pacing anxiously, gripping a pudgy baby in her arms. "You've got another customer."

Meghan's stomach drops.

"She hit her head!" The mother howls

hysterically. "Oh my GOD! The cracking sound! I almost had a HEART ATTACK..."

On exam the baby girl is quietly sucking a pacifier, tugging at her mother's thick brown hair, intermittently bouncing and kicking her legs. She peers over at Meg inquisitively. A crooked Band-Aid lay across her forehead. There is no obvious bleeding. When Meg takes a peek the baby starts wailing, but otherwise seems unfazed by the evaluation.

"What did you make the baby?" Bill asks when she finishes.

"A Level Two."

"Why?"

"Head injury."

Bill chuckles. "A head injury who is now bouncing on her mother's lap?"

"The kid was howling."

"A crying baby is expected especially when a stranger is prying a bandage off her head. Be cautious, Meg. According to our census beds are tight and we have no idea what's on the way in. Do you truly believe that patient can't wait?"

Meg pauses, thinking. "I guess she can wait."

"Then she's a Three. I dare say a Four. Remember Threes and Fours are exclusive to how many tests you estimate the doctor will order. This kid might, and I stress *might,* get a scan. That's *one* resource which makes it a Four."

"But the mom, she's so freaked."

"We're not here to evaluate the mother's anxiety level. You need to see past the emotions and deceit."

"What do you mean by deceit?"

"Let's see..." Bill smirks. "I've caught sweet old ladies shutting off their oxygen tanks right before check-in so their numbers drop. Word has gotten around that if you rank your pain higher than a seven, it gets you seen faster. And let's not forget about that chest pain incident."

"What incident?"

"When that moron newscaster announced on television that patients having chest pain automatically cut the line. If our job isn't hard enough, now we've got to weed out the bullshitters."

"Did a reporter actually do that? That can't be true."

"It's true, alright. She has no idea how much damage that commentary has caused emergency departments nationwide. Let's hope she never shows up as my patient. No fucking pillow for her." Bill growls. "But seriously, Meg, this is important. Only patients in imminent danger cut the line. Everyone else waits. I don't care if it's Mr. John K. Scott himself. If he's got a bogus story, then he sits his ass with the rest of the fools. Remember Meg, your primary goal as a triage nurse is to sort and..."

Meg finishes the sentence. "...treat in order of severity."

"Wrong."

"What do you mean, *wrong*?"

"Your primary job Megs, my dear, is to keep everyone in the waiting room ALIVE. Someone dies out front and it's *your* funeral, the end of *your* career."

"But..."

"That's why *you're* the bitch. Everyone waiting sees you as the enemy. You're the obstacle between them and the doctor. They will lie straight to your face, cry like babies, hyperventilate, scream and point blame. You're hindering their care on *purpose*. Moreover, what are you physically doing? Nothing but sitting on your ass, milking the time clock."

"That's not true!"

"Sure it is. At least that's the perception. But enough blab for now. We got a live one. Check the oldie coming through the door. He's gray."

"There's someone before him with a complaint of chest pain."

"What a shocker." Bill mumbles as he opens the triage door. "I want you to *look,* Meg. Really take a gander. Tell me who you think needs the first evaluation."

Meg visibly inspects the two gentlemen. The one with chest pain is talking on his cell while registration attempts to get his information. He holds up a hand at the clerk haltingly as he finishes his conversation. The second man is hunched and swaying, his shirt completely drenched.

Bill doesn't allow Meg to choose. He leads Mr. Sweaty to the triage bed. "What's going on today, sir?"

"I think it's my gallbladder. I ate these chicken wings about two hours ago and I've got heart burn something fierce. AAAgghhheeoOO*WWW*" The man moans and pushes a fist against his chest. "It's up in my throat. I tried Maalox but...I barfed. The *PAIN*...it's something *else*."

During the man's explanation, Bill is strapping him with EKG leads and Meghan is typing information.

"The funny thing is," the guys continues, "that I don't *have* a gallbladder. It's been gone five years."

Bill picks up the phone and dials. "Yeah, it's me. I need a bed. Room fifteen? Thank you." He turns to Meg. "I'm taking this guy back. Keep triaging and remember what I said—hear the words but listen with your eyes. Weed out the drama."

While Meg calls for the next patient, an overhead page announces "*CODE STEMI. ROOM FIFTEEN.*"

Meg cringes. Mr. Sweaty is having a heart

attack.

"What brings you in today, sir?" Meg asks the recently skipped patron.

"I'm having chest pain."

"Where exactly are you hurting?"

He points vaguely to his torso. "Right here. And my head is throbbing too."

"The headache started today?"

"No. It's been going on about a month, maybe longer, but today the pain distracted me from my job."

"Did you fall or hit your head?"

"I've been getting migraines since my car crash last June. I hit my head on the dash and messed up my back pretty good. Now I get headaches and need cortisone shots in my neck. I'm still waiting to hear about workman's comp. I can't *function* like this."

Meg pauses, confused. "So…so why are you here *today*, sir?"

"I just told you, my chest."

"Chest? But you're telling me about your head? Which hurts most?"

"All of it. All of it's bothering me the most. I'm blurred. My vision is blurred, I tell you…"

By the time Meg finishes with Mr. Everything, six people are waiting. She triages the next four relatively quickly. Back pain. Wrist pain. Dental pain. Urinary pain. Straight forward simple complaints. She begins skewing her line of questioning in attempts to limit long-winded explanations. Customers continue to arrive at a steady stream and she falls behind. There's an aggressive knock on the window. Flustered, Meg jumps and turns to see. It's the lady with the baby, who is now perched on her hip chugging a bottle of milk.

"Yes, ma'am?"

The woman glares at her. "How *long* is this going to take? You said I'd be going back *soon*! I've got other children at home, you know. I can't be sitting here *all* day! I need get out of here!"

Meg presses a smile. "We'll get your daughter back as soon as we can, ma'am." Right as she says it a forty-something man marches through the door, his clothing blood splattered. His left hand is balled up in a towel and he's cradling it with the other. A bag of ice is balanced on top.

"Excuse me, but I need to take this patient."

"NOT BEFORE YOU GO CHECK MY WAIT TIME!" The woman shrieks.

Meg pulls back, shocked by the outburst. She responds by pointing at the bloody towel. The livid mother, clearly not impressed, mutters obscenities as she slinks away.

Before Meg closes the triage door the man blurts, "Circular saw snaked up and got my thumb. It's hanging from a tendon. And my forefinger, that's another story altogether."

Meg reaches for some gloves, ready to unwrap the wound. The dude stops her. "I'll bleed all over the floor."

"I need to see it."

"No problem." The man places what the nurse initially believes to be a simple bag of ice in Meg's gloved hand. Inside contains a severed index finger. Meg shrieks, composes herself, and picks up the phone. "Yeah, I need a bed. I got a finger in a bag."

Charge's response surprises her. "We can't save it, Meg. They don't sew on well."

"His thumb is also hanging on by a thread."

"Fine. Room eighteen."

"Thank you."

"And Meg."

"Yeah?"

"That's my last bed."

No sooner does Meg return to triage when the next disaster hits. She's calling for a patient with "female issues" when a gasper rushes the door. His face and arms are red and blotchy, puffed up with hives. His lips are swollen and Meg can hear audible wheezing from a distance. She halts the young girl, who is leisurely strolling up to the booth wearing pajamas and slippers, thinking *what kind of fool comes to the hospital in jammies?*

Meg restrains her inside voice and promptly apologizes. "I'm sorry, ma'am, but you'll have sit back down, for just another minute."

"Oh, you've GOT to be *KIDDING* ME!" A voice howls from the corner. It's the mother again. Her baby is now waddling around the waiting area roughing up magazines. "Are you going to COMPLETELY IGNORE THE REST OF US? This is ABSOLUTELY *RIDICULOUS!*"

Another woman pipes up. "Stick a cork in it, will ya! I've been here longer than that baby. My stomach is *killing* me!" Dorito Lady shouts at the mother and then promptly slugs back another chug of Coke. *(So much for nothing by mouth.)*

Meg is about to reply when the chick in jammies offers assistance. "It's okay. My sister has breathing problems. That man needs help."

Several waiting customers nod in agreement as Bitch Momma and Dorito Breath face off. Meg doesn't have time to play referee, and she internally kicks herself for ripping on the young girl for her choice in clothing. Hive Man is gasping.

"I...(gasp)...got a flat tire out on 42, driving my mom to work. I fixed (cough) it, but (wheezing) putting back my jack...I wasn't paying attention. I caught myself (more spasmodic strider) ...standing in an ant pile. *Red* ants. I'm highly allergic."

Meg picks up the phone. "Yeah, it's me. I need a bed."

"I don't have a bed." Charge replies. "Finger Man got the last one."

Meg huffs, anxiously. "I need *somewhere*. Bad allergic reaction."

Charge sighs, defeated. "Start him in the hall."

Bill resurfaces. "How's it going?"

The flustered look on Meg's face says it all. "I need to take this guy back but another person is signing in."

"No worries. I can handle poor old Douglas, speak of the devil. Last week's emergency, rolling in with his half-dead girlfriend, must have freaked him out. I suspect he's found Jesus, once again."

Meg flashes over to the stranger standing at the registration booth, visualizing naked balls and a plug-in fan. What she finds is a clean-shaven young man, donned in an over-starched Polo, slightly hunched, gripping dramatically at his frontal lobe. A fluffy- in-the-middle female in full-make up and perfectly coifed hair, dressed in bright polka-dots, is checking him in. Busy as she is, Meg can't resist comment. "Is that his *wife*?"

"Sure is. Catering to her cheating husband's heroine withdrawal headache, no doubt."

"I'll be right back."

"Take your time. Douglas isn't going to die tonight, not with Peaches looking after him. I'll hold down the fort."

As she wheels past, Bill mutters in her ear. "Makes you want to sit your bitch ass in triage everyday, doesn't it?"

Meg blurts out an abrupt laugh and keeps walking.

Chapter 24

Jamie rifles down six Tums attempting to quiet the burning rage tormenting her esophagus. She waits for the sensation to pass but it doesn't, so she follows it up with a long swig of Maalox, her very own private stock buried deep within in her locker. Jamie moves to the bathroom, splashes cold water on her face and automatically checks the time. *Eight fifteen. Damn. Two and a half hours to go.* Losing control of her emotions, she suddenly cusses at the mirror, berating Lashon and that stupid bitch nurse for dying on her watch...

*

The shift had started so well. With the deposition behind her, Jamie couldn't recall a day when she had felt so relaxed. Everyone was pleased with her; management, the lawyers. Jamie handled that aggressive defending attorney with ease. So confident under fire, Betty and Molly thought she'd breeze through trial, if it even went that far. (Betty continued to remain hopeful for an out-of-court resolution.) Jamie hadn't realized that settling was an option. The possibility of NEVER laying eyes on Betty or Molly again both inspired and revived the anxiety ridden nurse.

The lawyers departed at deposition's end, promising later contact, assuring Jamie that she had a couple of months to chill. "Law is not like television," Molly had explained. "Court dates take months. Expedient litigation, truthfully, is an oxymoron."

The sheer energy Jamie expended preparing for the deposition-interrogation had been both physically and mentally exhausting. Never did she want to repeat that drama no matter how well the attorneys said she'd managed. On a more positive note, the stress had fucked with her stomach so badly; she dropped three dress sizes from not eating. Jamie was popping Tums like breath mints and swigging antacids like tequila shots, but that was beside the point; she was down to a size six! The last time she remembered ever being that small was her sophomore year in high school. So, to celebrate the end of deposition hell and her trim new waistline, Jamie spent the entire weekend at the mall shopping for new duds.

And today, Charge designated her as the float nurse. *Bonus*! Jamie loved to float. Not that it was any easier. The float nurse assisted colleagues by tasking— jobs like transporting patients, popping in lines, covering lunches, changing diapers, dispensing meds. The list of requests was never ending. What Jamie appreciated was the freedom. Floating lacked responsibility. She helped everyone, and yet, wasn't primarily responsible for a single person.

Except, of course, for the occasional hall patient…

Seeing that she wasn't being rushed, Jamie decided to eat lunch in the cafeteria. (Yes, being the float nurse had its advantages.) Upon completion of her thirty-minute sabbatical, she ran into Henry, a friend from respiratory, and waited while he fixed a coffee. Together they strolled leisurely down the hall, Henry babbling about his recent vacation to Key West, offering highlights to Jamie who was considering a similar venture.

Henry's beeper went off. He paused to read. "Breathing treatment in hall bed three. A-bay."

Jamie groaned. "Hall? Damn it! When I left

for lunch the joint was half empty!"

Henry grinned. "You've been gone a whole thirty minutes. What did you expect?"

Jamie hears the stridorous wheezing prior to turning the corner and her first visual isn't promising. The patient is young, maybe twenty, with a tall, lanky build. His skin is tight and red, blazing like a buffed apple, and his upper lip is so swollen that it's shadowing his nose.

Right then, the kid's mother flies through the entrance blubbering and agitated. She's wearing a faded *Poppi's Diner* uniform with an apron already in position. "Sorry! I had to park the car. What a *day*! My son drives me to work. We get a flat tire and now *this*. Oh, *Lord*, this is going to cost me! But what can I do? His lips are *enormous*!"

The boy points to his mouth and repeats for the doctor who is already at bedside, "Reb Ants."

"Red effin' ants! Can you believe my luck? Fifty bucks for a new tire and possibly thousands because of an ant!" His mother scowls. "I told you to pay attention, Kyle! Those infested dirt piles are everywhere!"

The doctor listens to the mother's rant while Meg works to inject the kid with medication. Although she'd never admit it, Jamie is impressed by Meg's speed.

"I've given Benadryl and steroids." Meg reports to Jamie when she notices her. Doctor Breezy, a transplant from Jersey with an easy presence, says to the patient. "You, my friend, need an Epi shot."

"Ebi?" The kid's voice sounds muffled. "Like the Ebi Ben?"

Breezy nods. "Exactly. Get that tongue back to a normal size so you can say your P's."

"I hab one of dose bens. It's in my baf'room."

"He has one of those pens but it's in the bathroom." His mother repeats the statement and then frowns at her son. "The hell good it'll do in the bathroom cabinet. I *told* you to leave it in the glove compartment!"

The doctor reaches over and places a confident arm on the mother's shoulder. "No worries, ma'am, we'll just give him a shot here."

The mother drops two meaty hands on full hips. "How long is this going to take?"

"That's the tricky part." Dr. Breezy smiles. "After we administer the medicine, we'll need to watch him for at least four hours."

The woman, clearly worn and disgruntled, halts abruptly. "Four *hours?* But I have to *WORK!* It's *Saturday!* I can't miss a weekend shift. You know how much MONEY I'll lose? Not that as a *DOCTOR* you can appreciate anything about being BROKE, but that's me. I'm *BROKE!* Besides, Poppi-the-prick doesn't give a rat's ass that my kid can't breathe. He'll fire me."

Jamie can tell this bitch rant aggravates Breezy, but his voice remains level and singsong. "Oh, I'm sure we can manage some kind of plan. Kyle's a big boy. What are you...like sixteen?"

"Seventeen."

"Mrs. Stone? Is it?"

"No Mrs., just Ms. Do you really think I have a *man* in my life? It's all friggin' me. Me and my rotten luck."

Breezy ignores her muttering. "Your son needs this medicine, ma'am. We'll get him settled nicely in a room. He can watch a couple of game shows to pass the time. You go to work and we'll call when he's ready. How does that sound?"

Ms. Stone coughs and shifts her footing, unsure how to tackle the physician's kindness. "I…I guess that'll be alright."

Meg cuts in. "So you want Epi?"

"Yes, Meg. But remember, shoot him in the muscle. Intra-*muscular*. Definitely NOT Intra-*venous*. And *why*, my aspiring nurse, do we *never* give Epinephrine 0.3 mg straight into the vein?"

While Meg ponders, Henry returns with supplies for a breathing treatment. Jamie is with him carrying the vial of 0.3 mg Epinephrine. They hear the tail end of the lecture but Jamie's barely paying attention, still flirting with Henry the hunk. Lashon wheels over the portable heart monitor and begins slapping on leads when Doctor Breezy cuts his teachings short to explain the process to mother and patient.

"Kyle, this is Henry from respiratory. He'll be giving you a breathing treatment to help combat the wheezing. Lashon here is hooking you up to our portable cardiac monitor because the medications can make your heart beat pretty fast. It's the best we can do until a room opens up." Turning to Meg, he reverts back to lecture mode. "So? Can you answer the question, Miss Ford?"

Meg flushes. "Ah, shooting 0.3 of Epi IV is a no-no, I'm certain of that. But the rationale…it's…uh…"

Lashon, the tech, cuts in. "Because intravenous Epi will cause a Myocardial Infarction. In English, that's a big fat heart attack."

"Two points for Lashon." Breezy says. "Nail on the head."

At this point, Lashon nods and nudges Jamie, who is whispering playfully to Henry. "We wouldn't want that to happen, would we Jamie?"

The nurse scowls clearly put off by the interruption. "What are you *badgering* me about, Lashon?"

Lashon reiterates, quietly this time, so only Jamie can hear. "*I said...*we wouldn't want to cause a big fat heart attack *pushing* Epi through the vein, now would we?"

Jamie pauses, startled. "What?"

Lashon winks. "At least...not again.

Jamie feels the blood drain from her face as comprehension settles around her ankles. She flashes back to that fateful afternoon, to the very instant that her colleague took a turn for the worse, all because of a tiny little blood pressure pill.

POOF!

Jamie's back in room seven again, arguing with Lashon over positioning...

"You need to move, Jamie. I have to get this EKG!"

"And I need to give these meds."

"So do it on the other side."

"The IV...DUH! You'll have to work from the left. It's not rocket science. I'm sure you can manage."

"What are you doing? That's not..."

Jamie's mind reels. Yes, she is certain. She pushed the Epi.

Then why wasn't it written that way in the chart? She asks herself.

Because you scribbled everything on a piece of paper, remember? Then Bev transcribed your chicken scratch and automatically assumed that the Epi was given as a shot. Every nurse in the world knows that IV Epi will cause a heart attack.

Yeah, every nurse but me…

Unexpectedly nauseas, Jamie turns white as a sheet.

"What's wrong, Jamie?" Meg asks, medically concerned.

Jamie stutters and shakes her head. "I…I'll be right back. I…I forgot to take my reflux medicine."

Chapter 25

Jamie rushes directly through me. I sense her angst but it's just the aftermath. I'm already stock still, emotionally frozen, attempting to digest the information.

Ever since the last lawyer meeting, I'd been hugging onto Jamie and Lashon like glue. I hadn't noticed it before, but they rarely worked together. In fact, this was the first time in months they've assisted the same patient. Now, it totally made sense. Betty and Molly had been keeping the two apart on purpose. I could see it in Lashon's face when he muttered the obvious. He'd been dying to call her out! And finally, he got his chance.

A thousand thoughts race through my mind, as my dead heart pounds and my stomach flip-flops. There is no denying...

Jamie the bitch killed me, and the lawyers knew about it.

My knees buckle.

I should still be alive.

Forgetting my already undetectable status, I rush the staff locker room. That's where I always hid, back in the day, when the job got the best me. Nobody frequented the tiny room mid-shift so it was a safe haven to de-escalate, scream and sob—to do whatever needed to be done without a captive audience. I forever despised getting tagged *emotionally compromised*, red-eyed and blotchy, attempting to conceal a friggin' drippy nose. When the "caring" nurses would gather 'round and get up in your business, all huggy and consoling, which only worked as a catalyst, tripling the response. It was much easier to hide. Hide and cry and hopefully get a handle on the situation.

Safely stowed away in my comfort zone like the old days, I medicate my collapsing nerves by way of inspecting lockers. Staff members were famous for plastering photographs all over their personal cubbies. The scene very much resembled a middle school locker room, except at Dixon Valley the pictures were taped to the *outside* of the cabinets for the viewing pleasure of anyone interested.

During my periodic blubbering events, I'd gaze at every picture and purposely scour my memories for individual specifics. Over the years colleagues have spewed loads of family juice, and retrieving such information was the perfect way to temporarily escape reality. In this respect, today is no different.

The first locker belongs to Elaine Mattern. The year I started at DVH, Elaine taped up a snapshot of her youngest son, Ryan, who was then entering his junior year of high school. I remember Elaine being so proud of her growing boy and sad just the same; life was moving way too fast. In the next photo young man Ryan is suited up and stern, posing in a military photograph. He was going to be an Airborne Ranger! Elaine's brave smile quivered with emotion. She was so proud of her baby and yet fearful for obvious reasons. In a third, Ryan grips a diploma. Four years of college done and gone.

Just recently, grown-up Ryan announced that he was getting married. I recall laughing out loud at Elaine's distressed response. *"Marriage?"* she shrieked. *"I think Ryan was safer jumping out of airplanes!"*

Second locker. Olivia Crutch, age two, lounges on a puffy pink cushion. She is wearing a floral print smock, white-ribbed tights and matching shoes. Her pose extends into the camera as she offers up a giant swirly lollypop clutched in a tiny fat fist. Mother Sara is pregnant again—a boy this time. No doubt future pictures will be adorable.

The third locker is Bev Martins. I sigh. Times have changed since my Sentence in Purgatory. Bev has made peace with her only son and is now the proud grandmother of two small boys. 'Meat Sticks', Bev calls them. Little men who have accomplished the impossible. *Neanderthal Bev* has transformed into *Gammie the Snugga Bug*. Everything Bev carries, from back pack to thermal lunch box, is plastered with photos of the chubby little dudes. Bev's locker is one massive collage of her loving babes, with a kitchen magnet slapped dead center that reads...KETCHUP IS A VEGETABLE AT GRANDMA'S HOUSE!

I inspect each photograph and read every catch phrase, one locker at a time. My dead muscles relax. My angst dissipates. Slowly. Very slowly...

Right when I start coming back to myself, I lay eyes on the ninth locker.

Taped to the front of the gray metal are four pieces of white paper. I stare at the blank sheets, momentarily confused, and then it hits me like a sledge hammer. My body immediately stiffens. There isn't a lock so I click the latch and peer inside. A pink backpack and a beat-up stethoscope dangle from one hook, a purple hoodie from the other. I grasp the jacket and hold it to my nose, inhaling. It smells like...is it *Obsession*? *Yes, that's it!* I smell it again. My thoughts cloud. The scent is too musky. Then it dawns on me. The fragrance is Obsession, alright. Obsession...for *men*.

My lip trembles.

This is my locker. I'm sure of it. And the sweatshirt smells of a man. *But is it because I had a*

man in life or did I just habitually don men's cologne?
I flip back to the front and touch the blank sheets in hopes of conjuring an image. *Are these pictures of my children? Parents? Is it a spouse? Did I have anyone? Did I have a single person in life that really cared?*

I crumble onto a bench drilled into the floor, just like you'd find in a gym locker room, and collapse into my hands. I'm sobbing even though I have absolutely no idea whom or what I've lost. *I wasn't supposed to die!* Now here I was trapped in *HELL* playing Good Samaritan, condemned to support the very people who failed me.

Stuck.

Forever.

I pause…leering at the locker with hungry eyes. *Why hadn't my family come to empty it?*

Because you don't have a family.

Then what are all the photographs?

Pet pictures.

Then who is suing the hospital?

A no good loser of an Uncle trying to make a buck.

No! NO! No! Don't think like that, Gloria. There is somebody! There has to be.

The locker door swings lazily on a hinge. Cautiously, I re-inspect the storage chamber. First thing that comes to mind: I wasn't the neatest person. There is junk literally smashed into the bottom half compartment. Tattered notebooks and folders slide out onto the floor as I begin my quest. Every piece of paper is completely blank. (Yep, I'm definitely in the right place.)

A flash of blue catches my eye. I reach in and pull out a pair of extra scrubs. (I forgot about that. I always kept a back up pair for the occasional truly *shitty* day). Under the duds I notice a shiny packaged bag. I retrieve an already opened note card jimmied into the top and reread the message. *THANKYOU FOR BEING AN AWESOME PRECEPTOR...Your friend, Marge*

    That's right! I trained Marge right before Meghan. This was her parting gift. I pull out a bottle of Clos Du Val, which, by the way, is an exceptionally delicious tasting red wine. It dawns on me. *I can remember.* I love red wine!

    Invigorated by the discovery, I hike the bottle under my arm like a football and hustle off to the break room in search of a wine opener. I hunt through every drawer and scour ever cabinet but my efforts prove fruitless. *What did you expect? This is a hospital, not a restaurant.*

    By now I'm salivating and suddenly wonder if this is how the Dickman feels when he's craving a hot dog. Temptation gets the best of me. I grab a plastic cup, a rainbow of utensils, and spend the next thirty minutes butchering the cork attempting to pry it out. I hole up in the broom closet to do this because it's getting close to dinnertime, and although I'm invisible my wine bottle is not. After much desecration, I successfully jam the cork inside the bottle neck. I dump a glug into my cup, fish out the floating shards of cork, and take a long delicious sip.

    I'm skeptical at first, unsure if imbibing spirits as a dead person will offer the same titillating effects. GOOD NEWS. It does! And boy, it kicks in fast. I spend the next several hours in total blackness lounging on a flipped broom bucket, savoring California's finest, feeding my stricken emotions with absolutely zero plans of stopping until I'm completely and unequivocally smashed.

Chapter 26

Dr. Gluck prides himself on meticulous professionalism. While his colleagues often joke and laugh between patients, discussing random life activities such as upcoming golf trips and attempted cooking recipes, Dr. Gluck works. Moreover, when there aren't any patients, a rare occurrence, he sits quietly at his desk and browses the internet. Rarely does Randall Gluck day dream or indulge in common chatter about whatever the topic.

Today is different.

Maybe it has to do with the secretary and the tech sitting behind him, quietly discussing the not-so-subtle ramifications of *Fifty Shades of Grey*. Or, possibly because his wife has been on holiday at Carolina Beach for the past month, visiting her sister. For whatever the reason, Randall Gluck can't stop thinking about sex.

But, then something really weird happens. Christine Zagak, a somewhat demure nurse with beautiful, red curly hair who Gluck has secretly fantasized about in the privacy of his own bedroom,; says…. "My favorite doctor? Randall Gluck, of course. He's so handsome."

Randall misses the beginning of the conversation, but is pretty certain Christine is teasing seeing as he's the only physician in A-bay. Randall flushes crimson more from his own deviance than Christine's statement and smiles in spite of himself.

The secretary, Ronnie, who has a knack for pointing out the obvious, adds, "Look Christine, you made Darth Vader blush."

At this, Dr. Gluck chuckles openly. Based on his silent stone cold stature and penetrating worth the nickname suits him well. He actually likes the attention, but would never admit as much. And, now, here it is˒ the middle of a quiet Sunday afternoon at Dixon Valley and he's all in a frenzy. Literally paralyzed by his own dirty and demented mind....

Randall Gluck, the man devoid of emotion, Darth Vader himself, is trapped at his desk with a hard on.

Great.

He tries rebooting his thoughts by scanning the internet for fishing gear and canned worms, but is now visualizing his wife, Hazel, donned in a red wig, slightly askew, straddled on his lap, panting nasty nothings while convulsing like a manic rabbit. As if she was already in position, the rocking sensation ignites a flood of seductive Hazel memories, when they were still living in that tiny apartment in Chapel Hill.

Ahh...the good old days! Sunday used to be Wiener and Wine Night. Randall had just started his residency and, of course, the young couple were dead broke. It was Hazel's idea to eat really cheaply on Sundays, so they could splurge on a decent bottle of wine. After a second glass, she was always good for a serious lap dance and a romp around the bedroom.

It had been a lifetime since Randall thought about that! When was it? Sixteen years ago? Shoot, now his wife wouldn't even let him *eat* hotdogs. The stoic physician tries crossing his legs, but it hurts to move. OH MY GOD! *Is this beast ever going down?*

Randall picks up the phone and dials.

"Hello?"

"Hazel?"

"*Randall?*" Hazel sounds shocked to hear from him. "I thought you were *working?*"

"I…uh…was just checking in."

"*You*? Mr. I'm-too-busy-to-make-personal-calls? *You* were checking in?"

Randall ignores the sarcasm. "When are you coming home?"

"Why?" Hazel spits. "Do you miss me?"

Randall Gluck cringes. After three miscarriages and too many disappointing obstetric visits, the couple has given up on children. The failing process has all but destroyed their sex life. Even smarty-pants Dr. Gluck can't seem to fix it. Today he has an idea. "Yes, Hazel. I miss you terribly."

"Really?"

Randall's chest clenches at the surprise in her voice. "Well…(cough)…yes."

"Oh…well, then…I'm heading home on Thursday…"

Before she has a chance to finish her sentence, Randall blurts, "I was thinking…being it's Sunday and all. Isn't it Wiener and Wine Night?"

The phone falls silent…and then he hears a rustling chuckle. "*You*…were thinking about *that*…at *work.*"

"I was wondering…maybe we could make Thursday Weiner and Wine Night. Or…maybe you could come back tonight? Sunday…technically it is the official day."

Another lapse.

There's a fullness in Hazel's voice when she responds. "I guess I'll get packing."

Randall laughs eagerly, so loudly that the Ronnie and Juanetta pause their gossip. *Is Dr. Gluck actually laughing?*

Before he hangs up, Randall whispers. "I'll have dinner waiting."

***

My slumber is thwarted by the sound of drums. (The tube system is jammed again.) There's drool on my chin and I'm curled up in the broom closet hugging onto a wine bottle. *Oh yeah, the wine!* That's weird. *Was I actually sleeping?*

I touch my head and discover something awesome. I don't have a hangover! Just the opposite, I feel renewed. My original plan was to suck down the whole vat, but after one glass I fell into such a serious stupor that my coordination went bust and I couldn't figure out how to wrap my fingers around the door knob. Suddenly trapped in the dark, I must have zonked out.

Upon awakening, I re-inspect the wine bottle and find the contents barely dented. Treading cautiously, I attempt the tiniest of sips and my lips pucker. The previously tender luscious fruity flavor that I had happily swished about my palate, hours ago, had transformed. Now the wine tasted sour, like it had been sitting. Regardless, in minutes my face goes numb and a tilting vertigo creates a stumbling affect. *Excellent!* Buzzed after one sip! I knock back another mouthful and stash the bountiful remains in my locker, absolutely certain that future fortified beverages will be hard to come by. Bad wine, I guess, is better than no wine.

Bleary eyed and adventurous, I take a stroll.

The first person that crosses my path is Marcy Campbell and...*what is this?* She's donned in Christmas scrubs. *Odd. Thanksgiving is still two weeks away.* Marcy never dresses out of season. *Maybe her washing machine is broken.* I trip past and head into A Bay. Tina Page is changing the bulletin board. She's stapling up an evergreen border infested with ornaments and plastic lights. She, too, is wearing a

209

holiday top covered in Mickey Santa's and Goofy helpers attempting to bind a screaming Donald Duck in bows and wrapping paper.

Confused, I check the date. *What the hell?* It's almost December! I'd been dozing in the broom closet for over a two weeks. Mental note to self: Drinking booze puts a ghost into a death snooze. The perfect ER get-a-way. *That's why I don't have a hangover!*

A bit giddy from my discovery, I skip over to where Ronnie and Juanetta are discussing some book called *Fifty Shades of whatever-the-hell.* I quickly discover that the story revolves around sex, sex, and more sex, which of course gets me too thinking about the nasty.

I spy Vader sitting in his little corner quietly scouring the internet for fishing bait. I wonder if Randall even has sex with his wife. The man is so up tight, I bet he could crack nuts with his butt cheeks. Out of boredom and drunken perversion, I crawl right up on his lap and whisper dirty nothings into his ear. He actually smells pretty good, so I nuzzle in really close and sneak my arms around his back absorbing his heat. *Breathers are so warm!*

I sense a change… I feel it- Dr. Gluck's erection growing at break neck speed. *Damn! The man is packing.*

I giggle out loud, enthralled, and suddenly remember my ghostly duties…*To help those in need.* I rock a little as I blow into Randall's ear. Then I say, *GET LAID, RANDALL. USE THAT WIENER FOR SOMETHING BESIDES PISSING. OFFER A BIT OF BLISS TO THAT WIFE OFF YOURS. AND BE A MAN ABOUT IT! NO PUSSY FOOTING AROUND. CALL HER RIGHT NOW. DON'T TAKE NO FOR AN ANSWER!*

209

I shouldn't be surprised when he picks up the phone, but I am, and his urgently flirtatious proposition bowls me over. *Amazing the secrets we keep.* You *go*, Dr. Gluck!

That's when I begin to appreciate the magnitude of my powers. Why not boost staff morale by spreading subliminal thoughts of the nasty? Television commercials use to do it all of the time, and people need to smell the roses on their roads to the crypt. We take way too many things in this world for granted. Simple human contact, for instance. Jubilant laughter. Elated joy. Blissful Sex. Unconditional Love. (Whispering true love may be a stretch, but what the hell!) I make a personal goal for myself just the same. If all goes as planned, employee satisfaction scores at the Dixon Valley Emergency Department are about to skyrocket.

Between trips to the locker for juicy sips and periodic week long naps, I take on my new role as Sex Whisperer with a vengeance. As anticipated, the change in atmosphere is palpable. Conversations shift from home repairs and work out trends, to dinner dates and new fuck friends. Vader no longer holes up in the corner, but stays encircled by staff, young and old, discussing anything from vacation plans to holiday gift ideas for his sweet wife, Hazel. On two separate occasions, I have to find another hiding place to drink because the new housekeeper and the old maintenance guy are making out in the broom closet.

I start referring to myself the *Love Doctor*, performing invisible strip shows in the middle of A-bay, belting out tunes in Vaudeville Fashion, rolling around the floor and gyrating like the recently appalling acts of a grown up Hanna Montana. The staff working around me are oblivious to my deviant renditions, and yet can't seem to resist my subliminal music selections.

"Hey! I was just singing that song." says Ray from respiratory.

"You must have heard me. I've been humming that tune all shift," replies Lisa, the nurse.

"Do you want to go dancing tomorrow night?" asks Ray.

"Can I dress like a slut?" winks Lisa.

Rays eyes go wide. His reply, "The sluttier the better!"

I giggle through wine goggles and give myself a hypothetical pat on the back. *The staff is so happy. And it's because of me!*

*

Like all good bashes, the thrill of lighting fires eventually wanes. (All of the erections in the department were beginning to skive me out.) I cut back on lap dances, saving sexual therapy for a chosen few depending on my mood. (*Don't hate. A girl's got to have her fun.*) Besides, having less than a few ounces of wine available keeps me selective. I also find it severely troubling, and slightly baffling, as to who does and does NOT warrant help in the love department. (For example: that quiet old timer that cleans the toilets definitely does NOT need any help!)

As for my destined duties, even with my careless carousing the emergency department appears to be running on schedule. No major tragedies. No deaths. Any slip ups are small. So irrelevant that neither nurse, nor doctor, nor anyone else took notice.

Kind of like the subtle mistake that killed you...

I pause, startled by my thoughts. Feeling guilty, I seriously contemplate giving up the love doctoring altogether when who shows up but the medical director himself. And he's smoking hot!

The first time I laid eyes on Dr. Gene Kassel

was closer to the beginning of my purgatorial sentence, before the Dickman's transfer to retrieval specialist. Decked out in a suit and tie, he came strolling out of the physician's lounge trailed by an entourage of colleagues. They were all slapping him on the back, offering condolences for obtaining the director's position, another unanimous vote by everyone present.

"Kassel! Kassel!" They chanted, before doubling over with laughter.

An amused Kassel responded by saying, "You get me for one year, boys. Then, well...I think it'll be Larry's turn on the chopping block."

Larry faked buckling to his knees. "No! Noooo!"

Gene smirked, show boating his arms like a circus trainer. "Yes, yes, you pain in the ass!"

Larry was Dr. Pierce, an old friend of mine in life, who secretly confessed that nobody, not one single physician, ever volunteered for the director's chair. There were way too many meetings and far too much bullshit paperwork, not to mention the never ending list of patient complaints. The prestigious job was more of a hassle than anything else.

When the archaic director, Dr. Purcell, finally retired the physician's group redefined the role as a requirement every partner would eventually have to endure. At the end of each one-year term, the doctor in office, if so wishing to step down, personally appointed the next stiff into the role. No one skirted this three hundred and sixty five day lashing, at least, not so far. Kassel was the first physician in awhile that continued holding the Chair after his initial obligation. I wasn't the only one surprised.

Still, even a dead nurse could see that the position had its perks. For starters, directors rarely worked patient care. Certain holidays or sick calls without coverage were about the only times the head honcho surfaced in scrubs. Truth be told, since Kassel's transition to director I had only seen him on the floor maybe a dozen times, today being one of them.

I definitely don't need booze to schmooze this guy, but I run to my locker just the same and knock back the last couple of swigs. My dead heart palpates in anticipation. Chuckling giddily, I reflect on my actions... *The perverted kicks of a dead ER nurse. Woot! Woot!*

My fantasy is struck down at the sight of an empty swivel chair. I frown. Kassel isn't at the desk. He's already running full tilt, knee deep in patient care. *Figures.* The one shot I get at the top dog and the department goes to pieces. I traipse about in search of my quest, but an argument in the break room between tech and nurse detains me. I settle that conflict and march right into a second disaster. A ninety something demented man is staggering down the hallway, half-naked, blood pouring from a dislodged IV, in search of a toilet. I just about get him straight when...

"CODE STROKE...ROOM FOUR", blares over the intercom.

I locate Kassel in the midst of the ruckus, performing a neurologic assessment on the victim. Nurses are buzzing about, obtaining blood samples and hooking up gadgets, preparing the patient for an imminent trip to the head scanner.   .

Kassel makes a bee-line for his workstation but gets cut off by Nurse Lee, who reports that her patient in five most likely has a bowel obstruction. A tell-tale sign is the large pink basin she's dumping, sloshing with putrid green bile. Off the doctor goes...

Damn!

Time slips away and my buzz disintegrates.

Only then do I find Kassel at his desk catching up on dictations. This is my chance. Except now I'm completely sober and feel utterly ridiculous snuggling the guy during such a crazy busy shift. *Go back to the locker.* The point is moot. My bottle of fun is completely gone.

Ahh…Screw it.

Without another thought, I climb aboard…

I'm not sure if the doc is married, but curling onto his lap, wriggling into that burly chest, I'd be pretty shocked to find that he wasn't. I give him a squeeze…

Under a loose fitting white jacket are strong corn fed arms, warm and inviting. His legs are solid like a chair and he smells of soapy cleanliness and a hint of after shave. My hands reach under his shirt and finger the muscles up to his neckline. I breathe deeply, intoxicated by his essence.

Then…the situation changes.

I falter.

Something is wrong. *Off.* I pull away which causes me to lose balance. I drop to the floor and rub at my person, attempting to eradicate the sensation. Unexpectedly frightened by his physical touch, I inspect Kassel at arm's length. Slowly, very slowly, my trepidation lessens. I inch closer….

…That's when I see it. In his eyes. In the creases around the face.

The doctor with the easy smile and casual stance is in trouble. He is sick somehow. Physically or mentally, I can't say for certain. Whatever the cause, it is withering his soul. The darkness is so distressing, I fear it. Still trembling from his touch, my stomach flip flops. I wonder… *Had there been others so emotionally compromised? So sickly? And I, too drunk on my manic sex whispering horse to notice?*

Traumatized by this sobering revelation, I reach out and squeeze his hand. I keep a tight grip as an overwhelming sense of destitute washes over me. The doctor startles and jumps up. He takes a few quick breaths and shivers, eyeing the swivel chair like it's a poisonous snake.

Stricken by possibilities, my knees buckle. What if it's *not* a someone? What if it's a *something? What if he's dying?* I immediately start praying that it is a *someone*. Time can heal pains of the heart, but diseases…not so much. Time becomes the enemy.

I move in close and force my arms around him, embracing him like a son. I nuzzle into his neck and kiss him softly on the cheek. My tone falters. *CALL SOMEONE WHO LOVES YOU.*

Kassel practically convulses and jerks back. He doesn't stick around this time, but turns briskly and marches towards the nurse's lounge.

At that exact moment Pauline Belcea races past like a runaway basketball. I hear it then. Faint drumming. Another jam at the tube station. The skin tone of everyone in viewing distance ripples between yellow and orange. *Mustard and Lil' Cuties.* Fear and uncertainty…

Forgetting Dr. Kassel, I transition into work mode and seek out Pauline. I find her gathering supplies and by the looks of it she's preparing to stick a small child. Happy to shift my thoughts back to something tangible, I touch her arm reassuringly. *IT'S OKAY, PAULINE. YOU CAN DO THIS.*

Pauline pauses coming out of the supply room. Out loud she repeats. "It's okay, Pauline. You can do this."

And off we go.

Chapter 27

Nobody likes sticking a baby. I remember back in the day, when it was common practice to extract a child from the embrace of their parents and take them down the hall to a treatment room for such debauchery. Times have changed. The newest trend is to keep families involved. Personally, I'm not convinced that this is such a good idea.

Let's face it, just hearing that their small child needs an IV causes such palpable angst, even the kid can sense it. Most folks can't even handle the preparation stage, let alone the insertion. A simple tourniquet initiates such fear and blood curdling screams from the babes, their parents try and talk down their own stress by spewing a stream of endearing phrases and promises, like the infant has any fucking idea what their bumbling about. *"It's okay, sweetie. Mummy is here! When this is over we'll gitchoo an ice cream. Don't cry, honey. Mummy loves you! The day you were born we celebrated with sweet treats. I'm gonna gitchoo a sweet treat when this is over! Let's sing...Mary had a little lamb, a little...Oh my God! How long is this going to TAKE?"*

Then comes the restraining part. Small children may not yet understood that needles are painful, but will resist and squirm the minute they're strapped into the papoose, (a wrapping gadget used to keep them still). This only escalates the hysteria. *"Okay...okay....okay..."* (The mother starts blubbering and weeping) *"...The wheels on the bus go round and round...round...sweet treats for babies! Sweet treats for babies! And round...round and round...Wheels on the bus. ALRIGHT...okay...HOW MUCH LONGER?"*

By the time the needle actually surfaces, the baby is ready for a nap and Mommy needs her own personal bottle of Valium. Let me just say that when the actual insertion is over, and the procedure complete, most children forget about the torture pretty quickly. Parents, on the other hand, are scarred for life.

*

I immediately cringe upon entering the room, yearning for the olden days of private treatment rooms and *No Parent Zones*. What a disaster. Pauline quickly assesses the situation, excuses herself, and runs off for reinforcements. I stay back, weighing my options, conflicted as to whether I should immediately whisper away the parents or let the nurse handle it. Under the circumstances, I hate to laugh, but the scene borders on comical...

Mom stands hunched over the bed, eyes wild, her naked bosom swinging like a pendulum. She has one hand placed behind the toddler's head, holding it in position so he can breast feed; the other grips a cell phone clamped to her ear. She's screaming into the receiver, something about diaper wipes and a very specific comfort blanky.

"NO, NO, *NO*! Will you *LISTEN*? It's his BOO-BOO blanket. The one for OUCHIES! It's green with tiny printed bears." A pause. "In the *crib*. Yes, that's right. You need to bring it me...*NOW*!"

Dad is pacing anxiously, but makes a grab at the receiver. "Tell her that the dog needs water."

Mom pushes him away. "We're here for the *BABY*! Your stupid DOG will *live*."

Dad ignores her and yells to be heard. "WATER TOBY!"

The woman scowls and literally whips the phone at his face. Her boob dislodges causing Junior to cry. "SEE WHAT YOU'VE DONE!" She snarls at the man, and then re-animates for the child. "It's okay, doo-doo. Mommy is here." Again, she slings her tit in gripping distance and the toddler flails for it with his one good arm (the other is snuggled loosely in a temporary sling) and clamps down hungrily with a full set of teeth.

Dad shakes his head, clearly mortified. "Try not to smother him, will you? Where the hell are the *bottles*? Put your shit away for *chrissakes*. We're in *public*."

The mother's face contorts spasmodically. "It's *COMFORTING*, you *ASS*." She's bursting with profanity, but suddenly hesitates. There is movement at the door.

Pauline reenters the room with her posse— Maria, Lee and Mylene. *The Manila Mafia*. I smile in spite of the escalating panic and realize my services are no longer required. I stay just the same. This crew is amazing to watch.

The parents can't see the hue, but it is immediately apparent that a commanding energy source has penetrated the room. Even the baby can sense it. He lets go of his mother's natural milk jug and peers inquisitively at the four strangers. Their presence borders on supernatural. Pauline's recent orange glow has transitioned into a vibrant fuchsia. In fact, the team of four shimmers in lipstick shades of Revlon pinks and I can't help but think *Spring Collection*. Standing side by side only enhances their aura. The room is so bright, I begin to squint.

By the way, pink signifies confidence.

Staff refers to these women as the *Manila Mafia* for a reason. They stand lean and petite, Maria and Pauline just over five feet, Lee and Mylene a half of foot taller, with not an ounce of fat between them. Not what you'd call brute strength, and yet something about the way they line up, side by side, legs planted at shoulder width, arms clasped loosely behind their backs, makes even the most aggressive of creatures second guess their actions. Filipino in origin, the "Peace Keepers" are exceptional nurses inept at caring for anything from trauma victims to neonates. They also happened to be trained killers; one veteran Air Force, two ex-Special Forces, and finally, the most terrorizing, a mother of four boys. Holding various degrees of black belts in Karate, Judo, Jujitsu and Tae Kwon Doe, all four ladies are very much so Martial Arts enthusiasts.

Put it this way, when shit hits the fan at The Dixon Valley Emergency Department, say a patient goes *Poco Loco* or a fight breaks out, the Manila Mafia usually has the mess contained before hospital security can even answer a page.

The primary nurse's tone sounds level and authoritative. "Hello, my name is Pauline and these are my colleagues. We are here to help your son. He has a broken arm that needs to be set. The doctor has requested that I place an IV for pain management and sedation during the procedure. The insertion may be difficult for you to watch."

As she speaks, the Peace Keepers move into position. Lee silently signals the father who pushes back against the wall in an attempt to clear the area. Maria whispers quietly in the mother's ear as she lifts her away from the child, explaining about the papoose and its obvious necessity. Within thirty seconds, Mylene has the baby's body snuggly restrained under a layer of intertwined sheets, while Pauline prepares her supplies at the bedside table.

"An IV," Pauline explains, "is a needle covered

in a plastic sheath. I will locate a vein, puncture the skin with the needle, advance the sheath and then retract the metal part. Think of it like a tiny arm straw for the baby's vein."

"Will it hurt?" These are the first words out of the mother's mouth since Pauline's introduction.

"There will be discomfort during the procedure, yes." Pauline doesn't attempt to sugar coat it. A needle is a needle. "At this juncture, I offer two choices: to stay or go. If you choose to stay, please remain calm and encouraging for your child. Babies can sense distress. Many parents choose to leave. That way the child doesn't associate those he loves with pain. It doesn't make you a bad parent if you choose to leave." At this statement Maria places a soothing arm on the mom's shoulder and Mylene repeats the action with Dad.

"But are you any good?" The father blurts.

For a second, I catch a ripple of green illuminate Pauline's complexion. *Anger*. Composing herself, she answers. "Yes, sir, I am one of the best. I will treat your son like he's my own."

All four nurses offer a single confident nod. The room shimmers like a pink disco ball as the parents exit, choosing to fetch coffee in the lobby. With the click of the door, Pauline's poker face dissolves. No doubt she is relieved not to be working in front of such a manic audience. She sighs and says, "Okay, little man. Let's get you fixed up."

The four work quickly and yet the puncture has to be precise. A little to one side and the vein is blown. (How can I put it? Placing an IV in a strong little toddler is somewhat comparable to pulling a sliver out of a feral cat.)

I inspect Pauline's options from a short distance. The baby's arm is meaty and the vein is deep. Pauline is going to have to search for it. *GO SLOWLY. SEE THE FLASH OF BLOOD...WAIT...ADVANCE.* I whisper as Pauline mumbles under her breath. "Go slowly. See the flash..."

Nobody else speaks as Pauline works and yet I can feel the team's auras directing a streamline of positive energy to the needle site, each member privately visualizing the flash.

By the time the parents return with the coffee, which isn't long, Junior's tiny arm is strapped to a board and IV fluids are running via pump. He is swaying on the bed, eyes locked on the television, transfixed on Dora the Explorer and her little monkey friend, singing about a map.

"BOOTS!" He points excitedly at the screen.

A tearful mom scoops him up, kisses his cheek, and then whips open her shirt attempting to smother the child with another hit of tit juice.

The father takes no time to comment. "The kid said *BOOTS*, Amy-Lynn. Not *BOOBS*. He's excited about the *monkey*! Put that fucking melon away..."

Chapter 28

Pleasantly amused, I head off to the lounge in search of a private sink to splash my face. I know that sounds weird, but even in death I don't *feel* dead. I feel sticky and sweaty as if it were me putting forth the effort and not Pauline. I take a running leap and lunge through the break room door. (Okay, so when I leap through wood, I kind of feel dead, but...oh, forget it.)

I falter. There's an argument in progress just around the corner. Again, forgetting my ghost-like qualities, I freeze.

"Lunch, Jillian! It's just lunch. We can talk. I...I miss you, Jilly-bean. I need to see you."

Immediately, I recognize the voice. *Dr. Kassel.* I wait for the response but there's only silence. "Don't be like that, sweetheart! I...I love you and I, oh I miss you baby. Why don't you just come home!" Another long pause. "I...I can't do that. I CAN'T FIX IT! I...we need to work this out...*together*!" p a u s e... "YOU'RE BEING UNRESONABLE! Okay, okay...I'm sorry. I'll stop yelling. I know... Don't hang up! No...Jilly! NOOO!"

BANG!

I turn the corner as Kassel smashes the ancient receiver into the wall phone. His face is flooded with longing and despair. Instantly enraged, I shamefully recall my last whispered order: *CALL SOMEBODY WHO LOVES YOU.*

I follow the cheerless director into the bathroom. He clamps both hands over his eyes and falls against the wall, sliding onto his haunches. His body visibly shakes as he weeps silently. Struck dumb by the man's physical state, I rush to his aide, draping loving arms around his person. We cry together.

Rousting abruptly, he moves to the sink and splashes cold tap water at his face. He peers in the mirror, no doubt inspecting for visible signs of his recent emotional outburst, and sighs raggedly.

Feeling completely responsible, I attempt a solution. *YOU NEED TO FORGET ABOUT JILLIAN FOR A WHILE. GET OUT OF THE HOUSE. CATCH A MOVIE. SHIT, HAVE A DRINK.*

Kassel sighs and slides a fingering hand through his hair. He speaks directly at his reflection. "You need to forget about Jillian for awhile. Get out of the house. Catch a movie. Shit, have a *drink*."

After washing his hands, I follow him out of the bathroom to the coffee station. A nurse is now sitting at the lunch table eating a bagel with sprouts and tomato, perusing the *Living Section* of the newspaper. I immediately recognize her as my sweet orientee from years back.

She waves casually, "Hey, Doc."

"Nurse Meghan." Kassel nods. "What's doin'?"

Meg shrugs. "Staying under the radar, I hope. Finishing up my last shift before the weekend."

"You and me both." Kassel says. "Any big plans?"

"Unless you call renting a movie and sipping wine on my couch big plans, then I got nothing." Meg rolls her eyes.

"That actually sounds relaxing. Shoot, I could use a glass of wine."

Standing next to the doctor, I have a sudden epiphany. *ASK HER OUT. NOW.*

"Uh...maybe we could go *out* to a movie together. I..." Kassel blushes. "I...uh, really need to get out of the house."

Both Kassel and I hold our breath waiting on the nurse's response. I'm absolutely positive that Meg isn't dating. Pretty sure that she works overtime out of boredom, and spends way too many nights gazing at the idiot box. My whispering, I believe, may help mend two lonely spirits.

Before Meg has a chance to let me down, I bark in her ear. *WHY THE HELL NOT? YOU NEVER GO OUT. IT'LL BE FUN!*

"You know...why the hell *not*?" Meg replies convincingly. "I never go out. It'll be fun!"

"Wow," Kassel says, unexpectedly. "What a whim!"

"Canceling already?"

"Heck no. I...uh, was just wondering if any of my jeans fit."

"Wear a stretchy skirt. That's what I might have to do."

"Oh, lawdy!" They both laugh. "So...tomorrow night?"

"Sure, Doc. What time?"

"Please, Meg. Call me Gene. I don't want to be anything resembling a doctor on the streets of Dixonville."

"As long as I don't have to be Nurse Meghan," she grins, "we'll get along just fine."

Chapter 29

"Let me grab another needle," Jamie mutters as she hurls a used angiocath into the sharps box and huffs out the room. *Looks like another two-stick friggin' day!*

All week Jamie's been screwing up. Just yesterday she mislabeled blood on a child, and the day before that she charted loads of detailed information on the wrong person. Truth is, the minute Lashon pointed out her error, Jamie's self-confidence went bust. Suddenly, her uncertainty bordered on excessive. Even choosing a vein became problematic. She'd mark one as decent, second guess herself, and then reposition over another without taking the time to feel or exact an insertion sight. *Boom!* Another miss. Another goddamned bruise. Another apology. Another *let me get someone else.*

Even the pharmacist, a voice at the end of a phone line, questioned her indecisiveness. Jamie used to be relatively trusting but now she *Google*-searched everything, or verified with pharmacy, and we're talking even the most common injections; meds she had given a hundred times before. Her excuse: *I thought I knew everything about Epi and look where that got me!* She triple-checked routes, re-calculated weight doses, and then vexed over side effects. Jamie used to sneer at nurses who were this anal, forever preaching a similar byline:

"Don't you realize that most listed side-effects are bogus? If even one person claims diarrhea then the Food and Drug Administration has to report it. Makes it seem like everything causes everything. Worry about the big stuff. You know...airway, breathing, and

circulation."

Jamie got so caught up recalculating a pediatric dose of antibiotics, a quantity already checked by another nurse and the doctor who ordered it, that she mislabeled the child's blood specimen. *What are the chances of two Jackson's being treated at the same time? A lot, you dumbass. Jackson is a popular name.* So Jamie accidently tagged Missy Jackson, age 8, with stickers belonging to Marissa Jackson, age 80. A simple blunder! And yet, per policy, the blood had to be thrown away. Not only did Jamie get written up, but a mislabeled specimen promised a day of lectures and remedial testing. The worst part, even more humiliating, Jamie was forced to face off with an already disgruntled mother, and explain why her daughter needed additional torturing.

That was yesterday. Today isn't going any better...

"What is this? Like our tenth conversation today?" Sam, the pharmacist, asks playfully when Jamie calls to question yet another medication. "Are you hitting on me or has little Miss Smarty Pants lost her edge?"

"Just answer the question," Jamie barks, clearly resisting the humor. "I'm busy down here."

"Easy, girl." Sam transitions to cautious. "I was just kidding. Are you okay?"

"Never better." Jamie mutters and bangs down the receiver.

Sam isn't the only one commenting on Jamie's new found anxiety. The once boastful, know-it-all fourth floor transfer, famous for scorning weak links and tormenting the indecisive, has in fact become the most indecisive weak link of them all. And in the world of emergency services, when seconds count, insecure delayed actions prove just as detrimental as over confident hasty ones.

The problem is obvious. Jamie can't stop obsessing about her fatal mistake. To think, six weeks ago she sat cocky and confident, suited up all swanky in a room filled with legal bigwigs, answering deposition questions with an exactness only an innocent person could manage. *"I am an ER Nurse, yes sir. I get the job done. We administer treatment by the book, on the dime, in the heat of chaos. Under the circumstances, the team was amazing! The heart and sheer energy we poured into that code...I cry thinking about it. The degree of intensity, the focus... Sadly, sometimes people die, no matter how hard you try."*

Jamie's deposition is now a printed legal document. She cringed when it arrived via certified mail, Betty phoning soon after to explain that she needed Jamie to re-read everything and fix any mistakes.

"Mistakes?" Jamie's throat tightened, *absolutely certain that Betty could sense her guilt. "Wha...what do you mean?"*

"Court reporters always make errors." Betty *replied bluntly. "Go through the text with a fine toothed comb. Confirm that none of your "no's" are typed as "yes's". Read it out loud. Take care that there are no questionable phrases—statements that can be twisted or interpreted hostility. We'll set up a meeting next month or so and compare notes."*

"Am I hearing you correctly? I can fix mistakes?"

"Sure, just not too many. Start striking through paragraphs and you'll look more like a liar than a timid nurse coerced into saying something she didn't mean by another self-serving attorney."

"Right."

"See you next month."

The idea of retracting her testimony and purposefully admitting that she was at fault seems physically impossible to the partially seasoned nurse. Confessing even to herself had been hard enough. How was she supposed to handle such demoralizing circumstances on a jury stand, with one hand placed firmly on a bible, in front of an aggressive audience? It sounded absolutely insufferable!

On numerous occasions, Jamie finds herself on the nurse manager's doorstep, ready to confess everything. *"It was me! I killed her. Yes...yes, I pushed Meghan out of the way as she attempted to look up the med."* Jamie replays the visual of ripping the Epi from Meg's hand, horrified by the memory of her smug and conceited tone as she sent the new nurse out of room. *"I'll take it from here. Uh...thanks, but now that your preceptor's down, it might be prudent to focus on your own patients."*

Damn! *Why didn't I let Meghan make the mistake?* Jamie pauses, cringing. A second thought creeps into the spotlight, more unnerving than the first. If Jamie was truly honest with herself, what disturbed her more than anything...

The newby would have gotten it right.

Chapter 30

Meg pretends that a single movie date with Dr. Kassel means nothing. But, as she undresses and climbs into bed, she can't deny that she feels something. *Gene.* Two days ago she didn't know his first name. Now, forty-eight hours later, it felt like they'd been friends forever.

Not in a million years would Meg have ever considered dating Dr. Kassel. For starters he was a doctor, and Meg considered all physicians the *boss.* A long standing rule in any business establishment: *If you like a job and want to keep it, never screw with the person directly in charge of you, mentally or physically.*

Meg isn't stupid. She recognizes that doctors don't sign paychecks. Nevertheless, comparable to the military, in the world of medicine there is a clear pecking order. Doctors, physician assistants and nurse practitioners write orders. Nurses and paramedics, (inadvertently assisted by a variety of ancillary staff, not excluding radiology, CT, and bedside technicians), implement. Everyone has a job. Everyone follows orders. And when they say shit rolls down hill, in the hospital business that means literally. The lower on totem pole, the more asses you wipe. Sorry folks. Generally speaking, health care is not a democracy.

*

Meg predicted an evening of random medical discussions peppered by awkward pauses. Not that she minded. Still very much a newby, Meg was like a sponge when the topic circled around emergency services. And yet, at the same time, she thought it might be wiser to steer clear of the subject altogether. That was the whole point of going to a movie afterall, to forget about the daily grind.

The good news was that Gene made the rule the minute they entered the restaurant. "No hospital discussions! I like to forget about that place when I'm drinking wine."

Meg laughed. "Probably a good idea. I have a hard time shutting it down, especially after a rough night. Truthfully, I'm surprised that I haven't started dreaming about IV's and ramming tubes into noses."

Gene nodded. "That's how it always is at the beginning. The adrenaline rush is like a drug, makes you feel unstoppable. But it's a heavy weight we bear. Our actions directly affect another person's life. That's why you're so freaked. You understand the severity of your job. Trust me. I've had many a sleepless nights. But now...well, after doing it awhile, you learn to shut it down. I walk out of that building and...poof! I'm no longer a doctor. I'm just a regular guy."

"So, what do you like to do, Mr. Regular Guy?"

"Ride motorcycles."

"Motorcycles?" Meg eyed him suggestively. "That's a surprise. What's your take on the Helmet Law?"

"Truthfully, if I ever get taken down on Interstate 95, I'd rather be *all* dead and not just half-way, but I wear a helmet just the same." Gene shrugged. "You know, for the minor accidents."

"What else do you like?"

"Movies, ice hockey, painting...I dabble in oils. Oh, and yes, at times I like to enjoy a good bottle of wine. Speaking of beverages, what's your flavor, missy?"

As they sipped cabernet and shared a plate of calamari, Meg was surprisingly comforted by Gene's presence. Conversation flowed easily. He asked about vacations so she expounded on the Vegas trip, even though it had been a while, which transitioned into a discussion about her life long friend, Katie, in California. Meg then rattled on about Kam's kennel job and her future plans of saving the four-legged world. The conversation flipped back to Gene, who playfully admitted that he'd rather be a cowboy than a medicine man.

Gene was born in Connecticut but after a nasty divorce, his mother, not a lover of snow and bundling jackets, dragged him off to North Carolina, her native home land. At first Gene wasn't very pleased about being whisked away from his life long Connecticut friends, but soon enough fell in love with the rural farms of his mother's childhood. He finished up high school in Granville County and then graduated from NC State as a respiratory therapist.

"What made you want to become a respiratory therapist?"

At this, Gene chuckled. "You're drinking wine in the *Smoker's Capital of the World*. Shoot! Half of my relatives labored on tobacco farms and my mother was raised on one—nicotine lovers the lot of 'em. Back in the day, puffin' was the thing to do. For me and my cousin, the repercussions meant lugging thirty pound canisters of oxygen, to and from the pharmacy, every other day, just so my granddaddy could breathe. Watching relatives rattle and hum, taking three steps to the bathroom, makes you want do something about it."

"Why the transition to physician?"

"Truthfully, doctoring wasn't a consideration until way later, after my degree. Then I started working in the hospital, personally observing the physician's daily toils and thought, *I could do that*. The good news: I was accepted into the Dixonville Regional Medical Program, which, as a staff member, was very cost effective. They paid the brunt of my tuition. Problem was that you couldn't stop working while you attended." Gene shook his head. "I was a hermit for the better part of five years. If it wasn't for my wife..." Gene stuttered and flushed a brutal red. "Look at me! Out on a date and talking about my marriage!"

"It's okay." Meg encouraged.

Gene eventually broke down and discussed Jillian, their broken relationship and his futile efforts to win her back. "At this point, I'd be happy with civil." He admitted. "Not two minutes in the same room and all hell breaks loose."

Meg placed an affectionate hand on his arm. "That must be hard."

So engrossed in conversation, they missed the movie and wound up having dinner at the bar. Afterward, Gene ordered a couple of roadie cappuccinos and they headed out for an evening stroll. Festive options in the rural town of Dixonville were always limited on weekends but, for a change, they got lucky. Every fourth Saturday Park & Recreation coughed up a dime and offered live entertainment on the town green. That night it happened to be *The Filipino Cowboy.*"

"My daughter loves *The Filipino Cowboy,*" Meg commented as they made their way down Main Street.

"Never heard of them or *him.* What do they sing?"

"It's kind of a mix between country and funk. Kam's got a couple of their CD's. She told me that the lead singer grew up in tobacco country, and that's why they play these local shows."

'I'm not sure that's allowed, country and funk on the same venue," Gene winked, "but I'll give it a shot."

They situated on a park bench at the edge of the

commotion so they could speak freely without screaming and enjoy the show at the same time. The topic transitioned to music, new and old. Meg and Gene agreed that both *FUN* and *Flo Rida* had great rhythm, but dually admitted that they could never point them out in a crowd.

Gene boldly announced that he was a head banger back in the day—a *METALLICA* guy. Jumping from the bench, he donned an air guitar and swung his head in a gyrating motion, shouting manically that his hair used to be really long and wild. "It was so kinky I had to spritz it with *Aussie Sprunch Spray!*"

Meg urgently divulged her love for the *Rolling Stones* and then proceeded to detail one very specific Greensboro Concert when her friend's older sister, Lonna, rented a school bus to transport a crew of forty. "They had lotteries back then and you needed a bracelet for placement in line. I guess the government was trying to avoid camp-outs by the ticket counters."

"I remember that." Gene agreed.

"Anyway, Lonna and her friends listened for that broadcast day and night, but when the announcement finally came, three of the girls were working. Suddenly desperate, Lonna turned to her youngest sister, my friend Neena, who was in the process of having a sleep-over. Lonna hustled us all into the back of her station wagon, promising of a free ticket with each secured bracelet—pending parental consent, of course. I remember my mother being so *jealous*. To think, that was my very first concert."

"The Rolling Stones was your first concert? And you were *how old*?"

Meg laughed. "Fifteen. A sophomore in high school. We all dressed in Mardi-Gras fashion, in fringed gowns with boas and masks, hoping to be chosen for the front row. The Stones were having a contest. Best costumes were escorted up front."

"Did you get picked?" Kassel asked.

"Nah, but we should have! We rolled into the parking area late on account of school buses not having bathrooms. Had to pull over like six times so we barely made it for the opening act. But everyone we met, they all kept saying *Wow! Ya'll should be front and center!"* Meg shrugged. "Still, it was super fun. One of those events that you never forget."

Gene reached over and squeezed Meg's hand. Meg returned the affection and, to her surprise, Gene didn't let go. Eventually they moseyed back to the parking deck, Meg only releasing his hand to seek out car keys.

Abruptly self-conscious, Kassel blushed and stuttered, kicking at the road. "Well...Nurse Ford, I have to say...that was quite an evening."

"Maybe next time we'll actually *see* the movie."

"Or maybe not." Gene winked. "Can't talk in a movie theatre. They have rules. How about a hockey game? I've got season tickets. Next Tuesday they're playing the King's at the PNC. Did you know that Sharan's son plays for the Kings?" (*Sharan's another nurse.)*

"I heard that." Meg paused.

"Do you want to go? Or, at least think on it?"

"I don't have to think about it. The answer is yes."

Gene flushed for a second time and then grinned. "Excellent. So, uh, I'll see you at work..."

*

Snuggling under cold sheets, reliving the grip of Gene's muscular hands, her mind keeps racing. *It's nothing, Meg. You're just friends.*

She hears an answer. That little voice from deep within that doesn't know how to shut up. *Yeah? Well, this nothing feels like a whole lot of something.*

Chapter 31

I'm craving me some booze. Now I know what I said before, that I was passed that business. Then I thought about it...*Why should I quit?* My liver's *been* dead for years. Nobody cares if I make an ass of myself. Moreover, I'm trapped on shit mountain without a view. Ollie Dick can keep the hotdogs and cupcakes; this ghost is hungering for something with a little more zest.

I start joining the staff at dinnertime, actually parking my ass on top of the break room table. My goal: To re-route discussions and make everyone thirsty. It didn't matter what they fancied, be it spirits or hops or fruity chick shit, at this point I'd take anything. During lulls in conversation, I'd holler out inquiries to get the ball rolling. Things like *WHAT'S YOUR FAVORITE COCKTAIL? DO YOU HAVE ANY SECRET INGREDIANTS FOR TASTY SANGRIA? HOW ABOUT A BEER EXCHANGE?*

But stirring up booze chatter turned out to be trickier than I thought. Dixon Valley is located smack dab center of the Bible belt after all, an area that bragged more churches per capita than convenient stores. Sweet tea is what they drink in Dixonville; sweet tea and Pepsi-cola. (North Carolina, by the way, is also home of the Pepsi Corporation.) All I can say is thank heaven for Yankee transplants and a few southern deviants or my mission for obliteration would've been toast.

One night I whisper in Beth's ear, a woman I am certain to be fond of sipping the occasional chardonnay. WHAT'S YOUR FAVORITE DRINK?

Beth promptly repeats my inquiry. "Anyone have any drink ideas? Got the in-laws coming down for a long weekend."

"I love me some Cranberry Orange Delight," Angela promptly replies. "I serve it religiously on Christmas and Thanksgiving with a mint cherry pie smothered in vanilla ice-cream. Dee-lish for any gathering."

My mouth waters at the possibilities. *Ooh! Gran Marnier is orange flavored! It sounded like the main ingredient.*

Then Angela adds, "It tastes absolutely fabulous over crushed ice, but on nippy nights, like tonight, I dare say that I appreciate it on the steamy side. Do you want a little sample action?"

DEFINITELY. BRING IT IN!

This time Angela responds directly to my order. "It's been sitting in my locker for months. Had planned on donating it to some organized gift basket earlier this year but forgot about it."

I peer up at the ceiling, joyfully optimistic. *There is a God!*

Then comes the hammer. Instead of hauling off to her locker where I anticipated a nicely wrapped bottle of high-end liquor, Angela opens a cabinet above the microwave and pulls out a small box. She says, "I busted into it last week when the temp dropped below fifty."

Cranberry Orange Delight is a brand of herbal tea.

Friggin' Teetolars!
What did you expect? They're nurses!
Yeah...so what? I was a nurse.

That's when I hunker down and really begin investigating, seeking out the lovers of fortification. I eventually mark my victims. Marge from Connecticut loves cabernet, as does Dr. Raj, who boasts an extensive collection of top notch vintages nestled deep in the shadows of his basement wine cellar. Bill from Wisconsin is the king of micro-brews, fond of transforming wheat and hops in the privacy of his own two-car garage, and Josh, one of our southern deviants, brags that his granddaddy's been distilling moonshine in his Fayetteville barn for the better part of twenty-seven years… *"White liquor strong enough to strip car paint and yet tantalizing to the tongue!"*

Hours later, I catch Bill and Josh swapping bottling tips over lunch and an opportunity finally presents itself.

LET'S MAKE A TRADE.

"Let's make a trade." Bill repeats. "You bring me a pint of Fayetteville's finest and I'll hit you with a couple quarts of my special brew."

"You working Friday?"

"Definitely!"

WOO HOO!

Josh pretends he's pulling a train whistle and repeats my phrase. "WOO HOO!"

*

A few nights later, I catch up with Marge and Dr. Raj in the nursing station. The ER looks like a ghost town. (When Raj works, he has nurses running like animals until the house is cleared. He'll crack the whip, and yet assist by expediting some of the many trivial nursing duties such as carrying specimens to the lab, transporting patients to X-ray; he'll even take telephone orders from other physicians if he thinks it's going speed up departure. In truth, Dr. Raj only relaxes when the department is empty.)

It is during one of these brief interludes, four a.m. on a Wednesday, when the facility is completely empty that I attempt to spark up another booze conversation. I get lucky when Beth asks Raj what wine she should buy for her upcoming dinner party. "Something reasonable," she says. "My in-laws drink like fish. They're Yankees, you know."

Raj starts in with his vintages and textures, which reels Marge into the discussion.

"There's better wine for cheaper, Beth." Marge cuts in. "Trust me."

Raj rolls his eyes. "Life's too short for cheap wine, but I dare say that if there is a deal out there, I'll be the one to find it."

The doctor's comment triggers a tempered argument. This is when I step in. *LET'S HAVE A COMPETION. YOU BRING YOUR BEST TEN DOLLAR BOTTLE AND I'LL BRING MINE.*

Marge pipes in. "I have an idea, Doctor. You bring in a couple of your best ten dollar bottles and I'll bring in mine. We'll let Beth decide."

"Deal." Raj chuckles. "You're going to lose."

Completely satisfied that I'll have some upcoming lockers to pilfer, I make a decision to check the other bay. Right then, a call transmits over the radio.

"EMS 72 calling Dixon Valley, do you copy?"

Dr. Raj, who is sitting an arm's breath away from the radio, answers it. (Taking EMS calls is another one of the many nursing jobs Raj performs. Personally, I think he likes the opportunity to give pre-hospital orders in hopes of speeding up inevitable departure times. I'm not kidding when I say he loves an empty department.) "This is Dixon Valley. Go ahead EMS."

"Coming in with a fifty-six year old male cancer patient in acute respiratory distress. Heart rate 32. Blood pressure 78/40. Saturation levels in the toilet. 79 percent on a non-rebreather. No line is established.

Six minutes out."

Dr. Raj flushes, immediately in bark-mode. "I DON'T CARE ABOUT A LINE! TELL ME THIS PATIENT IS INTUBATED!" Raj continues muttering for everyone's listening pleasure. "They'll line a twenty year old that pukes once, but won't intubate a man with zero oxygen levels."

EMS replies, "That's a negative, sir."

"INTUBATE *NOW*."

"Uh…this is a Hospice patient, Doctor."

Dr. Raj convulses wildly and then spins around to face the staff, flapping his arms like a violent duck. "What on earth are these fools *doing*?!"

"That'll be direction on arrival." Beth completes the transmission and then turns to the physician. "Guess we'll find out when they get here. Until then, I suspect it's best to be prepared."

All chatter stops as the staff gathers in room sixteen, the unofficial code room, to await their next guest.

(Let me take a moment to explain why Doctor Raj is so bullshit. The Hospice Organization was founded many moons ago, set up to assist and support not only the terminally ill but any others who choose to end life's journey with less intrusion from the medical process. An array of caring personnel offer emotional support for both patient and family, and provide basic medications such as pain and nausea relief in hopes of easing some of physical suffering during the transition. At this point, patients are not trying to be cured, they are expecting to pass. Very few exclusions bring Hospice patients to the emergency department, and dying isn't one of them. Hence, the reason for Dr. Raj's spasmodic upheaval.)

EMS arrives. A swarthy man with a country accent is guiding the stretcher, a skinny female coming up the rear, is doing the pushing. The patient is pale as a sheet, guppy breathing through an oxygen mask. His body is swollen like a tick and he's hoisted high on the stretcher, sitting at a ninety degree angle, to promote breathing. No doubt about it, the man is drowning in his own bodily fluids.

Raj is waiting for them with arms crossed. The EMS crew members cringe at the sight of him. Confrontations with Dr. Raj are most often inevitable. The skinny female ignores him completely and reports off to Beth. Marge and Bill undress the patient.

"This is Andrew Redman, age fifty-six. He was diagnosed last June with an aggressive form of Pancreatic Cancer, which has already advanced to his bones and brain. According to statistics, he should've passed months ago. Wife reports that he ate dinner at the table on Sunday. Monday he went to bed early with indigestion and stayed in it all Tuesday because he was feeling so weak. Now here it is Wednesday and he's swolled up like a tick. The patient signed Hospice papers three weeks ago."

Beth and Bill exchange glances. I can practically read their thoughts. *Heart Attack Monday. Full blown Congestive Heart Failure on Wednesday.*

"Why are you *here*?" Raj asks flatly.

The fat guy drops a hand on his hip and with the other wipes his brow. Shaking his head he says, "It's the wife, Doc. Very sad."

"Get her in here." He responds dryly. "I need to speak with her."

"I'm here." A shaky withdrawn voice emerges from the doorway.

The doctor jolts at the sound. When he locks eyes on the weathered spirit, Raj transitions to a more agreeable form. It is clearly evident that her husband's illness has taken a toll. The woman is shivering and pitiful, hugging herself tightly for tonight she walks alone.

Dropping his usual façade, Raj immediately extends an arm and wraps her in a hug. "Hello, dear."

The woman stumbles sideways, but he catchers her. Tears begin before the words. "They gave Andy three months to live six months ago. He's supposed to be dead. But...well, he isn't. A few weeks ago I thought we were close. He fell like four times trying to get into the bathroom, then he started talking about letting out our cat, Ruthie, whose been dead since 2004. Right after that he had a full blown seizure on the bedroom floor. *Horrible*! I took him in to Dr. Steve, his oncologist, who immediately scheduled an MRI. The report showed that his brain is riddled with tumors. Andy was lucid that day. He said he was sick of tests and hope and all that jazz. Tired of being tired.

"The kids flew in—Justin from Arizona, Samantha from Texas and Nick from Chicago. They stayed for ten days. We all expected Dad to pass, but the minute they showed up it was like he got a second wind." The woman heaves and Marge presses a small box of tissues into her wringing fingers. "Justin and Samantha headed out Saturday, and Nick on Sunday morning. I don't blame them. They had to get back. They've got kids and bills and families to run."

Raj breaks in quietly. "I don't think we can save him, baby."

The woman nods aggressively. "I *know*! It's not *that*! I contacted the Hospice nurse, but I waited too long! She was with another patient. Said she'd call for back up, but couldn't give an exact time. And...my *HUSBAND*...he's going to pass any MINUTE. I...I...the kids are *GONE*! Andy is DYING and I...I can't *HANDLE* IT! I can't be *ALONE!* Not tonight."

Bill pulls over a chair and Marge wraps the fragile creature in a heated blanket. Raj speaks caringly. "It's okay. Let us medicate your husband, to help with his pain and breathing. I'll get in touch with Hospice and Dr. Steve."

The woman's eyes glisten. "My Andy was a physician. Had a private practice out in Benson. Pediatrics. Kid's called him Dr. Red. He kept hours up until January, before the pain consumed him." She reaches out desperately and grips Dr. Raj with a trembling hand. "I realize we're not supposed to be here. This isn't *your* kind of an emergency." Her bottom lip quivers. "But…well…it's an emergency…to *me*."

The woman's devastating confession has a profound affect on the physician. He spins on a heel and barks a quiet yet determined order. "Administer IV Morphine 2mg every ten minutes until we get him upstairs." As Raj exits, he adds, "If you'll excuse me, I have a mountain to move."

Chapter 32

Wait times are the biggest complaint in emergency departments nationwide. We have our expedient moments, but usually, most OFTEN, seeking medical attention via emergency services transforms into an all day affair. I refer to it as the *Hurry and Wait Syndrome*.

Hurry to get to the ER. Wait to check in.

Hurry to see the triage nurse. Wait for an evaluation room.

Hurry to get undressed. Wait for the doctor.

Hurry to complete the testing. Wait for results.

Hurry for a consult. Wait for a call back.

Hurry to get admission orders. Wait for a hospital bed.

Hurry, hurry, hurry....wait, wait, wait.

People don't mind the hurry parts, but are always stunned by what they determine as unreasonably lengthy delays. (These wait times, by the way, are when nurses and doctors are tending to everyone *else* in the department. Damn those *other* sick people! I would also like to add that medical personnel, *especially* medical personnel, those who actually *understand* the system, are the absolute worst when trapped on the sick end of the spectrum, and freak out more than anyone when time seems to freeze.)

Sorry folks. Emergency care isn't like fast food. Tests take awhile. Medications have to be mixed and administered by time-specific guidelines. CT scans (hundreds of images) need to be read. Diagnosis and treatment are based on a person's physical exam, taking into account their current drug regimen and medical history. A lawyer once explained it to me like this: *If it were simple, like cookie cutting, then everyone would be a licensed physician.*

Wait times escalate irritability and I dare say animosity to the messenger, (which is always the nurse), especially after hours of lying on a cramped stretcher with nothing but a flimsy blanket and no pillow. However, let's be honest: If the evaluations were rushed and something potentially debilitating missed, how swiftly would the tables turn? Fingers would get pointed, the blame game would commence, and the only person in the room grinning from ear to ear would be the money-pilfering lawyer. Sorry peeps—some things should never be rushed.

There are a few exceptions to the Hurry and Wait Rule, but none of them are good. A fading pulse. Shallow gasping respirations. A circling blood pressure. True life-ending situations will always light a firecracker under even the slowest and laziest of asses. That's because healthcare workers have been ingrained to share one common goal: To keep the patient ALIVE and get them where they need to be.

And where is *that?*

"That" is situational and depends on who you ask.

Let's have an example:

A man gets ejected from a car on Interstate 95.

Paramedics and EMT's arrive at the scene. Their goal: Stabilize the spine, tape up holes, electrocute, bolus, drug, and drive HOT. Move mountains (or drive over them), do whatever it takes to get the patient to the trauma room. ALIVE.

The torch passes. Nurses, physicians, techs, dozen of caregivers lay in wait. The victim arrives and the room explodes into a frenzy. Clothes are cut off, pictures are taken, and organs are prodded. The goal:

Find the problem. Keep the patient ALIVE.

The torch passes. Surgery's turn. Time to cut, sew, sever, administer blood and FIX HOLES. Stabilize. The goal: Get the patient through surgery. ALIVE.

The torch passes. Recovery comes next. With a nurse less than a foot away, pacing three steps forward and three steps back, checking drains and pumps, hanging fluids, recording vitals, watching for signs of deterioration. The goal: To get the patient through recovery and up to a room. ALIVE.

If a healthcare worker delivers a patient to the next department with a pulse then...well, that's a successful day! So ingrained is this concept, so innate, even now while caring for a Hospice patient that is SUPPOSED TO PASS, the frenzy begins.

The current goal: Get the Hospice patient to the floor. ALIVE.

You may ask: *Why can't the patient just pass in the emergency department?*

Any ER nurse's response: *Where's the dignity in dying behind a curtain? He should have a room with a proper bed and door, where his family can grieve in private. Have you no empathy?*

This statement is true to some extent, and yet that isn't the only reason nurses want them out of the department.

For starters, death is emotional. Everyone cries. Even the warhorses shed a tear when Grandma or Momma or Brother Simon shows up. It's almost impossible to keep a dry eye in a mourning crowd. Weeping, as we all know, is physically exhausting; a stamina sucker when you're expected to stay sharp for twelve hours. Most nurses, whether they'll admit to it or not, would rather avoid such life ending dramatics.

Secondly, families of the deceased get special

privileges. Nothing *Four Star*—a tray of sodas and juice, cups of ice, a basket of saltines and cheese— whatever can be conjured from the patient refrigerator. Sometimes there's a supervisor or case manager able to assist in the process, but not always. The task of passing out refreshments lands in the lap of the primary nurse, who, by the way, still happens to be responsible for *living* customers in adjacent rooms. It's probably the one time a nurse can't shirk a simple blanket request or spew on about priorities. A loved one has passed. It's best not to piss off the family.

The next step involves a mandated conversation with the organ donor people, who expect notification within one hour of death so they can send out a specialist to, oh so cautiously, discuss the matter of plucking organs from the recently departed. (God forbid anyone gets buried with corneas these days.) I often wonder how this organization goes about hiring for such a position.

Help Wanted: Organ Retriever. Must close within the hour and remain empathetic and caring while discussing the expedient harvesting process. A people person...

Thankfully, nurses are not allowed to breech the subject of organ donation, which has always been fine by me. Although, during my years of service, I have fabricated many a scenes...

Hello Mrs. So and So...yes, dear, the old man is finally down. Here, sweetie, have a tissue. Blow for chrissakes, you've got a juicer protruding from that left nostril. Who am I? Oh, right. I'm here for the old boy's kidneys and a bit of skin. No worries. Its best that you don't have an open casket anyway because...damn! What a snout on that one. I hope your children didn't inherit that muzzle...

(You'll be happy to know that the organ donor

people are far more professional than my demented imagination.)

Anyway, moving on…

Paper work for the deceased is maddening but doable. The really freaky part for me has always been preparing the body. If the loss is unexpected or traumatic, the carcass is sent to the medical examiner. I feel a bit guilty admitting it, but I never minded an ME case. Nothing gets removed. Nothing gets cleaned. You just wrap 'em up and ship 'em out.

Never the less, ME cases are rare. Most of the time death *is* expected. Anticipated. *Craved.* For a normal passing, all wires and gadgets are removed. That includes plastic airways, angiocaths, urine tubes, skin drains, wound covers, Band-Aids, diapers— everything. The only thing *inserted* are teeth. I'll never forget my nursing instructor's comment, back in the day, as I assisted with post mortem care for the first time. Her remark, *"Get those dentures back in Grandma before she's rock solid. That's right, cram'um right in there. Time is of the essence. The family will have a fit if she's toothless for the funeral."*

The duty of body preparation always feels a bit supernatural. You're in the room pulling lines, cleaning off dried blood, wiping ass, getting caught up in the experience, and somehow forget that the body is soulless. Then peripherally, you catch a glimpse of…something. *Was that a blink? Did she just exhale?* I often wondered if the souls were among us, leaning over shoulders, watching us sponge and fluff while discussing ordinary bullshit like soap operas and weather changes. Transforming to nurse whisperer protected me from witnessing any of the scrubbing and zipping of my own dead remains, but I'm not sure if that's the case with every departed soul. So now, *especially* now, hearing such nonchalant conversations during post mortem care always makes me cringe.

Next comes the actual packaging. If you're lucky, the hospital doesn't cheap out on end-of-life wrappings. Body bags come in a variety of sizes and gradients, kind of like garbage bags. There's the top-of-the-line double-graded *Hefty,* with pull strings and stretch-ability, all the way down to the bargain brand *Econo Sack*, that rips when prying it from the roll. Body bags are no different. You've got the high-end zip shroud, that maintains similar qualities to that of a protective garment bag, and the not-so-sturdy *Flimsy Flicker,* made out of cheap plastic and secured with wiry paper clippings.

Dixon Valley carries the top dollar zip bags for a reason.

And that reason is Anna-Marie Wellington, RN.

Anna-Marie retired soon after my arrival to Dixon Valley, and maybe that's why she had such enormous cahoonas. One could never be certain. She was one of those poker-faced broads, doubled over in hysterics one minute, stone cold serious (I dare say bordering on bitch) the next. With Anna-Marie, you never quite knew what to expect.

Back then, Dixon Valley cheaped out on body shrouds. Instead of the *zippem' and go* wrappers, we used the *roll-em and twist* bullshit that really didn't roll without stretching, or twist without ripping, and very rarely secured what needed to be contained. Needless to say, the task of packaging the dead was considered exceptionally laborious.

On the particular day in question, I marched into the bay, slung my bag over a chair and stood at attention anticipating report. Anna-Marie moved purposefully, tying up loose ends, tidying her assignment. At pre-shift, there was talk about a morning code; a long, ugly, drawn-out affair that ended poorly.

I figured Anna must be exhausted and anxious to hit the road. I asked if there was anything I could do to assist with her departure.

Without looking up from the computer, she said. "Mrs. X in room eight has asked me for a drink like ten times. Can you get her a coffee?"

"Decaf? Probably shouldn't be offering up Regular."

"Whatever," Anna shrugged. "She's had a rough day. I'm sure she'll take anything." Anna continued to beat on her key board as I hustled off to acquire the life-sustaining beverage.

Coffee in one hand, a pile of creamers and sugar in the other, I tapped on the door before entering. "*HELLO*-O! Is anybody home?" When I didn't get a response, I moved ahead cautiously thinking perhaps the old bird had a hearing issue. "Hello? I come bearing gifts!" My voice transitioned to singsong, on the verge of shouting. Still no answer. I dramatically flipped the curtain and advanced boldly, holding forth the well intended *Cup o' Joe* like a peace offering. Grinning zealously, I announced, "ROOM SERVICE!"

Staggering…I *YELPED*…and spilled the hot mixture down my shirt. And then, to be totally honest, I collapsed into a fit of belligerent laughter.

The visual was absolutely ri-*DONK*-ulis.

Sitting in an upright position, crammed onto a skinny ED stretcher was Mrs. X, dead as a door nail, wrapped in a blinding yellow shroud. It was one of our squeaky cheap plastic *roll 'em and twist* bags that didn't quite fit the woman's horizontal stature. Plump by nature (and my best guess, too many mashed potatoes), the nurse was forced to get creative and bind the edges and flaps with duck tape. The head now simulated a saran-wrapped frozen turkey, misshaped and bulbous, with a twist tie shooting out the top *Alfalfa* style. More duck tape strangulated the neck, securing the slippery material, and the bottom was so encapsulated with layers of the same sticky tape that it appeared as if the victim donned vinyl gray shoes. The body was bound like a Tootsie-Roll, but I couldn't stop thinking banana flavored salt-water taffy.

This was my first time laying eyes on the end product of a dead person bound in a Flimsy Flicker, and I'm telling you there was absolutely nothing pretty or reassuring about it. But that's not why I yelped, and definitely not the reason for my uncontrollable hysteria.

Due to such a wide girth, Anna Marie was forced to leave one arm out of the slippery yellow packaging. (I suspect that may be what ignited her demented sense of humor.) That same arm, rigged in position, was balancing a scribbled sign taped in place to the front of the carcass.

Scrawled in black Sharpi, the message read....

TAKE ME TO DUNKIN DOUGHNUTS.

The good news—all family members had been gone for hours and no management actually witnessed the debauchery. Still, I'm pretty certain that Anna-Marie Wellington, RN is going to have a lot of explaining to do before entering any such pearly gates.

*

To reiterate, the end of life process basically sucks. The experience is emotionally exhausting, weird as hell, extremely laborious and a horrible strain on the lower back. Seriously, taking the "empathetic route" has its advantages. The family is happy, the patient is comfortable, the doctor presents like a super hero, and the nurse avoids a visit to the chiropractor.

All joking aside, deep in our hearts we all believe that no man, woman or child should die in an emergency department. There's too much chaos and background noise; buzzing phone calls and over head pages, folks shouting out for bed pans and turkey sandwiches, people complaining about waits and delays. To be trapped in such a hole during our last moments on earth is just plain wrong.

Chapter 33

So…back to our Hospice patient. Usually, I'm all for racing the clock. Usually, I'm whispering urgent messages to doctors and secretaries, nurses and clinicians, cracking the whip to get a move one. Usually.

Today, I'm frozen. Stunned. Shocked. Deliriously hopeful. *This is it. This Dr. Red is my replacement!. It's time for me to move on! To somewhere. Hopefully UP! I was totally ready for UP.*

Besieged with possibilities, I'm jilted back to reality when Raj plunges into the room and barks, "Bed 225 is ready. Call report."

My ghost body goes rigid. *No! That can't be right.*

Labs need to be run.

Tests completed.

Consults placed.

Orders taken.

A bed assigned.

Hurry, hurry, hurry. Wait, wait, wait.

What the heck happened to the wait part?

My brow furrows as I regurgitate. *Dr. Raj is what happened.* So caught up in my reverie of options, I forget who I'm dealing with—Dr. Speedy Gonzales himself. Standard Raj—calling for a consult, writing orders himself and dropping the bomb on bed control in less than a minute. *Boom.* It's what he does.

What did you expect, Gloria? Red doesn't need lab work. Red doesn't want an MRI. Red wants to die, you dip shit it…right the fuck now.

On the physician's command, the staff explodes

into action.

Andy begins to shimmer. His eyes have glazed over and he's no longer focusing on his wife. He's searching past. We lock eyes. I'm the angel in the doorway now. He sees me and smiles. Andy lifts a staggering arm to point, but his wife takes hold. Clutching desperately, she whispers, "I'm here, baby. I'm right here."

He tries to speak but the words won't come.

She answers for him. "It's okay, my love. I'm with you."

Beth barrels through me, moving deliberately, quietly packing up the bed preparing for departure. She speaks soothingly to the weeping near-widow. "Marge is calling report right now. We'll be leaving shortly."

I momentarily stiffen and plunge through the door, unfazed by the oaky textures and lacquer taste, desperately seeking Marge. I find her punching numbers into the phone, attempting to call the floor.

I shout directly in her ear. *DIAL EXTENSION 6645.*

That's not the number but she tries it anyway.

DIAL EXTENSION 6645.

She punches the wrong number again.

DIAL EXTENSION 6645.

After her third try, she hollers over to the night secretary. "Darlene! What the heck's the number for the fourth floor?"

"3-3-4-5." Darlene doesn't bother looking up. She's used to stupid questions, and yet never fails to answer.

"Why do I keep dialing 6-6-4-5?"

Another stupid question. Darlene responds accordingly. "Quit smoking dope before work. That might help."

Marge tries again, this time she punches the

numbers correctly, but I'm one step ahead. I've managed to snatch the phone cord from the socket. She eventually figures it out and plugs it back in. Attempting to dial, I dislodge it a second time.

"What's the hold up?" Beth cries, exacerbated. "The man is gasping in there!"

"It's the phone. It's dead."

Beth holds up the cord. "Have you tried plugging it in?"

Marge's eyes go wide. "I…I just checked that!"

Darlene jeers, "Sure you did."

"No. Really! I swear!"

Beth rolls her eyes. "Fax report, please. We need to go."

I spend the next five minutes jamming papers in the fax machine. Completely flustered, Marge's complexion is fluorescent green as she opens the machine's inner workings and starts prying out the lodged pieces. I take a second to peer in on our patient. He's guppy breathing and his soul seems to be shifting. Death is minutes away.

Right then, Dr. Raj exits another room and absolutely flips out when he realizes that his Hospice patient is still in the department. "WHY IS DR. REDMAN STILL HERE?" He whisper barks at Marge. "You need to go!"

"It's the fax machine! The fourth floor will have a COW if I don't send report. I'm beside myself! And *look* at the patient? He's probably going to die en route. Maybe we should just keep him here."

"NO! No way!" Raj grabs the crumpled report sheet from Marge's hand and rushes back into the room, determined. "I'll take him up myself."

Oh, shit. Now I'm screwed.

"We're going. Now!" Raj growls and gets into position.

As Raj pushes, I start jumping on the side break, which causes a frenzy of sudden jerking halts. Doctor Raj rams his abdomen with each pause and mutters out loud. "What the heck is wrong with the steering on this thing?" He doesn't wait for an answer. Like I said before, Raj will do just about anything to empty the department. He gives up on analyzing the problem and puts his body into it, sliding the bed in the locked position. In no time, he's almost out the door.

I'm beyond desperate. Searching. WHAT CAN I DO? Then I see it. The fire alarm. Hell yeah! If I slam it down the automatic doors will stop working. It'll take time to slide a bed with no wheels through a manual double door. At least three people will need to assist. It might be just enough time for Andy's soul to pass.

I   grip   the   handle,   ready   to   pull, and...*WHAM!*

Something hard slams into me from behind. I'm hurled to the floor. *What the hell?* Cursing and out of time, I scramble to stand. Raj is too quick. The ED doors are already open.

POOF...the patient is gone.

"NOOOOOOooooooOOOOOOooooooOOO!!!" Completely disheveled, I drop to the floor kicking and screaming like a spoiled three year old. "FFFFUUUCCCCKKKKK!" I swear because it feels good. "MOTHER FUCKKERR!" Banging my fists and thrashing my heels, my intentions are to desperately ANNOY. But nobody is listening. Nobody hears me. Nobody gives a rat's ASS about the Queen of Shit Mountain. Flat on my back, flailing like a snow angel, I use the ceiling as a sounding board. "THIS PLACE SUUUUCCCKS!"

And then...I think about it.

"What the hell plowed me over?" I ask the ceiling. "I'm a GHOST! Nothing can move a ghost except maybe…"

"…another ghost." A voice replies.

I yelp from sheer surprise.

My eyes go wide as the head of Ollie Dick looms above me. "Again I find you laying on that disgustingly filthy floor." He shakes his head. "My, my, are we in a state."

"Ollie? What…what the fuck are *you* doing here?"

"I missed you too, sweet heart." Ollie chuckles.

Brooding, I respond to his greeting with silence but deep down I'm happy for the reprieve.

"You know why I'm here, Gloria," he continues, unfazed by my sour attitude. "To pick up old Red. I'm a *retriever*, remember. I've come to retrieve."

"Thanks a *LOT,* by the way. Red was mine. He was a DOCTOR! He could've been my *REPLACEMENT*! My ticket to ride. And you..." I pause, suddenly dumbfound. "Why did you *tackle* me?"

Ollie coughs, shifting his feet. "Yeah, right. Sorry about that. The good news; ghosts don't bruise."

"But *why*?"

"I didn't need you to make a similar mistake."

"It's not like I was going to KILL the guy. He was practically dead." I stop abruptly, suddenly taken by Ollie's comment. "What do you mean *similar* mistake?"

Ollie's mouth draws thin. "Uh…"

Then it dawns on me. A rush of memories knocks me hard in the gut. I practically dry heave from the visual. Pointing a determined finger, I jab at Ollie's hot dog induced abdomen. "You!"

"Hey...easy. *I* didn't kill *you*, either." Ollie remarks defensively.

"You might as well have! How could I have missed it? YOU WERE IN THE ROOM! You LET Jamie push that Epi! You could've stopped her. Instead, you danced through it. I remember now. It was that *Moves Like Jagger* song. You were HAPPY! Not only did you let me drop dead, but you RUINED Jamie's life! Not my favorite person, but have you seen her lately? She can't give a med without having a friggin' panic attack. That's what Deloris meant when she said *doing nothing wrong* isn't the same as *doing everything right."* I gasp, totally floored by the revelation. "If...if you had done your JOB, I'd be alive right now!"

"You're mistaken, Gloria." Ollie's response turns solemn.

"*MISTAKEN*?" I cry. "How can that be?"

"No...no, no...well, you're kind of right. I should've stopped that nurse. Not helping Jamie is the very reason I'm stuck between worlds. But you...you were definitely a gonner."

"I WAS A GONNER BECAUSE OF JAMIE. I'd be ALIVE. I could be home..."

"No, baby." Ollie grips hold of my shoulders, his voice full of emotion. "That's not true."

"You were friggin' DANCING! And....and *SINGING!*"

"Don't kid yourself. If I hadn't tackled you just now, you'd be doing cartwheels." Ollie scowls. "My job was OVER. You don't seem to get that part, Gloria. I was dancing because I was ALREADY free."

"I WAS STILL ALI..."

"You....were...*NUMBERED!*"

The comment throws me. "*What*?"

"Soul 674."

"That…that's my case file."

"And that's not a coincidence, Gloria. 674 is also your life number."

"My what?"

"Remember the old timer, Bobby, and his wife Lorraine? The digits shimmering across Lorraine's forehead? We suspected the Broken Heart Disease, but couldn't say for certain? Her soul was already marked for death. Just like yours." Ollie pauses. "The digits on your forehead surfaced twenty-seven hours before your allergic reaction. I had been following you around like a puppy dog, but had no idea what to expect. Or…or *when* to expect it. A person can last up to seven days in such a state, but that's about it. One minute you were good and the next…WHAM!"

"I…" My eyes water. "I don't *believe* you!"

"It's *true*! That's why I wasn't thinking about Jamie. Tickets are rarely rescinded. Somebody had to pass."

I stumble suddenly, but Ollie catches me and wraps me in a hug. "I'm sorry, Gloria. There was nothing I could do. It was your day to die."

Chapter 34

Friggin Flu Season should be over thrice fold and still the retching and shitting continues. Jamie flings herself out of another filthy room, whips off the mask, balls up her contact gown and dumps it in the trash. She rushes the sink and scrubs her already chafed hands. Tonight she'll have to grease up with Vaseline and sleep in gloves just to get through tomorrow's shift. *What a nightmare.*

Fevers and vomiting are bad enough, but when it's spewing out both ends, the stomach flu takes on a whole new meaning. Hospital brand diapers just don't secure like they're supposed to, which makes every accident a full on disaster. Jamie has been elbow deep in shit, rolling and wiping, fluffing and tucking, for the better part of nine hours. As soon she fixes one problem, the next call bell goes off.

Jamie sighs. At least her patients are appreciative. Elderly folks usually are. They say *thank you* and *please*, and many even *apologize* for having accidents. How can Jamie get angry with a sweet old lady or loveable grandpa who acts indebted by her very presence? No, debilitated seniors are definitely not the problem. It's the healthy people that drive her insane.

Hundreds of ragged customers flock to the ER every year, coughing and hacking, sniffling and sneezing. They roll in wearing robes and nighties, shivering in comforters, crying out for footies and blankies, requesting private cots in the waiting room so they can lie down. (FYI: A cot is a ROOM, people. If there was a room available then you wouldn't be waiting.) These whiners monopolize every wheelchair in the lobby and demand to be pushed to and fro like it's an ankle injury and not a sore throat. They wheel into the treatment area sniveling and horking like nurses and techs are immune to such infections. Holy shit COVER YOUR MOUTHS people! A second grader could do better. Jamie can understand toddlers being resistant to masks, but if one more middle-age histrionic man coughed in her fucking face, things were going to get ugly.

Giving up on manners and basic human etiquette, Jamie assumes that every complaint of body and joint pain, every generalized weakness and sniveling honker, is most likely a case of the flu. Wearing a mask becomes second nature. She starts covering up before entering any new room. Her tactics seem to be working. Jamie has managed a perfect attendance so far this year, but after today's wrath of snots and leaking shit she begins to question the stamina of her immune system. *And it's April already! Is this bug ever going to quit!*

The call bell rings in room nine. It's Mr. Henry again reporting another pile of the thick and nasty. Resigned to a day of filth, Jamie gathers supplies, latches on to the nearest tech, and together they head in for a cleaning. The mess is bigger than usual. Mr. Henry has attempted to make the bedside commode. That's where Jamie finds him, trailed by splattered chocolate stool that is smeared all over the bed sheets, dribbled across the floor, and staining both of his legs.

"I'm sorry, dear. I was trying to help." Mr. Henry apologizes immediately.

Jamie struggles to compose herself, but with every soiled towel, every filthy sheet, it gets harder to maintain civility. Counting back from five in her head, a lesson she has learned from practicing for trial, she composes and formulates a more respectful response.

"Next time use the call bell, Mr. Henry. You could've fallen."

Twenty minutes pass before the room is back in order. By the time Jamie strips out of her contact gown and rescrubs her already raw hands, a new patient has been assigned to room ten.

Charge bustles past, offering her condolences as she goes. "Sorry, girl. You had the only open room."

Never a good sign. "What is it?"

"*What* isn't what you should be asking." Angela mutters as she hustles away. "It's the *who* part that's going to make you cringe."

Jamie scowls and enters the room cautiously. "Hello?"

Rita Robertson, the Crohn's Queen, is perched on the bed. Covered in worn, ratty blankets from home, face down in a vomit bucket, she promptly wretches. The foul smelling contents are a putrid green and projectile in nature. She groans and wipes her mouth, slaps a wet towel across her forehead, and drops back against the pillow.

It's been awhile since Jamie has cared for Rita Robertson, but can see that their days apart have not been kind. Rita's face is swollen and slightly discolored, no doubt from a life long regimen of steroids. She appears malnourished in the legs and her stomach is tight and protruding, kind of how life long drinkers present. Jamie knows better. Crohn's disease is an intestinal issue, inflaming and twisting the GI tract, causing nausea, vomiting, pain, sometimes drug dependence, and in today's case; obstructed bowels. Mrs. Robertson is only forty-eight years old and already has survived sixteen abdominal surgeries. Today may very well turn into unlucky number seventeen.

She peers out from under the wash cloth and groans. "Yee hah. Nurse Uppity. *Christ.*"

Jamie's hair stands on end. Her eyes flash and a thrashing of not so pleasant replies resound on the tip of her tongue. *What a dreadfully foul creature!* Jamie checks herself. She's too tired to fight. Too damn sick of vomit and shit and getting berated. The whole process was old. Too friggin' old already and she's barely out of the starting gate. Statistics proved that the average nurse only makes it about three years working patient care. When Jamie first heard these reports she thought they were preposterous. *Only three years?* Now she understands. How is she ever expected to make it twenty years? *I'm not. I'll never make it.*

She slumps down in a chair next to her arch enemy, defeated. Counting back from five like fifty times, she's fearful to speak, sure that anything she'll say will convey her true feelings—ugly and hateful.

The moment of silence lasts too long. Mrs. Roberston takes another peek. After a good three minutes, she removes the cloth altogether and huffs quietly, holding out her arm. "Go ahead, kid. Begin the torture."

"That has never my intention," Jamie speaks softly, "to torture you."

Rita guffaffs. "And it was never my intention to be a life long patient. Never my plan to be cut up and tortured. Never my dream to get hooked on the juice. But it is what it is so I guess we're both screwed."

This is the first time Jamie hears Rita laugh sarcastic as it may be, but for some reason it strikes a nerve. As if seeing the woman for the first time, Jamie imagines a day in the life of Rita Robertson. Stuck in the hospital for months at a time, endless doctor visits, hundreds of needles poking and prodding. Jamie suddenly wonders how many nurses walk into her room and cringe on sight. The visual is especially disturbing because Jamie imagines her very own sour and contemptuous reflection.

Holy shit. What am I doing?

Rita comments. "Are you okay?"

"No. Not really. I've had a shitty day. Literally." Jamie pauses and her response softens. "I'm sorry that you have to come here, and I'm sorry for all the times I've been ugly. It's frustrating. I see you and know that I can't get your line, and yet I still have to try. And you...well...you're not always the most pleasant individual."

"Not that burst of happy sunshine you were expecting?" Rita raises an eyebrow.

"No. Not really."

Mrs. Robertson points to the bucket between her legs. "I'm puking black shit. You try friendly and radiant while throwing up this crap."

Jamie laughs, but then promptly apologizes.

Rita throws up a flippant hand. "Don't bother apologizing. I've been an ass. In fact, I'm *always* an ass. I know that I'm not well liked. Don't think I can't hear your conversations behind closed doors, or visualize arguments through pane glass. I've watched nurses actually flip coins, and from a hundred feet away I can tell who the loser is.

"At the beginning of my illness, people were nicer. Empathic. But it's been years since I've been treated with any real compassion, forget about basic respect. These days nurses and doctors alike are down right hostile. I'm a drug addict, don't you know? A manipulating miserable junkie. Which is true. But it really sucks having another bowel obstruction when *nobody*, and I mean *NOBODY*, gives a shit." Rita stops abruptly, and coughs to avoid the tears. "I could be nicer. I *should* be nicer. Then again, so could you."

A moment of silence ensues. The woman's confession is humbling somehow and Jamie is suddenly overwhelmed with guilt recollecting interactions from year's past. "I definitely haven't won any awards, as of late, for my friendly demeanor." (Pause.) "Maybe we can start over?" The nurse holds out a hand. "Hello, my name is Nurse Uppity. Some folks call me Jamie."

Crohn's Lady grins. "Hello. I'm Rita. Most people call me Bitch."

"Hello, Bitch."

"Hello, Nurse Uppity."

"Now, how can I help you?"

Rita sighs, "Bring me some Dilaudid, straight up, with a side of Zofran. On second thought, make it a double."

Chapter 35

All I can say is Josh's daddy distills some potent white liquor. Although, even in death, acquiring such a taste has taken a record amount of time. I would have much preferred slugging back Bill's garage microbrew, but pinching and actually enjoying bottles of beer has proved ridiculously problematic.

Open beer doesn't store well, which translates into consuming a complete bottle at each sitting. Sadly, in the case of the nonliving, one ice cold frosty turns out to be one ice cold frosty too many. I discover my dilemma ten days later when I wake up crammed in the broom closet, drool congealed in my hair, snuggling a mop end as a pillow. Not one of my finer moments.

By the time I risk a second microbrew, a month later, it's piss warm. I consider my options. Sneaking booze into the lounge freezer could be seriously risky. It isn't like the olden days, when cocktail distribution was Standard of Care in most hospitals; when beer and airport liquor bottles were readily available and prescribed for the alcohol dependant patient. If that were still the case, I'd be in great shape.

Attempting another tepid sip, I almost vomit. Screw it. *I need ice*! But the last thing I want is to get a staff member canned because of my wrongdoings. So I lay in wait for a lapse in lounge traffic before making a break for the fridge. Five minutes into the chilling process, the clinical administer surprises me by plowing through the entrance, blabbing into a phone, informing the recipient that she is on her way up with a stack of frozen dinners. She opens the icebox and finds Bill's finest standing at full salute, chilling nicely smack dab in the middle of the compartment. Due to a lack of options and nervous adrenaline, I smack her in the head with the swinging freezer door. She yelps, clutches at her skull, and by the time she returns to the task, my beer bottle and me is gone.

Enjoying cold brewskies just isn't working out. And truth be told, Wisconsin Bill was pretty bent about the missing six-pack. He let his anger be known by scribbling hate notes on the fridge and sending hospital wide emails discussing integrity and basic etiquette. Even now, weeks out, there is still a sign hanging on the lounge door announcing that *SHOPLIFTERS WILL BE PROSECUTED.*

Thankfully, I was smart enough to heist some white liquor the same day I snagged Bill's microbrew. Josh was preparing to trade a glass quart of Grandpa's moonshine for Bill's soon-to-be-missing six-pack. I didn't steal the whole container, just switched out the contents of a water bottle. Nobody, and I mean *nobody*, will ever notice the dilution. I swear, even in death, ingesting the spirits has put hair on my chest.

Even so, I've been spending long intervals holed up in the broom closet testing out my newest concoction: cranberry juice and moonshine. It's hard to believe, but I've been in a funk since Ollie's departure. After the initial drama of losing Dr. Red and Ollie's devastating confession, we visited for awhile and I realized how much I missed the sorry bastard.

While Red was up on fourth on the brink of transition, Ollie lingered, complaining about his new dead life as a retrieval specialist. "We sit around in this narrow hallway covered in seventies wall paneling. The room is lined with pleather orange chairs and boxed off with a couple of end tables that are stacked with crossword puzzles and vintage magazines. The magazines were cool for awhile, but they never get updated, and Barry Manilow is *always* playing in the background. There's a broken coffee machine in the corner, and dirty ashtrays stink up the joint even though there's nothing to smoke. Our only saving grace is the one chess board. All we do is play tournaments; best out of a hundred games. What can I say? Eternity is *fore-verrrr*." Ollie chuckles sourly. "Oh, and I almost forgot, there's no friggin' food. Remind me to load up on turkey sandwiches before I go."

"At least you have company."

"Losers, Gloria, fuck ups of the in-between. Not what you'd call illuminating conversation."

"They can play chess."

"Not very well." Ollie says.

"How many retrievers are there?"

"In my office, a dozen or so, but there are a lot of offices. And let's not forget about the guest retrievers."

"Guest?"

"That's right. Angels put in requests to pick up specific loved ones, so they can personally guide them through the pearly gates. Husbands retrieve wives. Sisters transport brothers. Neighbors welcome neighbors. A loving face always softens the blow."

Confused, I ask, "How do they know when they're needed?"

"I would think that'd be obvious."

"Well, it's not."

Ollie shakes his head disappointingly. "Have you not a single ounce of religion in you?"

"What's *that* supposed to mean?"

"Think about it. Use that dead brain of yours. What is the one similarity all religions share?"

"They believe in a god?"

"All of their gods are *different*. What is the *same*?" .

I shrug.

"What's the first thing people do when someone falls ill? Or gets mortally injured?"

"I don't know...cry?"

"They *PRAY* you fool. Even non religious folks, they all pray like crazy. During these moments of homage and desperation, some people send very specific messages to friends and family that have already passed. *'Hey, Leah...do me a favor and watch over my baby girl. Dear Gran, keep my Charlie safe.'* If a person prays hard enough, the angel can sense it. A request is put in and *bam*...guest retrieval specialist at your service."

"That's pretty cool."

"*Very* cool, Gloria. The more I learn about life after, after *this*, the more I yearn to be on my way."

"How long are you trapped there?"

Ollie frowns. "I've been asking around, questioning every ghost I can. They all say the same thing. Until I fix my mistake, I'm stuck."

"Mistake?"

"Not helping Jamie. I need to get her back on track or I'll be playing chess for eternity."

"How can you do that as a transporter?"

"I can't, but like I said I've been talking to people, explaining my situation."

"And?"

"And I'm told that *you* need to glow, sister. If *you* get out, then I can be reinstated and try to fix my problem."

"Is that all?" I huff. "Well, when the next circling caregiver shows up, you'll be the first to know."

"That's the problem," Ollie says matter-of-factly. "You need to get out *without* anyone dying."

"Is that why you rushed off old Red?"

"You're a pain in the ass, Gloria. I was *helping* you."

"You keep saying that, but I'm not feeling it." Attempting to annoy, I add, "If nobody dies, how exactly am I supposed to do that?"

"The *other* way." Ollie growls. "FIND OUT WHO YOU ARE!"

Find out who I am. The idea thrills me and yet everything I try, every memory I conjure, brings with it an entourage of syringes and shit pads. Nothing clicks. I return to my locker in hopes of a seeking out a hint of a clue and discover that it has finally been cleared out and reassigned to our newest hire, Alyssa Day. Alyssa is actually rifling through it when I enter, her preceptor close at hand (another nurse that started way past my time), waiting for her to unpack. I make a lame attempt at whispering comments, resurrecting a discussion about my death.

DID A NURSE REALLY DIE HERE, ON THE JOB?

"Did a nurse really die here, on the job?" Alyssa repeats.

"Two of them." Naomi replies. "One choked to death on a hotdog, the other had an allergic reaction."

Alyssa frowns. "Did I get a dead chick's locker?"

Naomi shrugs. "Maybe."

"What if she's pissed that I took her spot?"

I am pissed. TELL HER I AM PISSED.

"She is pissed." Naomi repeats. "Uh…that was weird."

"What?"

"I didn't mean to say that."

"Why are we *talking* about this?" Alyssa adds.

"You started it."

"I didn't mean to."

Both women giggle nervously and hustle out of the room.

So much for whispering.

Frustrated and out of ideas, I track down my hidden bottle of moonshine water (crammed deep within the depth of the fridge, labeled with a SHOPLIFTERS WILL BE PROSECUTED sign), snag a couple of cranberry juices, and head for the broom closet. Within minutes, I'm belligerent drunk and talking out loud to myself like a crazy person. It dawns on me. "I've lost it," I mutter. "I'm a friggin' nut case. Off my rocker. Crazy as... Crazy as..."

I have no interest in prancing about drunk, flirting, or even lap dancing my favorite staff members. I don't want to stew over lost love or the *Promise Land* or monitor anything medical EVER again. My goal is to be knocked out cold. Lifting the 'shine directly to my lips without a chaser, I take a glug...and then...catch myself. "Wait. Waiiittt a minute. Wait, wait, wait! That's...thassssitt!" One last thought crosses my synapse before completely blacking out. "...crazy as Geraldyne Dixon."

My only hope.

Chapter 36

Meg has been unofficially dating Gene for six months. If she was counting, and she is, Gene has accompanied her on twenty-seven different days to twenty-seven different places. By numbers alone, this should make them a couple. At the beginning, Meg didn't care. She had committed to the first movie offer out sheer of kindness. With Gene's invitation, Meg had sensed his despair, an underlying sadness that she now better understood. Never had she planned on falling head over heels for the guy, and yet, there was no denying it. Meg is enthralled. *Obsessed*. A friggin' basket case.

Meg is also very confused. Has she been reading Gene completely wrong or did she truly sense his reciprocation? Surely twenty seven dates with the same person had to mean something? But to what extent? To what degree? Meg kept putting off the discussion, certain that the subject would breech itself. Then, well, the shit hit the fan and Jillian had everything to do with it...

*

They were having lunch at Subway after finishing up a three mile walk in the park. Meg was heading back to the soda fountain for a refill and a stack of napkins when Gene's phone rang. Upon her she return, Gene's face was flushed and his brow deeply furrowed. He flashed a practice doctor smile, held up a finger, and moved away from the table to finish the conversation. At first, Meg thought nothing of it. Gene was continuously answering the telephone (a job faux-paux), but for some reason this exchange sounded different. From across the room, Meg could hear the battering. A professional, no matter how angry, would never berate a medical director so obnoxiously over the phone. The conversation had to be personal.

Upon Gene's return, the silence was impenetrable. Meg passed over a couple of napkins pretending not to notice. Finally he sighed and erected a half-hearted smile. "Well, that's that. Cat's out of the bag."

"What do you mean?"

"About us."

"Who was that?"

"Jillian."

"Uh, oh."

Gene shrugged. "She knew I'd have to start dating sooner or later, but well," Gene pressed another smile, "now she knows."

The afternoon soured after that. Gene promised to call and Meg tried to remain positive, but their departure felt permanent somehow. For the first time Gene didn't wave when he drove off. He just climbed in the car, flipped the switch, and hauled ass.

*

Two weeks pass with no text messages and zero phone calls. Meg puts on a pretty convincing act for herself that it doesn't matter, that it has always been a simple friendship and nothing more. Gene has issues, afterall. *Huge* issues. Meg reassures herself that she doesn't need a man with *that* kind of baggage in her life. That it's better this way. Besides, on-the-job relationships rarely work out. *What's that saying? Don't shit where you eat?*

Then comes that tiny inside voice. That pain in the ass whine that never quits. *But twenty-seven dates?*

Meg has never been to Gene's house or vice versa. They had always met out in public. Up until

Subway, Meg never gave it much thought. Now, she can't help but wonder it these actions weren't calculated. Meg is pretty certain that Gene's place is in some well-to-do neighborhood like *The Hills* or *Markham Village,* where Meg only ventures at Christmastime to check out the high end light shows. *How serious can our relationship be if he's never invited me to his house?*

That tiny voice. *Have you ever invited him to your place?*

Well...no.

She tries not to stew over the subject and focuses on the positive aspects of her life. Like yesterday, when Meg received written approval for a home loan. She had always wanted her own place, but tipping jobs rarely offered reasonable loan rates. Now, *finally*, it was time go house hunting! Technically, she had her heart is set on a town house, certain that paying a homeowners fee would be far more manageable than caring for a quarter-acre lot. *I'll plant a bucket garden on the back deck. That'll be my yard!*

Megs has been thumbing through real estate pamphlets and browsing neighborhoods for months, excited to start hunting, eager to choose. But the kerfuffle with Gene has put her in a serious funk. Meg can't seem to do anything but lay around the couch and click through movie channels.

Screw it! Clutching the stamped letter of approval, she rises from her sofa prison with renewed determination, rallying herself with an internal pep talk. *What is wrong with you, girl? Are you really falling sideways over a man? After all of your struggling? After years of tolerating pompous customers and condescending managers just to keep a beat-up roof over your daughter's head? Now, when you can actually qualify for a decent loan? Is one silly fool really worth souring a lifetime of dreams? Of course not! So get your stinking ass in the shower, put on some clothes and contact a realtor. It's time to go house hunting!*

The shower feels incredibly relaxing. With hot water drumming against her skin, Meg daydreams about amenities. *Spacious granite counter tops, a spare bedroom for Kam, a healthy-sized back porch. But what color scheme?* Tans? *No! Too apartment like.* Blues? *Ahh...maybe.* How about greens? *Definitely some emeralds and jades, maybe pale lime. Nice and soothing. Ooh, and a fire place!*

As Meg dries off and fluffs, she constructs a mental list, stopping only briefly to schedule an appointment with the first available real estate agent. *Two o'clock today? Perfect. I can definitely make it in one hour.* With no time to waste, Meg plunges in her closet and pulls out a bright printed sheath dress and matching sandals. Suddenly in the mood to feel pretty, she rifles through her make-up bag in search of that magic touch. *You're gorgeous! That's right....shoulders back.*

Time has run out. She's got eighteen minutes to get Downtown. Meg reaches for her keys, purse, and the realtor magazine that she's marked with possibilities. Deep in thought, she rushes the front door and flings it open.

Gene Kassel is standing on her stoop, his arm in knocking position.

Meghan yelps.

Gene jumps.

Nervous laughter follows.

"Gene...oh, hey. How did you *find* me?" Meg's tone sounds guarded and surprised.

"Ingrid. Ingrid gave me directions." Gene is gripping a bag of *Snoopy's* hotdogs. At a loss for words, he holds it out. "I brought lunch. Wanted to see if we could talk?" Abruptly, he drops the bag down to his side. "But...uh, by the looks of things...maybe you already have a lunch date. So, uh...I'll just go."

Meg catches her reflection in his sunglasses—definitely way too dressy for a simple trip to Target. It dawns on her that Gene thinks she has date. *Let him believe what he wants, the ass. Not calling for two weeks! What does he think I'm going to do? Wallow away on the couch, drowning my sorrows in a tub of ice-cream?*

The annoying tiny voice: *Isn't that what you've been doing?*

She recognizes it then, Gene's secret physician's façade. The same pressed smile and rigid stature practiced and executed during moments of professional duress, when he's struggling to keep cool. But his tone betrays him. After twenty seven different dates and hours of engaged conversation, Meg can read him. Her stomach flip-flops when she realizes. Gene Kassel is heartbroken.

Yeah...well, tough shit.

Annoying tiny voice again: *You're being a pompous fool, Meg.*

As he turns away, Meghan reaches out. "Wait. Don't go." Gene's skin feels hot. Radiating. "I...I've missed you."

He grins shyly. "Really?"

Meg sighs, resigned to honesty. "Yeah. Too much."

"Too much is good."

"So you say."

Dropping the Snoopy's bag, Gene turns suddenly and grips her in a burning tight hold, kissing her hard on the lips. He pauses and whispers urgently in her ear, "I've missed you, Megs. Too much. I dare say that I don't want to miss you anymore. I've been thinking a lot lately. About you. About Jillian. I've come to a conclusion."

Meg lowers her gaze, unsure. "What's that?"

Gene takes a finger and lifts her chin. He peers directly in her eyes and they seem to swallow her whole "I want to be close to you, Meghan Ford. Today. Tomorrow. Whenever you'll have me."

Flooded with emotion, Meg breathes deeply and whispers thickly into his ear. "How about now?"

Gene kisses her again, softly this time. Tenderly. Abruptly he sweeps her into his arms and carries her back across the threshold, his intentions made clear.

The uncertainty and angst of Meg's recent separation dissipates with each step. By the time Gene lays her on the bed and presses against her, she feels everything but despair.

Joy.

Anticipation.

Lust.

POOF!

Everything is as it should be.

Chapter 37

Seven p.m. shift change is always chaotic, especially on Friday the 13th during a full moon. Jamie arrives five minutes early, shimmies through the congested room and slumps into a shabby recliner hidden in the far corner. Immediately, she pulls out her phone and starts fiddling.

Jamie used to park front and center at the main table, always chatty and sociable, re-living frenzied shift moments and off day events. Now she avoided frank conversations and disassociated with crowds, forever fearful of being questioned about her looming trial. It was sad, really, how estranged she had become. All because of one off decision.

Betty, the lawyer, made repeated attempts at convincing her that when the trial was over, no matter what the outcome, she could chalk it up as a learning experience; reporting that it would make her a better nurse. *Yeah, right.* In Jamie's very personal and hostile opinion, being on the wrong end of the legal process sucked horse shit. If she could rewind time and switch career paths, she would have most certainly opted out. *I should've been a florist!*

Her thoughts are disrupted when Elaine Mattern, day charge nurse extraordinaire, breezes into the lounge gripping a list of penciled-in assignments. "Welcome Night Staffers and Day Staffers and Mini-shifters. It's Friday. Hope ya'll are wearing your big-girl panties because it's a shit show out there. "

Confused, Victoria the float nurse asks, "Are you working the over night, Elaine? That's odd. What did I miss?"

"You missed the fact that tonight our sweet little golden child, Serena Grady, is getting married."

"You're *kidding!*" Victoria's eyes go wide. "The *virgin* has finally settled?"

The room erupts with laughter.

Mary Catherine pipes in, "Serena Grady did *not* settle."

"Oh, come *on!*" Victoria retaliates. "You're telling me that she's landed a virgin that's never drank or smoked; a man that would rather pass out food at a soup kitchen than lounge in the comforts of his own home, scratching his balls and watching Sports Center?"

"She sure did." Lee comments, shaking her head. "By the way, Vic. You're shit ain't right. "

Victoria giggles. "*Tell me.* I'm serious. Where did she *find* such a pure bred? Mail order?"

"For your information," Elaine cuts in sarcastically, amused and yet clearly ready to get back to work. "Serena is marrying a pastor."

Victoria gasps and immediately cackles. "Now that makes *way* too much sense!"

"It definitely does." Maria says.

"Wonder why I didn't get invited?"

"Tormenting the poor girl with your personal tips about mastering the perfect blow job, Victoria," Bev replies, "probably didn't help."

Again the room explodes and Elaine cat whistles to calm everyone down. "Settle in folks. We've got work to do. First, I'd like to thank Jamie and Bev for picking up the overnight. The two of you and the Blow Job Queen," Elaine points an exaggerated thumb in Victoria's direction, "will join Amanda in B-bay. If, in the tiniest of slightest chances, patient flow diminishes, I will try and shut down the bay and send ya'll home.

"The Manila Mafia will take over A-bay. Lee: fourteen, fifteen and twenty five. Mylene: sixteen, seventeen, and eighteen. Maria: nineteen, twenty, and twenty-one. Pauline: twenty two, twenty three and twenty four. Figure with it being a full moon and all, I'll want the Peace Keepers together."

"Who are the docs?" Maria asks.

"Dr. Rodriguez has B-bay and Dr. Kassel will take over A-bay at eleven o'clock. We've got the Candy Man until then, and tonight's clientele have him in rare form."

"Candy Man!" They all chant. (Side note: Generally speaking, physicians that pass out narcotics ever so freely usually acquire the nickname *Candy Man*. In the case of Dr. Channon, it is the exact opposite. He doesn't tolerate seekers and manipulators very well, and refuses to succumb to their continuous whining and begging. The reason Channon has been renamed the *Candy Man* actually has nothing to do with narcotics, and everything to do with his sweet tooth. Staff can always tell when Channon is on the clock by the scattered movie-size boxes of *Sweet Tarts* and *Gobstoppers* surrounding his work station.)

"The full moon has the department bursting with psych holds, chronic painers and total freaks." Elaine shakes her head. "The Candy Man has pissed them all off and I dare say, ladies," Charge is now speaking directly to the Filipinos, "it will most certainly become your personal problems."

Pauline pump fists the air. "I love a full moon!"

"*WHOOP! WHOOP! WHOOP!*" The staff chants sarcastically.

"As for triage, Mary Catherine will join Jeanne until eleven. When M. C. goes home, I'll cover second triage, float, and act as Meg's resource."

"Resource?" Meg questions. "For what?"

"It's time to get your feet wet, my dear." Elaine winks. "Tonight, you train for charge."

Meg's eyes go wide. "But...I'm not *ready*."

Lee playfully slaps her on the back. "Who ever is?"

"OKEY DOKE. LET'S GO PEOPLE." Elaine barks. "It's party time."

*

As the staff trickles out of the cramped meeting area, Jamie makes a beeline for the manager's office, practically knocking over Tina Page as she rounds the corner. Tina yelps. "Whoa! Slow down, girl, before you kill someone."

Jamie spews a heartless apology and pushes past, determined to catch up with administration before they've gone for the day. Boy, is she bent! Absolutely *seething! What the fuck is management thinking letting Meg train for charge? What about me? I've been ER nursing longer than her! Two solid years longer!*

Charge nurses at Dixon Valley are like legends. The same few people have monopolized the job for years. However, with Josh transitioning to flight nurse and Angela accepting a clinician's role, rumors have been circulating about perspective trainees. Jamie is next on the totem pole. *It should be me training for the position, not the fucking waitress.*

So what if her game was a little off? Nobody knew about her deadly mistake except Lashon, whom, by the way, had transferred to Same Day Surgery. Half the staff hadn't even worked here during the code kerfuffle. No matter. In Jamie's very self-absorbed opinion, she is definitely *way* more qualified than Meghan friggin' Ford.

It's because the bitch is screwing Kassel. That's why she jumped line. The couple went public, when? Yesterday? A week tops. *BAM*! And looky there,

Meg-the-waitress, *you do know that she's dating Dr. Kassel*, is getting trained for charge! *She's so sweet. So nice. She totally deserves it!* Unbe-fucking-lievable.

Jamie bangs on the nurse manager's door. *She better be in!*

Sure enough, Winnie is planted at the computer, coffee in hand, catching up on emails. "Hey, Jamie." Waving her in, she says, "Have a seat." As always, the manager's tone conveys relaxed. Rumor has it that even when she fires folks, or writes people up, Winnie does it so calmly that people sign the detrimental paper work with a smile.

Today Jamie isn't going to let Winnie's positive attitude slow her down. She nods smugly, drops abruptly into a chair, and unleashes. "I have been working in this hospital for a long time, Winnie. A long time! In the ER and before that, up on the floor. I'm next in line for charge! I'm sure of it. And I definitely deserve to train before the friggin' waitre..." Jamie catches herself. "...before anyone else."

"Of course we're going to train you." Winnie's replies promptly.

Jamie halts. "You...you are?"

"Yes, ma'am. I'm pretty sure we already had this discussion, at your annual review. Don't you remember?"

Winnie's response catches Jamie off guard. She stutters. "Then why is Meghan training today and not me?" *It's because she's banging a doctor, isn't it?*

Winnie reaches over and touches her sleeve. "I sensed that your hands were full, with the trial and all. The director and I figured it'd be best to let you get through court before tackling another project."

Court. Just thinking about it made Jamie's stomach lurch. *The goddamn trial.*

"Have they set a date yet?"

Jamie pulls back and crosses her arms. "They keep saying next month. Just when I build up my guts to go through with it, they delay again. I'm at my wits end. I want this crap *over*."

"You're not the only one." Winnie shakes her head. "Half a dozen staff members are going through the same thing. Sandee Jean, Tina, Bev, Dr. Bennet...everyone on the chart has been deposed. They're all stressed."

Yeah, but none of them pushed a life ending medication.

"The process affects each of us differently," Winnie continues, "but I dare say it has affected you the worst."

Jamie's eyes fill. She bites her lip to keep from trembling. "What if...what if I made a mistake?" Jamie pauses thinking now is her chance to fess up. "And didn't realize? What if they nail me at trial?"

Winnie shakes her head. "Jamie, Jamie, Jamie...you tried to *help* her. Your *intent*, when you walked into that room, was to *do no harm*. That is the Standard of Care. Did you abide by that practice?"

Jamie's voice is a whisper. "I tried to."

"Then stop second guessing yourself. Whatever happened on that tragic afternoon, it wasn't an act of malice. Trial is always horrific, but let that thought keep you steady while you're taking the stand. Your intent was to *help*."

Jamie shrugs.

"I don't think you realize, but the lawyers have interviewed over a dozen of your colleagues questioning your skills and character. You should read their testimonials. How you're their "go-to-girl" for tough IV sticks; the nurse you hope shows up during a deteriorating situation. One reported that you were self-motivated and tough as nails. The best one,"

Winnie grins, "is the letter administration received a few weeks back boasting your compassion. Haven't you been reading your emails?

Jamie shakes her head. "Uh, not as often as I should, I guess."

"Let me just say that when Rita Robertson takes the time to type up a very cohesive and endearing letter about a nurse's extraordinary bedside manner, it's hard *not* to be impressed."

"Rita?"

"The Crohn's Lady, whom, for the record, has sent Mr. Scott so many notices of complaint over the years that the two are on a first name basis. Never, and I mean NEVER, has Robertson forwarded a single pleasant report. Mr. Scott was so ridiculously shocked, so enthralled, he cart-wheeled down the hall and practically kicked in my door to report the news. He kept talking about framing the damned thing, and truthfully, I couldn't tell if he was kidding."

Jamie cuts in. "She called me Nurse Uppity."

"Who?"

"The Crohn's Lady."

Winnie chuckles. "You must have done something right to make Mr. Scott attempt acrobatics."

Jamie's eyes well up. "The deposition...this court business...has weakened me."

"Trial is a humbling experience. Trust me, I've been there. You feel weak now but in years to come the experience will transform into a valuable lesson. Like that song, *what doesn't kill you makes you stronger...*"

"That's what my lawyer keeps saying."

"Remember, every practicing caregiver in the world is on your side. Trial can happen to any one of us at any given time."

"I guess so."

"So get through it," Winnie nods reassuringly. "When it's over we'll train you for charge. Now tuck in your big girl panties, toughen up, and resurrect that confident nurse from deep within."

Jamie sighs, flicks a weary military salute and turns on a heel.

Chapter 38

I wake up to the sound of drums. Again.

From my closet position, lodged sideways under a mop bucket, I hear a muffled radio call. Still gripping my water bottle of moonshine, I stumble out the cramped space forgetting, once again, about my ghost-like abilities. I trip over a broom and slam into the opposing wall, the mop bucket wedging the door ajar. Nobody notices. The department is in chaos. I move slowly, hugging the wall, attempting to recall my last train of thought before checking into la-la land. It's pointless. My memory is toast.

Nobody appears too stressed in B-bay, although every curtain is drawn and door closed—a telltale sign of a full house. I turn the corner and the atmosphere changes. A-bay transitions into what feels like one giant psych hold. Buzzers are blaring, one chick is screaming "ASSHOLES...FUCKING *ASSHOLES*" from her doorway. Another dude is whining into his phone to someone named Yvonne, promising change and permanent employment.

Lee and Pauline are holed up in room fifteen, catheterizing an old woman who tripped in her driveway while checking the mail (at ten p.m. in pitch black). The woman's femur is completely snapped, tenting the skin above her right knee. She, too, is screaming hysterically, from pain and need to urinate, although her more warranted cries are far less irritating.

Maria, Mylene, Dr. Channon, and Deb, from respiratory, are zipping around room nineteen tubing an unresponsive female found guppy breathing in the bathroom of *The Southern Delight*, a gentleman's club located just off Highway 51. Mary Catherine is helping settle Maria's other sick patient, in room twenty, a man who is shitting blood like most people piss urine. I hear Mary Catherine's comment as I pass. "Ingesting cleaning solution can have this effect on your bowels, sir. Drinking bleach is definitely not the smartest way to get the attention of your ex-wife, or the least painful. Maybe next time try sending flowers…"

Elaine drives a stretcher right through me as I turn the bend, wheeling some blood-spattered papa with an impressive head gash over to get his noggin' scanned. By the looks of her flip-flop patterned work shirt, I deduct that it's most likely summer. Checking a calendar over the secretary's desk, I verify. It's Friday June 13th. A circle symbol in the lower corner of the thirteen box causes me to cringe. Friday the thirteenth…*and* a full moon!

Meghan Ford takes the corner at a run. She appears determined, so I follow. She signals Jamie, who is cutting through the B-bay carrying a bag of IV fluids. "There's an EMS coming into ten, five minutes out. Fifty-something female knocking on random doors, exhibiting belligerent and erratic behavior at the local trailer park."

"Trailer park?" Jamie groans, rolling her eyes. She hollers over to Dr. Rodriguez who is perched at the computer. "Hey, Doc. Your BFF is on her way. She must've caught wind that you were working tonight."

Rodriguez shakes her head. "Poor Geraldyne. Will she ever behave?"

*

"I wonder why she likes you so much, Doctor?" Victoria asks, before the crew heads into the room.

Rodriguez shrugs. "She works at the convenient store near my house." "Really?" Bev says. "I always thought she met you here."

"That's when we had our first conversation, but I think she probably recognized me from working at the 7-11. Last year, the gas pumps were down so I went inside to pay. Sure enough, old Geri Mae was manning the register."

"Did she recognize you?"

"At first, I wasn't sure. I never single out patients in public because of confidentiality issues. I played dumb and ordered twenty bucks on Pump One. Of course I over shot by a penny and returned to pay. That's when Geri held up a coin and waved me off. *No worries, Doctor,* she said. *I got you covered.* She knew it was me the whole time."

"Did you switch gas stations?"

Rodriguez smiles. "Nope."

*

Geraldyne arrives in her usual freak-out attire. She's wearing another platinum blond wig, *Marilyn Style*, a polka-dot shirt, a scarf tied around her neck, pencil legged jeans and saddle shoes. The outfit is cute enough in a early fifties way; and I flash a visual of Geri Mae prancing away from her apartment, clip purse in hand, dolled up and on a mission. But the full moon has taken a toll. Geri's wig lies slightly askew, mashed up to one side. Eyeliner is leaking down both eyes prompting a visual of a rabid raccoon, and bright fuchsia lipstick is smeared haphazardly over weathered lips. Tragically, disheveled Geri presents better than usual.

For a change, she isn't strapped down in four point restraints. A young paramedic with an easy smile proudly reports that he coerced Miss Dixon into trading her half-bottle of Mad Dog for a shot of Haldol. Instead of a dramatic screaming rant about Joey and a missing diaper bag, Geri is belting out a throaty mixed-up version of Loretta Lynn's song, *Crazy*.

"Craaazzzy...Crazy for feeling so pho-NEEY...crazy for wanting to scaa-REWW..." Without further ado, Geri slides off the gurney, kicks her saddle shoes wide apart, plants a hand on each knee and starts butt-rolling to another set of hacked vocals. Mimicking the rhythm *Crazy In Love,* by Beyonce', she sings, *"Got me hooking so crazy right now...love's got me looking so...Uh oh Uh oh Uh oh I am a ho!"* before repositioning on the hospital stretcher. She finishes with a snatch of Van Morrison's ballad, *Crazy Love,* in vaudeville fashion...*"HE GIVES ME LOVE, LOVE, LOVE, LO-UUV CRAZZEEEYYY...yeah, whatever."*

Bev and Victoria clap enthusiastically. Geri giggles and continues to hum as the nurses take vital signs and help her undress. She puts up little resistance even as they remove all personal items from the room. "Just leave my goddamned lipstick," she hums. "A girl needs color you know."

Bev's is too tired to argue. The late night has taxed her exuberance. She passes over the tube and comments sarcastically. "Is there anything else I can get for you?"

"Yeah, I'll take a vodka tonic with a twist." Geraldyne cackles. When Bev frowns, she smacks at her. "Oh, forget it, doll. When can I see the doctor? And don't send me Dr. Hot Shot. I want Miss Eva."

"Who's Dr. *Hot Shot?*" Victoria asks.

"Kassel, baby. King-of-da-castle. King-of-da-castle." Geri chants like the dude in *Borat.* "You know, the good looking one."

Victoria grins deviously. "King of the *castle?* Ha! That's hys*terical!* He should be here any minute. Speaking of time, my four hour princess shift is *OVA!'"* Victoria playfully palms the ceiling. "Have fun drooling over the night doc, but I'm outta here."

"Oh, posh!" Geri is slurring now. The Haldol

has taken full affect. "Now that he'sssgot a girrffriend, he's no use to me."

"*Girlfriend?*" Victoria shrieks. "Kassel's got a *girlfriend?* How would *you* know?"

Geri's eyes go wide. "My *GOD,* girl! How do you NOT know? A fool could pick up on that sizzling heat. Besides, I saw the two of them at the Food Show last weekend *holding ha-aands.*" Geraldyne's voice rings singsong before abruptly flicking her wrist as if to shoo off an imaginary fly. "The King is dead to me. Bring on Rodriguez."

Chapter 39

Geraldyne Dixon...that's it. That's what I'm supposed to remember. It dawns on me as I watch the scene play out from the doorway of room ten. Acutely aware of her supernatural abilities, I don't want Geri to see me yet, absolutely certain that showing myself prematurely will only aggravate her situation. (For the record, I find it strangely coincidental that I wake up at *exactly* the same time Geri's EMS call penetrates the radio. Pondering these thoughts, I wait for Victoria and Bev to exit the area.)

Geri is attempting another application of lipstick when I enter. Bev has refused to let her keep the compact seeing it has a glass mirror and can potentially be used as a weapon, so Geraldyne is relying on her reflection in the darkened window to beautify. I stand directly behind her and, once again, notice both reflections. Our conversation proceeds through the glass.

"Great." Geri rolls her eyes. "You again."

"Ah! So you *can* see me."

"Because I'm *crazy*. Thanks for the reminder. It does wonders for the self-esteem." Geri rolls her eyes. "Now skedaddle. My friend is coming to see me and I don't want the visit spoiled."

"I need your help." It dawns on me that Geri isn't nearly as smashed as usual. Sure she has a buzz, but it's most likely Haldol induced. When the nurses depart, Geri's posture shifts. Her actions become deliberate. Kind of like...*the curtain has closed, time to relax.*

Geri marches over to the sink and, with her back

to me, starts washing up. When I refuse to leave, she sighs and says, "I *told* you. This is a *social* visit. Why don't you and that ridiculous Indian just back off for once."

My jaw drops. "Indian? Is there *really* an Indian?"

"Yeah. Actually. If it's not you then it's him, banging those friggin' drums. Is there no *end* to you people?"

"I thought the banging was the tube system?"

"Think again, sister. Worst part, Indie never speaks which is really irritating. He just jumps around, waving his arms and pointing, like in a bad game of charades. That reminds me, he has a message for you."

"Me?"

"Yeah, you. If I got his mime act right, he wants you to lay off the bottle. Says he's sick of picking up your slack. Every time you get hammered he has to pull shift. His final words...*Sober up.*"

"You got all that from charades?"

"Not an easy task, I'd like to add. I kept shouting out phrases and he'd shake his head, hold up two fingers, and then flap around with another clue. Nurses kept coming in and pumping me full of drugs, thought I was hallucinating. I slept for two solid days after that and woke up in the crazy house, which was fine by me. The Indian can't leave his burial ground."

"That...is so...*crazy*. I didn't know. I've never seen him."

"Aren't you *listening*? He only shows up when you're slacking. He's the *back up* guy."

"I heard you, but still." I pause. "I wonder if it's like this at every hospital. How about the sanitarium? Any ghosts at the crazy house?"

Geri nods. "Charlene Kopowski. She's an ex-psychiatrist, but I don't thinks she's trapped like the

Indian. Charlene's in love with some homeless dude named Ned, an ex-patient of hers. She seeks me out whenever he's committed and begs me to relay messages." Geraldyne shrugs. "Charlene's always good for a cigarette or two. Oh yeah, I almost forgot; the Indian gave me a second message."

"What's that?"

"If I did what he said, you're supposed to give me a drink."

"Is that right?"

"Nah, I'm just fucking with you," Geri cackles. "But I'm gonna need a cocktail soon if you want to continue this banter. I'm sobering up."

"So?'

"So, when I'm sober I can't see you." Geri winks. "You're starting to fade."

I can't tell if she's messing with me so I play it cool. "I'll tell you what, Miss Dixon. I'll get you a drink if you promise to help me."

Licking her lips, Geri eyes me suspiciously. "Help you with what?"

"I need you to…"

Geri halts me with a twitch of the finger. "Cocktails first, doll. I want to see a ghost pull off an alcoholic beverage in the middle of an emergency department. Take your time, sister. My favorite doctor is on her way in and I don't want my visit spoiled with your hovering."

Ten minutes after I serve up Geri's cocktail, Jamie marches into the room. Jamie has cared for Miss Dixon on multiple occasions, but treats her indifferently. Geri is sitting on the bed sipping *Cranberry Surprise,* completely naked, wrapped in a sheet, gown strewn across the floor.

"Hello. My name is Jamie and I will be your nurse today. I need to get some blood and urine

A.S.A.P."

"Where's my doctor friend?"

"She's detained at the moment by an actual *sick* patient."

Geri's brow furrows as she sips my mixture. "Oh, posh!"

"This isn't cocktail hour, Geri." Jamie adds. "It's an emergency room."

"Says you."

"I'll be back in five with my supplies and I expect you to be *wearing* the gown."

"The gown doesn't match my lipstick."

"Nothing matches that lipstick, Geri." The nurse turns on a heel. "For the record, fluorescent pink has been out since 1985."

"For the *record*," Geri rebuts, "it's FUSCIA!"

*

As Jamie heads out the door I have an epiphany. I can kill two birds with one stone! Redirecting my attention to beat-up Marilyn, I say, "Geri! Geri, pay attention! Listen to me. *She's* the girl." I insist. "Relay my message to Jamie."

"That...that color blind *bitch*?" Geri snaps. "Fine. As long as I can be mean."

"You can't be mean *or* nasty. That's the most important part. You need to be genuine."

"That, my ghost friend, is going to cost you another drink." Geri holds up the cranberry juice laced moonshine. "This shit's pretty tasty."

"You can have the rest of the bottle but this is serious, Geri. Stick with me."

"Deal...*hiccup*..." Geri replies. "Whatever you sa...*hiccup*...ay. Damn! I got the hic...*hiccup*...cups."

I can hear squeaking wheels from the IV cart. Jamie is right outside the door. Time is limited. My initial intentions were to exact my life name and get the hell out of Dodge. But when Jamie enters, I am reminded of the lesson preached by Deloris, the ghost administrator, about *doing everything right*.

"Tell Jamie that my death wasn't her fault." Forgetting my original intentions, I blurt. "The Epi didn't matter. *Tell her*. It was my day to die."

Geri's jaw goes slack. "Who the hell is Ep...*hiccup*...i? Oh, my gosh, I need wat..*hiccup*...er. I can't stand these hicc...*hiccup*...ups."

"Not *who*! EPI...Epinephrine! It's a medicine. Jamie thinks she killed me."

"Epineph...*hiccup*...rine?" Geri repeats.

Jamie enters. "What's with you?"

"Water. I need water for these...*hiccup*...sss."

"After, Geri." Jamie cuts her off. "Let's draw your blood."

"You really don't like my lipstick? I think that's the first time...*hiccup*..."

FOCUS GERALDYN! TELL HER NOW BEFORE YOU FORGET.

Geri glares at me through the mirror. "Fine."

NOW!

"Who are you talking to, Geri?" Jamie grins. "Is it the Indian?"

"No. It's that nurse you killed but not really. She...*hiccup*...'s been tormenting me, and she's like a total pain in the ass."

"What?"

"GL...*hic*...LORI...*cup*...A."

Jamie blanches. Her voice a whisper. "*Who*?"

"The nurse. She's got a mes....*hiccup*...sage for you. Epi...yeah, him. He didn't matter. It was her day...*hiccup*...her day to die." Geri turns to me. "Happy now?" Switching gears, she says to Jamie. "If pink is so offensive then what lipstick color *should* I be wearing?"

Jamie's face shimmers a blazing yellow. Fear. "What…what did you say?"

"I said," Geri huffs dramatically. "What's so terrible about *fuchsia*?"

"No, no, no… Before that?"

"Oh, *that*. Sorry." Geri waves a finger and replies in a singsong tone. "No more messages until I get my second *dri-innkkk*…"

"How do *you* know about the Epi?" Jamie growls. "Nobody knows! Nobody, except…."

TELL HER TO CONFESS. IT'LL SETTLE HER SOUL.

Geri turns to me and frowns. "Yeah, sure it will. That's exactly what I *wouldn't* do." Back to Jamie she says, "Every time I admit to hearing voices, they throw me in the funny farm. Keep your trap shut. Don't confess shit."

YOU'RE NOT HELPING, GERI! Then I add. *I'M GONNA DUMP THE BOOZE.*

"Alright, already!" Geri rolls her eyes and redirects to Jamie. "The ghost wants you to fess us. Tell the tru…*hiccup*…th and settle your soul." Geri pauses and holds up a finger. "Although, I'm not too sure I agree with that last statement. Settling the soul…*hiccup*… is *very* tricky business."

SHUT IT, GERI.

"Fine. But that's two you owe me, ghosty." Geri winks. "And now…Jamie, is it? Back to more urgent matters. My spring lipstick color."

Geraldyne's voice falls on a deaf ear. The nurse has gone.

Chapter 40

"Okay, Meghan, it's one a.m. Let's you and me huddle." Elaine says, after delivering yet another admission to the floor. "Everyone else is too darn busy. So," she pauses, "how does it feel to take charge? You seem very much in your element."

Meg smirks. "Feels like I'm back in the steak house and everyone expects a free dessert."

"Nail on the head, sister. A full moon always promises an entourage of insufferable whiners, but I dare say so does any given Monday so let's not dawdle on the obvious. What's the game plan? Enlighten me on your assignment specifics."

"As you can see, we're running a full court press in A-bay." Meg begins. "Maria is trapped with the intubated patient in nineteen, who keeps trying to yank out her breathing tube. Pauline is changing the umpteenth bloody diaper on bleach man who, by the way, is also getting a blood transfusion. Mylene and Kassel just dumped ASSHOLE chick in four-point restraints after she tried gnawing off the doctor's finger. Surgery finally picked up Lee's femur fracture so she's been floating, helping me contain everyone else. We've got four psych holds and only two sitters, so I've rearranged them to be next to each other. It's the best I can do."

"What about B-bay? Are you planning to close it?"

"Nope. Shot that down when Dixon showed up. A-bay can't handle another psych hold. Thankfully, she's better than usual so Geri will have to go without a sitter. Amanda and Victoria clocked out at eleven so I systematically closed off rooms as their patients departed. Bev and Jamie will have to hold down the fort until B-bay empties, or seven a.m., which ever comes first. I've already broken the news."

"Good for you, Megs." Elaine says. "Most newbies feel bad about retracting promises, but there are no guarantees of a short shift in the emergency department. What else?"

"The waiting room has finally cleared and I'm about to send Jeanne to lunch. Maybe you can relieve Maria? I'll bet she's ready for a break."

"Controlled chaos," Elaine smiles and punches her lightly in the arm. "Good job, girl. Remember, it could always be worse..."

Elaine's comment is cut off by the hospital-wide intercom.

...*ATTENTION, ATTENTION! CODE BLUE. ROOM 384...*

...*ATTENTION, ATTENTION! CODE BLUE. ROOM 384...*

Meg groans, "Murphy's Law. You spoke too soon."

"Screw Murphy," Elaine huffs. "Get the med box and meet me upstairs. I'll run ahead with Rodriguez."

"Do we both need to go?"

"Training is by the book, sister. Charge goes to all codes and technically, I don't exist. It's important to understand how far you get stretched. Now hustle. Remember, time is muscle."

Meg shouts over to the triage nurse as she heads for the med room. "Cover me, Jeanne. Elaine and I are going with Rodriguez to the code."

As Meg races through B-bay, Geraldyne Dixon's voice booms from ten's doorway. "PARTY IN ROOM 384!"

Chapter 41

I follow Jamie into the bathroom. She is flaming yellow and shaking so badly I have to grab her in a bear hug, squeeze tightly and shout directly in her ear. *CONTAIN YOURSELF, JAMIE. GET A GRIP.*

She continues sniveling as I persecute myself for being so stupid. My translated confession has made the situation ten times worse. Nurse Jamie has come absolutely and completely unhinged.

She stands in front of the sink, smacking her face, drenching it, mumbling hysterically to her reflection in the mirror. "I'm crazy as a shit bird! I need to see a doctor. I need *medication.*"

YOU ARE NOT CRAZY! I slap her face.

Jamie pauses as if sensing the invisible sting. Her eyes narrow and she points a trembling finger at her image. "You are NOT crazy." More hysteria. "Then why are you SCOLDING a mirror!"

STOP FEELING SORRY FOR YOURSELF. IT'S WASTED ENERGY. FIX THE PROBLEM. STOP THIS MADNESS.

Jamie is hyperventilating now. She suddenly halts and points a second determined finger. "Stop feeling sorry for yourself! It's wasted energy. You need to fix the problem." Jamie grips the side of the sink and shakes her head. "I can't confess."

YOU CAN.

"I can't."

YOU CAN.

Jamie's excessive head shaking transforms into slow determined nods. "I can." She takes another deep gulping breath, her body pulling out of the hunched position, rising to full height. "I definitely can."

From up above, the hospital intercom sounds.

...ATTENTION, ATTENTION...CODE BLUE...ROOM 384...

...ATTENTION, ATTENTION...CODE BLUE...ROOM 384...

*

Code Blue. *Great*. Jamie digs around her fanny pack, pulls out a tiny bottle of *Visine* and flushes both eyes. She needs to get back on the floor *without* the inquiries. Red eyes and blotchy skin always cause a commotion. *The fools*. Nobody gets that it's best to leave a teary-eyed person alone. Discussing an incident prematurely will only resurface the drama.

Thankfully, she's in B-bay with Bev Martin. Jamie can only imagine Neanderthal's response to Geri's statement. *A bunch of malarkey! Geri has got you boo-hooing like an imbecile. Did you forget the part that she's 'Coo-coo for Co-Co Puffs?'*

Trapped in thought, Jamie turns the corner and runs smack into Dr. Kassel. He's standing beside the staff fridge chugging a four-ounce container of orange juice.

"Woah! Nurse Baxter. What's the rush?" The medical director smiles and leans to the side so she can pass.

"Oh...errr...why aren't you at the code?"

"Rodriguez went."

Jamie's knees suddenly wobble and her arms feel like lead.

"I've been dying of thirst for two hours," Kassel continues, and then pauses. "Hey, are you okay? You look...I don't know...pale."

"It's nothing. I need to get back." Jamie passes him and then stops short. *Now is your chance!* Without facing him, she says, "I need to tell you something, sir. Something work related. Something bad."

"Rest assure, there is nothing we can't get through together."

"I don't know about that."

Kassel smiles easily. His demeanor has always been respectful and kind. "Tell me, Jamie. What's on your mind?"

"It's…uh…about the code."

"The code upstairs?"

"Uh…no, the other one. The court case."

Their eyes meet and Kassel flushes as if the subject embarrasses him. "Yes, well, it still may not happen, Jamie. I'm trying to shut it down. You know I am. It's just…trial is a horrible thing."

"It's not the trial," she whispers. "It's worse."

Dr. Kassel's mouth draws thin. "Okay, then, tell me. What is it?"

"I think….I mean, I *know*…" Jamie coughs and her eyes sting. "I mean I'm absolutely *positive* that I…I pushed the Epi."

"It was a code, Jamie. That's what you were supposed to do."

"No. I pushed the zero point three milligram Epi. I caused the heart attack. I…I didn't even do it on accident because I thought I was *supposed* to push it. Her tongue was so BIG! Her skin was turning blue. I knew she needed the medicine fast. I *thought* I was doing the right thing. But…I learned later…only *after* my deposition did I realize… I had no IDEA I did anything wrong!"

Terror flashes in Kassel's eyes and his body goes momentarily rigid. He catches himself and settles into his practiced role as levelheaded administrator. "Jamie… Jamie… Stop."

The nurse is on a roll now, blubbering like an

idiot. "I met with the lawyers and answered so confidently. Everything I said was a lie. It was me. I *killed* her."

Kassel drops the façade and pulls her close. Jamie collapses into hysterics and the director whispers quietly in her ear. "She's never coming back, Jamie, no matter what you think you did. No matter how much we question our actions. *You* need... *I* need... *We* need to let it go. But, I want you to hear me out on this. It's important."

Jamie retreats, hugging herself. "Yeah?"

"The airway. Her airway was never secured. Autopsy reports showed that anesthesia's tube had completely perforated the trachea. No matter what you think you did, she died from lack of oxygen."

"*Secondary* to my Epi causing heart attack."

Kassel grips at his head and sighs sadly. "Everyone tried, Jamie. You tried. Bennet tried. We had the heart and soul of ten caregivers in that room, and yet... That's what quiets my nightmares. That's what keeps me sane. It's what makes this trial so absolutely unbearable. To think of the team's exhausting efforts, mentally and physically, only to be forced to succumb to such intolerable accusations from a bunch of pencil pushing lawyers and my very own... The situation sickens me. Medicine...it's not perfect. We're *human beings*.

"All you did, Jamie, in my professional and most personal opinion was try and help. And I...I want to *thank you* for trying." He clenches tightly onto Jamie's arms and faces her full on. "I never said thank you, did I? Well," Kassel huffs abruptly, "back then I was pretty lost. I...but *now*...now I want to *thank you*, Jamie. Thank you for trying."

Kassel's emotional response startles the nurse. So forthcoming with sentiment and gratitude, it both confuses and settles her somehow. Before Jamie has chance to respond, another overhead page goes off.

DOCTOR KASSEL ROOM THREE! STAT!

Kassel releases her and attempts a professional tone, but the façade has been shattered. He speaks now like a friend. "I'll call you tomorrow. We can talk. But now," Kassel sighs, "we need to worry about the living."

*

I watch the whole scene play out at an arm's breath. I'm pretty shocked when Jamie decides to confess to the medical director rather than the nurse manager, but what the hell. It's obvious that Kassel has kept close tabs on the case, and yet as we all three hustle over to check the commotion in B-bay, the good doctor's demeanor has shifted inward. He seems lost in thought.

So much for that new MRI machine, huh Gene? Guess will be paying off the family after all... I smile in spite of the situation. I know it sounds crazy, but for a change, I'm not stressing about my family and the anticipated blow they will be forced to endure by such a discovery. Or whether they will even comprehend what Kassel just admitted. My airway was never secured. Nobody survives without an airway, no matter how much medicine was administered incorrectly. I was a cooked bird. The ticket for Soul 674 had expired.

In all honesty, I'm smiling for the bitch. You know what? I don't even want to call her that anymore. Jamie really isn't that much of a bitch. Behind closed doors, within the secrets of the curtain, her humanitarian efforts have come to surprise me.

I'll never forget that night she offered a homeless guy a shower. (Try that in an ER with zero showering facilities.) It was a rainy, muddy November

Eve. The man lay shivering and dirty, chilled to the bone in soiled damp clothes. Self initiated or not, it was crystal clear that life had not been kind to the pathetic soul of room fourteen. Normal ER standard of care for homeless patrons that showed up complaining of back pain or stomach pain or all of the above, seeking shelter from inclement weather, usually consisted of a blanket and a turkey sandwich. I had zero reason to believe that Bitch Jamie would alter this course...

...The ED was dead quiet that night. I can still hear Jamie's grumbling when Charge relayed the specifics of her newest assignment. She stormed off. Minutes later, Mr. Dirty Drawers was following her down the hall wearing nothing but a hospital gown, his hairy butt flashing with each stride. Jamie was carrying soap, towels and a rolled up bundle of clean clothes. (We have a donation closet specifically for the homeless.) I suspected that she was sending him into the bathroom to wash up in the sink. Then she surprised us all by dialing security and requesting keys to the ambulance bay. Sternly, she ordered Dirt Man to follow.

Dumbfounded, I watched as Jamie personally rearranged the Decon Room. (Every ER has a decontamination area for potential chemical hazards. In truth, the area is rarely utilized and proves more beneficial as an unofficial junk drawer.) It took about five minutes for Jamie to push everything to one side. She flipped the water switch and held a hand under the spouting water head, checking the temperature. Finally, Jamie cracked a smile. "You're in luck. It's hot." As she made her way to the exit she said, "Take your time, dude. There's no reason to hurry."

Respecting his privacy, I listened from the door to make sure he didn't fall. (Some things even ghosts don't need to see.) Soon enough, the man started scrubbing down. Then he began to hum. Eventually, he transitioned to singing. *"Scooby Dooby Doo, where are you? We got some work to do now... "*

I smile remembering the incident, thinking *miracles can come true.*
People can change.
Jamie Baxter does have a heart.

Chapter 42

As Kassel and Jamie hustle to room three, the overhead page is repeated. *KASSEL TO ROOM THREE. KASSEL TO ROOM THREE.*

Someone is screaming hysterically. (Side note: room three and four are separated by curtains so the area can be adjoined to form one giant space. This serves a great purpose during codes and deteriorating situations. Problem is there are no walls to suppress the noise.)

"OH MY GOD! DOUGLAS...*BABY*! BABY....DON'T *LEAVE* ME!"

As we enter the bay, Lee emerges from behind the drape with the screamer in tote, waltzing, practically dragging the frantic creature away to the family room. The woman is resistant until she discovers that the tiny waiting area is only paces away.

Kassel and Jamie flip the material and enter the madness. Jeanne is zipping about with a pair of cutting shears, removing a very expensive three-piece suit in a not so pretty fashion, ripping and cutting, prying to unclothe. Mylene is attempting to insert an IV and Bev is at the head of the bed, squeezing an ambu bag, forcing oxygen into the Smurf-colored patient laying glossy-eyed and limp on the stretcher.

Kassel jumps right in. "What do we know?"

Jeanne pipes up. "Heroine, sir."

Jamie doesn't wait for an order. She immediately fetches the crash cart, cracks it open, whips out the reversal agent for opiates, and pops the cap. (During this time, Jeanne continues to report.)

"According to his wife," Jeanne flips a thumb at

the curtain, "they stopped to drop off a tool on their way home from a dinner party."

"So late in the evening?" Kassel questions.

"Red flag number one," Jeanne nods. "Not five minutes after getting back in the car, he goes unresponsive."

"What's the certainty about heroine?"

"Because it's *Douglas*, sir. You know, Mr. Naked, jumping-on-the-bed? He loves all the bad stuff. PCP, heroine…"

Kassel frowns. "This is Douglas? In *that* suit?"

"Dr. Jekyll and Mr. Hyde," Jeanne says. "With his wife, he's a peach. With the girlfriend, a beast. I'm betting that "tool" delivery was a sneak visit to the girlybeast."

"Where's the EMS crew?"

Jeanne shakes her head. "No EMS. The missus pulled up to the front entrance. With help from Security and his wife, we dragged him out of the car. Thankfully, I ate my *Wheaties* today.

"Track marks up and down both arms," Mylene cuts in. "I've got a shitty line, Doc, but it flushes."

Kassel points to Jamie. "2mg of Narcan, please. IV."

As Jamie administers the reversal agent, Bev complains openly. "I knew I shouldn't have picked up this shift. Friday the friggin' thirteenth. Who gets married on Friday the friggin' thirteenth *during* a full moon? Once again, I'm reminded that no good deed goes unpunished."

A commotion breaks out on the other side of the curtain. Two strange voices erupt in hostile argument. One sounds very much like Peaches, the recently removed shrieking wife. The other…"

Jeanne rolls her eyes. "Great. Beastie just showed up."

"YOU! WHAT ARE *YOU* DOING HERE?"

"I'M HERE TO SEE MY *BOYFRIEND*!"

"AFTER PUMPING HIM FULL OF THE DEVIL'S JUICE? BE GONE, YOU *TRAMP*! YOU'VE RUINED OUR LIVES AND PRACTICALLY KILLED MY BABY!

Bev mumbles sarcastically to the crew. "That's right, blame the other woman. The problem couldn't possibly stem from her screwed up husband."

"HOW ABOUT YOU RUINIED *OUR* LIVES. DOUGIE LOVES ME! HE HATES EVERYTHING ABOUT YOU! ...'CEPT MAYBE YOUR MONEY AND YOUR COOKING, YOU...YOU STUPID FAT TWAT!"

Ouch.

Right then Jeanne points to a squiggling monitor. "Houston, we have a problem. Douglas just lost his pulse."

Mylene immediately jumps on Dougie's chest and starts CPR. Bev continues bagging the patient and Jamie prepares for imminent medication orders.

"Charge to 200 joules." Kassel barks. "Prepare to shock."

As Jeanne prepares the machine, the chick fight continues. A lot of F-bombs and slut inferences.

"CHARGING AT 200 JOULES." Jeanne announces. "Everyone steer clear of the bed...I'M CLEAR, YOU'RE CLEAR, WE'RE ALL CLEAR..."

The verbal skirmish intensifies. Lee's voice booms from just outside of the curtain. "Ladies, SHUT IT *DOWN*."

Lee focuses on Beastie, a hardened shell of a creature, tougher in mouth than body. This proves a fatal error. Peaches is in love, remember, and there is nothing in the world more dangerous than a pissed off spouse.

As Jeanne shouts *I'M CLEAR, YOU'RE CLEAR, WE'RE ALL CLEAR*, a barbaric roar simultaneously emanates from the pit of Missus Douglas as she charges the anorexic, heroine-addicted girlfriend. Her strong, corn fed bones slam into Beastie full force. Beastie goes airborne and smacks against the curtain, dislodging staff members working the code on the other side. It is at this exact moment that Jeanne unleashes 200 joules of electricity....

A crashing ZZAAPPP follows. The bed shifts and caregivers tumble.

"WHAT THE *HELL*?" Bev growls as she switches places with Mylene and continues CPR. "LEE!" Bev roars. "GET THOSE EVIL BITCHES OUT OF HERE BEFORE SOMEONE DIES."

Dazed, Jamie checks the perimeter. "It's okay....I think we're all okay. OH MY GOD!"

Everybody turns.

"WHAT? WHAT IS IT?" Bev says.

"Doctor Kassel. He's down."

*

(SIDE NOTE. Let's back up a minute to the beginning of this story. How I expressed the importance of not touching any part of a bed while a shock is being executed. Touch a zapped bed and get zapped yourself. In the case of the fat twat versus the skinny drug addict: When Beastie hits the curtain it is Dr. Kassel who takes the brunt of the slam, which causes him to fall into the stretcher. ZZAAPPPP!)

*

Jamie pounces on the doctor who is out cold and jams two fingers into his neck. His breathing is ragged and the pulse, "NO PULSE."

Everybody starts hollering at once, but Jamie cuts them off as she begins CPR on the floor. "Bev, you and Jeanne stick with the dumbass."

Jeanne shouts to Bev, "This guy is still in V-Tach."

"PREPARE TO SHOCK AGAIN." Bev retorts as she continues to pump on Dougie's chest. Jeanne is now in charge of bagging and working the monitor. (Charting, by the way, will have to be done by memory, until either nurse grows a third arm or someone else shows up.)

"LEE! Grab another defibrillator." Jamie orders. "AND HAVE THE SECRETARY CALL A HOSPTIAL WIDE CODE."

Mylene slaps the extra pacer pads stored on top of Douglas's crash cart on to Kassel's chest. She's working around Jamie's CPR while Kassel makes a strange sucking sound, turning purple at the same time. Seconds later, but what feels like eternity, Lee returns with a second defibrillator.

Jamie is in a zone. *The* Zone. The zone that sets her top priority to GET BACK THAT PULSE and KEEP THE PATIENT ALIVE. Like all emergency department nurses, she has been trained and retrained in Advance Cardiac Life Support (ACLS). She has taken and retaken tests, sat though hours of re-certifications and practice sessions, and has always been acutely aware of the faint but now certain possibility that if a physician is unavailable to run a code then it falls on the primary nurse. Today is that day. Today Jamie is Top Dog.

"CHARGE AT 200 JOULES."

Jamie and Lee lock eyes as Lee repeats the order, "CHARGING AT 200 JOULES."

If Jamie had time to think about it, to really wonder if it was such a great idea to take the lead, then maybe things would've gone differently. Frankly, taking full responsibility of a situation puts a health care worker in the line of fire. Any mishap, any tiny mistake, translates into meetings and inquiries up the ass, a full on assault by a bunch of suited administrators and lawyers who have already spent hours dissecting the chart in search of imperfections. If Jamie had time, if Jamie even for a second was reminded of her looming trial and her very recently torturous deposition, then maybe she would've chickened out.

But you know what?

She didn't.

You know why?

Because ER nurses don't have time to chicken out.

They only have time to act.

Chapter 43

As the Nurse Whisperer, I'd like to say that I had a lot to do with Jamie's resurrection. However, that was not the case. Jamie Baxter's determined and authoritative actions were all very much her own. Of course, initially, I had great intentions to assist. But that all changed the second Beastie slammed into the curtain.

I was on the outside with Lee and the cat fighters. Peaches was so bent that no amount of whispering was calming her down. When Beastie got hurled into the curtain, I could actually see the bed shift and hear everybody go flying. It reminded me of a Saturday Night Live skit, absolutely amusing in a sick ER sort of way. Until, of course, it was followed by Jamie's sobering announcement: *Dr. Kassel. He's down.*

*

Forgetting my ghost-like abilities, I flip the curtain. Nobody notices. Everyone is struggling to stand and get back to more imminent tasks. Jamie is kneeling next to the body, feeling for a pulse. Kassel's eyes are glazed over and he's staring at the ceiling. The very instant Jamie reports NO PULSE, his gaze shifts to the left. Our eyes meet...

Jamie immediately jumps on his chest and starts barking orders. But I just stand there, motionless. Alarmed. I stumble backwards, head spinning, heart in my throat. Everyone is racing about. Mylene is ripping off his shirt, slapping on pads. Jamie is calling orders. My head is in a bubble. My body is frozen.

A strange declining yelp releases from my dead

vocal cords as Lee zaps Dr. Kassel with a scorching 200 joules...

Kassel blinks.

"We've got a pulse." Lee reports.

There is more banter. More orders. Jamie is on a roll now. But I'm not listening. I'm trapped in my mind. Bombarded with vivid memories of...of...

I know who I am.

My name is *not* Gloria House.

It is Lori Kassel.

My husband is Gene Kassel.

We got married on Topsail Island, barefooted in the sand, the year Gene started medical school. Fourteen months later, I delivered a headstrong baby girl. Our daughter, Jillian Marie—*Jillian the lawyer.*

I don't care about any of that now. Not Jamie or blue Douglas, or the fact that my daughter is most likely suing Dixon Valley Hospital. I have eyes for only one person. As soon as the initial shock passes, I scramble over to where Gene is laying on the floor and kiss his forehead and lips and cheeks and anything I can touch. Rodriguez has returned, and after a moment of duress reclaims her role as Top Dog. The nurses shift Gene onto a backboard and lift him up on a stretcher. All I can manage are blubbery sobs and whispering endearments.

The room is exploding with action, but I fail to notice. Strangled with panic, I keep shifting my vision to the lift-and-fall of Gene's chest. *He's breathing. He's sleeping.* I climb onto the stretcher. Tears flow as my dead heart thumps frantically. My head is spinning and I clamp tightly to my rock of a husband in hopes of resolution. I need to stay level. Calm.

I whisper thickly into his ear. "I'm here, baby. I'm right here."

*

Time is strange in the in-between. Nurses keep prodding and checking Gene's pupils, running blood pressure checks every five minutes. I barely notice. I lay squeezed in next to him, Eskimo style, like the way he used to wake me up on cold Sunday mornings after working the late night. He'd lumber into bed like a big loving dog and wedge his body in so close that our noses touched.

Inhaling his intoxicating scent, a mix of men's Obsession and bodily sweat, I rub at his nose until Gene opens his eyes. It is the same sheepish half-lidded gaze I so fondly remember. He grins and says, "Hey, girl. Where have you been?"

My eyes sting. "I've been around."

"What's with the tears?"

"I was worried."

"Don't be." Gene's response is sluggish but sincere. I'm half shivering, half trembling, and Gene steadies me in strong arms. I weep quietly, cradled in his embrace. For the first time in forever, I naturally drift off to sleep.

*

"I'm here, baby. I'm right here."

"Hey, girl. Where have you been?"

"I've been around."

"What's with the tears?"

"I was worried."

"Don't be."

Déjà vu? I smile behind closed lids.

Then, to my horror, the conversation continues.

"Electrocuted and still telling jokes." A voice says. "Unreal."

My eyes shoot open. I'm still in the nose-to-nose position staring into Gene's half-lidded gaze, but he's looking straight through me. I'm invisible once again. The conversation, OUR conversation, Gene is having with another.

I go rigid and roll out of the bed, (right through the side rails). Scrambling to my feet, I seek out my predecessor who sits hunched and anxious at the bedside.

Meghan Ford.

A sense of helplessness consumes me. I'm jealous, heartbroken...and sadly comforted. A thousand emotions flicker though my dead synapses as I resist my final act to do what's right.

But, this is my husband!

No, Lori. Not anymore.

I suddenly remember my wedding vows. Gene's solid hands gripping mine. Me smiling. Gene grinning. Both of us trying not to laugh, thinking the final declaration is a bit over the top. *Until death do us part.*

Numbly, I turn and stumble from the room, unsure where to go and yet certain just the same. I force myself not to look back.

Chapter 44

Meghan's heart pounds up into her esophagus as she hugs herself. Less than an hour ago, she was on top of the world, determined and confident. Taking charge made her feel like a superhero. Unstoppable. Even as she raced off to the code, four flights up, she ran like a teenager. Taking the stairs two at a time, bounding through the corridors like an Olympian, she concentrated on the mission at hand—to save a life. *A little different from racing off for a side dish of creamed spinach!* Meghan thinks as she rounds the corner.

Unbelievably Meg continues to have waitressing nightmares. Hurrying anxiously down long winding roads, hot rolls in one hand and a water pitcher in the other, so worried that her customers will be upset. What amazes Meg is how rarely she dreams about nursing. Not even the really screwed up stuff like codes and near death situations, or, more specifically, the very recent hypoxic post-op patient in room 384. It was Meghan who pointed out the tracheal deviation, a sure sign of a collapsed lung. Dr. Rodriguez inserted a needle in the patient's chest wall, reversing thoracic pressure, which caused the lung to immediately re-expand. *SHAZAM.* Another saved life. Another win for the good guys.

The team was all patting each other on the back when they heard the overhead page. *ANY AVAILABLE DOCTOR TO THE EMERGENCY ROOM...STAT!*

You didn't hear that announcement very often, and Meg was ticking off the possibilities as she hustled back to the ED. With only one doctor available, there had to be an emergency involving more than one patient. Meg never expected…

When Meg flipped the curtain and found Gene on the stretcher, all of her nursing skills went out the window. She stumbled out into the hall, gasping. Suddenly light headed and dizzy, she slid to the floor.

"Put your head between your legs, Meg, and stay down until you feel better. We're out of stretchers for staff members." Maria winked as she rushed over with a plastic container of juice.

"Is he…is he going to be okay?"

"Right now his color looks better than yours. We're moving him to room five. Kassel's going to be fine."

"Can I stay with him?"

Maria smirked. "Lucky you. Tonight we've got a back up charge nurse."

*

Maria leads Meghan to a chair parked by Gene's bed. At first Meg is afraid to touch him. Her vision keeps shifting between his face and chest wall. *He's breathing. He's sleeping.*

Gene seems at peace lying in the fetal position. He starts mumbling and then chuckles. Whatever he's dreaming about brings a smile to his face. Meg sighs, relieved. Gene talks in his sleep. She knows that about him. She reaches for his hand and squeezes.

"I'm here, baby. I'm right here."

Gene opens his eyes. "Hey, girl."

"Hey."

"Where have you been?"

Meghan's heart swells. "I've been around."

"What's with the tears?"

"I was worried."

"Don't be."

"Electrocuted and still telling jokes," Meg attempts a relaxed tone, but her voice sounds alien.

"Unreal."

Meg lets down the side rail and drapes her arms over him. His eyes water and he begins to shake. Meg uses a soothing voice. "Hey, you're okay. It's going to be okay."

"I had a dream about Lori."

Meg momentarily freezes and then reassuringly squeezes his hand.

"She was just laying here with me on the stretcher. It felt so real, like a regular old Sunday morning."

Meghan smiles sadly and nods.

"I really thought that if I just blocked her out, I could extricate the pain. She was so close. I could smell her."

"She was your wife, Gene. You love her."

"I wouldn't allow myself to miss her, Meg."

Meg's eyes fill. "It's natural to miss her. It's okay."

"Dad? DADDY?"

Meghan jumps to the sound and automatically releases her embrace. She turns to find a well-manicured woman standing in the doorway. Her hair is long and silky straight, but her face is red and blotchy. Stricken.

"Jillian?" Gene croaks, "What...what are you doing here?"

Jillian coughs out a wobbly chuckle, suddenly unsure. "A nurse called me. She explained what happened and...I...I didn't want to come back here EVER again. After Mom. But I needed to see you. To be sure that you were okay. I...oh, Dad!"

As father and daughter embrace, Meghan quietly exits the room. Meg is certain that Gene hasn't seen Jillian under decent circumstances in forever. Every meeting revolved around Lori's court case. Gene didn't want to sue his colleagues for something that could never be changed, and Jillian... Well, as it has already been explained, sudden death brings out the worst in people.

Meg takes off the girlfriend hat as she leaves and replaces it with her nursing cap. Checking her watch, she realizes that it's only four in the morning. Weary or not, she's got three hours to go.

Chapter 45

"Let me guess? You finally figured it out?" Geri says as she peers at me through the mirrored glass.

Without planning it, I have wandered back into room ten. Geri's comment jars me back to reality. "I...I...yes. But...how did you know?"

"I didn't at first. Never put two-and-two together. But I'm *crazy*, remember. People talk about everything near me like I don't exist. Nurses, doctors, paramedics, even my own traitorous family. They all think that just because they shoot me up with a couple of milligrams of Haldol that I'm oblivious. Like I'm a piece of friggin' *furniture*." Geri points to her brain. "They talk about sex and daycare, boyfriends and yes, Dr. Hot Shot's wife, the nurse who dropped dead from a tiny blood pressure pill. This noggin harbors a million conversations, not to mention the LIES and the DECIEPT. I KNOW WHAT MY FATHER TOOK FROM ME!"

I pause, forgetting how quickly Geri could lose it. Before I have the chance to redirect, Geri's thoughts transition. Her voice is suddenly calm. "He's dating that restaurant nurse."

"I know. I set them up."

"*You*? Ain't that a kick in the ass." Geri chuckles easily, but she stops short when I don't join in. Then her tone turns serious. "Deep down you probably knew. That's why you set them up. You want him to be happy."

I drop into the chair next to her and silently shake my head.

Geri nudges me. "Answer me this? Is it better

to love and lost, or to completely forget that anything good in your life ever existed?"

"I don't know." I pause. "Is that what happened to you?"

Geri sighs. "That's been the battle of my brain since the beginning of time. The reason I exist. The reason I snap. The reason why I come here. If I could do it over, would I change things? Maybe. But then I wonder, I *fear* that my alternative actions would screw up *her* life. The life she has now. I wouldn't want to mess that up. "

"Her?" My eyes go wide. "Okay, Geri. Fess up. What the hell are you talking about?"

Geri smiles sadly and shakes her head. She points at me. "Look at your hand."

I hold it up. Sure enough, it's shimmering gold.

Geri rolls her eyes, cringing. "Oh, shit."

"What?"

"I smell hotdogs."

There's movement just outside the room.

"KNOCK KNOCK. Transport for Soul 674 ready and waiting." I turn and find Ollie Dick leaning against the door chewing a mustard splattered foot long. He holds it up to me and grins, "One for the road, baby. The last one."

My eyes go wide. Ollie is shimmering metallic. "Ollie? But how?"

"It was you, Lori." He comes over and squeezes me in a bear hug. "You did everything right. You selfless bitch, you. You fixed Kassel *and* Jamie. Now we both get to move ON."

Trembling, I say, "What if I don't want to go? What if I want to stay?"

"Stay?" Ollie frowns. "For what?"

"For *what*? My husband! My daughter! I need to watch over them. I MISS THEM!"

Ollie tilts his head and sighs. "Of course you miss them, Lori. Like I miss my family. Like they miss us. Staying trapped in purgatory isn't going to change any of that. Besides, now that you've discovered your identity, Gene will be able to sense your presence and it'll hold him back. Is that what you want? Do you want Gene to turn out like..." Ollie points to Geri. "like her?"

"Hey," Geri frowns. "Easy!"

My throat tightens. "Maybe. No...uh, sorry Geri. I can't just LEAVE. I'll never see them again."

"Says who?"

"What do you mean?"

"The Universe is one great continuum, my dear. Ends and beginnings are only a matter of perspective."

"Really?"

"Really." Ollie grins. "And there are others, you know."

"Others?"

"Old friends. Relatives. Your sister is totally excited to see you. She's been waiting a loonnnnnggggg time."

My brow furrows. "Sister? I don't have a sister."

Ollie laughs. "Not from this life."

My eyes go wide. "What?"

Before Ollie has a chance to speak, the tube system jams and the sound of drumming beats in the distance.

Ollie rolls his eyes and hollers out the door. "FINE! WE'RE GOING ALREADY!"

He turns back to me. "Now or never, Gloria. I mean Lori."

"If we both go, then who's going to whisper?"

"The Indian, of course." Ollie shrugs. "At least until the next death."

Ollie reaches for my hand and this time I take it. We walk out of B-bay and through A-bay, where things haven't quite settled down. Some nurses are charting while others are racing to-and-fro, fending off the next disaster. Dr. Rodriguez is calling for consults, barking out verbal orders and moving room to room with great deliberation. The secretary has the phone clamped to one ear, talking, typing and scanning at the same time. Techs are pushing about linen carts in a frantic attempt to restock by morning.

As Ollie leads me towards the EXIT, for the first time I catch sight of the Indian. Except for the long silvery locks of feathered-woven braids, he looks younger than I expected. Tall and muscular, robed in colorful patterned skins, he's sitting dead center of the nurses station with legs entwined around a rawhide-tethered drum. I offer a shy wave. With the palm of his hand facing me, he pauses in half-salute, nods, and then begins yet another slow and powerful beat.

The nurses freeze. I catch the dilatation of their pupils, the rigidness of their stands, as adrenaline courses their systems. The moment lasts a few seconds and then, once again, the department explodes into action. It is 5 a.m., ten hours into the shift, and the staff is working a full court press. To think, only hours before, they had saved the life of a colleague.

So? What did you expect? An actual *break* in patient care? A little celebratory party? For *what*? Nobody *died* or anything. Even Douglas will live to see another day. And as I have already explained since the beginning of this story, there is no final curtain in the emergency department.

The Show must always go on.

The End

Thank you!

I'd like to take a moment to thank all of you for reading my story! A special salute to my local and cyber friends for their pre-reading and grammatical expertise, whether I used their suggestions or not! Thank you Kristi Bettilyon, Patti Conway, James Kizer, Debbie Gallagher, Nette Eifler, Julie Ann Smith, Shoopman, Michelle St. Clair, Jennifer DelSesto, Lisa Bennett, Winnie Walker, Stacy Parr, Jennifer Sollami, Janice Felciano, Cathy Felton and Lenore Beebe.

P.S. The dangers of pushing Epinephrine 0.3mg IV are very real. Thankfully, the medication now comes in big cartridges making it physically impossible to administer the drug incorrectly. I have heard rumors that there is a national shortage on these cartridges so the little dangerous vials may resurface. Nurses, new and old, BEWARE!

P.S.S. Hospitals and mental health facilities nationwide are always accepting new and used clothing, shoes, jackets and definitely underwear for the indigent population. The "closet" is always in need.

"SCOOBY DOOBY DOO!"

Made in the USA
Lexington, KY
02 January 2015